"God, it looks like a damn battlefield."

He shook his head. "No. We're only two days from McAlester. Help me wrap the bodies, and we'll send them home on the train." He blew out a weary breath. "And give me back my damn rifle."

She passed over the Winchester, the familiar letters, R-A-B, carved in the stock. "Found it yonder where ya dropped it. Now ya can point it at me an' threaten to shoot me iffin I don't do like ya say."

His dark brown eyes narrowed. "Are you ridiculing me?"

Johnny stared at him, her brow furrowed in concentration. She shifted her feet, glancing down as she swatted at the tips of grass with her manacled hands. "Don't reckon I know what re-dic-u-cule means."

He blew out a long sigh. "It means to make sport of someone."

She shrugged.

He tried again. "I wondered if you were laughing at me, outlaw?"

This time her shoulders snapped back, and she lifted her chin to squarely meet his dark eyes. "I reckon iffin I had call to be a-laughin' at ya, I'd be a-doin' it right in yer face, so there'd be no wonderin' about it." Spinning around, she stomped off.

Richard couldn't stop the grin that tugged the left corner of his mouth. Despite the pain in his leg, despite the grief pressing against his heart, despite the tenuous grip he held on his sanity, that obnoxious little outlaw could still make him laugh.

"And it's ridicule!" he yelled.

A clod of dirt came hurling out of the blue and landed with a thunk against the toe of his left boot. For a moment his laughter rang out to mingle with Johnny's sputtering curses.

Praise for *LOST HEARTS*

Winner of Third Place in the
2008 Utah Romance Writers of America
Hearts of the West Contest

Lost Hearts

by

Kathy Otten

Lost Hearts

Cover Art by *Nicola Martinez*

The Wild Rose Press
PO Box 708
Adams Basin, NY 14410-0706
Visit us at www.thewildrosepress.com

Publishing History
First Cactus Rose Edition, 2010
Print ISBN 1-60154-860-5

Published in the United States of America

Dedication

For my mom, who made me believe that
Lucky The Dog and *The Lost Uranium Mine*
were the greatest pieces of literature ever written.
Thanks for your constant encouragement and
your unwavering faith in me.
Love you.

Special Thanks to Thurman Shuller, M.D.,
at the Pittsburg County Genealogical and Historical
Society in McAlester, OK.
Thanks for the maps, articles and photos.
Sorry it took so long to write the book.

Chapter One

Don't think about it. Don't think about it. U.S.
Deputy Marshal Richard Bennick repeated the
words in his mind as he lay hidden in blue stem
already tall enough to reach his chest. Even his
bones ached for a swig of bourbon from the bottle of
Old Crow in his saddlebag. Just one swallow would
calm the anxiety which ate at him. One swallow
would curb the restless energy which flowed through
his body and pulsated from every nerve ending. He
could almost smell the faint whiff of caramel and
vanilla as he popped the cork. Feel the tingle along
his tongue as the familiar burn crept up the back of
his nose when he swallowed.

With his horse ground tied out of sight, he was
forced instead to draw a deep breath of warm,
morning air. Slowly he exhaled, reminding himself
to focus on the crumbling sod dug-out in front of him
and wait for fellow deputy, Martin Brady to give the
signal to advance.

He peered through the swaying prairie grass at
the open door of the outlaw hide-out less than one
hundred yards away. In front of the dug-out, three
bedrolls lay spread in the grass as low snores
rumbled from beneath the colorful mounds of quilts
and blankets.

Resting his finger on the trigger guard of his
Winchester, he shifted his hip off a lump in the
ground. A single bead of sweat trailed slowly down
his forehead, and though he itched to swipe away
the annoyance, his left arm—a casualty of a war
long over—had been amputated just above his

1

elbow, leaving only his right hand to support the weight of his rifle.

Another bead of sweat worked its way along the length of his nose, hung for a moment from the very tip, then dropped. He glanced down at the tiny splat, dark on the gray metal breech of his Winchester. A black fly wandered up the barrel and stopped to drink from the tiny spot.

While lying in this grass was hot and uncomfortable, he'd gladly choose dripping sweat and whining mosquitoes if only to avoid the inevitable gunfight should Brady wait until the outlaws were awake and armed, before demanding their surrender.

He could almost hear the shooting in his head as dark images pushed their way forward from the back of his mind, obscuring the reality before him.

Tears blurred his vision to protect his eyes from the sting of the thick gray haze while his heart thumped painfully against the wall of his chest.

No, he admonished himself, squeezing his eyes tight. *Don't think about it. Don't think about it.* He drew a deep breath, released it slowly then took another and expelled the unwanted memories. The sky was blue once more.

Perhaps Caroline was right. His new job as second assistant to her father, District Attorney Benton Caldwell, was just what he needed. There would be no more killing. He would still be part of the judicial system, helping, as Caroline said, "...to rid society of its undesirable element, yet without the ugliness." Such a change, she'd insisted, could only be what was best for him.

He cocked his head, and with a roll of his left shoulder, wiped a bead of sweat from his cheek. A mosquito whined in his right ear. He ignored it.

Ahead, a young boy crawled from the farthest bedroll and stretched. With practiced efficiency, he rolled up his blankets and carried them to the sod house where he tossed them down and picked up a battered wooden bucket from where it sat on a bench beside the open door. Wearing his wide brimmed hat pulled low, he wandered toward the stream where Richard lay hidden. The bucket swung from the boy's left hand, as he whistled tunelessly under his breath.

Another bead of sweat began its long journey down Richard's nose. Twin beads slid down either side of his face to twist through the thick stubble of his beard. He frowned, realizing that despite the heat, the boy wore an oversized, white-linen duster. The garment hung to his ankles and swallowed his hands inside long tattered sleeves.

Squatting at the edge of the water, not twenty feet from where Richard lay, the boy reached up and removed his battered hat, revealing short, shaggy blond hair. Shoving up the voluminous sleeves, he leaned forward to splash water on his face and neck. For several minutes the boy stared out across the tips of the swaying grass, seemingly lost in some daydream.

"Johnny!" bellowed an angry voice from inside the sod house. "Where the hell's the water for my coffee? Get your sorry little ass in here!"

Muttering under his breath, the boy scooped up some water, plopped his hat on his head, and tromped back to the crumbling dug-out.

The commotion roused the other men in their bedrolls. Where was Brady? They could still catch the outlaws unaware if they moved in now. But there was no signal. Had the deputy dozed off? Richard cursed under his breath. This was one of the many reasons he preferred to work alone.

No sooner had the boy reached the soddy when a large, burly man, clad only in sagging underwear, stepped through the open door. Richard had seen the craggy features and narrow eyes of that face staring back at him from the flat plane of a hundred wanted posters.

Pierpont Bodine.

The outlaw had started his career during the war riding with the notorious Bloody Bill Anderson. After Anderson was killed, Bodine wandered through the western frontier taking what he wanted when he wanted it, without regard for human life. He'd held a reputation for ruling his men with an iron hand and using his long barrel Colt swiftly, without feeling or conscience.

Two weeks ago, Marshal Upham received word from the Chickasaw Indian Police that Peirpont Bodine was in the Nation. Richard immediately volunteered to bring him in. Though the area west of the Boggy was the wildest part of the Chickasaw Nation, he knew it like the back of his hand.

Seeking information in a small village, he and Brady were told Bodine and his men were holed-up, two days ride, northwest of Smith Pauls Valley. Once they located the hide-out, they waited until dark before taking up their positions on either side of the soddy then bided their time until dawn.

Bodine snatched the bucket from the boy's grip, sloshing water over the sides. "Go check on them horses." He gave the kid a shove that had the boy stumbling backward, barely able to catch himself from sprawling in the grass.

"Yes sir, Paw." The boy gave the man an obedient nod before scurrying off to the make-shift corral attached to the side of the soddy.

Paw? Richard frowned. This boy couldn't be any more than fourteen. Maybe Johnny was a younger son. Richard shifted in the grass. God, he didn't want to believe someone not even old enough to shave could be sentenced to hang.

Judge Parker hadn't known the name of

Bodine's son, but he'd been seen with the gang during a few of their stage robberies, so the warrant included a detailed description; average height, blond hair, blue eyes, early twenties, seen wearing a white duster, riding a large brown and white paint horse.

Smoke curled from the crooked stove pipe as the aroma of coffee drifted through the open door. The two other men were awake now, joking good naturedly with each other as they rolled up their bedding and headed inside. Any moment now Bodine would send someone to relieve the sentry and all hell would break loose.

Earlier, after the last guard change, Richard and Brady had crept up on the sentry who'd been dozing against the narrow trunk of a lone hackberry tree on a knoll less than a quarter mile away. Brady knocked him unconscious, then he and Richard tied the man up and dragged him back to where he and Brady had hidden their horses.

Damn it, Richard cursed to himself. How long was Brady planning to wait?

Having finished his chores, Johnny tromped back toward the front of the dug-out, where a lean man with long blond hair stepped into the early morning light. A cup in one hand, he paused for a moment to scratch his shirtless belly. As Johnny approached, he set his cup on the bench then turned and urinated against the crumbling wall of the dug-out.

"You best get in there, your pa's pissed." He chuckled at his crude joke while he buttoned his fly. "We're ridin' out soon to meet Calvin, and I want somethin' to eat before I gotta spell Willis from guard duty."

"We ain't got no supplies."

"Don't give me none of your sass, you little bastard." The outlaw drew back his fist to hit the boy, but Johnny ducked and darted inside.

Immediately, the muffled but irate voice of Pierpont Bodine penetrated the thick sod walls and drifted through the grass to Richard's ears. The tirade was punctuated a few minutes later by a loud thump and the splintering sound of breaking wood. After lengthy silence the smoky scent of bacon wafted outside. His stomach rumbled.

All the outlaws were now inside. Finally, Brady issued a low, soft whistle, signaling Richard to move closer. Adrenalin pumping, he dashed across the clearing to take up a new position at the corner of the corral. Again he waited.

The clank of buckles and the uneven scuffing sound of someone walking toward him through the grass tightened every muscle in his body. In one smooth motion, Richard shouldered his rifle and dove behind a broken barrel, praying he hadn't been seen.

Head down, Johnny rounded the corner of the soddy with a bridle looped over his shoulder, lugging a saddle and blanket in his arms.

The boy tossed the saddle onto the top rail then ducked between the poles. For the first time Richard caught a glimpse of Johnny's face.

Something undefined in the boy's features momentarily captured his attention, but he didn't have the time to wonder what, for he became distracted by the ugly bruise which marred the boy's left cheekbone. The deep purple and black bruise had evidently been there a day or two for the skin around it held a yellowish cast which spread all the way up to Johnny's eye. In addition, fresh blood oozed from a cut in the corner of the boy's lower lip.

In that instant, an urge to barge into the cabin and confront Bodine over his mistreatment of the boy washed over Richard, but he quickly shook it off. Johnny certainly didn't deserve any pity. His father was one of the most notorious outlaws in the territory, and from all reports this kid was following him straight to hell.

"Damn it all, Jack," the boy muttered softly as he smoothed a Navajo blanket over the back of a big brown and white paint. "I don't want to join up with Uncle Cal. An' I sure as hell don't want to be a-robbin' no stage." He swiped at the blood on his lip with a quick shrug of his shoulder, before heaving the bulky saddle onto Jack's muscular back.

"Why in hell does Paw want me to go?" he asked the horse as he rubbed his left elbow. "Prob'ly 'cause he ain't got Henry to tend the horses no more. Shit, Paw don't even like me. 'Course he weren't none too fond a Henry neither."

Johnny reached under the horse to grab the dangling cinch, then threaded the long leather latigo strap through the ring on the saddle, pulled it snug, and dropped the stirrup back in place.

"Prob'ly end up a-ridin' hell bent fer leather with some damn posse doggin' our heels. Jest promise ya'll see to it I don't get left behind, an' I promise to take real good care of ya."

Johnny patted the horse's neck. He lifted the bridle off his shoulder and offered Jack the bit. "Reckon we ought'a jest be glad Paw ain't a-leavin' us here alone." Johnny dropped the reins, leaving the horse ground tied while he climbed through the poles and returned to the soddy. After a moment he reappeared, the stirrups of another saddle bumping against his shins.

Richard hunkered down as Johnny moved in his direction. Damn. As soon as the kid moved to the next horse Richard would be spotted for sure. Unsure if the boy had a weapon hidden in his baggy duster, Richard waited until the boy had turned his back to heave the saddle onto the horse. Richard leaned his Winchester against the side of the barrel and slipped between the rails of the corral fence. The thick dust made his footsteps silent, as he crept up behind the unsuspecting boy.

Just as Richard stretched his arm out to clamp his hand over the boy's mouth, Johnny whirled around.

Frozen, they did little more than blink at each other for several heartbeats. Richard found himself mesmerized by eyes so intensely blue they were violet. They drew him into their depths and held him captive, though he didn't comprehend how.

That moment of insanity cost him. Johnny bolted. The abrupt movement jarred Richard from his daze. He realized his mistake and threw his body forward, ramming his shoulder into the kid's lower back. The pair slammed into the ground, with Richard on top of the thrashing boy.

"Posse!" Johnny yelled as they hit the dirt and rolled across the corral.

The scrappy little outlaw kicked Richard's legs and pummeled his back with small fists. The startled horses danced around their rolling bodies.

"Pos—"

Richard clamped his hand over Johnny's mouth, pressing the back of the boy's blond head firmly into the ground. But doing so left Richard vulnerable to the kid's clawing fingers.

A shot rang out from the front of the sod house. Brady's deep voice carried across the prairie. "Pierpont Bodine! This is U.S. Deputy Marshal Martin Brady! I have warrants for you and your men. Put down your guns and come outside!"

Johnny tried to scramble free, but Richard yanked the kid down and straddled his hips. Leaning forward, Richard pressed his right hand against Johnny's left shoulder, pinning him to the ground.

Gunfire began in earnest.

"Give it up, Bodine!" Brady ordered above the din.

With his free arm, the boy landed a weak punch to Richard's jaw, but because of his missing arm, he was unable to block further onslaught. With gritted teeth, he suffered pounding abuse to his ribs, back, and head.

"The water's out here, and we got you surrounded!" Brady yelled. "Surrender or we'll fire the house!"

Just as the boy heaved his upper body toward Richard's face, Richard lifted his head. Instead of Johnny driving his forehead into Richard's nose, the kid slammed into Richard's chin instead, knocking his teeth together with a sharp click.

"Okay, Marshal!" Bodine's gravelly voice rang out. "We give up!"

At that moment the kid turned his head and chomped down on Richard's forearm.

"Sonofa—" Richard reared back, releasing the kid's shoulder, while still managing to maintain his position across the boy's hips. Spots of blood had already seeped through the sleeve of his faded blue shirt.

The instant Richard lifted his weight off the kid's shoulder; Johnny twisted onto his stomach and tried to crawl away. Richard forgot about his bleeding arm and lunged for a fist full of linen duster. "Oh no, you don't."

"You men," Brady commanded. "Line up right along that wall. Hands up. Bennick! Get over here!"

The kid snatched up a fistful of loose dirt, churned up by the horses and threw it over his shoulder into Richard's face. Immediately, he slapped his hand over his burning eyes as Johnny squirmed to free himself from beneath Richard's weight. At the end of his patience, he grabbed the kid by the back of his collar and hauled him to his feet.

Spewing curse words with every breath, Johnny wriggled around under his layers of baggy clothes, trying to escape, even as Richard, while maintaining his hold, pushed the boy across the corral.

"Give it up, kid." Richard squinted through the well of tears, against the painful glare of the sun. Then, whether it was fatigue or resignation, Johnny ceased his struggles. At the corral fence, Richard grabbed his Winchester and used it to gesture the kid toward the front of the sod house.

Johnny glared daggers at him.

Though tears leaked from the corners of his eyes, Richard found himself strangely exhilarated by their little tussle. As he met the spitting-mad glare of his opponent, he couldn't suppress the mischievous urge to provoke the kid a little bit further. He flashed him a quick grin and winked.

Johnny's eyes narrowed into slits. He drew his small frame up, shoulders square, his chin high.

"What the hell are ya a-laughin' at lawman? Ya didn't whup me. Why yer friend there had to call ya off afore I ripped off the rest a yer sorry hide. So stop a-standin' there a-lookin' so... so..."

"Smug?" Richard finished, amazed that he was enjoying himself.

"So goddamn happy." Johnny whirled around and stomped off.

"Give 'em hell, Johnny." The blond outlaw cheered as the pair approached.

Another man, older and heavier than the blond, leaned against the sod wall of the house. He held his right hand pressed against the muscle of his left bicep, as blood dripped from between his thick fingers.

"Didn't know you was such a scrappy sonofabitch." He grinned as Johnny approached.

"Why the hell didn't ya use yer knife?" No

lighthearted teasing inflected Bodine's harsh voice, only cold condemnation. "Why didn't ya grab his gun, 'stead a hittin' him an' throwin' dirt like some goddamn girl? I swear, I don't know how I could a sired a bastard as a dumb as you."

"That's enough," Richard snapped when he noticed the kid's shoulders slump and his gaze lower to the ground.

"Sorry, Paw, I didn't think."

"Didn't think? Didn't think? Henry weren't no smarter than a box a rocks, but he was a damn sight brighter than you, ya goddamn worthless piece a shit. Ya never think."

"Shut up." Richard commanded, swinging his rifle back over his shoulder as he stepped in front of the outlaw.

"Ya cain't do nothin' right." Bodine continued to rant. "Couldn't even grab his gun. Ya must a had half a dozen chances. Could a saved us all, but no, ya didn't think. I swear to God, Johnny, ya cain't tell yer ass from a hole in the ground."

"I said, shut up." Richard drew back his fist and drove it square into Bodine's jaw.

The outlaw appeared to lift off the ground for a moment before he fell back against the wall of the soddy and slid to the ground unconscious.

Richard wondered if anyone had ever defended the scrawny kid before. Judging from the slack-jawed, wide-eyed expression on Johnny's face he guessed not, and for some odd reason, outlaw or not, Richard was pleased he'd been the one to do it.

"Bennick," Brady ordered, "Keep your eye on these varmints." He slid his revolver into his holster then strode off toward the chokecherry thicket some distance away, where the deputies had hidden their mounts. He returned several minutes later with two horses. Flopped over the back of one horse was the sentry, who groaned when Brady grabbed him by the back of the shirt and yanked him to the ground. A sack of manacles was then thrown into the grass beside him. Richard trained his Winchester on the outlaws as Brady tossed hand cuffs at each man and ordered them to put them on.

"Johnny," the blond outlaw called. "Come see, can ya fix up Warren here. He got creased durin' the ruckus an' needs tendin'."

The heavier man lifted his gaze to meet Johnny's. "It's just my arm. Not bad, but it burns like hell an' now I'm trussed up tighter than a Christmas goose."

Johnny nodded and since he had yet to be handcuffed, started toward the open door of the soddy.

"Hold it, kid!" Brady yelled. "Where do you think you're goin'?"

Johnny halted then swung around, a scowl on his face. "To fetch my yarbs an' sech."

The older deputy grabbed Johnny by the arm and snapped the iron manacles around his narrow wrists. "Bennick, go get what the kid needs. And be careful. Someone might be waitin' in there to blow a hole through your middle."

Richard turned to Johnny waiting for instructions, but all he received was a belligerent glare. "Come on, outlaw, I haven't got all day."

"I got yarbs hangin' from hell to breakfast in there. 'Lessin' ya know about sech things, ya won't know what to get."

Richard studied the boy trying to decide if the kid was telling the truth or if it was a ploy to attempt an escape. When he saw the boy's chin lift stubbornly, he felt the corners of his mouth twitch in response. "He can come with me."

"Okay, just be careful."

Using the barrel of his rifle like a pointer, Richard motioned to the boy. "Come on, kid."

Part of the sod house had been built below ground level, and Richard had to step down as he ducked through the doorway.

The odors of gunpowder and wood smoke assaulted his senses as soon as he stepped into the hazy, cave-like interior. He staggered back a step. Nausea rolled his stomach. Blood pounded in his head, reverberating in his skull like cannon fire.

****

Thick gun smoke hung between the trees like heavy fog. Bullets whizzed past his head, each one accompanied by a dull thunk as they pelted the scraggly underbrush and low-limbed trees around him. The afternoon light had faded, the dense woods growing so dark, that as the smoke lifted, he still couldn't see more than twenty feet in any direction. Branches snapped around him as the rest of his unit stumbled through the underbrush. He tried to move forward, through the muck at the bottom of a little gully, but another Minnie ball slammed into the oak tree beside him, and he dropped to the ground.

****

Johnny grabbed a chair and positioned it beneath the closest rafter of the low ceiling, from which hung rows of bundle tied herbs. While fear of lawmen had been drummed into her head since she learned to walk, it couldn't compare to her daily terror, that her father or one of his men would discover her secret.

As far back as she could remember, Johnny's mother had told her pretending to be a boy was a special, secret game, just between the two of them. However, it wasn't long before Johnny saw first-hand, exactly how her father and his men treated women. Only then had she understood why her mother had been so insistent.

As she grew older and started her woman's cycles, Johnny made certain to layer on the clothes, avoiding men as much as possible. After nearly six summers of binding herself, she sometimes forgot to which gender she actually belonged.

But today, with the arrival of the one-armed deputy, came the possibility that for the first time in her life she could actually be freed from her father's control. Hopeful, she touched her fingers to the locket that rested against her skin, beneath her many layers of shirts. With her father and his men in prison, maybe she would finally have a chance at the life she always dreamed. Whistling happily under her breath, she pulled down an assortment of dried herbs, roots, and flowers.

She had just extended her hand toward a bundle of goldenrod when she heard a soft thump behind her. Glancing over her shoulder, she saw the deputy had flattened himself against the floor. With his Winchester in hand, he pulled himself forward as though he were a Comanche brave stalking his prey.

She hopped off the chair, set her bundles on the seat, and stepped over to where he lay.

"Hey, lawman."

He didn't respond.

He seemed so blind to her presence, she wondered if she could actually step over the man and walk outside without him noticing.

"What the hell are ya doin'?"

He stilled at the sound of her voice.

Curious, she squatted directly in front of him. "Hey, lawman." She reached out and poked him in the shoulder.

He gasped and reared onto his knees, his rifle pointed at her chest.

Startled, she leaned back, lost her balance, and fell onto her butt with a thump.

Wide-eyed, the deputy's dark gaze darted around the interior before coming to rest on her face. His complexion was ashen and beads of sweat dotted his forehead. They blinked at one another for several seconds. Then swinging his rifle over his shoulder, the deputy drew his shaking hand down his face and exhaled several ragged breaths.

Johnny recovered first and rolled to her feet. "I must a whomped ya up-side the head harder than I figgered. Yore lookin' a mite addled."

The deputy's brown eyes were dilated to almost black as he stood and glanced around the interior. Striding to the table, he snatched up a nearly empty bottle of whiskey. With his teeth, he spit the cork onto the floor and downed the contents in two quick gulps.

"How can you stand living in this filth?" He snapped when he caught her watching him.

"Ain't got no choice." She shrugged and moved to a cluttered corner of the shadowed interior to retrieve a large doeskin bag decorated in a colorful beadwork pattern. Ignoring the deputy's black glare, she slid the herbs she'd already pulled down into the bag then stepped onto the chair. Though it was awkward with her hands joined at the wrists, she soon filled the bag with all the dried plants.

Stopping before him, she lowered her gaze to the scuffed toes of her boots. "I can tend that arm iffin ya want."

The small bloodstains on the deputy's shirt sleeve were nearly dry, and though he said nothing about what she'd done to him, she wouldn't neglect his wound. Placing the bag on the table, she stepped away to rummage through the piles of clutter near the stove.

With the crook of her arm soon overflowing with an assortment of bandages, Johnny swung back toward the table and froze. The deputy stood before her with his rifle once again pointed at the center of her chest. She gasped, nearly dropping the clean linen onto the dirt floor. She studied his intense brown eyes for several moments and sighed with relief when she realized he wouldn't pull the trigger.

A lifetime with her father and his men had honed her ability to read people. Like an expert shootist, she knew exactly when that trigger would be squeezed or when the next punch would fly. Pointedly ignoring the barrel of his rifle, she stepped around it and dropped the bandages onto the table beside the doeskin bag.

"Ya damn lawman, iffin I'd a-wanted to kill ya, I'd a done it afore now."

She lifted her gaze to meet his and saw in his eyes that he was aware she'd had her opportunity a few minutes ago and had chosen not to take it.

"Well, do forgive me," he groused, "but I never trust an outlaw."

Johnny narrowed her eyes into a mutinous glare. "I ain't no outlaw. My paw's an outlaw. Uncle Calvin an' them others is outlaws, but I ain't. I'm jest a...jest a... "

"Just an innocent victim? Ha! Now finish what you're doing and let's go."

Annoyed he didn't believe her, she moved to the stove and reached for a small tin on the shelf. She placed the tin on the table then leaned over to grab the chair she'd been standing on while she collected her dried herbs. "Here. Set your ass in this."

The deputy complied, as the tension in his features eased. Confused by the fact she even cared, Johnny stomped off to retrieve the bucket of water and dropped it on the table with a thump. "Is ya goin' to put up that rifle-gun? I don't want it a-goin' off ax-ti-dental-like if this here salve stings."

"Then you'd better make sure it doesn't sting," he snapped. "And it's accidental."

She scowled, waiting as he looped the rifle over his shoulder. She easily pushed up both the unbuttoned sleeves of his shirt and long drawers.

Picking up one of the smaller cloths, she dipped it into the water, wrung out the excess, and gently dabbed the blood from the wound. "Ya know'd my meanin'."

"You said it wrong." He grumbled. As he leaned close to examine the circle of teeth marks, Johnny caught a whiff of soap. She took a deep breath, inhaling the faint scent of sandalwood. This deputy sure smelled nicer than any man she'd ever known.

"Accidental." The deputy prodded.

Johnny picked up the tin. Her father and his men always smelled sour, a mixture of sweat, horses, and dirt. Their body odor turned her stomach; it never stirred a desire to lean close and breathe deep.

"Say it, Johnny."

"Sonofabitch. Don't ya never quit?"

"Accidental."

She blew out an exaggerated breath that was more like a growl, then pried off the tin lid, and tossed it on the table so hard it skidded across the wood and hit the dirt floor with a ping. "Ask-did-dental."

"Ac-ci-den-tal."

"Who the hell cares?" She scooped up a blob of salve and smashed it into the raw wound.

"Yeow!" The deputy shoved the chair back and glared at her. "You did that on purpose."

Johnny scowled right back. "The hell I did, lawman. It was plum ax-ti-dental."

The deputy's brown eyes narrowed dangerously for a moment then gradually his harsh expression eased into a quick half smile. A large dimple appeared to crease his left cheek, and for just an instant his white teeth flashed like a ray of sunlight through morning fog.

She stared at him for several seconds marveling at how handsome he was. She ignored the tiny prick she felt in the region of her heart as she wondered if he might instead, be laughing at her inability to say the word right. Shoving aside her doubt, she picked up another cloth, folded it, and gently pressed it over the wound before wrapping it with a long strip of linen.

"Hey, Bennick!" Deputy Brady yelled from outside. "Everything all right in there?"

"Yeah, we're coming!"

Hastily, Johnny stuffed the pile of bandages and the tin of salve into her bag. She turned for one last look around the sod house then started for the door.

"Hey, outlaw."

She stopped and sighed, before she slowly turned to face the deputy.

"I'll take that knife of yours now."

"Damn lawman," she muttered as she bent over to raise her left pant leg and remove from her boot, the small skinning knife her father had cursed her for not using.

"Now nice and slow, put it on the floor, and kick it over here."

Annoyed, she kicked it so hard the knife skidded past the deputy's feet, bounced off the dwindled pile of wood and Buffalo chips, and slid under the closest bunk.

"Brat. Now turn around. Let's go."

"But ain't ya a-goin' to fetch my knife?"

"Believe me, you aren't going to need it anymore."

"How the hell do ya know that? 'Sides, Uncle Henry give it to me."

"I'm not taking my eyes off you long enough to crawl under there, and I'm sure as hell not letting you get it. For all I know you've got a Gatling gun stashed under that bed."

"A what?"

"Come on." He used his rifle to gesture toward

18

the open door. "Let's go."

Johnny looped the strap of the wide doeskin bag over her head to hang diagonally across her chest, where it caught awkwardly on her handcuffs. She stomped through the doorway, right past the older deputy, to the corral fence where the blond man, Machler, sat chained beside her father, Warren, and the groggy sentry, Willis. Ignoring the rifle Deputy Brady held aimed in their direction, Johnny dropped down beside Warren and treated his wound.

Afterward, she moved away to sit alone against the fence. Reaching inside the neckline of her shirt, she withdrew her locket. Carefully, she popped it open and gazed longingly at the familiar faces staring back.

On one side was a beautiful young woman with dark hair parted in the center and twisted into two knots on either side of her head. She wore a pretty lace collar and a simple smile of joy. In the opposite oval rested the photograph of a young man. His expression was stern, but his eyes were gentle. Johnny knew he never yelled, or swore, or hit anyone, no matter how badly he was provoked.

Images of that illusive place called 'home' rose in her mind. A soft bed with real sheets and a pillow. Maw singing lullabies and reading stories. Paw holding her hand as they walked up the street of the busy town.

Her horse wedged his nose between the poles to nudge her in the back, but she ignored him. Instead, she closed the locket and slipped it back beneath her layers of shirts.

A few feet away, the deputies stood talking. When they finished, Deputy Bennick walked to the horses and took some empty sugar sacks from his saddle bags. As he headed toward the soddy, he told Deputy Brady he was going to search for evidence.

Never in her entire life had she met a man like

this one-armed deputy marshal. After her mother and Morning Song died, Uncle Henry had been the one to look out for her, although none of them had ever dared go against her father. But this deputy hadn't been afraid. He had slammed her paw right into the wall of that soddy. She'd never been so astonished in her life. And the outdoin'est thing of it all was that the deputy had done it for her—worthless little Johnny Bodine.

Chapter Two

Deputy Brady strode through the grass toward Johnny. After removing a small notepad and pencil from his vest pocket, he towered over her firing questions at her about her father's plans and the whereabouts of Calvin. But she refused to say a word. She was well aware of what would happen if she let slip even the tiniest bit of information.

"Damn it, kid, would you rather swing from the end of a rope alongside your father?"

A shadow fell across her. She looked up to meet the brooding gaze of Deputy Bennick.

"Leave the kid alone, Brady. Can't you see he's more afraid of what Bodine will do to him if he talks, than anything we can threaten him with?"

"What the hell's eating you?" Brady snapped.

Deputy Bennick shrugged and looked out past the stream. "How long before this Uncle Calvin person wonders where Bodine and his men are and comes looking? That's why Bodine hasn't put up much of a fight. I just want to get out of here before we end up getting picked off like tin cans on a fence."

"I don't like it either, but we'll leave when we're ready." The two men walked away still talking.

Deputy Bennick returned a minute later and tossed Johnny the hat she'd lost during their tussle in the corral. Snatching it up, she jammed it over her head and pulled the brim low, instinctively hiding her eyes in its shadow.

The deputy then pulled out his own notebook and pencil. He was taking an inventory and issuing receipts to the prisoners for their personal possessions, but all Johnny owned besides the clothes on her back were the knife under the bed, a worn Bible her mother had given her, the doeskin bag filled with dried herbs, and Jack.

Another twenty minutes passed before her father and his men were all mounted and handcuffed to their saddle horns, with their feet fastened by a chain that crossed beneath their horses. Sitting against the corral fence, Johnny waited her turn. She lifted her head and watched the deputy who stood a few feet away beside a red roan gelding.

Holding a bottle of whiskey by the neck Deputy Bennick raised the bottle to his mouth and with his teeth, pulled out the cork. Then he tucked the bottle between his side and the stump of his left arm, spit the cork into his palm, and held it with his pinky and ring fingers, while he grasped the neck with his remaining three fingers, and tipped the bottle to his lips.

She shifted her gaze from his face to his arm as he raised it for another drink. The sleeve of his shirt pulled snug over the thick bandage. In her mind, she could feel the brush of fine brown hair against her fingertips as she'd tended his wound and could still see the raised, gray-blue veins that twisted their way beneath the skin of his muscular forearm, to spread out across the top of his broad hand. She glanced at his empty sleeve and wondered what had happened.

He corked the bottle then stuffed it into his saddle bag as Brady motioned for Johnny to mount. With her manacled hands gripping the saddle horn, she shoved her right foot into the right stirrup and pulled herself into the saddle.

"What are you doing?" Deputy Bennick snapped. "You're mounting from the wrong side."

She frowned. Was the man always so surly?

"How the hell can a horse have a wrong side?"

"You're supposed to mount from the left. Indians mount from the right."

"What the hell's it matter so long as ya get on the damn thing?"

He gave her a pointed glare as he looped his own reins—which were knotted together at the end—over his horse's neck. Then standing at the shoulder, facing the rear of his horse, he twisted the left stirrup around, stepped into it with his left foot, and with his right hand reaching across his body to grasp the saddle horn, he swung himself into the saddle. Picking up his reins, he nudged the roan forward.

When she saw him lift his chin in that superior way, she wanted to knock him right to the ground. "Iffin ya wasn't stubborn as a Missouri mule," she said as Deputy Bennick motioned for her to fall in line behind Willis. "Ya'd see it'd be easier fer ya to be a-gettin' on from the other side."

"I am not mounting like an Indian."

"What the hell difference does it make? On is on. Ya only got one arm, seems like ya'd be a-wantin' to do it the easiest way ya can."

"With your mouth, no wonder Bodine hits you."

His heartless comment dropped Johnny's chin to her chest as the unexpected impact of the deputy's words hit her with the same force as one of her father's blows. She drew her lower lip between her teeth and began to chew, distracting herself from the pain of his betrayal. It was her own fault anyway. Just because he'd taken her part against her father didn't mean he was different. He was a man, and except for Henry, Johnny had learned early in life that all men were the same.

The older deputy rode past the two of them, shooting them a pointed glare before taking up his position at the lead. Next came Bodine and Machler, then Warren and Willis.

She glanced over at the deputy a couple of hours later, and though he met her gaze he said nothing. She looked away then, stubbornly maintaining her silence until dusk when the small party rode into the deputies' camp, one day's ride west of Smith Pauls Valley.

****

The prison wagon waited in the sparse shade cast by a narrow copse of brush, which hugged the eastern slope along a dip in the rolling prairie. Two men rose, bracing their rifle stocks against their hips, as Richard and Brady rode into camp with their prisoners. At the back of the cook's wagon, two more men stood talking near the fire. Brady had hired the guards days earlier as they neared the area where Bodine was reported to be hiding.

With the guards training their rifles on the prisoners, the chains were removed and the prisoners dismounted. After they were given time to relieve themselves, they were shackled in pairs. The shackles each passed through a ring in a long, heavy chain, the end of which was then locked around the rear axle of the prison wagon.

Richard hobbled the prisoners' horses then turned them out to graze with the extra mules and horses they'd brought from Fort Smith. He stripped the saddle from the red roan he'd been riding, then grabbed a curry comb and stiff brush from his saddle bags and scrubbed the dried sweat from the horse's back. Though he never made eye contact with Johnny, he could feel that wide, violet gaze boring a hole right between his shoulder blades.

He'd regretted his harsh words to the boy as soon as they'd left his mouth that morning. Over the years his tendency to snap out such cutting remarks had lost him more friends than he could count, but he never mourned their loss. With Caroline he carefully chose every word. She was such a gentle, innocent, young woman, if he did slip up and say something rude, he automatically apologized.

But Johnny was an outlaw and the chance that he might have hurt the kid's feelings shouldn't have gnawed at him all day. As a deputy marshal he had no business becoming friendly with the prisoners, or developing any relationship other than what was allowed within the parameters of his authority. What he needed was to keep up his guard. Calvin and whatever followers he had were still out there. Richard couldn't allow the injured feelings of some scrappy kid distract him from the focus of this mission.

Yet, despite his assertions, he found himself detaching the kid from the others prisoners. He'd even allowed the kid a few minutes of privacy in the bushes to attend his personal needs before putting him to work peeling potatoes.

Once the meal was ready, Richard took some time to wash up and change his shirt. As he approached the fire, Miles, one of the two guards, tossed the last of his coffee into the slop bucket hanging from the back of the chuck wagon, and with his rifle in hand, took up a nearby position against a steep section of the slope to watch the prisoners.

"Where's Tyler?" Richard asked as he grabbed a plate and cup from the chuck wagon and joined Brady by the fire.

"Sleeping." Brady gestured toward the other side of the chuck wagon where a mound of blankets indicated the second guard. "He's got the next watch."

"We heading to Fort Smith?" Richard set his plate and cup in the grass then poured some coffee.

Brady nodded as he drew on a cigarette. "I know we talked about searching Wildcat Thicket to pick up a few bootleggers, but I got me a funny feelin' about this trip."

Returning the coffee pot to the coals of the fire, Richard spooned beans and fried potatoes onto his plate. "Yeah, me, too." With a sigh, he dropped to sit cross-legged on the ground beside Brady.

The older deputy flicked the length of ash from the end of his cigarette. "Sides, this way we'll make it home by the end of May. Plenty of time before you turn in your badge."

Richard scooped up some potatoes. In truth, he didn't want this trip to end. He never told Caroline he specifically requested the long assignments, that he preferred working by himself, away from people. A certain measure of peace came over him while riding alone, through miles of open land. There were no judgments, no pressures, just his horse moving beneath him, the swish of the grass, the wind, and an endless sky.

But Caroline worried. The last time he'd returned from one of these extended trips she'd run, crying hysterically, down Garrison Avenue to the jail where he'd been logging in his prisoners all because she'd dreamed he'd been shot and killed.

To please her, he accepted a job as a second assistant to her father, District Attorney Benton Caldwell. Richard would be nothing more than a glorified errand boy, working in a job created by an indulgent father to pacify his pampered daughter. But Richard needed to keep her happy.

She would keep him sane. Her innocence and purity would balance the evil that lurked inside him. He couldn't risk losing her, for the thought of what he would become without her goodness in his life terrified him.

He stole a quick peek over his shoulder. Johnny sat against the wheel of the prison wagon with his knees drawn up and his forehead resting on his crossed arms. Richard turned back to his coffee, took a sip, and replaced his cup in the grass. Though the boy hadn't moved or given any indication that it was true, he knew Johnny watched him.

Balancing his plate on his right knee, he jabbed a few chunks of potato onto his fork. Brady scowled and tossed his cigarette butt into the fire.

"You an' that kid been settin' off sparks all day. What's goin' on?"

"Nothing."

"Kid's a brat," he grumbled. "Someone ought to take a switch to his backside."

Richard's gaze jerked to Brady's. Couldn't the old man tell from the bruises on Johnny's face the boy had already endured years of abuse far more harsh than just a few swats with a switch? Yet somehow, Johnny hadn't allowed that bastard of a father to break his spirit.

"Would you quit worryin' over that damn kid an' listen to me." Brady snapped. "That kid's no different from the rest. Remember, there's reasons we got warrants fer these men." Brady's voice took on a hard edge. "Think on the folks they robbed. Folks what never did nothin' but go about their lives. Think on the money they took. Life savin's of honest hard working families.

"An' think on that little gal Bodine raped an' murdered. An innocent girl who never got the chance to be courted proper nor fall in love an' have a family of her own. An' if you think that kid over there didn't have no part in any a that, well then I'm glad yer turnin' in yer badge. 'Cause yer puttin' me an' the rest a these men in danger."

No longer hungry, Richard rolled to his feet. He tossed his dishes into the bucket with the others to be washed and walked over to his bedroll. He sat down and pulled out his bottle of bourbon. His hand shook as he took a steadying swallow. He could feel Brady watching him, wondering about him, judging him. They all judged him, Marshal Upham, Reeves, even Wade Hollister. He was so damn tired of it.

One last swallow and he returned the bottle to his saddle bag. Then as was his habit every evening, he pulled out the small leather bag which held his gun cleaning supplies.

He glanced at Johnny's huddled form as he used a small rod to push an oiled cloth down the barrel of his Smith and Wesson Top Break revolver. There was strength in the kid which drew Richard. It was reflected in the way Johnny looked directly into your eyes. Those blue eyes should have sparkled with laughter. Instead, they held a wariness that came from years of mistrust. He felt a twinge of remorse that someone so young should be so old.

Rather like himself in some ways, for he'd been that age once, just before he'd gone off to war and traded his innocence for a gun. However stupid, he'd made his choice. But Johnny hadn't had a choice. Raised by a brutal man to believe that violence was a way of life, Johnny should be helping his family on a farm somewhere, wrestling with his brothers, going to church, and taking pretty girls to socials.

A part of Richard raged at the injustice of it all. And yet, despite the harsh reality of Johnny's life, his blue eyes held what Bodine's, what Machler's, what Warren's did not. Compassion. Buried deep beneath that gruff exterior was gentleness.

He glanced at his arm. The sleeve of his clean shirt fit snug over the thick bandage. And for Richard it was that hidden streak of caring which separated Johnny from the rest of the outlaws.

He wiped his oily hand down the front of his pants then tucked one revolver into his holster. The chamber on his second gun didn't rotate when he pulled the trigger. He took it apart, but the light was poor, so he reluctantly put the weapon back together, wrapped it in a piece of toweling and stuffed it in the bottom of his saddlebag.

Rising from his bedroll, he picked up his Winchester then located Brady leaning against the side of the cook's wagon, smoking a cigarette.

"I'm riding out to check our back trail." Richard said. Don't worry, I'll take my turn at watch."

The older deputy shook his head. "Don't suppose it'd do any good to point out clouds are movin' in.'"

Richard shrugged. "Billy's a good night horse, and I'll sleep better knowing no one's following us."

"Sleep? Bennick, ya never sleep."

"Don't worry, I'll be at your back when you need me."

****

Steady rain woke everyone well before sunrise. Rain ponchos of India rubber were thrown on and plates of cold beans passed around for breakfast.

Miserable without rain gear of her own, Johnny stood at the end of the chuck wagon, beneath an open-sided, water proofed canvas tent, washing the breakfast dishes while the cook packed up the camp. The tension that had twisted her stomach muscles into a knot when the one-armed deputy rode out last night, eased when she saw him ride up alongside the wagon.

Beyond the circle of lantern light, he was nothing more than a black silhouette against a backdrop of dark gray sky. He dismounted, leaving his horse ground tied, then grabbed one of the lanterns hanging from a pole and strode past her on his way to the front of the wagon. It tipped to the left when he climbed inside.

A moment later, the large, burly man who'd been hired to drive the prison wagon, brushed by. "Don't I get a gun?" he asked from outside the wagon.

"I thought you drove a prison wagon before," the deputy snapped as his silhouette bent and shifted behind the canvas.

"Sure, I rode a few posses an' such, but I always had me a weapon."

There was a slam, hollow and solid, like the lid on a wooden box. The wagon lurched again. The deputy swung his legs over the seat and jumped to the ground.

"The driver for the prison wagon never carries. It's too dangerous."

The glow from the lanterns reflected off his black poncho and rain dripped from the brim of his dark hat. The low light deepened the circles which underscored his red rimmed eyes. She doubted the man's surly mood would improve during the day.

"Come on, Deputy, can't I even have me a little pig sticker tucked in my boot for comfort?"

"No. You were told no weapons. That's the rule."

"Can't ya bend the rules? That Bodine's a dangerous man."

"Look, Hobbs, is it? I don't bend rules for anyone. Ever. And because Bodine is dangerous is precisely the reason you are not to carry a weapon."

"I guarantee the only way Bodine will get it is to kill me first."

"Then he'll still have it won't he?"

"But—"

"No weapons. You don't like it, get your gear and get the hell out of here." The deputy swung around and slammed into Johnny. "What do you want?" His broad hand clamped onto her shoulder, then he spun her around, and shoved her toward the back of the prison wagon where Brady had the other prisoners lined up.

Afraid of what might happen if she were trapped with her father and his men all day, Johnny veered off toward the horses and her big paint, Jack.

"Hold it!" Brady yelled. "Where are you going?"

She lifted her manacled hands and pointed toward the horses. The wet sleeves of her duster stuck to the tops of her hands. She'd rather be soaking wet all day than ride one minute in that dry wagon. "To fetch Jack."

"Sorry kid, everybody's in the wagon today."

She stiffened. "I done tolt ya, I ain't no outlaw." She hoped her father hadn't discerned the trace of panic in her voice.

The one-armed deputy moved up and stepped between them. "It doesn't matter what you claim, kid. We still have a warrant for your arrest."

Looking beyond the deputy's shoulder, she saw Brady raise the barrel of his rifle. Her heart pounded and her mouth went dry. She turned back to the one-armed deputy.

He denied her silent plea with a slight shake of his head. "Sorry. Your horses have been confiscated and later they'll be sold at auction."

Her anxiety over being chained in the prison wagon with her father vanished. "What do ya mean, sold?" she asked. Henry had given her Jack, and the big paint was the only friend she had left in this world. "Y'all cain't sell my horse."

"All your personal property has been confiscated by the court," the deputy explained as Brady lowered his rifle and gestured Johnny forward.

"What's that, conif-skate?" she asked, taking a few steps toward the prisoners who were being shackled together at the back of the wagon.

"Con-fis-cate. It means your horses have been appropriated as a penalty for your crimes. They will be sold and the money will go into the treasury."

"But I ain't done no crimes." She stopped and turned to meet his gaze. "Ya'll cain't sell my horse. That's stealin'."

"Shut up and fall in line." Brady ordered.

"It's not stealing, Johnny. It's legal," the deputy explained as he walked beside her.

"Why is it stealin' iffin I take a horse, but it ain't

iffin ya'll do?"

"We're not taking your horse. The court is."

"What's a court?"

Coming up from behind, Brady gave Johnny an impatient shove, which forced her feet to quick-step in order to keep her balance. From the corner of her eye, she saw the deputy's single arm stretch toward her, but at the last second, he jerked it back to his side.

"But Jack was give to me by my uncle Henry. I ain't a-goin' to let ya'll sell him."

"Shut up." Brady snapped as he slammed her against the corner of the iron prison wagon.

Pain exploded through her shoulder and radiated across her chest. Stumbling back, she dropped her gaze to the ground, the inside of her lower lip clenched between her teeth. If she hadn't been so afraid of losing Jack she never would have done anything so stupid. Men were men, reckon it didn't matter if they wore a badge. Brady grabbed her arm and pushed her into line beside Willis.

The outlaw raised his manacled arms and rested one hand on her shoulder. "You okay, kid?"

She nodded.

Bodine regarded her from his place a few feet behind the back of the wagon. "Now yer finally beginnin' to understand how the law works. Ya ain't so high an' mighty now is ya? The law can shoot ya an' say ya had a gun. The law can steal yer horse an' sell it all legal like. An' the law can hang ya right along with the rest of us, even iffin ya ain't never done nothin'."

"But Paw, I didn't steal Jack. Henry give him to me."

Bodine growled. "Ya stupid kid, how the hell do ya think Henry got him? The horse was stole. Ya ain't got no bill of sale. Ya'll be standin' on the gallows right along with the rest'a us when that new hangin' judge gets done."

As the severity of her situation dawned on her, her mouth went dry. Until that moment she hadn't actually believed she would be punished, knowing she was innocent of any crime. It hadn't occurred to her that no one would believe her.

The blond guard, Tyler, wrapped the other end of Willis's leg iron around her left ankle. She lifted her gaze to the one-armed deputy, hoping against hope he would deny her father's prediction.

Once again, the lawman seemed to possess the ability to read her mind.

"You'll have your say before Judge Parker. If you're found innocent he'll let you go and you can have your horse back."

Ahead of them, Brady ushered the prisoners into the wagon. Chained together, Willis and Johnny were the last ones to climb inside. Once they sat, Brady pulled down small doors on the sides of the wagon, and reaching in under the bench seats, he secured their leg irons to rings on the floor.

Richard swung onto his horse, while the burly driver climbed onto the high seat of the prison wagon and headed the mules east. Brady mounted and jogged his horse to the head of the line. The guards, Miles and Tyler, rode armed on either side of the prison wagon. Watching the wagon pass, Richard wondered why the kid was the only prisoner who hadn't had a slicker rolled up in his bedroll.

The wound on his forearm itched beneath the bandage. He fiddled with his reins, pretending to ignore the prisoners until the chuck wagon rolled by, with the extra horses strung out behind it. He reminded himself the kid was no good, that searching for signs of Bodine's men was more important than worrying about how wet and cold Johnny felt.

Tugging his hat low, he pulled up his collar and

turned his horse west, for a quick check of their back trail. But because of the continuous rain there wasn't much to see and unable to shake the edginess that tickled the hair on the back of his neck, he rejoined the procession.

Rain water filled gullies and swelled small streams, in some places bogging the wagons down to their axles. The prisoners ended up marching alongside, chained together in pairs to relieve the weight and to be available for pushing.

The tall, wet grass quickly soaked through the kid's pants and duster as he tromped along beside Willis. Richard wondered how many layers of the boy's clothing were wet. Johnny raised his arm and sniffed, wiping his nose across his drooping sleeve. As he did, he tripped and would have fallen flat on his face if Willis hadn't jerked him up in time.

Unable to stand it a moment longer, Richard dropped his knotted reins behind the saddle horn and pulled off his slicker.

"Hey, kid," he called riding up beside him.

Johnny looked up, causing rain to channel off the wide brim of his hat.

"Here." Richard tossed his garment at the kid. "You look like a damn drowned rat." He leaned out of the saddle and dropped the poncho over the kid's head. The hem hung nearly to his ankles and when Richard leaned down to tug it into place, he couldn't even see the boy's hands. Rather than try to adjust all the extra cloth with a piece a rope around the kid's waist, Richard gave his head a shake and swung his horse around.

****

Dusk arrived early as the sun lowered unobserved behind the thick gray storm clouds. Out most of the afternoon checking their back trail, Richard caught up with the procession at the wide red banks of the Washita River. Brady sat on his horse, looking through the brush and leaves at the swirling muddy water. He turned his head as Richard rode up beside him.

"I'm sick of this rain," Brady complained. "We're all wet and cold and hungry. Let's make camp and cross tomorrow. Maybe by morning the rain will have stopped and the water gone down."

More than anyone, Richard longed for dry clothes and a cup of hot coffee with a splash of bourbon, but his anxieties gnawed at him, making him restless, urging him to keep moving.

"If it keeps raining we won't be able to cross in the morning, and we'll have to wait for the water to go down while Bodine's men catch up. I say cross now, before it gets any higher. We can camp on the other side."

The older deputy frowned. "You ain't seen no sign of anyone all day, have ya? Ya don't even know if there is anyone. And if there is, they're likely holed-up someplace dry. An' look at you. Damn fool, givin' away your slicker. Don't know what the hell good it's gonna do if ya take sick."

"I've been wet before."

Brady stared at him for several seconds. "All right," he relented. "Reckon I don't feel like a cold swim first thing in the mornin'. But let's hitch the extra mules to each wagon so we don't have any trouble. If we do the prisoners can push."

The guards kept watch while Richard helped add two mules to each team. Brady took the horses across first, using them to clear a path down the bank. Hobbs followed next with the prison wagon. Water immediately covered the axles. The wagon had almost reached the far bank when the rear wheels mired down in the silt bottom. The mules strained. For several seconds Richard wondered if he'd have to send the prisoners into the water to push. Then the team gave one hard lunge. The wagon pulled free from the bottom, and the mules scrambled to haul the iron vehicle up the slippery incline.

Richard mounted his bay gelding, Billy, as the chuck wagon, loaded down with extra supplies and ammunition, rolled down the bank. Water swirled around the wagon box, and he prayed it wouldn't get any deeper. It would take a full day of hot sun to dry everything out. The wagon had nearly made it to shore when, an invisible rope seemed to tug the rear wheel slightly downstream and drop it into the same hole which had bogged down the prison wagon. Yanked off balance by the sudden shift, the mules struggled to keep their footing in the soft red sand as the driver cracked his whip. Above, Brady fumbled to remove his wet rope from his saddle.

"Get in there and start pushing!" Richard yelled to prisoners. "Miles, go help Brady!"

Miles charged his horse into the water, his rope already in hand. The prisoners, still shackled in pairs, waded into the river behind him. Johnny and Willis slogged into the water behind Bodine and Machler as debris swirled around their waists.

Richard urged his horse forward, flanking the prisoners on the downstream side, while Tyler guarded them upstream.

The wagon team, fought to pull the heavy load up the bank, lost their footing in the soft red sand and the wagon rolled back, tugging, them toward the water and settling the wheel deeper into the hole.

Having reached the back of the chuck wagon, Warren and Machler immediately leaned into the job and pushed.

At the top of the bank Miles and Brady scrambled to secure their ropes from the wagon to their saddle horns.

When Richard shifted his attention back to the prisoners, he saw Bodine grab Willis from behind and shove the man's head under the water. Frantic, Willis latched onto Johnny, pulling the boy down with him. Johnny popped back up, but the drowning outlaw's fingers clawed desperately at the boy's arm and the front of his poncho.

For a stunned moment Richard could only blink in disbelief. Then he kicked his horse forward, but the river bottom was soft and the water not deep enough for Billy to swim.

Though Machler and Warren stopped pushing to watch, neither man attempted to intervene.

"No one falls asleep on guard duty," Bodine declared, pushing Willis under once more. "Not iffin ya ride with me."

Coughing and spitting, Johnny was sucked under again, just as Richard jumped from the saddle. Reaching beneath the surface, he hauled Willis up by the back of his collar and towed the limp outlaw to shore. Because Johnny was attached, the boy half swam, half stumbled along beside them.

Richard dropped Willis face down in the grass then started pushing on the man's back. Though his action forced water from the outlaw's nose and mouth, he didn't revive. Furious, Richard whirled then charged back into the river.

"You sonofabitch!"

"Whacha gonna do?" Bodine sneered. "Hang me twice?"

Richard drew back his fist and drove it square into Bodine's jaw. The outlaw appeared to lift from the water for an instant, then fell back with a splash. He surfaced, cursing and sputtering.

Richard grabbed the front of the outlaw's slicker and leaned close, and with his nose nearly touching Bodine's, he bit out. "I ought to kill you right now and save the court the trouble."

Bodine smiled, a slow, malicious, leering smile.

The rage surging through Richard's blood was

suddenly sucked from his chest as an evil grin curled up the corners of the outlaw's lips.

When Bodine spoke, his voice was low, and he drew his syllables out in a seductive taunt that conjured an image of the serpent in the garden of Eden. "Go ahead, marshal. Kill me. Do it. Come on. We both know ya want to."

And the sickening truth was that Richard did want to. He could almost imagine how it would feel to wrap his hand tight around Bodine's wet, stubble-coated neck, while he slowly squeezed the outlaw's throat. In his mind, he could hear the outlaw's wheezing little gasps for air as his eyes bulged from their sockets in his desperation to breathe, but instead of letting go, Richard only imagined himself pushing his thumb against the fragile cartilage until it collapsed inward with a soft crack.

His blood turned to ice as a deep chill, which had nothing to do with the rain or his wet clothes, racked every bone in his body. Richard released the outlaw with a shove, more repulsed by his own vile thoughts than by the evil which was Bodine.

He felt detached from his body as he slowly backed away, even as he remained unable to tear his gaze from the outlaw, terrified that the next time he looked in a mirror he would find Bodine's face looking back.

A maniacal burst of laughter erupted from Bodine's throat. "Come on, marshal, yer no diff'rent than me," the outlaw jeered. "Ya know how it feels to kill. But go ahead. Hang on ta yer rule book and yer code. See if that'll save yer soul."

The backs of Richard's thighs bumped against the bank. His knees buckled, and he dropped heavily onto a submerged portion of the grassy slope. The muddy water swirled around his waist. A cold shudder shook his body.

"Are ya aimin' ta set in the river all night?"

Richard blinked and turned his head. Johnny sat huddled on the bank, in the oversized poncho, looking very small and very wet. Rain poured off his matted hair and ran down either side of his face.

"I'd sure be obliged, iffen ya'd unlock me."

Damn, the poor kid was still shackled to the dead man's ankle.

"An' don't go a-tellin' me that deputy over yonder got the keys." With a nod, Johnny gestured upstream, where Brady and the others had just pulled the cook's wagon up the bank.

Exhausted and ashamed, Richard hauled himself from the water and stood dripping as his numb fingers fumbled to remove the small brass key from the pocket of his vest.

As he stepped forward, Johnny leaned back on his elbows and stuck his foot in the air, making it easier for Richard to insert the key. As soon as Johnny was freed from Willis, the kid rolled to his feet and started up the bank. He had just reached out to grab onto a small bush, when he heaved a weighted sigh and turned around. Tilting his head slightly, he fixed his gaze on Richard.

"Ya ain't nothin' like my paw, an' yer a damn fool fer thinkin' so." Then with his chin high, he swung around and climbed up the bank.

Kathy Otten

Chapter Three

Disbelief anchored Richard to the bank as he stared at the empty spot where Johnny had been. The kid possessed such piercing eyes; had he seen something worthy in Richard to inspire such an adamant declaration? No, Johnny couldn't know all the sins Richard had committed.

Dismissing the boy's words, he climbed up the bank and returned with one of the extra horses to bring up the body. Then, before heading back, he took a short walk along the bank in search of Johnny's hat. He wasn't even sure what prompted him to look for it, except the kid seemed a bit lost without that wide brim pulled low to hide his face.

That Johnny sought to go unnoticed, sought to become invisible to watching eyes, was a need Richard understood. And after a brief search, he found the light colored Stetson caught in a tangle of sticks and debris not too far downstream from where they'd been sitting.

He waded into the river and leaned over to untangle it from the snag. He shook off the excess water and walked back to the horse. At the campsite, he found the kid standing by the horses, apparently forgotten by Brady and the guards while they secured the prisoners and set up a big open-sided tent. The wet grass muted his footsteps as he approached, and he could hear the kid whispering to that big paint of his. The horse lifted his head and perked his ears forward.

Johnny swung around and gasped.

"Here's your hat." Richard extended his arm.

40

Their gazes met for several long seconds, as Johnny searched his face. Finally he stepped forward and took the hat.

"Obliged," he said as he jammed the hat on his head.

Unsure of what to say, Richard nodded then turned away, leading the horse which carried Willis's body.

Unable to build a fire, everyone was forced to eat cold food. Later they spread their damp bedrolls out in the wet grass on waterproof gum blankets, beneath the canvas roof.

The rain stopped during the night, and the next two days passed uneventfully. Richard hoped they would be able to make up some of their lost time, though they were still eleven or twelve days out from Fort Smith.

That evening, the prisoners were once again chained to the wagon axle. Bodine whispered softly with Machler and Warren, while they played cards. Occasional chuckles and crude remarks drifted to Richard's ears on the night air as he sat near the campfire cleaning his rifle and revolver.

Though it was quiet, he was restless. Earlier, he'd ridden back toward the Washita looking for signs they were being followed, but all he'd seen was a distant flock of black birds swarm into the sky then swoop down again. He wondered what had spooked them. His gut instinct warned him it was the rest of Bodine's men, if so, why were they hanging back? There had been hunts for Bodine before, but the outlaw had proven as elusive as dust in the wind. The ease of his capture now, nagged him. McAlester was three days away.

The terrain had become more rolling and less open with scattered hardwood forests, valleys, and ridges. If Bodine's men were going to make a move, it would be soon. Trouble was coming. The question was—when?

Carefully, he repacked his gun oil, cleaning rods, and cloth, then checked his ammunition. With a quick glance toward Johnny, who was busy scrubbing pots and pans, he padded softly out of camp.

****

A heavy fist slammed into Johnny's ribs and jerked her from a sound sleep. With her hand pressed against her side, she blinked and sat up, keeping a wary eye on the outlaw who had delivered the blow.

Beside her, Warren held the dangling chain of his handcuffs in one fist to keep it from making any noise which might draw the attention of the nearby guard.

"Listen," he hissed.

Johnny shivered, knowing she was going to hate whatever Warren had to say.

"Breed signaled your pa while you was washin' dishes. Cal's waitin' up ahead to spring us tomorrow afternoon. So listen good. Your pa wants you to use yer bag a medicines to make that Deputy Brady sick, so's you can get close enough to lift the keys for these chains."

"How am I s'posed to do that?"

Quick as a snake, Warren's big hand was around her throat, squeezing hard enough to cut off her air. She should have known not to argue.

"Look, you stupid little shit!" He bit out between clenched teeth. "Your pa don't care how. Just get the damn keys!"

Gasping and coughing, she rubbed her aching throat.

"Hey!" the guard yelled, as he strode toward the prisoners, his Winchester aimed at Warren. "What's going on here?" He stopped just out of their reach and gestured toward Johnny with the barrel of his rifle. "What's wrong with the kid?"

Johnny shook her head, unable to respond with anything more than coughs and ragged breaths.

Instead, Bodine replied from the other side of Warren. "The boy's prone to these spells." He shook his head. "Purely a shame ain't it? Ya know I sure do hate sayin' this, him bein' my boy an' all, but it jest might be more merciful fer him to get his neck stretched, than to watch him waste away, coughin' up blood like his maw, God rest her soul."

The guard sent Johnny a long, pitying look. "Yeah, well try to keep it quiet over here," he mumbled before he returned to his post at the rear wheel of the chuck wagon.

As soon as the guard's head began to nod, Bodine leaned across Warren's bulk and grabbed Johnny by the front of her duster, jerking her close. "Ya understand what yer s'posed to do?"

She swallowed the bile that climbed up her throat as the stench of her father's breath slammed into her face. She nodded vigorously, ignoring her instinct to pull back.

"'Cause I got me a plan an' iffin ya mess it up, I swear to God I'll leave ya alone out here in the middle a the friggin' prairie."

As her father's thick fingers released their hold, Johnny scooted back, pressing her spine into the spokes of the wagon wheel as though she could somehow disappear into the wood. With her knees drawn tight to her chest, she huddled deep in her oversized duster too terrified to sleep.

A couple of hours past midnight, the deputy returned to camp. Johnny watched him ease himself down before the fire. A strange ache grew to choke her throat almost as painfully as Warren's hand had earlier. She longed to sit in that small circle of light where the deputy poured himself a cup of coffee then added a splash of whiskey. She wished she were as tough as she pretended, instead her chest hurt with the pressure of bottled up tears.

Outlined in shadow by the orange glow, the deputy set aside his Stetson then combed his fingers through his hair. A short lock flopped down across his forehead. He brushed back the annoyance, but without his hat the hair fell over his forehead again. Resigned, he rubbed his hand over his face and yawned. It seemed almost like spying to watch the man like this when he was so unaware, but she couldn't help it. Fascinated, she watched as he first drew his arm across his chest, then raised it over his head and stretched. The left side of his shirt tail popped from the waistband of his pants. She was forced to curl her fingers into fists, clenching them against the strange desire to reach beyond the distance and touch him.

Finally, he tossed the remains of his coffee into the grass and set his mug on the end of the chuck wagon. He rolled himself up in his bedroll and pulled the blanket over his head as they all did, to keep away the mosquitoes. Secure, knowing the deputy slept so close, Johnny, too, drifted off to sleep.

****

In the dark gray of pre-dawn, the deputies rose to eat a quick breakfast and break camp. A brisk wind snapped the canvas of the cook wagon and tipped the flames of the campfire sideways, delaying the time it took to prepare the meal. Immediately, Bodine snatched the coffee and biscuits meant for Johnny, right from the hands of the young guard, Tyler.

"Bodine, you had yours. Let the kid eat."

"What the hell's going on over there?" The one-armed deputy demanded from the other side of camp where he paused in the act of rolling up his bedding.

"Nothing," muttered Tyler. "I'll just fetch the kid some more."

44

A minute later he returned with a new plate. Johnny exchanged a quick glance with her father and surrendered her meal.

Recognizing the impatient stride that swished through the tall grass, Johnny dropped her gaze and focused on the scuffed brown boots that stopped before her, certain if she looked up the deputy would see the lie in her eyes. "I ain't hungry."

The deputy shifted his weight. Johnny silently prayed the lawman wouldn't ask questions.

"Boy's feelin' a mite poorly this mornin'." Her father's explanation was garbled as he spoke around a mouthful of food.

The young guard who had first watch that night, wandered over. "Yeah, the poor kid had a bad night of it."

"What do you mean?" the deputy demanded.

"Kid's a lunger. Had a bad spell of coughin' last night."

Rolling his weight forward onto the balls of his feet, the deputy hunkered down in front of her. Johnny found herself staring at faded walnut-brown pants, pulled tight across flexed knees. The deputy's right forearm rested on his thigh. She stared at the back of his hand, fascinated by the network of raised veins. The cleanliness of his hand was amazing, especially around the fingernails, even after all this time on the trail. It wasn't fair, she suddenly thought, that this magnificent man before her should have only one arm.

"Are you okay, kid? Do you need anything?" His low tones rumbled almost level with her ears.

There was such concern in his voice she was tempted to throw herself on his mercy and confess all. But Pierpont Bodine had given Johnny her orders. If she failed, she had no doubt her father would leave her behind. And only one thing terrified Johnny more than being left alone.

"Johnny?" the deputy gently probed. "Are you sure you don't want anything?"

Johnny lifted her gaze to the center button on the deputy's blue shirt. "Maybe a cup a chokecherry tea would help some."

The deputy slowly rolled to his feet, and Johnny suddenly found herself staring at the soft bulge beneath the button fly of his britches. Mortified, she dropped her gaze to his dusty boots. After a moment he turned, and she watched the back of his legs disappear into the swaying grass.

She heard Brady's voice a moment later. "I don't care if the kid has TB, he'll be swingin' at the end of a rope come fall. We're not waitin' around to brew tea."

She couldn't make out all of what the one-armed deputy said, but she did hear him say, "...it's not right. You don't know what Parker will do. Johnny's just a kid."

Striding toward the horses, Brady yelled, "Fine, coddle the brat, but I'm not waitin'. You can catch up."

A few minutes later the one-armed deputy returned with the keys and separated Johnny from the others. "Come on. I'll get your bag of herbs."

Eyes downcast, she trailed behind him, while Brady yelled for the guards to help him load the prisoners.

Hobbs stood at the back of the cook wagon holding an arm full of canteens. He dumped them into Johnny's arms. "I gotta go. Can ya fill these for me?" He didn't wait for her answer before striding over to the prison wagon and climbing onto the high seat.

At the water barrel, which rode strapped to the side of the cook wagon, she dropped the canteens on the ground. Then using both hands she lifted the lid and dipped them one at a time into the water. The silver chain, looped between her wrists, glistened in the early morning light as she screwed on the last cap and set the canteen on the ground.

"Don't ferget to bring back my pot." The cook said in passing as he handed her a dented saucepan, then climbed onto the wagon seat as the deputy jumped down with her doe skin bag over his shoulder.

He passed her the bag. "Don't move," he snapped and strode over to where his bedroll still lay in the grass. He snatched up his canteen, tossed it to her, and spun back to finish tying up his bedroll.

His aim was true, and she easily caught the strap. As she untangled it from her manacles she noticed three letters painted on the outside of the canvas cover. Wondering what they spelled she traced the first letter with her finger—R.

"Hurry up back there," the cook called impatiently. Johnny barely had time to fill the canteen and secure the lid on the barrel before the cooked moved his team in line behind the prison wagon.

Cursing under his breath, the deputy dog-trotted after the departing wagon and tossed his bedroll under the seat.

Turning away, Johnny walked to the campfire and set the pot in the remaining coals. Next she pulled a thick, leather bound journal from the doeskin bag and sat cross-legged on the ground.

It had taken her years to create this book, and though there were no words, the pages were still organized in sections. A precise drawing of a particular injury or illness was followed by pages of brightly illustrated plants, beneath which were step-by-step colored pictures for preparing the plant.

A breeze tossed the pages forward and back, giving her time to think as she racked her brain for a plan. After a few moments, she stopped and began rummaging through her bag for the small bundle of dried plants that matched the illustration on the page.

"Where did you get this?" The deputy asked, picking up the book as he squatted beside her.

"Uncle Henry give it to me," she replied, distracted by his nearness and the scent of sandalwood.

"Well your uncle is very talented."

"It was me done the renderin's. Uncle Henry jest give me the book an' Morning Song showed me how to make the colors."

He shot her a surprised glance then set it down, open, on the ground in front of him. Flipping through the pages, he paused every so often to study different paintings on the pages. "These are beautiful," he murmured. "Amazing."

Her gaze shot to the side of his face, but his attention remained on the book. Her fingers clenched around the dried leaves in her hand. Having spent her life doing everything wrong, he couldn't know how his simple compliment warmed her insides. She tossed the crushed curly dock, into the pot and swallowed the lump that climbed up the back of her throat. Her eyes burned with an unexplained need to cry, though she hadn't even been hit. She shot to her feet.

"What's the matter?" he asked.

Her mind raced. She shifted nervously from foot to foot. "I gotta go," she finally choked out.

"What? Right now?" Suspicion immediately replaced the warmth in his voice.

She nodded.

"All right," he acquiesced after a long moment, "just hurry up." He gestured vaguely to the right where the ground sloped downhill. "You've got two minutes."

She really did have to go and certainly didn't

want to do it where he could see. Spotting a lone bush a short distance away, she hurried toward it. When she finished, she headed back, swatting at the swaying tips of the waist-high grass as she walked.

For him to say her simple artwork was both wonderful and amazing left her feeling more mystified than the day he punched her father. She was forced to stop and press the heels of her hands against her eyes just to stop the burning.

When she lowered her hands and looked, the odd sensation she was going the wrong way washed over her. She swung around, searching for the bush, but she saw only scattered trees and brush. Fear clamped like a vise around her chest, squeezing so tight she could barely draw a breath. Her pulse pounded, roaring in her ears like a north wind, as her palms began to sweat. *Think! Think!* The voice in her head screamed.

Her trail through the blue-green grass was still visible. She whirled around to follow it back, but the wind had picked up, sifting through the stems and erasing her trail. She told herself to just turn and go back up the slope. But when Johnny swung back, the ground sloped in every direction and all looked the same. Rolling hills, scattered trees, and sky. Pink and orange streaked the horizon in one direction, but she couldn't remember which way that was.

She searched for the head and shoulders of the deputy, but if he was sitting by the fire coals, the height of the prairie grass hid him from view. She wanted to yell, but it was impossible to draw enough air. She turned and ran.

No. She skidded to a stop at the edge of an old buffalo wallow. This wasn't right. She should have found the camp by now. She altered her direction. This wasn't it either. She changed course again, but couldn't remember which way she'd just tried. A sob caught in her throat. Oh God, she was lost!

She heard a soft swish behind her and whirled around. That goddamn wonderful deputy was striding straight toward her. Relief nearly drove her to her knees. She longed to run to him and throw herself against his broad chest, to grab hold of him and never let go, but all she could do was stand there and breathe.

"Where in the hell do you think you're going?" he yelled, his long legs devouring the distance between them. He halted a few feet from where she stood. Angry creases furrowed his brow. "I asked you a question. Where are you going?

She swallowed. "I..." She glanced around confused. "B-back to the c-camp," she squeaked.

"I'd have to be pretty stupid to believe that wouldn't I? The rest of your father's men are out there aren't they?"

The blood drained from her face, leaving her feeling cold and clammy.

"You were hoping to get to them before I noticed you were missing. Weren't you? How did you know they were here? Did they signal you last night?"

Suddenly, she was yanked forward as the deputy, reaching to grab her duster, caught her faded silk bandana in his fist and gave it a jerk.

"Tell me," he hissed. His dark brown eyes had hardened like chips of stone. He gave her a quick shake.

Johnny knew that look. The fist would come next. Terrified, she wrenched away. The worn material ripped, tearing free in the deputy's hand. Johnny stumbled, poised to run, but the deputy was quick and had her by the arm before she could escape.

Though she struggled to free herself, his grip was too tight. Bravely she lifted her gaze, trying to read in his expression what he would do next. His dark brown eyes narrowed into an angry glare which had her heart thudding against the wall of her chest, until his rage gradually faded into confusion. He released his grip on her arm and raised his hand to wrap lightly around her throat. She swallowed nervously as her pulse thrummed wildly beneath the calloused pads of his fingers.

Richard frowned. As he suspected, his fingers were an exact match for each of the purple ovals on the boy's neck. Someone had tried to choke the poor kid.

Suddenly the faded yellow bruise on Johnny's cheek seemed more pronounced, even through the smudges of dirt. Once again the urge to protect stirred inside him. For an insane instant, his arm ached to draw Johnny into the comfort of an embrace. An image of Caroline's slender white neck flashed through his mind. Unconsciously, his thumb moved back and forth to lightly stroke the underside of Caroline's jaw. He closed his eyes and leaned close.

He felt her shiver, then stiffen. He blinked, and found Johnny, not Caroline, staring at him with wide violet eyes. He snatched his hand away.

Slowly, Johnny brought his own smaller hand up to cover his neck in the exact places Richard's own fingers had just been.

Richard's face burned, mortified by what he'd almost done. He reached behind his neck and pulled free the knot which secured his oversized neckerchief. "Here!" He snapped as he thrust the blue calico silk into the boy's hand. "Cover your damned neck."

Johnny stared at the bandana.

"Hurry up," Richard snapped. "Put it on and let's go."

Quickly Johnny tied on the new neck cloth, adjusting it to cover the bruises, then turned and started walking.

"Not that way, east."

Johnny swung around.

"Up the hill, toward the sun." Richard pointed. Though the two horses weren't immediately visible because of their distance from the fire, the angle of the sun and the height of the grass, they hadn't gone so far as to become lost. He couldn't help but wonder if the kid was trying to escape.

Johnny adjusted his direction, and they walked back to the camp fire in silence.

"I put those canteens next to your bag so we don't forget them. They should have been put in the wagon, but that damn cook took off so fast..." Richard pointed to the steaming pot. "Hurry up and make your tea. I'm going to get the horses, and you damn well better be here when I get back."

His own horse had already been saddled, and he just had to grab the lead line attached to the halter of Johnny's big brown and white paint. He rode up as Johnny poured some of the remaining tea from the pot over the coals. They hissed as the water rose into steam, then he stirred the coals and poured out the rest.

"Pass me those canteens and let's get out of here." Without a word Johnny handed him the canteens, and he looped each strap over his saddle horn. Then he tied the pot and the cup Johnny had used on top of his saddle bags.

Turning, he watched Johnny struggle to mount the big paint. Without a saddle, he kept jumping up and sliding down. Finally, with a shake of his head, Richard nudged his horse sideways, close enough so he could give the kid a little boost when he made his next attempt to mount. After what happened earlier, Richard was reluctant to put his hand on the kid's butt end, but the boy was already starting to slip so Richard leaned over and gave him a shove that nearly pitched him off the other side of the horse.

The kid shot him a dirty glare once he'd adjusted himself on the horse, but Richard ignored him. He rubbed his palm up and down the thigh of his pants trying to use friction to erase the lingering sensation of his hand pressed against Johnny's nicely rounded behind.

They caught up to the rest of the procession a short time later, and Brady insisted Johnny be returned to the wagon with the rest of the prisoners.

"Let me help ya boy." Warren offered as he leaned down from his seat near the back door of the wagon, grabbed the length of chain between Johnny's wrists, and gave it a sharp jerk.

Unable to break his fall, Johnny hit the dirty floor face first. Bodine and Machler burst out laughing.

"Shit! I'm awful sorry boy." Warren apologized, but his tone lacked sincerity.

Slowly, the boy pushed to his knees. Blood trickled from his reopened split lip.

Suppressing an urge to intervene, Richard swung his horse toward the cook wagon while covertly watching the boy from the corner of his eye. The horses shifted in their traces just as Johnny stood. Off balance, he stumbled against his father.

"Get off me, you stupid little shit!" Bodine shoved him toward the opposite bench. Johnny stumbled, and tangled in the length of chain, he fell to the floor, while Warren and Bodine sat laughing.

"Leave the kid alone!" Brady ordered from outside the open door.

From the back of his horse, Richard couldn't help but wince at the pain reflected in the boy's dirty, blood smeared face. He had to get away. "I'm going to check our back trail."

Brady nodded.

"I'll catch up around mid-morning." He left the pot and canteens with the cook, then swung his horse around and cantered back the way they'd come. Once out of sight, he halted his horse and dropped his reins around the saddle horn. Reaching behind, he pulled his bottle of Old Crow from his saddle bag and took a long swallow.

He wondered if he was actually crazy and didn't know it. Only through supreme force of will had he been able to ride away and leave the kid alone with that bunch of worthless pond scum. But what happened earlier had shaken him to his core. He tried to convince himself that his reaction had been caused by prolonged celibacy. He'd been faithful to Caroline since that day almost a year ago, when he'd asked Benton Caldwell for permission to court his daughter.

The vulnerability he'd seen in Johnny's vivid blue eyes should have brought out his normal need to protect, not this insane lust. He took another swallow, trying to forget the feel of his own thumb caressing the soft skin on the underside of the boy's jaw.

He was almost too terrified to admit it, even to himself, but in the early light of dawn, U.S. Deputy Marshal Richard Bennick, had very nearly kissed Johnny Bodine, son of the most notorious outlaw in the territory. Between the nightmares, the unpredictable flashbacks, and this new, unnatural attraction to Johnny, Richard seriously doubted his own sanity. How much longer before he completely lost control?

Chapter Four

In the distance a covey of partridges soared upward against a backdrop of clear cerulean sky. He returned the bottle to his saddle bag and rode a couple of miles north to investigate. The tracks he intercepted showed several riders heading east. He followed the trail for a few miles, wondering why whoever he was following was riding parallel to the posse. Uneasy, Richard turned his horse away and dropped down, riding southeast, in order to catch up with Brady and the others.

Uneasiness gnawed at his stomach, and he pushed his mount into a lope. That kid had known this morning something was going to happen. Richard cursed himself for a fool. He should have stayed focused on the job and questioned Johnny when he'd had the chance. Instead, he'd felt sorry for the kid and allowed his own unbridled lust to over ride his instincts.

He caught up with the posse at mid-morning. Nodding to the guards on either side of the prison wagon, he forced himself to avoid looking at Johnny as he rode past to join Brady at the head of the procession.

"See anything?" The older deputy asked as Richard rode up alongside.

"Riders shadowing us to the north. I don't like it." He dropped his knotted reins around the saddle horn and lifted his canteen. He tucked it next to his body and held it in place with the stump of his left arm as he unscrewed the cap.

"Got a bad feeling myself," Brady agreed as

Richard gulped some water. "Considerin' he'll probably hang, Bodine sure ain't put up much fuss."

Twisting the cap back on, Richard couldn't help but notice how unusually pale the older deputy looked. "You feeling all right?"

Brady nodded. "Stomach's acting up a little."

"Too much worry."

"Yeah. We'll be stopping for a bit later this afternoon. There's water ahead and woods. Get out of this sun for a while. Give the horses a break."

Richard shifted in his saddle. He swallowed. Damn trees. The landscape had been steadily changing, since they crossed into the Choctaw Nation. Hills and hardwood forest were outlined on the horizon as they headed east toward the outer edge of the Ouachita Mountains. If he'd been alone he would have gone miles out of his way to avoid their dark, leafy canopies.

"Okay, but I'd like to borrow your spyglass for a while. I'm going to ride ahead. I want to make sure we're not riding into an ambush."

Brady nodded and they rode in silence for a few minutes. Then Richard asked the question he'd been battling with himself not to ask.

"How are the prisoners?"

Brady cast him a shrewd glance. "Knew all along ya was wantin' to ask about that damn kid." Brady frowned. "Well, ya ain't gonna be happy."

Richard turned sharply in the saddle. The light-colored duster was easy to spot inside the prison wagon, but with his head down and his hat pulled low, it was impossible for Richard to discern the boy's features.

"Now don't go gettin' yore back up 'er nothin'. They just been shovin' an' pokin' him. Teasin' like, only they ain't funnin'."

Despite his personal admonition not to get involved, every muscle in his body had tensed, and he found himself swinging his horse toward the prisoners. The guards turned in their saddles as he rode up.

Concern etched Tyler's features with deep lines. "They're givin' that kid a real hard time. Ain't never seen the like."

Richard held his bay parallel to the wagon and the young guard moved ahead to ride alongside Brady. Ignoring Bodine's cocky grin and Machler and Warren's chuckles, Richard silently regarded Johnny. The boy's head remained down, but he could feel those unusual eyes watching him from beneath the brim of that battered hat. To ask Johnny how he was would be pointless. The kid was too afraid of his father to admit to any abuse. But Bodine's smug look was the only answer Richard needed. The outlaw had deliberately mistreated Johnny, but to what purpose Richard couldn't decide.

A few minutes later, Brady called a halt. Curious, Richard rode up to the head of the line. He glanced at the quiet young guard. Tyler was as pale as Brady.

"I'm fine," Tyler snapped in reply to Richard's silent scrutiny. "Guess I ate too many a them beans last night."

Richard swung his gaze to Brady as the older man shifted in his saddle. If anything, his face had grown more ashen.

"We're fine," Brady snarled. "Get up there an' scout ahead like you was goin' to!" He turned to Tyler. "Go see if any of them prisoners want a drink 'fore we get movin' again. An' see how Miles and the drivers are doin'."

With a nod Tyler turned his horse around and headed back toward the wagons.

Johnny's heart pounded as Tyler dismounted and walked toward them with a handful of canteens. She'd tried several times this morning to tell her paw what she'd done, but every time she opened her mouth to explain she'd been hit, kicked, or shoved, much to the delight of Warren and Machler. She was actually tempted to let the three of them drink their fill. It would serve them right, but she couldn't do it. She knew what would happen to her if her father became as sick as the others.

Tyler passed two canteens through the bars. Bodine grabbed one, Warren another.

"Paw!" Johnny lunged for the canteen, caught the leather strap and jerked it from his beefy fingers. It landed on the dirty floor. Water trickled from the loosened cap.

"Why you worthless little sonofabitch," he snarled and slammed his manacled fists into her face.

Johnny didn't cry out, even as the impact flung her to the floor. She'd learned long ago that crying only got you hit again. Blood gushed from her nose, quickly soaking the blue bandana the deputy had given her that morning.

She recalled how his dark brown eyes had softened with concern when he'd seen the bruises. He'd guessed where they'd come from, but he never asked. Instead he'd given her his own bandana so no one else would know.

Tyler's shout had that deputy swinging his dark bay around and loping straight toward them.

"The kid only wanted a drink." Tyler explained as the deputy halted his horse.

"Johnny, are you all right?" he demanded from beside the bars.

"Yeth," she answered with her hands pressed tight against her nose.

"Johnny?"

She lifted her hands from her face to see how much blood soaked the bandana. Then she gingerly touched the end of each nostril with her finger tip to see if the bleeding had stopped. "Quit yer fussin'. It ain't nothin' but a damn nosebleed."

"What the hell's all the ruckus about?" Brady demanded as he joined them.

"Brady, I want that kid out of there. He can ride his horse."

"Ya damn fool, they're doin' it to rile ya."

"I know that, but at this rate the kid will be dead before we reach Fort Smith."

Beads of sweat stood out across the older deputy's forehead as he glared at the one-armed deputy. "They ain't gonna kill him. An' so what if they do? Kid's gonna hang anyways."

"You don't know that, and it's our job to protect the prisoners, not stand by and watch one of them be beaten to death."

Brady drew a shaky hand across his brow. "Look Bennick, I don't know what's goin' on between you an' that damn kid, but I don't need this. You let that kid loose and he'll just be one more thing to watch. An' right now I ain't feelin' too good, an' neither is anyone else."

"Well, I won't stand by and do nothing while that kid is abused."

"Okay. Have it your way. But he's your responsibility."

Miles and Tyler leveled their rifles on the prisoners as Brady reached through from the outside to unlock Johnny's leg iron from the floorboard, and she was freed from the confines of the wagon.

Without another word the deputy followed as she headed toward the horses grazing to the right of the procession.

She kept her head down, afraid of what he would do. He said nothing, just sat on his horse beside her as Miles went to retrieve her saddle from the cook's wagon. She could feel the deputy's dark gaze boring through the top of her head. Then she felt the light pressure of his index finger as he leaned from his horse and reached out to gently turn her chin toward him. The pit of her stomach gave a funny little flutter just as it had hours earlier when the deputy had similarly lifted her chin and stared into her eyes.

Now, he lifted a corner of the blue bandana around her neck, leaned close, and tenderly wiped away the blood smearing her face. Her cheeks were sensitive from her father's earlier blows, and she flinched when the cloth touched her skin, but once she lifted her gaze to meet the deputy's eyes, she was lost.

Regret and sympathy filled his dark brown gaze. Not even with Henry had Johnny felt such an affinity, and the intensity of this odd connection scared her.

"Bennick," Brady's voice disrupted the current.

The deputy blinked and jerked his arm back as he straightened in the saddle and swung his attention to the older deputy.

Brady snapped. "What the hell's wrong with you?"

"Nothing."

"Ya ain't gettin' sick?"

"I'm fine."

Johnny watched the deputy's dusty boot as his weight shifted in the stirrup as if he were uncomfortable with the older deputy's questions.

"Okay then. You're responsible for the kid."

"Damn it, Brady, this isn't the time. If I don't scout ahead we might miss an important sign."

Miles approached with Johnny's saddle and bridle. She intended to saddle her own horse, but even though she knew the young guard was feeling poorly, she stepped back and waited when he insisted on saddling the big paint.

Brady turned his tall sorrel around. "You

wanted the kid, take him with you. Just don't lose him."

"You know I can't do that, it's not procedure."

"Do what you want. We've wasted enough time." He kicked his horse into a canter and returned to the lead.

In turn, the deputy snapped at her. "You keep those big blue eyes of yours looking straight between your horse's ears. Move wrong and you'll be dead before you hit the ground."

Johnny jerked her chin up and shot the deputy a nasty glare before she gathered the reins in her hands and flipped them over Jack's neck. Turning, she stuck her foot in the stirrup and pulled herself into the saddle. The cook rolled by next with his team, followed by the prison wagon. Johnny and the deputy came next.

They rode in silence for two hours before Brady called another halt and trotted his horse back toward them. Johnny couldn't help but notice the beads of sweat that dampened the brow of his pale face. A glance at the prisoners confirmed the fact that her father and his men weren't fairing any better.

Brady dismounted and stood clutching his saddle. "Damn, must have been something in the water."

"The water," the one-arm deputy mimicked dully.

Johnny tensed as he swung toward her.

His narrowed gaze was filled with suspicion. "Why aren't you sick?"

"Cause I ain't had nothin' to drink all day."

"Why? You filled those canteens. What did you do?"

She shifted in her saddle. "Nothin'. I was tolt to fill them canteens, an' I filt 'em."

"And what exactly did you fill them with,

besides water?"

"Nothin'."

"Damn it, Johnny. You were alone with the canteens and your bag of herbs. I know you put something in the water."

"No, I didn't. Iffin they's somthin' in the water it come from whcre ever ya'll filt the barrel."

"Then why haven't I gotten sick?"

"How the hell do I know? Yer belly's prob'ly made from the same rock as yer head."

"Damn it. I know you poisoned our water."

"Ya can think whatever yer a mind to, but I can fix up some tea to soothe yer bellies iffin ya want."

The deputy's dark gaze narrowed suspiciously. "What are you up to now?"

"I ain't up to nothin'. Iffin ya want I should fix the tea, I'll fix it. Iffin ya don't, it's ya'lls belly aches."

"I want some, Johnny," Machler moaned pathetically from where he sat in the wagon with his knees drawn up close to his chest. "I can't take much more a this pain."

"Me neither," Warren complained. "Forget them deputies an' take care of us, Johnny."

"You have a tea that'll take care of this?" Brady asked, holding his stomach.

"Yes, sir."

"Don't trust him, Brady," the deputy cautioned. "It's part of their plan to weaken us. Whatever this illness is, it will pass. If you trust this kid you could wind up dead."

"I'll take that chance." Hobbs volunteered from the prison wagon seat.

"This is a mistake."

Johnny glared at him. "Then why would I be lettin' my paw an' them other no accounts take sick?"

"I'm not sure, but I am sure you poisoned that

water."

"Iffin I was a goin' to poison anyone it'd be you, ya goddamn Yankee, lawman."

"Enough, Bennick. You made your point. Look, the kid fixed up your arm." Brady rationalized. "Let him make his tea. He can give it to his pa first, if it'll make ya easier, but I got to tell ya, my stomach can't take much more a this crampin'."

"All right. All right, but I don't like it."

"That's cause yer gut ain't rippin' in half," complained Hobbs from the wagon seat.

Out voted, the deputy dismounted and shadowed her to the cook's wagon. "I'm watching you." He growled in her ear.

Tyler started a small fire with the supply of sticks and buffalo chips they had collected in the sling suspended from the bottom of the cook's wagon. The skinny man who drove it passed Johnny her doeskin bag.

"Ya still got that pot?"

"A pot? Yeah, sure." He turned to retrieve one from the wagon and thrust it eagerly into her hand.

She carried the pot around to the other side of the chuck wagon where the water barrel was strapped and lifted the lid. Suddenly the deputy's hand lashed out to capture her wrist in a painful grip.

"What are you doing?" His eyes narrowed dangerously.

"Fetchin' water."

"You're not using that."

"I ain't? Well, where the hell else am I s'posed to get water fer tea?"

She knew he didn't have an answer for that. There was nothing around for miles except the rolling wind-swept grass of the prairie. Away in the distance low hills rose above the rolling plain and tree tops formed clusters of green against the blue.

63

"But you poisoned that water. I won't let you use it."

"I didn't poison ya'lls water. 'Sides, I'm gonna be a-cookin' it first."

"Hurry up, Johnny!" Warren called from where he sat with the other prisoners behind the prison wagon. "My gut is killin' me."

"Yeah," Machler pleaded. "Help us."

Tyler moaned and bent forward at the waist. "I don't care, kid. Help me first."

The driver of the chuck wagon dropped beside Tyler in the grass. He moaned and pressed an arm against his lower abdomen. "Uuuhhhg, it hurts. Help us first, Johnny."

****

"Help!" The wounded called out. Fellow Confederates or Yankees, he couldn't tell, the woods were as dark as the bottom of a well, but like him, they were in pain and so thirsty. In the distance the orange glow of one of the many scattered fires, caused by the spark of a bullet igniting the dried leaves, accelerated his heart beat. Were the flames crawling his way?

"Help!" Their moans and pleas for water echoed throughout the night, reverberating in his head until the sounds overwhelmed him, and he clamped his good hand over his ear to mute the horror.

****

"Hey, lawman!" Johnny frowned at the deputy. His normally tanned complexion had gone pale. His dark brown eyes stared off in the distance, as though he saw images no one else could see. His right hand was pressed tight against his ear.

"Lawman. Ya havin' a spell 'er somthin'?" Johnny waited for a response then punched him in the arm, only hard enough to jar him back to the present.

He blinked and shook his head. She watched the

wild beat of his pulse as it flickered against the skin beneath his jaw. His Adam's apple bobbed up and down several times, and his hand trembled as he wiped it across his clammy face.

In those brief moments, Johnny saw fear in his dilated eyes. Whatever happened to the deputy during these spells scared him to death. And as awareness refocused his dark brown eyes, she saw the deputy knew that she'd once again witnessed his drift away from reality.

Breaking free from the strange connection that drew them together, she scooped up her water and returned to the fire. She mixed the crushed leaves and tossed them into the pot to steep. From the corner of her eye, she watched him stride through the waving grass to his horse. His back was to her, but from where he stood at the back of the saddle, she suspected he was going for his bottle of whiskey.

A minute or two later, he returned and squatted beside her. Immediately, that brooding dark gaze fixed itself on her face, intense and alert, seeming to penetrate all the way to her soul.

"Hurry up," he snapped.

She shot him a glare.

The deputy scowled right back. "I don't like sitting out here waiting for your father's men to pick us off like tin cans on a fence. At this rate it will be dark by the time we stop to water the horses."

"Well, hell," she grumbled. "This should brew a mite longer, but since yer in sech a all-fired hurry to see us all hang, ya best fetch me some drinkin' cups."

She had no sooner finished speaking than Tyler was tapping her on the elbow with a battered tin mug. After pouring the young guard a half a cup she carried another cup to Deputy Brady who stood, still clutching his saddle.

"Why don't ya jest set down, 'stead a hangin' on yer horse like that?"

Brady nearly managed a smile. "'Cause if I do, I prob'ly won't be able to get back up."

Johnny just shook her head. Then with her wrists linked together and the cup in one hand she managed to help Brady sit more comfortably on the ground.

"Brady, wait." Deputy Bennick's deep voice rang out as he strode through the grass toward them. "Give it to Bodine first."

"Well, hell," she grumbled rising to her feet. "Yer the most pis-icious damn deputy I ever did meet."

"What?"

"Ya don't trust no one do ya?"

"No. Especially not scrawny little outlaws who poison our water."

Johnny drew herself up indignantly, just before she swung around and stomped off toward the prison wagon.

"And it's suspicious!" He yelled after her.

"Here, Paw," she offered as she passed him the drink through the bars. As his hand closed around the cup, she gave her arm a little shake and the ring of keys from Deputy Brady's pocket dropped from inside her baggy sleeve onto the backs of her father's wrists.

With a quick jerk of his head, he signaled Machler who leaned over and quickly placed his hands over the keys then slipped them into her father's pocket.

To disguise the movement in case the deputy was watching, she said, "Hold yer horses Machler, I'll bring yers directly."

Her father downed his drink in a few quick swallows then snarled at her in a harsh whisper. "Ya stupid little shit! What the hell's wrong with ya, poisonin' us all?"

"But Paw, I tried to stop ya..."

"I don't want to hear none a yer damn excuses."

"Hurry up over there!" The deputy yelled.

Snatching the cup, she hurried back to the fire. When she returned to the wagon she carried two.

"Ya think them sticky fingers a yers can fetch me back a gun?" Bodine whispered.

"A gun? How am I s'posed to steal a gun?"

"An' be watchin' fer my signal."

"But Paw, I..."

"An' be ready to cause some kind a ruckus so's we got time to get the horses."

"But Paw," she protested. "I don't know what to do. I cain't..."

"Ya damn worthless piece a shit, fer once in yer life use that little piss pot brain a yers fer thinkin'. Fetch me a gun, then watch fer my signal. Do whatever the hell ya want, jest cause a commotion. Do it ya stupid little bastard, or I swear to God, I'll leave ya a-standin' in the middle a the friggin' prairie an' never look back."

Chapter Five

A gun! How was she supposed to steal a gun?

Anxiety continued to churn her thoughts an hour later as she rode beside the one-arm deputy. The lawman wore a Smith and Wesson .44 Top Break on his right hip and carried a Winchester rifle in the scabbard on his saddle. He cleaned them so often he'd notice if she left so much as a smudge, let alone steal one of them. Afraid his perceptive brown eyes would recognize her guilt for her part in her father's plan, she kept her gaze on the ground.

Her empty stomach gave a low rumble. How could she possibly think of a way to get her father a gun when she was so hungry? The chilling intensity of his cold, gray eyes boring into her as she rode along beside the prison wagon caused her to shudder. Slowly, she dropped back so her father couldn't see her. Maybe, if she didn't see his signal, she wouldn't have to create a diversion. Then again if her father did manage to escape, he would be true to his word and leave her all alone out here in the middle of nowhere. The mere possibility had her as jumpy as a pregnant fox in a forest fire.

Sometimes she wished she could just bawl like a baby. Maybe a flood of tears would be able to ease the terrible pain that even now pressed against the inside of her chest. But Johnny had spilled her last tear when she was four years old and learned that boys didn't cry and tears only got you back handed across the room.

Damn, she hated her life. Uncle Henry and Morning Song had made it bearable, but now they were both gone. Johnny slumped lower in the saddle. Her stomach growled again.

Her horse stumbled. Her chin bumped against her chest, against the old locket she wore tied around her neck by a thin strand of rawhide. The weight pressed against her sweaty skin and brought to mind an image of the two faces hidden within.

"Hey, outlaw."

The deputy's deep voice startled her back to the present. She lifted her chin and met the gentle concern in his dark gaze. Just like the man in the locket. Her heart nearly burst from the pain.

"What's wrong?"

"They ain't nothin' wrong. Jest a mite hungry is all." Actually now that she thought about it, she hadn't eaten anything yesterday either, except a meager portion of beans and even those her father had snatched before she could eat them.

The deputy dropped his reins around his saddle horn, the knot in the end preventing them from falling to the ground, and reached behind to rummage through his saddle bags.

"Here," he said after a minute. Johnny stared at his outstretched hand. He held two biscuits and a piece of jerky. She hesitated, instinctively waiting for permission to eat. Her mouth watered.

The deputy frowned. "Go on, take it before I drop it."

Quick as a striking snake, she snatched the food. He grinned as she greedily stuffed the biscuits into her mouth.

"Sorry there's no safe water to wash it down."

She shrugged. "Ith okay," she mumbled around the piece of jerky she had just torn off with her teeth.

The deputy grinned, and when that big dimple appeared in his left cheek, her heart skipped a beat, and she forgot to breathe. Immediately a piece of dry biscuit caught in her throat, triggering a short bout of coughing.

"Slow down," he cautioned. His grin faded into a sympathetic half smile. "Are you all right, kid? Do you want to stop and make some tea?"

"Tea?" she asked puzzled. "What fer?"

"Like you made this morning. For your...damn, Johnny, I'm sorry. It must be hell being so young, knowing you're so sick."

She stared at the deputy for several seconds struggling to understand what he was talking about. Finally, it dawned on her. His concern added to the guilt she already felt, and she couldn't lie to him any more than she had to.

"Naw, I ain't sick. My Paw, he jest said them things to cover up what Warren done to my throat."

The deputy's dark eyes fell to the blood stained scarf around her neck, staring at it for several seconds seemingly lost in thought.

"Damn it, Johnny, how'd you ever end up with Bodine for a father?"

Her gaze locked with his. Suddenly it was vital that he not think badly of her, that he understand she wasn't like her father or any of the men who rode with him. Slowly, she reached inside the neck of her shirt with both hands and withdrew the small locket. She stared at it for a moment as her finger traced the worn design pressed into the dull tin. She removed her hat and pulled the rawhide cord over her head.

"Where did you get this?" The deputy asked, dropping his reins and reaching out to accept it.

Johnny nudged her horse closer. "Open it."

He worked his thumbnail into the seam and flipped open the two halves, revealing the miniature photographs of a young man and woman. He looked back at her, puzzled.

She shrugged. "They's my real Maw an' Paw."

His brown eyes widened. "Your real Maw and Paw?" he repeated incredulous.

She nodded.

"Pierpont Bodine is not your father?"

Johnny shook her head. "Nope. Paw, he swiped me from my real folks when I weren't no more than knee high to a jackrabbit."

He stared at the images for several moments, his mouth agape. "Johnny do you know what this means?" He turned his head and looked straight at her. "You're not an outlaw. You were a victim, coerced into participating in those robberies. The jury will have to show leniency. Can you tell me anything about your parents? Anything at all about when Bodine took you, or where you lived? Anything to help us find them for you?"

Her gaze drifted out over the procession in front of them. "My real maw an' paw live in a big white house with a strong fence around the yard so's I cain't get lost when I go outside. An' they eat fine meals ever' day. My paw, he works in a bank an' looks after other folk's money. An' he got a passel a big strong guards at his bank so's no mangy cur dog outlaws ken take it away from him. An' my paw, he comes home ever' night an' helps me with my cipherin' so's I ken do good in school. An' the teacher likes me 'cause I'm so smart.

"An' my maw, she sews purty dresses..." She paused and rubbed her forehead against a sudden throbbing. "'Ceptin' yeller ones, cause I don't like no yeller dresses." She added quickly. "An' she sews pillows with fancy stitchin', an' cooks sweet smellin' pies, an' stack cakes, too, with sugar icin'. An' Paw likes to walk down the street with me a-holdin' his hand, 'cause he's so proud a me."

With his thumb and forefinger the deputy snapped the locket closed and passed it back. "Johnny?" he asked. "How long has it been since you've seen your parents?"

She slipped the rawhide loop over her head. "Long time I reckon. Years an' years. I was just a baby when them outlaws took me away."

"I thought you said you were in school."

She rubbed her forehead then explained. "Reckon I was little, just startin' school."

He nodded then said carefully. "Your parents must have given you up for dead by now."

"Oh, no." She shook her head. "My maw an' paw, they won't never give up on me. Why they got a whole passel a them Pink-in-ton men out a-lookin' fer me right now. An' one day they's a-goin' to find me an' kill Paw, shoot him dead. An' then they's a-goin' to take me home so's I don't never get lost no more."

"Do you remember anything else, like your last name or where you were born?"

She shook her head. "Don't rightly know. Afore we come here we was down in Texas fer a spell with Uncle Cal. An' I know we lived in the Ozarks wunst. Paw an' Uncle Cal, though, they been all over."

"Johnny?" he began. He glanced away for a moment then back again. "I'm sorry I accused you of poisoning our water. I should have believed you when you said you weren't an outlaw. I'm obliged to you for making the tea and fixing up my arm." He flashed a quick grin, his dimple carved deep in his left cheek. "Even though you were the one who bit it.

"I'll make it up to you, Johnny. As soon as we get back to Fort Smith, I'll start looking for your parents."

She looked away and rubbed her forehead again.

"We'll find them Johnny, I promise."

When the deputy said nothing further she glanced over to see what he was doing.

He had dropped his reins over the saddle horn and twisted around to untie his saddle bags. With a quick tug, he hefted them onto his right forearm and before she realized his intention, he dropped them across the front of her saddle.

"Help yourself. If you find anything else to eat it's yours." Then he picked up his reins and nudged his horse forward to ride alongside the blond haired guard on the right side of the prisoners.

She studied his broad back for several seconds then turned her attention to the saddle bags. They were made of good quality leather with letters carved into each flap. The same three letters she'd noticed on the deputy's canteen. She wondered briefly what name the letters spelled.

In the right pouch, she discovered a round tin of tooth powder, the deputy's shaving gear, and a bar of sandalwood scented soap. With a quick glance to see if anyone was watching, she deftly slipped the razor into one of her many pockets. Next she found a toothbrush, comb, and a bruised apple he was probably saving for one of his horses. Still ravenous, she devoured the apple, core and all. The juicy fruit helped relieve some of the dryness in her mouth. At the bottom she found a small, bone pocket knife, again with the same three letters carved into the side. She looked up, half expecting the mind-reading deputy to turn around. When he didn't, she slipped the knife into another pocket of her baggy coat.

Turning her attention to the opposite pouch, she found a bottle of whiskey, nearly half gone. Beneath it lay a small notebook and pencil. She moved her hand to the side and bumped a tin of peaches. The picture of a tree dotted with peaches started her mouth watering. She considered using his pocket knife to pry open the can, but she couldn't risk what would happen if he turned around and caught her. Her hand burrowed deeper, then froze as her finger tips grazed the cold steel of a pistol barrel. Heart pounding, she looked up, half expecting the deputy to race back yelling, "I knew I couldn't trust you!"

But he kept riding, apparently unaware of her discovery. Cautiously, she ran her fingers along the barrel, half expecting it to spring like a mousetrap, because deep inside she didn't believe the deputy had forgotten that either the knife or his gun were in his saddlebag. It was likely a test to see how far he could trust her. A twinge of guilt pierced her heart for disappointing him, because for some reason she craved his approval, but Paw wanted a gun and come hell or high water she'd do what she could to get him one.

She glanced toward the prisoners, bumping along inside the wagon and saw her father with his head turned, watching her with those piercing, gray eyes. Though it seemed impossible, somehow he knew. Carefully, she eased the revolver from the towel it was wrapped in then slipped the weapon beneath her baggy duster, into the waistband of her pants.

A few minutes later the deputy dropped back to ride alongside her big paint. "Find enough to eat?"

She nodded afraid to meet his eyes. Did he know? Guilt twisted her stomach into a queasy knot. Unnerved by the intensity of his penetrating gaze, she nearly blurted out the whole scheme. But when she finally dared to lift her head, the deputy had already turned his attention to the terrain ahead. His jaw clenched as he stared at the thick line of tree tops which followed the horizon in both directions.

They rode together in silence for another hour. Then she heard it—the call of a meadow lark, followed by the shrill cry of a hawk. She stiffened. That was the signal Breed had used for years when someone approached their hideout.

At the sound of the hawk, the deputy tilted his head to scan the empty sky and frowned. He glanced in her direction, but she pretended not to notice. The deputy nudged his horse into an easy lope and caught up with Brady at the head of the procession.

Seizing her chance, Johnny trotted up alongside the prison wagon and carefully maneuvered her horse between the guard and her father.

"I was jest noticin'," she mentioned casually to Tyler, "That yer horse seems to be pullin' up lame on his left fore."

The young man leaned over and studied the left foreleg of his horse.

"No," she corrected, "I meant the other foreleg."

He scowled at her for a moment then leaned over to study his horse's right leg. As soon as his attention was diverted, Johnny pulled the revolver from beneath her duster and shoved it through the bars into her father's raised hands, just as the guard straightened.

"There's nothing wrong with his leg."

"Sorry, I reckoned it looked like he picked up a stone."

Johnny glanced at her father. He gave her a subtle nod.

Think. Her mind was spinning. Somehow she needed to distract the guard, cause a diversion, and not get shot doing it. Think.

She dropped her horse back a half a length, while maintaining a leisurely pace. Hiding her hands she retrieved the deputy's pocket knife from her coat and opened the blade.

Nudging her horse forward, she leaned over and jabbed the tip of the blade into the rump of the guard's chestnut. The horse bolted. Johnny veered her horse to the right, and leaning low over his neck, raced straight through the extra horses Miles was driving. They scattered in four different directions. The report of a rifle cracked behind her. She urged her horse to greater speed. A bullet whizzed past her head. The big paint galloped faster.

"This here horse can run like hell an' high light'nin'." Henry had explained when he'd given him to Johnny four years earlier. *"Yer paw, he won't be able to get shed a ya too easy iffin yer a-ridin' him. An with his colorin' the rest a them bastards won't take him from ya, cause durin' a robbery they'd be as noticable as a chicken ridin' a mule."*

Now Johnny had Jack racing hell bent for leather toward the distant trees. Glancing over her shoulder, she spied the one-arm deputy giving chase. The bay the lawman rode was a fast horse, but there were few that could catch Jack. She looked back again. The distance between them had grown.

She faced forward and charged into the trees. Branches scraped her arms, and her right knee brushed against a trunk. A few minutes later Jack splashed through a shallow creek, splattering water onto her legs. She ducked low over his neck, avoiding the low limb of a Blackjack tree.

The trees and brush gave way to patches of grass, which should have been pretty in the golden glow of the lowering sun, but all she could think about was the pounding of her horse's hooves against the hard ground taking her farther and farther away. They burst through the trees and raced flat out over the open plain. She jerked back on the reins. Jack slid to a stop, pivoting on his hind legs, to spin in a tight circle, and Johnny was lost.

Every direction suddenly felt the same. Straight ahead and on either side, a world of blue sky and waving grass. Panic swelled inside her chest. She swallowed against the mounting terror. What if the deputy gave up? What if he left her here all alone? She reminded herself that the deputy was almighty stubborn. He wouldn't quit the chase easily.

Her breath came in short ragged gasps as though she, not Jack, had just made the mad dash through the trees. Cold sweat chilled her forehead as her gaze swung in every direction, hoping against all hope that the deputy hadn't given up. Her shallow breathing made her light-headed. Desperate to stay calm, she tried to think.

Focused on the sound of her own breathing, she didn't even hear the deputy's horse thundering up behind her until he had maneuvered his horse to a stop in front of her.

"Where in the hell do you think you're going?" he roared.

He dropped his reins, allowing the knot to catch on his horse's neck then yanked her reins from her manacled hands. Twining both sets through his fingers, he swung their horses completely around.

There on the horizon, outlined against the pink, cloud-streaked sky, the dark green, tree tops rose just above the line of grass. She should have turned around. In the back of her mind she could hear her father's voice ranting, "Ya stupid piece of shit."

Fury radiated from the one-armed deputy like the glow of the setting sun, but he said nothing.

Overwhelming relief left her speechless as she rode mutely behind. She didn't care that he was furious. She didn't try to lie or justify her actions. She was only grateful he hadn't left her alone.

For several minutes, they jogged in silence toward the tree line, with only the swish of the horses through the grass, until the loud crack of a rifle shot shattered stillness. An instant later, there was another, then another, until the sounds of a gun battle reverberated through the trees in front of them.

"Goddamn!" The deputy cursed, jamming his heels into the sides of his bay, urging his flagging mount to increase his speed.

Though only minutes had passed since the first shot, it seemed an eternity before they rode back into a world of green and black. A cloud of smoke sifted through the trees ahead. In one smooth motion the deputy slid his horse to a stop, dropped both sets of reins, yanked his Winchester from its scabbard, and slung it over his shoulder.

"Stay here!" He snapped as he leaped from the saddle. Bending low, he dashed off, zig-zagging his way through the trees toward the thickening gray cloud.

Johnny waited only a half a second before she jumped off her horse and ran after him. Ahead she saw one man topple from a horse as the deputy fired his pistol, his aim accurate even through the gray haze. Heart pounding, she dove behind the log from which the deputy returned fire.

She landed in the leaves beside him, and he swung around, his revolver in hand, poised to shoot. He scowled when he recognized her and returned his attention to the outlaws. She lifted her head just enough to see over the top of the log. While Uncle Cal's men kept the deputy pinned down, her father and his men climbed from the prison wagon. Beside her, the deputy fired, and one of Uncle Cal's men, who had extended his hand toward her father, tumbled to the ground clutching his thigh.

Johnny dropped flat beside the deputy as gun fire ceased from the direction of the wagons as the remaining gang members now focused their ammunition on the lone deputy behind the log.

Rolling onto his back the deputy tucked the barrel of his gun between the stump of his left arm and the left side of his body. The Top Break he carried hinged. Though he snapped it open, and reloaded the cylinder in less than thirty seconds, for Johnny who tried to squirm her way deeper into the leaves as bullets pelted the ground around them, thought it seemed to take forever.

"Damn it, lawman! Cain't ya load that gun no

faster?"

He shot her a nasty look as he slid the weapon into his holster. Without a word of explanation, he spit into his hand, dug down beneath the log, and began smearing his face with dirt. In moments brown smudges coated his forehead, cheeks, nose, and chin. Baffled, Johnny watched him remove his hat and send it sailing to the right of their position behind the log. Immediately, the gunfire diverted away from them.

"Stay here." He grabbed his Winchester as he rolled onto his stomach, and crawled away, quickly disappearing into the smoke and brush.

Alone, Johnny wiggled herself parallel to the log and covered her head with her arms, praying she wouldn't get shot. After several seconds the shooting stopped.

More seconds ticked by, before she heard the sharp report of a rifle.

"Shit!" The voice sounded like Machler.

"Where the hell did that come from?"

"Over there!" Her father yelled.

Several shots rang out. Johnny squiggled herself deeper into the leaves. The rifle fired again from somewhere in the trees opposite the outlaws. Gun smoke burned the inside of her nose.

"Damn it, where is he?"

"Somebody get that sonofabitch!"

"What about Bodine?" Machler yelled.

"Forget him! He's gut shot!"

"Damn you, Breed! Get back here!"

"We'll be back with Cal!"

Johnny recognized Breed's deep voice.

A horse crashed through the brush, heading straight for her log. *Please don't see me. Please don't see me*, she chanted to herself as the pounding of horses drew closer. Two horses raced past on either side of the log. The third jumped over both it and

Johnny. The white socks of the animal's back legs as he flew overhead were familiar. She raised her gaze to the rest of the black gelding and the moccasin clad feet of Uncle Cal's right hand man, the Mexican-Comanche man called Breed.

At the ambush site, she heard the report of another rifle shot.

Crack!

Someone cried out in pain.

"Where is he?"

"He keeps moving!"

"Damn, he's picking us off one by one."

"Where's the horses?"

"Half way to Fort Smith by now."

"Grab a horse from one of the guards. Damn it, Warren, stay down!"

Again, she heard the sharp crack of the rifle.

All was quiet.

"Machler, what are ya doin'?"

"Makin' a smoke screen so's we can unhitch the horses from the wagons."

Curious, Johnny wiggled forward and peered around the end of the log to see what they were doing. A haze of gun smoke blocked the outlaws from sight. A moment later the orange glow of what looked like a campfire appeared through the wall of smoke. The shadowy form of a man, the size of Machler, tossed leaves and other mulch on top of the flames. Thick, choking smoke rolled out in all directions, blending with the gathering dusk, until she could no longer make out any of the men. A moment later the flicker of orange flared up, higher and brighter than before.

"Damn it, Machler," Warren yelled. "You're gonna set the woods on fire."

"Then ya best drag your ass down to the creek. I'm leavin'."

There followed a chorus of cuss words, then all

was quiet. The horses stamped and squealed. She wondered if Warren and her father had stayed behind, or gone with Machler.

Crack!

Someone scrambled through the underbrush.

She heard her father chuckle, then cough. "Ya stupid bastard, now ya got us pinned down 'twixt the deputy and the fire. I reckon what we got here is a genuine Yankee sharpshooter."

Her father coughed again. "One a you boys best grab them wagon teams, afore the fire—"

A horse whinnied and the heavy sound of a wagon and horses crashing through the trees followed. Machler yelled and swore. She wondered what was going on, but the deputy had said to stay put and that was what she planned to do.

"Johnny," her father called out, his voice weaker than a moment ago. "Are ya out there?"

Johnny raised her head above the log. The smoky fire had widened its area, licking at the base of a tree. Though she could hear her father, the smoke and the trees were too thick to make out any shapes.

"I'm righchere, Paw," she called.

He coughed and drew a wheezy breath. "Git yer ass over here, boy."

She scooted out from behind the log and crawled toward his voice. Through the haze, she saw him sitting propped against the rear wheel of the chuck wagon, a revolver in his hand. Worried the fire would spread, she pulled off her duster and beat out the low flames where they crept close to the trees.

Thankfully, it was more of a smoke fire than a blaze and after several minutes of kicking dirt and stomping on the bits of flame, the fire died out and all that remained was a blackened patch of ground and a thinning wall of smoke.

Johnny turned toward her father. The entire

front of his shirt, from mid-chest down past his waist, was soaked in blood. A shot rang out and a chunk of dirt kicked up two feet in front of her boots.

She froze. "What the hell are ya a-shootin' at me for? I ain't done nothin'!" she yelled.

"Ya stupid piece a shit," her father mumbled weakly. "He ain't a-goin' to answer. He'll give away—his position." He drew a raspy breath.

After several moments passed and nothing else happened, she inched her foot forward. "Now, I ain't a-plannin' to do nothin', lawman!" she called, moving slowly toward her father. "Jest a-fixin' to tend my paw."

Looking around, she saw for the first time the carnage that littered the area in and around the trees. One of the guards lie slumped over the body of a dead horse, behind which he had apparently taken cover. She couldn't see his face, but his features were ingrained in her memory none-the-less.

Not far off, the younger guard, Tyler, lie in a small patch of grass. His blue eyes stared sightlessly at the tree branches above. A warm breeze gently lifted the corner of his shirt tail and sifted through his wheat blond hair. If not for the dark, crimson stain in the center of his chest, he might have been watching birds flitter from branch to branch.

Near the chuck wagon, Deputy Brady lay dead. His left sleeve was soaked with blood from a shoulder wound. Another bullet had creased his temple and a third wound bloodied the center of his green striped vest.

Hobbs lay unconscious not far from her father, blood oozing onto the grass from a head wound and another in his upper arm. And a man she knew rode for Uncle Cal, bled from his thigh beside a bush close to the creek. Waving her hand, she fanned the dissipating haze of smoke and coughed.

Warren sat with his back pressed against the

gray trunk of a red bud tree. Shackles still wrapped around his ankles. Blood dripped from his shoulder and fury gleamed in his shadowed gaze as he watched her every move. His hatred was as palpable as the carnage around them. Uneasy, the acid in her stomach began to churn.

Somehow things had gotten turned around, and she'd become aligned with the deputy. She stood for a moment, avoiding his gaze, gnawing on her bottom lip. Instinctively, she wanted to help them all, yet, she worried what would happen if she helped the wrong man first.

The crack of a rifle shot rang out from the creek. The deputy must have had Machler pinned down.

She stepped toward the chuck wagon where her father sat propped against the rear wheel. His grizzled face was waxen, his gray eyes dull. Blood soaked through the front of his shirt and seeped down his pants.

"Jest let me fetch my bag a yarbs. Then I can help ya." She didn't wait for his reply but dashed to the front of the cook's wagon and climbed over the seat into the crammed interior. In the fading light, she rummaged through bedrolls, cookware, and sacks of supplies before she found her doeskin bag.

"Jest leave me be." Her father coughed as he fought for breath.

"Paw, I can help ya," she called through the canvas.

"Ya best...see to yerself boy. Yer kin. Calvin'll come fer ya."

Her fingers wrapped around the strap, and she looped it over her head as she climbed back over the seat. "But Paw, I don't—"

As she jumped off the wheel hub, she turned, and slammed smack into the solid wall of the deputy's chest. His right hand held his Winchester.

Lifting her gaze to his she grumbled, "I swear ta

goodness, lawman, ya sure do got a way a sneakin' up on a body."

Deep furrows etched his brow. His brown eyes were bleak, and the muscles along his jaw bunched with tension. She stepped around him and started toward her father, but his voice called her back.

"Johnny."

Swinging around, she saw him swallow as though he were about to say something but didn't seem able to find the words. He blew out a heavy sigh instead.

An awkward silence hung like the gun smoke in the air between them.

"I'm right sorry 'bout yer friends. I'll help ya bury 'em, but I got ta go tend my paw first. He's bad hurt."

When the deputy said nothing more, she walked past him and dropped down beside her father.

Chapter Six

They were all dead. Brady, the guards, the drivers, all dead. Richard locked his knees to stop their shaking. His head throbbed, and his stomach rolled with nausea. Images of outlaws and Confederates swirled around in his head, to blend with those of flames crackling through the underbrush and gun smoke so thick he couldn't see the trees beside him. The scents of blood and damp earth filled his nostrils and fused together. Past and present jumbled into a mixture of reality and flashback so that he couldn't separate one from the other.

His head hurt. There was something—something happened in the smoke. The pain started to build. No, he'd think about it later. Right now he had to focus on what needed to be done next. His friends were dead. Guilt tore through his stomach like an artillery shell.

He'd promised Brady he'd be at his back. He promised the men in his unit he'd clear out the Confederates on the ridge. What had gone wrong? Why was it so hard to recall what had happened just minutes ago? Or had it been minutes? How much time had passed? His head pounded like a hammer against an anvil. The vibrations reverberated in his skull. He wanted to rub his hand across his forehead, but he didn't dare put down his rifle. His skin felt cold and clammy. Not now. Think about it later. He focused on Johnny.

The boy knelt beside his father. It was obvious the man was dying.

"I'll fetch ya somethin' to ease ya, Paw." Johnny soothed placing his hand on Bodine's shoulder.

Gathering his strength, Bodine lifted his arm. In the outlaw's right hand wavered Richard's revolver. The one he'd had in his saddle bag. Damn that kid. Stupidly, he had hoped the brat could be trusted. Never trust an outlaw.

Somehow Bodine managed to point the barrel directly at Richard's chest. Focused on what he was doing, Johnny seemed unaware of the gun in his father's hand as he leaned closer and tried to wipe away the blood to better examine the wound. The man was gut shot and bleeding to death, and while Richard told himself it was wrong not to care, he wondered why he should.

"Johnny, fetch one a them...guns an'...come over here."

Johnny glanced up and stared at the gun in his father's hand.

"Go on boy, fetch...a gun from one a them dead men."

As if he were detached from himself, Richard watched as Johnny diligently obeyed, slowly inching past Richard, until he came to the body of a man Richard didn't recognize.

Bending down, the kid carefully pried a Colt revolver from the dirty fingers of the outlaw. Slowly the boy circled around to stand beside his father.

"Shoot him, boy," Bodine whispered weakly.

Always obedient, Johnny pointed the barrel at Richard's chest. Oddly, he wondered if he should care.

"Shoot," rasped Bodine.

But the kid hesitated, and Richard suddenly realized as he stared into those wide violet eyes that Johnny Bodine had never shot another human being in his life. Curious, Richard wondered if he would be Johnny's first, and part of him almost wished the boy would pull the trigger. But the damn kid must have seen something in Richard's eyes, for Johnny's brow drew together as though slightly puzzled then he gave his blond head the barest of shakes.

Taking advantage of Johnny's vulnerability, Richard raised his arm, pointing his Winchester straight at the boy's chest. Johnny stiffened and backed up a step, the gun he held pointed at Richard apparently forgotten.

"Ya stupid little shit... He's bluffin'...rifle is empty... " Bodine coughed. The blood which trickled from the corner of his mouth looked black in the gathering dusk.

"Why don't you shoot me yourself, you sonofabitch?" Richard challenged the outlaw. "Could it be your gun doesn't work? Or should I say my gun?" He switched his gaze back to Johnny. "Did you think I wouldn't recognize my own gun?"

Johnny swallowed and backed up another step.

"Shoot...him," Bodine rasped.

Richard stepped toward Johnny, raising his arm, exposing his chest as an easy target.

"Shoot him." Bodine ordered with a surge of effort.

Richard stopped. "Why don't you shoot me yourself Bodine?"

Richard locked his gaze on Johnny's face. "Tell me, Johnny, did you look to see if it was loaded before you stole it? Did you check to see if it would fire? Because it doesn't, does it, Bodine? The mainspring is broken and the chamber won't rotate."

The boy backed into a tree.

"Damn it, Johnny." Bodine called weakly. "That rifle is...empty."

"Is it?" Richard flashed Johnny a nasty smile, sadistically teasing the kid like a wolf toying with a rabbit. Suddenly, he turned and aimed his Winchester at Bodine's head. "I hope you rot in hell," he bit out just before he pulled the trigger.

From the corner of his eye he saw Johnny jump as the rifle exploded. The boy gasped when he realized his father was still alive, and that Richard had deliberately missed.

"I'm sorry," Richard taunted the outlaw maliciously. "But I'd rather enjoy watching you die a slow death." He smiled again; his attention returned to Johnny.

The boy gulped and inched around the tree.

"Now what are you afraid of? Are you wondering if my gun has another bullet?"

"I ain't done nothin'."

"You ain't? Why I must be mistaken then, about how you stole my gun and you poisoned our water."

Johnny retreated.

Richard advanced. "You stole Brady's keys."

"Stay back!" Johnny's voice quavered as did his hands, still desperately clutching the butt of the gun. The chain from his manacles hung in a loop between his wrists. Johnny stumbled back.

Richard moved forward. "And after I trusted you. What a goddamn fool I was. Letting myself get sucked in by that sad sap, bullshit story you told me. Giving you my food. Believing in you." The betrayal he felt sliced its way through every word. He wondered briefly at the sudden return of his ability to feel.

"But I won't ever make that mistake again will I? You and those violet eyes be damned to hell." He advanced toward Johnny, his rifle pointed at the boy's chest. Terrified, Johnny stepped backward.

"Go ahead, Johnny, shoot me. Put me out of my misery."

"Jest you stay back, damn yer hide!" Johnny kept up his steady retreat.

"You can't do it, can you Johnny? I see it in your eyes. You've never killed. You lie. You steal. You can

88

act the innocent victim, but you cannot kill."

He spotted the dark outline of the dead outlaw behind the boy just as the heel of the kid's boot caught on the man's leg. As the boy fell backwards his finger must have squeezed reflexively on the trigger and the gun fired. A sharp ping followed, as the bullet ricocheted off a rock, then tore into his right thigh.

Right before her eyes, the deputy dropped. Horrified, Johnny stared at the empty place where the deputy had stood.

"Oh God! I kilt him."

Scrambling off the dead man, she realized her fingers were still wrapped tight around the butt of the revolver. Repulsed, she threw the weapon into the brush and raced to the place where the deputy had fallen.

The deputy rolled into a sitting position as Johnny dropped to her knees beside him. Fresh blood welled through his fingers which were pressed against his lower right thigh. Johnny shoved aside his hand and tore open the worn canvas pants to quickly examine the wound.

"It was an ax-ti-dent!" she cried, untying the bandana from her neck and pressing it against the bullet hole. Warm blood quickly soaked the thin material.

Jumping up, she dashed to the chuck wagon and scrambled inside. The cramped interior was already in shambles from her earlier search. Now she stumbled over the bed rolls, tossed aside tin ware and crates of food, and dumped out the contents of drawers until she found two large towels. Vaulting from the wagon she raced back to the deputy, the white cloths clutched tight in her manacled hands.

She dropped to her knees beside him and pressed one of the hastily folded towels on top of the bandana. "Hold this." She took his blood soaked fingers in her hand and pressed them down on the thick pad. Then she rummaged through her many pockets until she pulled out a small pocket knife.

"Damn it, Johnny," the deputy hissed through clenched teeth. "That's my knife."

Ignoring him, she used the knife to notch the end of the second towel and tore it into strips. She wrapped two of the strips around the padding to hold it in place with a quick knot.

As the bleeding slowed, Johnny rocked back on her heels and wiped her hands with the left over piece of towel. "I need to fetch my yarbs and dig out that bullet," she said lifting her gaze to meet the tight expression on the deputy's face.

"This is all your fault," he hissed. "So just keep your sorry little self and your bag of poisons the hell away from me."

"I-I'm sorry," Johnny stammered. "I didn't mean to shoot ya. It was a ax-ti-dent."

"Yeah? Well you've been nothing but one big accident since I met you. Now get the hell away from me."

Confused and oddly hurt, Johnny stood and slowly backed away. Not knowing what else to do, she returned to her father.

"I tolt ya...to shoot...that damn deputy." Bodine rasped weakly as she pulled aside her father's bloody shirt. Bodine coughed and drew in a ragged breath. "I'm sorry...say ya was even my youngin...worthless piece a shit..." He closed his eyes briefly. "Damn boy, I'm cold."

"Don't worry, Paw, you'll be right as rain wunst I get the bullet out."

"Remember Henry, boy. My whole body's numb. Cain't feel a damn thing. I seen enough gut shot men ta know...my number's up. Jest sit tight...an' wait fer Cal. Yer...kin... He'll...take carrre...aaa...yaaa..." His last words trailed off with the air of his last breath.

Johnny was left staring at her father's dull gray eyes. "Paw?" She already knew, but she reached out and touched her fingers to the side of his neck anyway. He was dead.

Though he hadn't been much of a father, Pierpont Bodine was the only father she'd ever known. First her mother, then Morning Song, then Henry, and now her father. Her whole family was gone. For the first time in her entire life, she was all alone.

A shadow fell across her father's body. She lifted her head.

The deputy loomed above her.

"About time the sonofabitch died."

Fresh blood darkened the pad tied around his thigh. The muscles along his jaw bulged with tension as he clamped his teeth tight. Beads of sweat coated his forehead and the pale cheek bones of his face.

"My paw's dead."

"Why the hell should you care?" He snapped. "He was sure no father to you. For God's sake, look around."

In silence, she watched the deputy swallow then run his blood smeared hand across his eyes. Slowly, he turned away and hobbled toward one of the bodies. Discretely, she rose and followed.

Flies crawled across the bloodied stomach of the blond guard, Tyler. More landed to walk across his face and into the corners of his dull open eyes.

"Get off!" the deputy cried dropping to his knees, heedless of the pain that must have ripped through his thigh. With his shaky hand he shooed the flies away, then gently closed the eyes of the young man. A black patch pooled on the ground around his knee.

Though she stood beside him, he seemed unaware of her presence. He stared out over the bodies, yet he didn't appear to actually see them. She thought it was almost as if his eyes were absorbing more devastation than his mind could comprehend.

Leaving him to mourn his friends, she moved off a little way. Spotting the deputy's Winchester rifle laying in the grass where he'd dropped it, she picked it up and returned to stand silent beside him.

"What the hell are you doing?" he snapped, looking up.

She shrugged, wary of his mood.

"Why haven't you hightailed your sorry little ass out of here?"

She shrugged again. "Got no place to go."

"No place to go?" He laughed. The sound rang hollow through the trees. "You've got the whole damn Indian Territory." He gave his arm a haphazard sweep to indicate the area behind her.

Johnny turned. There was nothing but trees and brush in every direction and beyond them empty miles of empty land. Every direction the same. Gangly tentacles of panic crept through her body, chilling her insides despite the summer heat, and slowly wrapping their length around her chest so that her breathing shortened to little gasps. Her stomach churned and blood pounded against her temples.

Paw was gone. There was no one left. Uncle Calvin might come back for her, but what if he didn't? What should she do? Sweat broke out across her palms. Should she stay here or go? But where? Tears pressed against the backs of her eyes, but Johnny never cried so she fought their growing pressure. For the first time in her entire life she was all alone.

A low groan rumbled behind her. The sound vibrated through her body the way a distant buffalo stampede rolled through the ground. The deputy. Relief washed over her and nearly buckled her knees. She tipped her face to the dark gray sky, closed her eyes, and drew in deep gulps of air. Gradually, the cleansing oxygen flushed away the terror that had clogged her every pore. Her heart beat restored, she turned around.

Sweat ran down the deputy's chalky face as he struggled to stand. The lower half of his pant leg was soaked in blood.

She started toward him. "Ya want I should tend that fer ya?" Still a bit shaky herself, her words were little more than a croaky whisper.

"No," he growled, swaying on his feet. "Leave me the hell alone."

"Well, then ya best set down, afore ya fall down."

"I can't," he said simply as he lowered his gaze to meet hers.

"Iffin ya got a shovel, I reckon I can see to a proper buryin' fer—"

"God, it looks like a damn battlefield." He shook his head. "No. We're only two days from McAlester. Help me wrap the bodies, and we'll send them home on the train." He blew out a weary breath. "And give me back my damn rifle."

She passed over the Winchester, the familiar letters, R-A-B, carved in the stock. "Found it yonder where ya dropped it. Now ya can point it at me an' threaten to shoot me iffin I don't do like ya say."

His dark brown eyes narrowed. "Are you ridiculing me?"

Johnny stared at him, her brow furrowed in concentration. She shifted her feet, glancing down as she swatted at the tips of grass with her manacled hands. "Don't reckon I know what re-dic-u-cule means."

He blew out a long sigh. "It means to make sport of someone."

She shrugged.

He tried again. "I wondered if you were laughing at me, outlaw?"

This time her shoulders snapped back, and she lifted her chin to squarely meet his dark eyes. "I reckon iffin I had call to be a-laughin' at ya, I'd be a-doin' it right in yer face, so there'd be no wonderin' about it." Spinning around, she stomped off.

Richard couldn't stop the grin that tugged the left corner of his mouth. Despite the pain in his leg, despite the grief pressing against his heart, despite the tenuous grip he held on his sanity, that obnoxious little outlaw could still make him laugh.

"And it's ridicule!" He yelled.

A clod of dirt came hurling out of the blue and landed with a thunk against the toe of his left boot. For a moment his laughter rang out to mingle with Johnny's sputtering curses.

He swayed as the ground tilted crazily, and his face seemed to drain of all blood. God, he thought, I don't even think I can stand up. Fort Smith was a good ten days away. And it would take a miracle just to get himself and what was left of his prisoners to McAlester.

"Hey, outlaw. Come here."

The kid turned and must have seen something in Richard's face, because he was beside him in an instant, his annoyance apparently forgotten. Clutching his Winchester, Richard draped his arm around Johnny's narrow shoulders.

Determined not to rest until he had checked the condition of every man, the two of them wove their way between the trees and around the wagons. In the end, Brady, Tyler, the second guard, and two outlaws were dead, including Pierpont Bodine. The skinny cook had apparently taken one of the horses from the prison wagon and lit out for parts unknown.

They found Hobbs still alive. A bullet had grazed his upper left arm, but he had evidently been knocked unconscious when he toppled off the high seat of the prison wagon and hit his head.

The outlaws Warren and Machler had been wounded. Machler was already chained to a tree near the creek, and with Richard aiming his Winchester at Machler, they brought him up and shackled him and Warren to the wheel of the prison wagon. In the brush near the creek bank, they discovered a tall, lean man, with greasy black hair and a long drooping moustache. Blood oozed from a gunshot wound to his right side and another in his left leg.

"Who is he?" Richard asked.

"I reckon he's one of Uncle Cal's men."

He'd been hearing the prisoners talk about Calvin since they arrested Bodine at the sod dugout. Now, he cursed himself for not having questioned the kid earlier.

"Who exactly is this Uncle Cal?"

Johnny hesitated and glanced around as though he expected his father to rise up and hit him for divulging information to a lawman.

"Paw's brother," he finally answered. "His proper name's Calvin. Calvin Everett."

"Calvin Everett? He's your father's brother?"

"Yup. 'Ceptin' they had diff'rent paws."

"Damn. I've heard of him." Richard leaned against the nearest tree. Could things possibly get any worse? "He runs wild down Texas, Arizona way. He deals white women with the Comancheros and guns with the Comanche. He's meaner than three Pierpont Bodine's. Do you realize that?"

"Course I do, I done tolt ya, he's my paw's brother."

He watched Johnny squat down beside the man to examine his wounds. "Uncle Cal never did cotton to me much, nor Henry neither. Cal come north to stay with Paw a spell. Texas Rangers was givin' him grief down there an' he—"

Richard snorted. "I'll just bet they were."

Johnny glanced up and scowled. "Well, ya best watch yer back, lawman, cause Uncle Cal's a-goin' to be pissed Paw's dead."

He pulled the man's shirt back over the wound in his side, then turned his attention to the wound in his leg as he continued talking. "An' I reckon Uncle Cal'll be a-comin' fer me, too, cause I'm the only blood kin he got left. Reckon it ain't a-goin' to matter none that I don't want to go."

Using the ground cloths from the bedrolls in the chuck wagon, Richard helped Johnny as much as he could, to carefully wrap the bodies of the dead. Exhausted, he eased himself down beside the chuck wagon and keeping his Winchester trained on the boy, watched as Johnny unhitched and hobbled the horses from the wagons. Next, he built a fire and did his best to tend the injuries of the wounded freighter and the outlaws.

Blackness filled the spaces between the trees before Johnny had the chance to whip up some bacon and biscuits for dinner, but no one was hungry. He did insist that they all have some of the tea he brewed and everyone was now asleep. Except for Richard, who refused both the bacon and the tea. Now, as he cleaned his revolvers, he watched the boy beside the fire as he continued fussing with his pots and herbs.

What a disaster. Not only couldn't Richard remember exactly what had happened today, he was badly wounded, and now responsible for protecting Johnny from the most notorious outlaw in the country. The thought did cross his mind that all he had to do was ride off, get his leg taken care of and be rid of the whole mess. But some inner force held him in place.

Duty demanded he finish the job. That he bring these prisoners, Johnny included, back to Fort

Smith. He had a responsibility to make sure these men who died today upholding the law, received a proper burial. It was a fine line he walked, between right and wrong. And half the time the damn line was so blurred he couldn't tell which side he was on.

He shook his head. The world spun crazily, as though he'd just climbed on the back of an unbroken colt. Johnny was beside him in a flash.

"I need to dig that bullet out. It's startin' to fester an' iffin I don't fetch it out an' poultice it fer ya—"

"Don't," he snapped. Then softer. "Don't say it. Please, Johnny. I already know."

The boy's eyes darted to Richard's empty left sleeve. Avoiding the pity he assumed he'd see in those eyes, he removed his Stetson and blotted the sweat off his brow with the sleeve of his forearm. A lock of hair dropped over his forehead. He searched the blackness beyond the light of the fire then looked at Johnny. There was no pity in the boy's expression, only that steady resolve that was Johnny; accept what couldn't be changed and move on.

Bone weary, he sighed, "I can't believe I'm trusting my leg to an outlaw."

The kid huffed indignantly. "An' I cain't believe I'm helpin' doctor a lawman. Why iffin he weren't already dead, my paw'd shoot me sure."

He didn't want to trust the kid, but he had to, just like he needed to stop looking into those eyes and remind himself that Johnny was an outlaw.

"Okay, outlaw, do it." He slipped his Smith and Wesson from its holster. "But I'll be watching you."

The kid scowled. "I sure do hope ya ain't a-fixin' to point that damn thing at me again. 'Cause it sure as hell is a-goin' to hurt this time an' I don't want no damn hole in my belly when it does."

Richard lowered the gun to the ground. A breeze sifted through the trees. He shivered. "Just do the best you can."

Johnny watched him for a moment then nodded. "Well, I reckon I'd best build up a fire, an' heat some water whilst I fetch my yarbs."

When the kid returned to the fire, he carried two lanterns from the cook's wagon, his doeskin bag, and a bottle of whiskey. After lighting the lanterns, he rummaged through the bag and pulled out some dried root.

"Yarrow," he explained as he mashed it into a pulp. Setting it aside, he carefully lifted the thick pad off the wound and applied the pulverized yarrow.

Then after a quick glance toward the prison wagon and the sleeping men, Johnny removed his battered hat and duster, and rolled up the sleeves of his oversized shirt. The kid seemed even smaller without the oversized duster.

"You don't have very big hands."

"Seems like ya ought to be glad I ain't a-goin' to poke around in yer laig with fingers as big as yer thumbs," he grumbled without looking up. Removing his book of drawings from his bag, he flipped through several pages then stopped.

His brow furrowed in concentration as he stared at the drawings for several minutes, then heated up the blade of Richard's pocket knife and passed him a new bottle of whiskey.

Richard took a few swallows and passed the bottle back, watching the kid pour the alcohol over his hands.

"Now don't ya fret lawman." His voice was low and reassuring as he bent over the wound. "I reckon I know more about doctorin' bullet holes than a jack rabbit knows about runnin'."

A hiss of pain escaped Richard's lips as the kid began to probe.

"Why do ya think my paw kept me around? I

learnt some doctorin' from my maw and the rest about yarbs an' sech from a Cheyenne squaw my paw was a using fer a while. She took a shine to me an' showed me how to use my knife an take care a myself incase one a them no account friends a Paw's learnt my see—.

"'Course Morning Song couldn't protect herself from 'em. Sometimes Paw would pass her around. That was hard on her. She birthed two babies, but they both died. I asked her wunst why she didn't run off. I'd a gone with her. We both could a got away. But she said she was shamed afore her people and didn't have no place to go. She took sick with winter fever a couple years back. I don't figger she tried very hard to get better. It's been kind a lonely since."

The steady drone of Johnny's conversation gave Richard something to focus on beside the agony tearing through his leg. He squeezed his eyes and clenched his teeth. Sweat ran down both sides of his face and moistened his neck. His right hand squeezed the butt of his revolver so tight his knuckles hurt, but he made certain his finger was nowhere near the trigger.

"Got it," Johnny whispered, sagging back on his heels.

Richard responded with a slight nod.

"Sorry, lawman. I reckon that yarrow root wore off quicker than I figgered."

He drew a deep breath and let it out slow. At least it was over. He opened eyes to see Johnny wiggling the cork from the top of the bottle.

"Now all's I got to do his pour some a this here whiskey in to clean it out good," Johnny said, and dumped a generous splash into the fresh wound.

Searing pain ripped through Richard's body in one great spasm as his whole spine arched off the wagon wheel. His breath escaped in one long hiss.

"Goddamn sonofabitch!"

"All done," Johnny soothed. "Now, soon as I get ya stitched up, I got some powdered flax seed and blue corn meal paste a cookin' on that fire yonder. I'm a-goin' to use it to poultice yer laig. Iffin ya rest up fer a spell, yer laig should be right as rain in a couple a weeks."

Their gazes locked for several heartbeats. Even as Johnny spoke the words, they both knew he wasn't going to rest.

Johnny turned away and scooted close to the fire. "I was jest a wonderin'," he began after a lengthy silence. "Iffin ya could tell me what yer name is. I reckon we's a-goin' to be together fer a spell an' I cain't jest call ya lawman or Yankee all the time."

Richard's spine stiffened. This was exactly what he'd been warning himself against. He needed to be firm. Don't look into those eyes. Johnny was a thief and a liar.

"I can't afford to rest up, and you don't need to know anything about me other than, I am a U.S. Deputy Marshal. Don't think for a minute that I'm stupid enough to sit here waiting for Calvin Everett to ride down on us. You and these other men are my prisoners, and I'm sworn to bring you back to Fort Smith for trial. First thing tomorrow we head to McAlester."

Chapter Seven

Richard never knew there were so many curse words as Johnny stomped around the camp, slamming pots and tin plates. The kid was furious, and he had every right to be. Richard felt like an ass, but he was losing control, and he couldn't allow that to happen. He didn't want to use each other's first names, to become friends with the kid, or to relax his guard. He didn't want to think about the guilt he knew he would feel if he allowed himself to care and the kid hung.

"Now get over here so I can chain you to the wheel and I can get some sleep." Slowly, he pushed himself to his feet.

Once he'd secured Johnny for the night, he took a lantern and limped through the area collecting all the guns he could find. He emptied the chambers and locked them in a box in the chuck wagon. Then sitting on his bedroll spread before the fire, he thoroughly cleaned his Winchester. Unable to help himself, he fell asleep.

The boy's stealth woke him. A lifetime of hard living had sharply honed his sixth sense. Like a whisper in a crowd or the silence of birds, the lightness of Johnny's footfalls startled him from a fitful dream. At first he was uncertain what disturbed him so he lie still, feigning sleep. No sounds came from the area around the prison wagon, except the snores of the prisoners. And allowing for an occasional snort or stomp, the horses, too, were quiet.

Ever so slightly he cracked open his eyes. There

was nothing to disturb the moonless night except for Johnny, creeping ever so slowly toward Richard's gear, which he'd piled neatly beside him. The little pick-pocket must have stolen Richard's keys when he chained him.

Beneath Richard's blanket the reassuring weight of his Smith and Wesson pressed against his throbbing right thigh. Blanket? He didn't remember pulling on his blanket before he'd fallen asleep. Damn, the kid was a mix of contradictions.

Though there was something endearing about the rough mannered kid, he couldn't be trusted. Even now, that fact was again proving true. Slowly, Johnny's hand stretched toward the Winchester, which Richard had placed across his saddlebags. There was a certain satisfaction in knowing the rifle was empty, yet his satisfaction was tempered with disappointment, because a part of him needed Johnny to be a better man than his father.

Richard's mind raced as he tried to determine what the kid was up to. Assuming Johnny's fear of getting lost was a ploy to evoke sympathy, the obvious plan would be for Johnny to steal a horse and escape, avoiding both the law and Calvin Everett. More than likely Johnny had removed the bullets from the revolver when he'd covered him with the blanket. But some niggling seed of doubt caused Richard to bide his time.

Holding the rifle and scabbard in one hand and the saddlebags in the other, Johnny scooted back to sit between Richard's hip and the fire. Johnny never even removed the Winchester from the scabbard to see if it was loaded. Instead, the kid sat cross-legged facing the fire, the rifle across his lap, his head bent low. Richard watched, puzzled by the intense concentration etched in the boy's shadowed profile, illuminated in the glow of the fire.

Johnny's finger caressed the dark wood of the

stock for a moment then traced the initials Richard had carved there years ago. R-A-B. Johnny's eyebrows tugged together below his feathery bangs.

Fascinated, Richard watched him trace the letters again, then do the same with the monogram etched in the leather flaps of his saddlebags. Over and over Johnny repeated this action until he took up a small twig and began to write in the scuffed dirt.

Now that he realized Johnny wasn't planning to run off, the tension knotting his stomach eased a few twists. But what exactly was the kid doing? Ever so slowly, so Johnny wouldn't notice the movement, Richard rolled onto his left side, bracing his weight with the stump of his left arm in order to get a better view.

First Johnny drew the letters B-A-R. Then with his left finger he retraced the letters on the saddlebags. Realizing they didn't match, he quickly brushed out the letters in the dirt with his hand. He tried again and rubbed them out. Once more, he traced the letters, copied them with the stick, and erased them.

Richard's own frustration mounted along with Johnny's at each failed attempt. He ached to help him copy the letters, but from the way the kid was gnawing on his lower lip, Richard decided to wait and see what the kid would do next.

After several more efforts, Johnny finally succeeded. R-A-B. Richard nearly cheered aloud he'd been so caught up in the kid's struggle.

But Johnny wasn't finished. His mouth worked as he softly sounded out each letter then pieced the sounds together. "Rrrr-Aaaa, Bah." Johnny blew out a long sigh, took a deep breath and started over. "Rrr-aab. Rab."

A grin born of pride lit his dirty face. Without his hat to cast shadows across his features, Johnny seemed younger, softer somehow. His jawline was fine, and his neck slender. Golden highlights from the flickering fire, reflected off his short blond hair. Straight white teeth were exposed by wide upturned lips. Why in the fading glow of the campfire, with the bruises and the grime covered by shadow, Johnny appeared almost beautiful.

Richard was pole-axed. The jolt vibrated him right down to his toes. Overwhelming desire exploded inside him. He felt himself grow hard. Denial warred with his body's sudden consuming need. *No!* This couldn't be happening to him. *Think of Caroline. Think of Caroline.* He squeezed his eyes tight and let his body roll away from temptation. His swollen thigh banged against the barrel of his revolver. A low moan escaped his lips.

The grass rustled. He felt the light brush of Johnny's finger tips push back the hair from his forehead, and he clenched his teeth against the feathery touch.

Then Johnny's palm, pressed warm and smooth and reassuring against his brow. "Rab," he sighed.

Richard felt the blanket carefully lifted off his wounded leg. He knew when Johnny stilled that he'd noticed Richard's fingers curled around the butt of the Smith and Wesson.

There was a small chuckle then, a whispered, "I bet ya got bullets in this one, lawman."

Opening his eyes just a slit, he watched as Johnny pulled a small knife from his vest pocket and began to slice through the makeshift bandage. The wound had started to seep through the thick wrapping, leaving a dark coin sized stain. Though Johnny was as gentle as possible, the pad stuck to the wound. Richard jerked and groaned.

"Damn it, Johnny." Richard pushed himself up to sitting and leaned over to inspect the damage. "What the hell are you doing? And stop stealing my knife."

"Well ya wouldn't let me fetch the one Uncle Henry give me. That knife had a real sharp blade. Fit nice in my boot, too. Henry got it from some folks ridin' a stage he robbed."

"Don't tell me things like that. And give me back my knife. Besides," he grumbled. "I found your knife under the bunk when I went back in the dug-out looking for evidence. It's in the chuck wagon with your family Bible."

Peering close, Johnny doused the bullet wound with another splash of whiskey.

A sharp hiss of pain escaped Richard's throat, "Damn it, Johnny, that hurts."

"Oh quit yer whinin' lawman. Yer laig needs cleanin' an' I need to fix ya another poultice so's it don't fill up with poison."

Before Richard could utter a word of protest, Johnny scooted back to the fire and lost himself with his pots and herbs.

"How did you know the rifle wasn't loaded?" Richard asked after several minutes, when he recalled Johnny's earlier comment.

Johnny's head jerked around. He leveled Richard with a hard stare. "Ya wasn't sleepin'?" It was more of an accusation than a question.

Richard shrugged.

"Why ya sneakin', lyin', Yankee skunk!"

"Johnny, you're avoiding my question. How did you know the rifle wasn't loaded? I never saw you check."

"Well, I'm the one fetched yer rifle-gun after the ruckus with Paw an' Uncle Cal's men. Reckon it was empty then. I seen ya cleanin' it, an' ya fell asleep afore ya loaded it. I ain't stupid, lawman."

"I never thought you were, outlaw."

Johnny smeared a strange smelling, dark paste of some kind on a soft cloth and placed it over the wound.

"Well, I ain't."

"I know." Richard spoke low watching through half lowered lids as Johnny then wrapped a strip of clean white linen around his thigh, right over his pants.

"My maw, she taught me my letters afore she died. I can read iffin I've a mind to. Bet ya didn't know that. Ya wouldn't tell me yer name, so's I jest read it. Ya had it wrote on all yer gear plain as day, jest a-waitin' fer folks to read it. Yer name's Rab. It's a pretty good name I reckon. Good an' short. Easy to read, easy to say. An' different, too, like you. Not diff'rent in a bad way mind ya, but diff'rent in a good way."

An odd feeling of tenderness swelled inside his chest. As Johnny pulled the blanket back in place, Richard swore he would die before he ever told this kid that Rab wasn't his name.

"Thanks," he whispered.

"Ya know, fer a low down, no account Yankee, an' a lawman to boot, ya really ain't so bad."

Richard chuckled softly. "For an outlaw you ain't so bad yourself."

****

Volleys of gunfire shook the trees in front of him as bits of bark splattered in every direction. Thick smoke enveloped him, burning his eyes. He swiped away the tears.

On a low ridge, just twenty feet ahead, he spotted a flash as an enemy musket fired. He peered through the sight of his Sharps rifle and squeezed the trigger. Another flash. Again he sighted and squeezed the trigger.

"No! Stop!" A voice cried. "Stop!"

The gray cloud evaporated. On the ridge stood the soldier he'd just killed. Brady. A small dark spot appeared in the center of his chest.

"Murderer!" Brady cried, his eyes accusing

"No!" Richard heard himself scream. Horrified, he jumped to his feet, backing away only to stumble over the legs of a dead man. Turning, he saw Tyler.

"Murderer!" the blond guard accused.

A shot whizzed past Richard's head to hit the other guard in the center of the chest with a muffled thud.

"No!" Richard cried as the guard fell forward over a decaying log.

"No!" he screamed. These men weren't the enemy. These dead men were friends!

****

Richard jerked upright, fully awake. Sweat dripped from his hair and drenched his shirt. His pulse reverberated in his head like the rumbling echo of cannon fire. Ragged gasps for air were all he could manage through a chest squeezed tight with terror.

He glanced around the camp to see if he had awakened anyone, uncertain if his screams had echoed through the night or only his head. The prisoners were quiet, and Johnny lay curled in a ball asleep.

He rolled carefully to his feet and limped into the dark, stopping near the edge of the narrow creek. He stared at nothing, trying to ignore the pain the short walk had caused and breathing deep to calm his racing heart.

Somehow he wasn't surprised when moments later, Johnny appeared beside him. It was almost spooky, this connection between them.

"I thought you were asleep," he muttered.

"Naw, all that thrashin' around ya was doin' woke me up."

"Well, do forgive me for disturbing you."

"I thought maybe yer laig was a-painin' ya. Iffin ya want, I can brew ya up some tea to take away the hurt."

A short, derisive laugh was his only reply. He raked his fingers through his damp hair, trying to brush back the lock of hair which had once again fallen across his forehead. "I don't think your tea will help."

"Figgered. I can brew a tea fer that, too."

He turned toward Johnny then, his gaze narrowed. "What?"

"I can mix up some yarbs to calm ya, so's ya can sleep."

"I don't need to sleep."

Johnny stood quietly beside him for a minute. "Maybe ya should jest talk about it."

He stared at the boy long and hard. "There's nothing to talk about. And even if I could remember my dream, why would I tell you?"

"I seen things, too, Rab, same as you. Things I want to ferget." Johnny turned away then, to stare as Richard had done, off into the inky nothingness.

"Last year we was down in South Texas with Uncle Cal." The boy began after several minutes of silence. "Cal, he has dealin's down there with a band of Comancheros. Mostly guns and whiskey. Sometimes he trades women. An' the ones they cain't sell, cause maybe they's too old or too ugly, they get passed around like a whiskey bottle, betwixt Uncle Cal an' Paw an' their men. The more them women screamed an' fought, the more they laughed."

He wondered why Johnny was telling him this. Maybe the kid needed to share the story with someone who would understand his underlying pain. A part of Richard wished the kid wouldn't tell him. He didn't want to think of Johnny as a victim, as someone who needed to heal as much as he did.

He stared at the boy, and though he could barely make him out, Richard was drawn by the softness in

Johnny's voice and the vulnerability not normally heard in the boy's usual brazen tones.

"One day, one a Cal's men drug home this little girl. She had long blonde curls an' big blue eyes an' freckles across her nose. She was a little younger than me, jest startin' to grow tits. An' she was a wearin' this real purty yeller dress, all full a ruffles an' lace an' sech.

"But Cal, he just tore it offin her an' threw it in the dirt. That little girl stood there naked an' cryin' fer her maw, whilst Cal an' his men stood 'round a-laughin' at her.

"Then she seen me. She seen I weren't part a them what was plannin' to rape her. An' she turnt them big eyes on me, a-beggin' me to help. She never said nothin', 'ceptin' with her eyes. I ain't never fergot them eyes, first a-beggin' me, then a-hatin' me cause I didn't do nothin' to help her.

"I couldn't help her cause—" Johnny turned.

Richard could barely make out the glint of white in Johnny's eyes, but he could feel that gaze, locked on his face, searching for understanding and maybe absolution.

After a moment Johnny began again. "So's I watched 'em take her right there on the ground on top a that purty yeller dress. One a the men, Jackson, I recollect, he picked her up, her an' that yeller dress an' drug 'em off. I seen buzzards a circlin' out a ways after that, but I didn't go check to see iffin it was her, cause I reckon I didn't want to know. I jest sat there a-thinkin' on my real maw an' paw an' what they was a-havin' fer dinner, anythin' to try an' ferget. But them eyes a hers is burnt right into my head an' I know I ain't never gonna ferget 'em."

"God, Johnny, I'm so sorry." His voice caught in his throat. He wanted to say more but didn't know what, so he reached out and squeezed the boy's shoulder, surprised by how narrow it felt beneath his fingers. "I'm such an ass."

Eventually Johnny relaxed but didn't pull away. Richard's leg soon could not support his weight so he carefully eased himself down to the ground. The kid sat, too, and fell asleep, curled up in a ball beside him.

But Richard's leg throbbed too much to sleep. In a way he was grateful. He didn't want to sleep. He didn't want to dream. So he stared at the black and watched over Johnny until the gray light of dawn silhouetted the trees, and pink tinted the horizon.

****

"Johnny, where's my razor?"

Reaching for the pot of coffee, Johnny swung her gaze away from the fire and over her shoulder. The deputy's silhouette stood slightly behind her, his body a shadowy form in the dark gray, pre-dawn light. "How the hell should I know?"

"You were in my gear last night." He held out his saddle bags as though their existence proved his accusation.

"I weren't neither." Distracted, she overflowed the mug of coffee she was pouring. She yelped and dropped the cup. The liquid hissed and sizzled as it splattered against the flames.

"Ya seen I never touched yer damn razor." She mumbled, sucking on the inside of her hand. "What the hell do ya think I'd be doin' with it? Shavin'? Ya prob'ly lost it."

Heaving an exhausted sigh, he returned his saddlebags to his pile of gear on the other side of the fire then limped back. She passed him a dented tin cup and began slicing bacon into a pan.

He accepted the cup, took a swallow, and instantly spit the warm liquid toward the ground. A misty shower sprayed down on her hat.

"I don't want any of your damn tea." He fumed.

With a jerk of his wrist, he tossed the remaining brew into the grass. "I want coffee." He hobbled closer to the fire and leaned over to set his empty cup on the ground.

"Coffee ain't a-goin' to help yer laig none, lawman."

"I don't care. I want a good, strong, cup of coffee." He unhooked the blue speckled coffee pot from where it hung over the coals then filled his cup with the dark liquid before returning the pot to the fire. He leaned over and lifted his cup from the grass. Scowling, he sipped the hot liquid and watched as she set bacon, beans, and biscuits on five tin plates.

"Where's my breakfast? I hope you're not feeding those damn outlaws first."

"I'm commencin' to serve it up right now, lawman, but you keep on, all horns an' rattle, an' I got a good mind to dump it in the grass." She slapped a spoonful of beans on a plate and passed it up to him.

Before he could accept the food, he had to lean over and set his coffee back on the ground. "Where's my fork?" he snapped, taking the plate. "How the hell am I supposed to eat without a fork?"

She rose and rummaged through the supplies at the back of the cook's wagon. "Now don't go gettin' all frothy, lawman. They's here someplace.

"Damn it, Johnny, I have a name and it's not lawman."

"I know that, but when yer actin' like this I sure as hell don't feel like a-usin' it."

He heaved a long sigh that caught on a soft groan. She swung around. He was staring at the ground as though he wanted to sit, but it was too far away. He drew another deep breath.

"Acting like what?" he demanded, lifting a piece of bacon off his plate with his tongue.

"Ornery enough to kick a cat."

"Damn it, Johnny," he mumbled around the bacon. He took a moment to chew. "I hurt, I'm tired, I'm hungry, and all I want is a hot bath and a shave. I hate being dirty."

"How are ya a-goin' to shave in the dark lawman? Ya'll sure as hell end up a-slittin' yer throat. An' I'll be obliged to doctor that, too."

"Damn it, Johnny, for once, can't you give that mouth of yours a rest? I'm not in the mood." His voice held a worn edge that sent her sharp gaze straight to his face.

Tossing down his plate, the deputy limped away.

Johnny stared after him. Her entire life her father had hated her. His men were constantly mad at her. Not a day passed where she wasn't being yelled at for something and she'd never cared. But the realization that Rab was annoyed with her caused her chest to tighten.

She knew his leg just plain hurt. Why did she have to be so gruff? She thought of her real mother in the locket. Her real mother gave away hugs and kisses like sweet treats. She was never cross. She was always kind and always smiled.

Johnny never thought about it before, but she suddenly wished she could be like that. Rab might like a smile right now, a kind word or maybe a hug. She wanted to follow him and offer a bit of comfort, but she suppressed the urge, not knowing exactly what to do, or even how.

She picked up her bandages and herbs and walked to the prison wagon to doctor the other men before giving them their breakfast.

The driver, Hobbs, was much better and some of his color had returned. Hungrily, the big man wolfed down two plates of food. Grateful to Johnny for her aid, he kept a Winchester braced against the front of his hip and followed her as she moved among the prisoners to check their wounds. Machler and Warren were doing better, although Machler had a very bad headache and Warren was running a fever.

The last man was burning up and delirious. She tried to get some tea into him to ease his fever and pain, but he thrashed around so much it was difficult. The bullet wound in the man's leg was swollen and infected. Concerned, she consulted her book, lanced the wound and mixed up a different concoction of herbs to draw out the poison.

Hobbs offered to clean up from breakfast, so Johnny picked up the deputy's plate and went in search of him. She came upon him unexpectedly as she rounded the side of the chuck wagon. He stood with his back to her, naked from the waist up, his suspenders looped down past his knees. He had evidently washed, because his skin and his hair glistened. A wet rag had been wrapped around the back wheel of the cook's wagon and Rab rubbed his arm over it as he scrubbed; first the outside of his arm then the inside. Somehow it never occurred to her that he wouldn't be able to wash his own arm, and she found an odd fascination in watching him maneuver himself over the fixed cloth. When he finished he unwrapped it, then rinsed it in a basin on top of the water barrel, retied it, and repeated the process to remove the soap. Knowing intuitively he would not want her watching, she silently backed away.

Giving him a couple of minutes, she approached again. His back was toward her, and as she walked through the grass, he whirled around with his revolver in hand.

Johnny froze. And though in some part of her mind she realized he'd drawn his gun, the sight of his bare chest held her solid in her tracks. She'd seen men naked as the day they were born, but never had her gaze been tempted to linger over the deeply chiseled grooves which sharply delineated the contours of each powerful muscle. Fine brown hair dusted the width of his chest then tapered into a narrow trail in the center of his abdomen drawing her attention down to where it disappeared behind the waistband of his pants.

"What do you want?" he growled.

Johnny blinked trying to remember exactly why she was standing here. "I fetched ya a fork." She held out a plate with a fork placed on one side.

The deputy shook his head. "I'm not hungry."

"Take it, Rab, ya got to eat."

At the sound of his name, his gaze shot to her face, his dark brown eyes softened with a touch of wonder. He opened his mouth for a moment, as though he were about to say something, then closed it as he accepted the food and turned away to set the plate on top of the water barrel.

"I got to change that poultice on yer laig afore we light out."

He shook his head. "It's fine, Johnny. I checked it earlier." He scooped up a fork full of beans.

She glanced at his right thigh. The wrapped cloth appeared a bit snug over the pad and was likely pressing on the wound. "Ya want I should loosen that bandage a mite?"

He shook his head, a biscuit held in his mouth as he passed Johnny the empty plate. He limped around to the fold-down table at the back of the wagon as he pulled the top half of his underwear over his head. With his thumb and forefinger he deftly pushed the buttons through the holes.

"Johnny, I need you to get our gear together so we can move out." He turned to Hobbs who had joined them to put away the last of the food and dishes.

"Round up as many of the horses as you can, and saddle one for me. You'll be driving this wagon behind the prisoners. Today you'll be armed." He picked up a clean shirt that he must have tossed onto the work table of the chuck wagon before he washed.

"Should'a had me a gun yesterday."

"No driver on the prison wagon carries a weapon. If I had it to do over I'd still do the same. Today your responsibility is to guard those prisoners until we get to McAlester. Take what weapons and ammunition you need, then we'll pack the bodies on horses and hitch up the teams." He tucked in his shirt tail as far as he could, but it hung out over the left side of his pants.

"Now, Johnny," he began once Hobbs was out of earshot. "Tell me exactly what you did to the water. We're still a good two days from McAlester, and we have nothing but the water in that barrel."

She could already spot tiny beads of sweat popping out across the deputy's forehead from just this morning's brief exertion.

"I didn't do nothin' to the water."

"Damn it, Johnny, I'm sick of your lies. I thought there was enough between us so that I could trust you at least a little."

She dropped her gaze to study each blade of grass. "Ya can, Rab."

"Then how did everyone get sick?"

"I put a bit of steeped curlydock weed in the canteens ya give me to fill."

"Can I trust you then, Johnny, to rinse out the canteens and fill them with good water?"

"Ya can trust me." She lifted her head. The deputy's dark gaze narrowed on hers, searching for the truth.

"I won't do nothin' no more to hurt ya." She started to turn away, but the deputy's hand lashed out, his fingers locked around her small wrist in a crushing grip as he yanked her close.

Kathy Otten

"How do I know? How do I know I can trust you?" His penetrating stare bore straight to her soul.

"'Cause I ain't got nobody 'cept you." She whispered. Her heart thumped against her chest as the seconds passed.

"All right, Johnny," he said finally. "I'm counting on you. And when we get to Fort Smith I'll do everything in my power to help you find your family and get the charges against you dropped."

A half an hour later, Hobbs had the teams hitched to the wagons. Johnny's horse, Jack, and four others, were tied to the back of the chuck wagon and draped with the wrapped bodies of the dead. The rest of the animals were either dead or missing. The wounded outlaws were ushered into the prison wagon.

Just before they were ready to head out the deputy approached her leading his big bay horse, Billy.

"Johnny, help me mount up."

She frowned, looking pointedly at his swollen leg. "Ya shouldn't be a-ridin' that horse."

"Look, I'm in charge and what I say goes. You're not going to manipulate me as easily as you did yesterday. Now, help me mount, and then climb up on that seat and drive the prisoners."

Johnny drew herself up indignantly and glared at him. "Well, I ain't a ma-nip-al-latin' ya. An' iffin ya wasn't stubborn as a Missouri mule, ya'd see that it'd be better fer yer laig iffin ya was to drive the wagon, 'stead a tryin' to ride. But iffin ya want to ride all over the damn territory with blood a-runnin' into yer boot, well, I ain't a-payin' ya no never mind. I'll jest haul yer carcass up off the prairie when ya keel over."

He stared at her for a long moment. His features softened, and a small smile tugged up the left corner of his mouth.

"I'm sorry, Johnny. I appreciate your concern, but I can't drive the wagon." He extended the stump of his left arm. "I can manage a buggy in town, but not two mules over this rough terrain."

She shifted uncomfortably as her gaze fell to the ground. "Well, hell, Rab," she grumbled, kicking at the ground with the scuffed toe of her boot. "Yer so damn bossy, an' smart as a barn full a owls, I plum fergot ya only got one arm."

"What did you say?"

Her head jerked up at the urgency in the deputy's voice. She searched his face, uncertain. "I said ya was bossy."

"And?"

"An' smart as a barn full a owls."

"And?" A thread of hope lifted his voice.

"An' I fergot ya only got one arm," she muttered.

"That's what I thought you said." The deputy leaned against the side of the chuck wagon. His wide grin pressed a long dimple into the stubble of his left cheek. "You are the first person I've met since I lost this," he raised his stump, "who didn't notice."

Embarrassed, she looked away. "Well, I did notice, Rab. That first day when we was a-fightin' in the corral, I seen right off yer arm was gone. It's just that yer always so damn sure a yerself, a thinkin' ya know ever' thing they is to know, like ya was God's own cousin. Well, it makes a body ferget is all, that maybe they's some things ya cain't do."

He laughed. "Johnny Bodine, I could kiss you."

Johnny felt her faced drain of all blood as she backed away. "Jest stay away from me, lawman."

The deputy's smile vanished as his face, too, turned white. He started to say something, but she whirled away from him and climbed up onto the wagon seat. She took a few moments to situate herself then collected the reins.

Curious, she stole a quick glance back. He was

stuffing his bottle of whiskey into his saddlebags. Guilt twisted her stomach as she watched him struggle to haul himself onto his horse, especially when the wind twisted through the trees and he shivered. Though she knew he'd been appalled by the thought of kissing her, it was so close to what she'd been wishing for when he'd flashed that dimpled grin, that she had to escape or risk exposing her secret.

Then almost as if Rab were punishing them, he pushed the group hard over the next two days until they arrived in McAlester.

Chapter Eight

A small crowd of men, women, and children lined the dusty street as their procession rolled past. They were mostly Choctaw, with a few whites intermingled, either leasing businesses from the Indians or having married into the tribe. Exhausted and flushed with fever, Richard was not in the mood for their curious stares.

Without a word to Hobbs or Johnny, he led the procession up Main Street to the undertaker, where he delivered the bodies of Brady, the guards, and the outlaws. He asked Johnny if her father's men had any family to claim the bodies, but the kid didn't know of anyone. Reluctantly, Richard paid the undertaker the cost of their burials.

Next, he dropped Hobbs and Johnny off at the doctor's office, along with the feverish prisoner with the leg wound, and promised Johnny he'd be back soon.

At the Tobucksy County Courthouse, Richard swung off his horse and took a moment to gather his strength before stepping on to the porch and entering the small frame building.

He talked to the local Choctaw police, seeking information on Calvin Everett, but the Light Horse officers knew no more than he did. Needing someone to guard Machler and Warren, Richard paid the Indian police to do the job and while he was relieved to leave the prison wagon with the Choctaw officers, he couldn't help but feel guilty for shirking his duty.

Afterward, he stopped at the small train depot and made arrangements to have the bodies of Brady and the two guards shipped home and have a telegram sent to Fort Smith.

Exhausted, he dragged himself back to the doctor's office. Hobbs and Johnny looked up as he came through the door.

"Hobbs." Richard tossed the freighter a silver dollar, which the big man deftly caught with one hand.

"Go get yourself something to eat. And when you're done, take some food to the prisoners at the jail. And bring me a receipt. I'll be staying at the Elk House."

"Sure enough, marshal." Hobbs hauled his bulk out of the wooden chair.

"How's the arm?" Richard asked as an afterthought. With all they'd been through he was grateful for the man's help.

"It's just fine, marshal, thanks to the kid here."

"Good. And Hobbs, I got you a room at the Elk House, too, and you won't even have to share." He managed a faint smile.

"Thanks, Marshal. An' if ya want my advice, I'd let the kid," he indicated Johnny with a jerk of his head, "tend your leg before that sawbones in there."

Johnny lifted her eyes to study the deputy as Hobbs left the doctor's office. Fever had flushed his cheeks and added a shine to his dark brown eyes. The fool lawman was pushing himself too hard. Though she'd changed the dressing as frequently as Rab would allow, she didn't doubt his leg was infected. What he needed most was rest, and lots of it.

Swaying on his feet, he nodded toward the inner door. "What's going on with that one?"

"That quack is a-goin' to take his laig."

Rab paled and grabbed the back of the nearest chair for support.

"I could save it, iffin' I'd had half a chance, but

the damn fool won't listen to no 'smart mouth, outlaw brat.'"

At that moment a soul wrenching scream erupted from behind the door. The pure agony of it radiated through the thin wall and sent shivers through Johnny's body. She glanced up. The deputy's complexion had turned the color of pond scum. He swallowed, then whirled, and bolted out the door.

She sat for a long time wondering what to do, when the door opened and Rab returned.

His face was chalk white and glistened with a sheen of perspiration. Limping across the room, he stopped in front of the chair beside hers and slowly lowered himself onto the scratched seat, extending his leg. He removed his dusty brown Stetson and wiped his brow with the back of his wrist. A lock of hair dropped across his forehead.

She studied him carefully. "Ya need to rest up, Rab."

A faint smile tugged up one corner of his mouth. "I will, don't worry." He set his hat on his left thigh and brushed back his hair. "I was just over at the train station and had the stationmaster send a wire to Fort Smith. Marshal Upham is sending some help. We'll stay here until the new deputies arrive. They can take the prisoners back to Fort Smith, and I'll rest here 'til I feel better."

"Why cain't we all go back on the train?" She'd always wanted to ride on one, and the thought of being separated from Rab had the familiar tentacles of panic creeping around her chest.

"Because prisoners are not allowed to be transported by train."

"Why the hell not? Seems like it'd make a heap more sense." She wondered if she could stay behind with him.

"Common sense doesn't enter into it. Believe me,

I've argued the point 'til I was blue in the face. I even sent a letter to Washington, along with a cost breakdown for transporting seventeen prisoners both ways. The train would have saved nearly three hundred dollars. Washington still said, no railroad."

"Seems like ya set great store by rules. Don't ya never break 'em?"

He dropped his head back against the wall and closed his eyes. "Some men break the rules. But I never do. They're too important."

"Why? They's jest rules."

"Because rules are based on a moral code of ethics that define right from wrong. They are the line society has drawn in the sand. I walk the edge of that line every day. I need those rules to hang on to, to keep me from stepping off the edge, to keep me from becoming a man just like your father."

A few minutes later, the inner door opened and the doctor stepped into the outer office. With a groan, Rab lifted his head away from the wall and blinked at the doctor.

The elderly man wiped his bloody hands on a stained towel. Half a cigar hung from his mouth. "It'll be a while before your man goes anywhere, if he makes it at all. That leg was pretty bad."

"Well, ya shouldn't a took it!" Johnny declared angrily, jumping to her feet. "Iffin ya kept a poultice on it an'—"

Rab's hand clamped around her arm. His fingers squeezed through her layers of clothes, halting her tirade in mid-sentence.

The doctor's gray eyes narrowed as he glared at her. "I told you, I'm the doctor, not you. During the war I took off hundreds of arms and legs."

Johnny felt the tremor that rippled through Rab at the doctor's words. She could feel the pressure of each finger tip as it dug painfully into the muscle of her forearm.

"Sorry, Doc, he's just a boy." He apologized in a low soothing tone. "He didn't mean any harm. I only stopped by to check on the prisoner. Now that I know he's in good hands, we'll be on our way."

"Why don't you stay and let me have a look at your leg. You don't look too healthy yourself."

"Ya damn jackleg sawbones! Ya ain't fit to doctor a mule." She lunged for the doctor, but the grip the deputy maintained on her arm jerked her back like a dog on the end of a tether.

"Come-on, Johnny."

Shifting his grip to her shoulder, the deputy managed to lever himself out of the chair. He swayed once, as he shifted his weight off his injured leg, then he pushed her out of the office.

She continued to sputter as they started down the dusty street, and it took a few minutes for her to realize the amount of weight pressing down on her shoulder had increased.

She stopped complaining about the doctor and glanced up. Sweat beaded across the deputy's forehead. Except for the two patches of dark pink coloring his cheek bones, his face had lost all color. The lawman was near the end of his strength.

"Ya need to lay down, Rab."

He closed his eyes briefly. "I've got a room at the Elk House. I was going to get you something to eat first, but I can't right now. I'm sorry."

"Hell, I don't give a shit. We'll fetch some vittles later."

The Elk House was a large two story clapboard house with a freshly painted addition. A balcony stretched across the second floor, and a white picket fence surrounded the yard. The pretty enclosure fascinated her, and she imagined it to be the perfect devise to keep any child from wandering out of the yard and getting lost.

Her fingers itched to reach out and bump along

the row of pointy slats as they passed by, but the deputy stumbled while she was distracted, and nearly tumbled them both to the ground. Taking more of his weight, she guided him through the gate.

"Ya'll feel better, wunst ya rest up. I'll change that dressin' an' fix ya up a new poultice. Damn, I need to fetch my bag."

"It's in the room. I had a boy from the livery take over all our gear."

She accepted more and more of his weight until her knees wanted to buckle, and she was nearly dragging him. Though he tripped on the stairs a few times, they finally made it to the room.

A double-size, brass bed was positioned against the front wall opposite the door. He collapsed, face down, across the mattress.

"I'm sorry, Johnny," he mumbled into the patchwork quilt. "Just let me get a little nap. Then I'll get you some food."

Somewhat drained herself, Johnny dropped beside him on the edge of the bed and watched him breath. "I need to check yer laig."

"Sure, Johnny," he murmured without opening his eyes. "In a minute, just give me a minute."

She looked around and thought she'd never seen a room so pretty. It was similar to the image she carried in her mind of her bedroom in her real home, with her real mother and father. All four walls were painted a wonderful shade of sky blue. To the left of the bed, lacey curtains had been drawn across the only window, softening the harshest rays of the setting sun. Beneath the window stood a small cabinet covered with a round piece of lace that almost matched the curtains. On top of that had been placed a kerosene lamp with tiny blue flowers painted across the white glass shade. And beside the window was a stuffed chair, made of a fuzzy, dark red cloth. Along one wall stood a scarred armoire and chest of drawers. A porcelain pitcher and bowl sat atop a small commode.

Scooting off the bed, she dropped to her knees beside the dresser where the deputy's Winchester and their saddlebags had been tossed. She set her hat aside and opened the doeskin bag.

Toward the bottom she found her book of drawings and set it on the floor beside her, then took careful stock of her remaining herbs, roots, and salves. Since the deputy wasn't likely to awaken anytime soon, she bravely shed her slightly singed duster, oversized vest, and long white shirt. She rolled up the sleeves of her second shirt, revealing her narrow, pale, forearms and wrists. Pulling the little book into her lap, she carefully reviewed all the pages she could find relating to wound infection.

Once she had formulated a plan of care, she returned to the bed. For just a minute, she watched him sleep.

This lawman was unlike any man she had ever known. Her heart did funny things when he was near, and strangely, he seemed able to peer straight into her soul. And while a part of her wanted to push him away before he discovered her secret, the rest of her wanted to pull him close and hold on tight so he could never leave.

Trying not to wake him, she kicked off her boots, climbed up beside him, and unbuttoned his suspenders. After flipping the ends over his shoulders, she carefully rolled him onto his back. Scooting off the mattress, she lifted each of his heavy feet and tugged off his tall boots. He moaned and rolled his head restlessly on the pillow. With a careless toss of her arm, the boots landed with a consecutive clump, clump in the corner of the room.

Next, she undid the buttons of his dark brown canvas pants and using his bone pocket knife, she cut the dirty dressing from around his thigh. A pinkish yellow stain seeped through the pad covering his wound. The stubborn man had been in such a hurry to get to McAlester he hadn't allowed her to change the dressing since dawn. All the walking he'd done today had caused his thigh to swell, and the discharge on the cloth confirmed the wound was filling with poison.

She pulled the stuck pad from the wound and winced when he moaned.

"Sorry, Rab, I had to do it."

Mindful of his wound, she carefully peeled his pants down his long, heavily muscled legs, pausing for several seconds when she saw how the area around the bullet hole had darkened from a healthy pink to an angry red and thin yellow discharge leaked from between the stitches. Pouring cold water from the pitcher into the bowl, Johnny wrung out a clean white cloth and laid the compress across his forehead.

"Now don't ya fret, I'm a-goin' to be real easy with ya from here on out."

A few minutes later, she donned her disguise and slipped from the room in search of some hot water. It was late enough she managed to avoid meeting anyone in the hallway or on the back stairs. The kitchen was dark except for the glow of a single lantern placed in the center of a large plank table in the middle of the room. Silently, she walked to the sink. But just as she reached for the pump handle, an older woman stepped from the pantry. Johnny jumped and the kettle she was about to fill clanged to the floor and rolled under the table.

The woman shrieked, "Ach du lieber Gott!" One hand pressed against her bosom, the other clutched the door jamb.

Johnny hesitated, caught between wanting to pick up the kettle and wanting to bolt from the room before the woman took after her with a broom.

Johnny inched toward the table. Keeping one eye on the woman, Johnny squatted and reached underneath to grab the handle.

Apparently recovered from her start, the woman moved toward the table and as Johnny stood, she took the kettle from her hand.

"I am sorry to frighten you, young man." She set the kettle in the sink and began to work the pump. "Did you vah-nt to make a cup of tea?"

Relaxing, now that she saw the woman wasn't angry, Johnny nodded. "Yes 'um. 'Ceptin' I got my own yarbs, upstairs in the room." She stepped back as the woman transferred the kettle to the stove.

"Yarbs?" She shot Johnny a puzzled glance as she scooped some coal from the scuttle beside the stove. "I am sorry, I do not know dis vord, 'yarb.'"

"Yarbs is jest willow bark an' sage leaves an' yarrow root an' sech. Fer medicine."

"Ach!" she exclaimed as she turned and waved her hand in Johnny's direction. "You are t'e young man t'at came in vit t'e deputy. Come, come, you sit." She patted a stool at the end of the table.

Feeling a bit uncertain, Johnny sat.

"Such a nice man, t'at deputy. He stays here every time he comes t'rough town." She unwrapped a half a loaf of dark bread from the center of the table. "I am Lena Sittel. My husband, Edvard and I, we run t'is hotel and restaurant. He told me your deputy vas vounded." She buttered two slices of bread and set them in front of Johnny.

"You eat."

She disappeared into the pantry and returned a few minutes later with a china plate, piled high with food. Johnny blinked as Mrs. Sittel set the odd looking vittles in front of her.

"A little sauerbraten and strudle. Eat, eat. You are much too t'in. I vill get you some clean bandages and v'en you are finish, my boy Fritz, he vill carry t'e kettle upstairs for you."

Johnny hadn't realized how hungry she was until she bit into the first slice of bread. The butter Mrs. Sittel gave her was sweet and every bite was heaven. The meat was so tender it nearly melted in her mouth and the strudel was the most delicious dessert she'd ever tasted.

It was almost as if she were being teased by her own dream. The big house with a fenced in yard, brothers and sisters, a kind father, and a mother who baked delicious treats. She wondered what her life could have been and what she would have become—if only...

Though she hadn't been in Mrs. Sittel's kitchen very long, reality greeted her as soon as she returned upstairs. Rab moaned and thrashed on the bed.

Fritz left the kettle on the floor near her doeskin bag and with only a quick glance toward the bed, he hurried from the room. Johnny tossed her armful of bandages on top of the dresser, shed her second shirt, pushed up the sleeves of her underwear top, and set to work steeping the tea and mixing a fresh poultice for the deputy's leg.

He muttered orders from battles in war she'd only heard stories about. He pleaded for God to forgive him and begged that they not take his arm.

She wondered how he'd lost it as she poured the steaming water into a cup with the pulverized willow bark. Leaving it to steep, she applied some blue cornmeal mush to his wound and wrapped it with a clean bandage. Then she returned to the kitchen and dragged up two buckets of cold well-water to try and lower his rising fever.

Johnny had seen bare-naked men many times in her young life, but stripping his shirt and cotton drawers from the deputy's body made her insides as jumpy as a toad on a hot rock. She forced herself to take calming breaths just to slow her racing heart.

As she ran the cold cloths over his heated skin, her own skin became warm and tingled each time she brushed against his body. She tried to convince herself that her skin felt all goose bumpy because it had been so long since she'd had a good scrub with soap and water. The deputy's bare chest and abdomen had nothing to do with her reaction. As soon as she bathed the feeling would go away.

Once he seemed to be resting, she decided to take a chance and wash herself with the remaining water. Longing to escape the confines of her smelly clothes, Johnny stood in the corner between the wall and the dresser, stripped bare, and began to scrub.

****

Around him scattered fires lit the blackness of the woods with flickering patches of orange. Underbrush crackled as flames devoured the thin branches. Screams and desperate pleas for help echoed through the night. In the distance, an explosion rustled the leaves of the trees above him as the blaze ignited the unused ammunition of some dead or wounded soldier.

Richard fumbled at his waist, frantic to pull free his own cartridge belt before he met the same fate, but he couldn't seem to find the buckle. The fire crept closer.

Heat pulsated through him from the inside out. His eyes burned in their sockets, his throat was parched, and his tongue hot and dry. He had to escape. He struggled to crawl, but he couldn't make his body move. His left arm throbbed where a Minnie ball had ripped through it, just above his left wrist, shattering the bone. Blood coated his hand and dripped from his useless fingers. He called for help and groped again for his cartridge belt. He still couldn't feel the wide strip of leather. Someone must have removed it.

129

He felt a presence close beside him, touching his face with something cool and wet. He tried to make out the man's face, but the darkness and smoke obscured his vision.

"Throw it away!" he rasped, the smoke clogging his throat so that it was hard to speak. He had to make the soldier understand. "It will explode. Throw it as far as you can."

"I done tolt ya, I throwed it clean into next week."

The soldier sounded irritated.

"It's gone. Yer safe now, Rab."

Richard relaxed against the damp ground. The pile of dried leaves behind the log he'd been using for cover, felt as soft as a pillow. The coolness pressed against his cheek and trailed down his neck. He longed for sleep, but was afraid to close his eyes.

A bullet thunked into the decaying log as others pelted the trees in back of him. He rested his rifle on the log and squinted into gathering darkness and smoke to draw a bead on the Rebs. Another shot plowed into the leaves in front of the log. This time he'd seen the muzzle flash. He aimed, waited for the next flash and fired.

Patiently, he lay watching for another, then aimed and fired. The flashes were like phantom targets, and his challenge was to find them when he couldn't see more than twenty feet in front of him.

He didn't wonder if he missed his mark, because he never did. His amazing accuracy with a rifle was why Colonel Hiram Berdan had accepted his lie about his age and welcomed him into his elite corps of sharpshooters at fifteen.

Twigs snapped and leaves rustled like crumpled parchment as someone charged through the undergrowth behind him.

"Stop!" the man screamed. "You're shooting our own men!"

The words slammed into Richard low and hard, like a Minnie ball tearing through his gut. Nausea erupted inside his stomach, and he shuddered as though he'd been doused with ice water. He lowered his Sharps and glanced back, recognizing the form of Sergeant Boyle as he emerged from the veil of smoke then shoved his way through the tangle of trees and brush.

"Our forward line is curved to the right. That's Billy Donovan's unit! Stop shooting!"

Horrified Richard looked toward the rise. Six muzzle flashes, six shots. Oh, God what have I done? He hung his head, and pressed his forehead against his arm. Drawing a deep breath, he inhaled the damp scent of decaying leaves then exhaled slowly, trying to suppress his need to vomit. A bullet thudded into the log.

He whipped his head around. "Get down!" he yelled.

There was a soft poof. Boyle stiffened and looked at his chest. Then slowly he shifted his gaze to meet Richard's. Confusion widened the sergeant's blue eyes for just a moment then he crumpled to the ground.

Richard crawled up beside him. Holding his rifle in his right hand, he stretched out his left hand and placed it on Boyle's chest. Wet warmth touched his skin through the sergeant's dark wool coat. Richard gasped.

Boyle moaned. "Christine..."

"Oh God, I'm sorry," Richard cried. Suddenly a bullet smashed through his left wrist.

Boyle jerked beneath Richard's hand and went still, as pain exploded up Richard's arm and shot across his chest. He rolled away and pulled himself back to the protection of the log. The acrid bite of burning leaves filled his nose. He tried to crawl away, but each time he left the safety of the log someone shot at him.

He turned his head and saw the orange glow of a distant fire. Would it spread in this direction? He stared at it, trying to decide if it was growing in size. At first he saw nothing but bright orange light with shadows of brown.

Gradually, the shadows shifted into a single silhouette, as the orange softened into a yellow halo and backlit the form of an angel.

She was dressed in what looked like his blue shirt. Unaware he was watching, her blonde head bent as though in prayer. A strand of rawhide dangled from her cupped hands.

"Angel," he murmured hoarsely.

Startled, her head jerked up. Something small and shiny slipped from her fingers to land softly on the rug at her feet. Her lithe form stiffened, and her wide-eyed gaze darted back and forth, as though she were poised to flee.

"No!" he croaked, his voice little more than a raspy whisper.

She stared back for several moments, her body gradually relaxing. He watched as she glided closer. One pale knee bent as she sat beside him. Her skin was white and smooth, almost luminous in the dark. He longed to touch her, to discover whether she were real or part of a dream, but he couldn't seem to raise his arm. Her small hand reached out to press against his cheek, and he turned his face into its coolness.

"Yer hot," she whispered

"Hell. We're in Hell."

"Ya ain't in Hell, yer in McAlester."

The flames of the scattered fires were gone, but heat still burned his eyes. He ached to close them, but he was afraid she would vanish. "Why are you here? There are no angels in hell."

"I'm here cause ya brung me. An' I ain't no angel."

"I'm sorry."

"Sorry fer what?"

"I'm sorry I brought you here. Angels don't belong in Hell."

"I ain't no damn angel."

"You aren't? You look like one."

The angel frowned.

He continued. "Why are you here? I'm a killer."

"Rab, ya ain't no killer an' ya ain't in Hell."

"I am. Can't you feel the fire?"

"Yer sick an' burnin' with fever. That's why yer a-havin' bad dreams. Jest ferget about 'em an' go to sleep."

"I killed them and never told anyone I did it. I'm a murderer that's why God took my arm. That's how I knew He'd send me to Hell."

The angel's cool hands moved to his shoulders. Lord, her touch felt good, though he did wonder why she was shaking him.

"Ya ain't dead, Rab. Ya ain't in hell. An' I ain't neither. We's in McAlester, at the Elk House hotel."

"Hotel? I'm in a hotel?"

She heaved a sigh and sat back on her heels. Her hands slipped from his shoulders. He missed their coolness, though her knee still pressed against his ribs. "Then why are you here? Are you my guardian angel?"

She sighed. "I done tolt ya, I ain't no angel."

He smiled. His eyes closed. "Angel," he murmured.

The pressure of her knee against his ribs disappeared. His eyes flew open. He couldn't lose her now. With an unexpected surge of strength his hand lashed out and captured her wrist, just as she was easing away from him.

Her eyes widened in panic. She tried to pull away, but he held her fast.

"Where are you going, Angel?" he asked,

confused.

She ceased her struggle. "T-to fetch ya some tea."

"Tea?" He wanted to rub his aching forehead, but he was afraid if he let go she'd run away. "Please, don't leave me alone."

She grabbed his wrist with her free hand and twisted her captured wrist back and forth until he felt his grip loosen. His eyes drifted closed.

"I'm a-goin' to fetch ya some tea. Drink it an' ya'll feel better." She tugged again, and her wrist broke free. His hand dropped to the mattress.

He dozed until the angel started shaking him and ordered him to drink. What did she call it? He had to think. *Tea.* It tasted bitter. He would have rather had whiskey, but he drank it because she told him to.

"Don't go," he whispered.

He was too tired to think anymore. Darkness was closing in, and he could feel himself slipping into it. Then he felt movement beside him, her coolness returned to press against his side, and her small hand lightly brushed across the tips of the hair on his chest. Before she could change her mind, he again grabbed her wrist. She stiffened. Her knee eased away from his side.

Too exhausted to speak, he could only utter the words in his mind. *Don't go. Please?*

Somehow she heard his plea. "I ain't a-goin' nowhere, Rab." She eased her body a bit closer and sighed.

Comforted, he let the darkness claim him.

****

A beam of sunlight across his face roused Richard from a sound sleep. He groaned and tried to roll away from the bright stab of light, but his arm was pinned to the mattress by the weight of a warm body. Reluctant to open his eyes, he squinted the one eye that wasn't being pierced by the sun.

A young woman lay curled against his side; her hand over his heart. He tipped his head slightly, savoring the silkiness of her blonde hair against his lips. Her breath streamed out in soft little puffs across his sweat dampened skin, tickling the fine hairs that dusted his chest. She felt so smooth and soft curled against him; he started to grow hard with wanting her.

Her identity mystified him for only a few moments before bits and pieces of memory dropped into place, and he realized the angel of his dream was asleep in his arms.

The knowledge Johnny was actually a girl left him grinning with relief. On some level, over the past two weeks, he must have sensed who she was. His growing attraction and his constant desire to kiss the little outlaw, he happily realized now, had been nothing more than his body's normal response to a beautiful woman. He was not insane. A self-depreciating chuckle rumbled in his chest. Well, at least not completely.

The familiar scent of sandalwood drifted through his nostrils as he breathed. She'd obviously found his bar of soap. He pulled her a little closer, then nuzzled his chin into her hair, closed his eyes and sighed.

She stiffened in his arms. His eyes popped open to discover her wide violet gaze staring straight at him. Inch by inch, she eased away.

"Johnny, wait." He reached out and wrapped his fingers around her wrist before she could escape. Her eyes dilated as she twisted and pulled against his strength. Confused by her reaction, he released his hold. She fell backward off the bed with a loud thump, but quickly scrambled to her feet. Confused by her reaction, he could only stare as she stumbled back against the wall.

Flashes of his dreams darted through his mind. He'd seen her standing beside the bed, backlit in a halo of light. He'd believed her to be an angel. She'd been wearing his shirt, an image he now found to be more erotic than angelic. She was still wearing his shirt, except now she was brandishing his small knife in one hand and his open razor in the other. Her terrified gaze shot from his face, to the obvious evidence of his morning arousal, and back.

His cheeks flushed with heat, and he drew up his good leg, tenting the blanket, although he was already shrinking in response to her panic.

"Johnny?" He was baffled by her fear of him. Had he hurt her in some way last night? His heart raced as the weight of dread pressed against his chest. No, he argued with himself, if he had, she never would have lain beside him all night. He pushed himself up higher on the pillows searching her face for an explanation.

"Don't ya come near me, lawman."

"Johnny, I'd never hurt you." He hoped his raspy voice sounded reassuring.

"Yer a man, ain't ya?" She accused. "I know what yer a-tryin' to hide. I seen how men is with women. Why else are ya a-layin' there a-grinnin' like a mule in a thistle patch?"

"I'm smiling because you're a woman. You can't know how relieved I am to know that."

She said nothing, but inched toward a low hanging clothes line that had been strung from the footboard of the bed to the top knob on the chest of drawers. Keeping a wary eye on him, she set her weapons on the floor and tugged her clothes off the line.

In just minutes, her entire body was once again hidden beneath the familiar baggy layers. The knife and razor remained on the floor. He chose to believe that was a good sign.

"Look, Johnny, you asked me once to trust you, and now you have to trust me."

For several long minutes, she stared at him as she searched every nuance of his expression.

An image of the girl in the yellow dress, being ravished on the ground right before her eyes rent his heart with such pain, he felt as though it were being torn in two. For the first time, he tasted a bit of the terror Johnny lived with every day, knowing that what happen to the girl, would happen to her—if someone discovered her secret. He longed to hold her close and protect her. He wanted her to know that with him she was safe.

But first she had to trust him. Because, if she believed him worthy of her complete trust, then perhaps it proved he wasn't as damned as he believed himself to be. He extended his arm, his hand held out in silent invitation, needing her to accept it even more that she did. Silent, he waited, her internal struggle reflected in her eyes.

Then, ever so slowly, like a frightened deer, her small sock-covered foot slid toward him. But she jerked it back and stood gnawing on her lower lip. His arm ached. He longed to rest it on the bed, but even the slightest movement might startle her.

He kept his gaze locked on hers as she took another cautious step.

First one and then another, until she stood beside the bed studying him, her lower lip caught between her teeth.

Then ever so slowly her hand reached out. Her fingers brushed his.

He felt a slight tremble. He didn't move, afraid she would bolt.

Gradually, she pressed her hand against his, and he closed his fingers around hers. He waited for a moment to see if she would pull away. When she didn't, he gently tugged, and she lowered herself onto the bed until she lay beside him once more.

He released a long breath and closed his eyes, already exhausted.

"Thank you," he whispered.

Chapter Nine

Johnny studied every fine line and blemish on Rab's face as he slept. The lock of hair he always brushed off his forehead, lay almost touching the bridge of his nose. She started to lift it back in place, but instead let it sift through her fingers and fall back. His hair needed a good washing, and his face needed a shave. She ran her index finger along his rough, stubble-coated jawline. Then, because she was so very close, she eased her face just a bit closer and pressed a light kiss against his cheek. His beard pricked the sensitive skin of her lips, and she pulled back.

He would want to shave when he woke. She drew her lower lip in between her teeth, wondering where she put his razor. She didn't want him yelling at her again if she couldn't find it. She smiled to herself. He might yell and swear, but in her heart she knew; Rab would never hurt her.

He was a good and decent man, like the man in the locket. And Rab being that kind of man gave her hope. Hope that not all men were like her father or Uncle Cal, and the life she'd always wished for could still come to be. One day, she might become part of a real family, and one day, someone out there might actually come to love her. As long as she held on to that hope, she could make it through another day.

In his sleep, Rab's thumb brushed lazily back and forth across her shirt, just below her breast. She'd been in such a hurry to escape beneath her clothes she hadn't bothered to wrap herself flat. She wasn't as big on top as her mother or Morning Song, but neither was she as flat as a boy.

Her gaze shifted to his face. The motion of his thumb stopped. Despite what her heart knew, her body still tensed, but his eyes stayed closed. His breathing remained slow and even.

She snuggled closer, and the movement started again. Slow and lazy, the end of his thumb slid back and forth over the cotton fabric with just enough pressure to make her skin tingle. Unable to stop herself, she squirmed. The tantalizing motion stopped, but this time he didn't start again. His warm breath sifted through her wispy bangs and tickled her forehead. She felt safe lying here beside him and eventually, she too, fell asleep.

****

Richard slept through the day and into the next night, waking only long enough to use the chamber pot or drink down the tea and broth Johnny gave him. Early the next morning, Johnny brought him his soap and a basin of water and left him alone to wash. Exhausted after the effort, he'd fallen asleep before he could shave.

When he next came fully awake, the unusual stillness of the room triggered a vague sense of unease, and he shifted onto his side to better see outside the window. From the height of the sun above the rooftop across the street, he judged the time to be late morning of what he calculated was their second day in McAlester.

He pushed himself up against the headboard, cursing his weakness. He glanced around the room wondering where Johnny had gone. Normally, she was at his side shoving a cup of tea at him, anticipating his needs before he even knew what they were. The clothes line was gone, but the contents of his saddlebags and her herbs and pots were scattered around the room. When several minutes passed and she still hadn't returned, a warning bell triggered an alarm in his brain, urging him to move.

Where was his gun? That sonofabitch, Calvin Everett, was still out there, eager for revenge, and not above using Johnny to get it. Had he grabbed her somehow and forced her to go with him? Would he bargain with her life to get his men released? What would happen if one of the men who rode with him learned her secret? Would they pass her around as they had the girl in the yellow dress, violating her until she no longer cared if she lived or died? The image had him tossing back the covers and surging to his feet.

The room tilted crazily, and he dropped to the edge of the mattress. He spotted the chamber pot on the floor and nearly toppled over trying to reach it. God, he was in no shape to go hunting outlaws.

Once again he tried to stand. The room didn't sway as bad this time, but he still needed the support of the bed post to steady himself. He stood for a few minutes, fighting the spiraling whorl of dizziness.

Nausea churned his stomach.

He staggered across the room and yanked his pants from the pile of clothes on the floor, then stumbled back to the bed to pull them on, too anxious to bother with his drawers. Beads of cold sweat popped out across his forehead as he leaned over to tug on his boots

The dizziness returned in waves when he straightened. He waited a moment to get his bearings then stumbled to the chest of drawers where he pulled his revolver from its holster and made certain each chamber was loaded.

Gun in-hand, he limped toward the door.

With a tray of food in her arms, Johnny carefully turned the knob and nudged the door with the toe of her boot, all without spilling a single drop of coffee. She froze as the door swung inward, and she came face to face with the deputy standing bare-chested and pale in the center of the room, his Smith and Wesson pointed straight at her chest. She swallowed, her eyes drawn not to his gun but to his britches, which hung low, just below the curve of his hips, to the 'V' of the undone buttons and the dark patch of hair it revealed. He was too weak to button them, yet the grim determination carved in his features gave him the appearance of strength.

"What the hell are ya a-doin' outta bed?" she demanded. She thought she'd glimpsed relief in his eyes when she walked through the door, but it disappeared so quickly she was no longer certain she'd seen it.

"I still have prisoners to check on," he growled. "Of which you are still one."

"Well, hell, lawman," she grumbled, relieved that he treated her the same way he had before. She'd been worried he would act differently toward her now that he knew her secret and they had shared the bed. He would never know how relieved she was to find him as ornery as ever.

"Where have you been?" he snapped, though it must have been obvious from the tray of food where she'd gone.

"Fetchin' vittles an' coffee. An' I can see from yer usual mornin' cheerfulness, I weren't none too soon in fetchin' 'em neither."

"How did you pay for them? Or did you just go down to Mrs. Sittel's kitchen and help yourself?"

"I give her some money I found in yer pockets."

"Fine. You've stolen everything else that belongs to me, you might as well take my money."

"Ya damn, ungrateful lawman. I brung this here food fer you. So why don't ya quit a-swayin' back an' forth like a damn penj-la-lum an' set down an' eat."

As she spoke, she set the tray on the floor and

moved across the room to slip one arm around his bare waist. "I swear to God, Rab, mules must come to ya fer stubborn lessons."

She eased him back in bed and propped him up with pillows.

"It's pend-u-lum," he grumbled. "And I was worried."

She turned to retrieve the wooden tray. "Pend-ja-lum," she mimicked, setting it on the chair. "Worried about what?"

"Pend-u-lum." He accepted a cup of hot coffee. "I was worried about you."

She froze with a dish of scrambled eggs in her hand and stared.

He set his coffee cup on the mattress beside his hip and reached out to accept the plate. "I thought your uncle had taken you."

He'd been coming to save her? Pressure suddenly swelled inside her chest. The familiar ache of tears closed off her throat, and she had to take shallow breaths to stop them from flowing. She felt an urge to throw herself against the solid strength that was Rab, but held herself back.

"Ya best eat up lawman. I got to check yer laig, so's ya'll need to shuck them britches. 'Sides, I can take care a myself."

"I know you can, but humor me. My parents raised my brother and me to protect women and children."

He held out his hand as he had yesterday. "Come, sit with me and eat. You can check my leg later."

She hesitated, afraid, maybe more now of herself than him. "Naw, I reckon I'll just set rightchere." She placed the tray on the floor, picked up a biscuit and dropped into the chair, pulling up her feet to sit cross-legged. "I don't want to bother yer laig none."

She wanted to trust him, as she had earlier. But

seeing him upright and moving, no matter how poorly, made him seem less vulnerable and more the virile man. A man to whom, against her better judgment, she longed to be closer. And that aching scared her.

"How'd ya end up bein' a lawman?" she asked after he'd taken his first bite.

"I thought I'd be a man like my brother, James, and join the Union army," he said. "I told them I was sixteen. I was barely fifteen. I was a crack shot so I joined up with Berdan's Sharpshooters, Second Regiment, Company 'G' in November of sixty-one.

"We were mostly used as skirmishers, out in front, hit and run. Officers mostly. Artillerymen. They were our usual targets. I was out in front for some of the bloodiest action of the war. The second battle at Bull Run, Antietam, Chancellorsville, Gettysburg, The Wilderness, I could pick off a man from seven hundred yards and not bat an eye. "

He watched her with wary eyes, as though he expected her to be horrified by how callous a killer he'd become. He still didn't understand. Her father and Uncle Cal were so much worse.

She shrugged. "It was a war, Rab. Reckon ya done what ya had to do."

"After James came home we sold the farm and headed to Texas. Most of the cattle were running wild, and we hired on at a couple places to round them up, but there wasn't much a man with one arm could do, so I kept doing what I was best at.

"I started as a guard for the Texas Pacific Railroad. I was twenty-one. I hunted down train robbers for six years, then in seventy-five, I started hunting outlaws for the judge.

"My brother has a ranch in Montana and wants me to come up with him and raise beef. He knows I hate what I do, but what good is a one-armed ranch hand?"

"Reckon about as good as a one-armed lawman."

He chuckled. "Your constant faith in my abilities astounds me."

She wasn't quite sure what he meant, but decided not to say anything, and they continued the meal in silence.

She frowned when he set aside his half eaten plate of food, but she looked away before she was tempted to say something he didn't want to hear.

A glimpse of silver under the bed captured her attention, and she rose from the chair to reach beneath. Her locket must have been kicked under the bed after she dropped it the other night. She sat back on her heels and carefully slipped her thumbnail along the seam to pop it open. With her index finger, she lightly touched each face. Funny that she hadn't noticed it was missing until now.

"It's very pretty. Who gave it to you?"

At the sound of his voice she snapped it closed and looked up. "Uncle Henry give it to me after Maw died."

"Henry?" His dark eyes narrowed.

"Yeah, he brung me somethin' from most every job." She glanced down, gnawing on her lower lip while she traced the design pressed into the silver.

"It's stolen. You told me they were your parents." Disappointment flattened the tone of his voice.

A sharp pain flared in the center of her chest. She'd always been a disappointment; to her mother, her father, and herself. After all these years she accepted it. So why did it hurt so much to hear it now?

She shrugged. "Reckon I ached so bad fer it to be true, I fergot it weren't."

She slipped the rawhide loop over her head and lifted her chin to meet his gaze. Though she wasn't certain what was going on behind those dark brown eyes of his, he didn't look upset. Instead of bawling her out for lying, he shoved that stray lock of hair off his forehead then patted the mattress.

She hesitated for a moment then rose and stepped toward the bed. He moved his coffee to the bedside table to make room for her, and she scooted up beside him, her heart nearly bursting.

His arm slid behind her neck to rest on her shoulder. "You and Henry must have been very close. When did he die?"

She wriggled closer, absorbing the comfort he offered like a dried sponge soaking water from a tiny puddle. "Back in the winter. Me an' Henry, we was the same. We cain't learn things an'..." She studied the dusting of fine brown hair across his chest, finding it easier to explain without having to meet his eyes. "Reckon we get lost real easy. We try to go back the way we come, but ever' way's the same in our heads."

"Is that why you never left?" The timbre of his voice rumbled beneath her ear. She stretched her hand out across his chest. His arm squeezed a little tighter, silently telling her it was okay.

"We tried to look out fer each other," she continued. "Henry, he know'd I was a girl an' he tried to protect me when he could, but he never went ag'in Paw."

"What happened?"

"We was hold up in a cabin in Wildcat Thicket with a whiskey runner an' his Chickasaw woman. Him an' Paw an' Henry was playin' cards one night, drinkin' an' tellin' jokes. Reckon the bastard had too much, 'cause he started pickin' on Henry, 'cause Henry was kind a slow to ketch on to his jokes. They wasn't funny jokes, but the sonofabitch was so drunk he thought they was. Well, he pulls out his pistol an' points it at Henry an' tells him to laugh. I don't figger he meant fer the gun to go off, but he was so damn drunk he didn't know he gut shot Henry 'til he seen all the blood."

Rab squirmed and rolled his shoulders, and she realized her fingers had been digging into his skin. "Reckon I can still see Henry a-layin' on the floor with all that blood a-soakin' his shirt."

His lips pressed against the top of her head. "I'm sorry, Johnny," he whispered.

A lump clogged her throat, but she swallowed it down. Part of her didn't want his sympathy. She'd seen death before and made it through with no never mind. Yet there remained that part of her which ached to let loose her bottled up grief and sob in the comfort of his embrace until there were no tears left to shed.

But Johnny never cried. So she drew a deep breath and continued, "Well, Paw was pissed, sure as hell. I mean he could rag on me an' Henry all he wanted, but none a his men was ever allowed, or Paw would shoot 'em dead. But that ol' bootlegger, he didn't know. Ya should a seen his face when Paw pulled out his long barrel Colt an' blew him clean to glory."

She drew a deep breath and let it out slow. "Henry, he tried to stay alive. He didn't want to go. I seen it in his eyes ever' time he looked at me. He know'd I was a feared to be alone, so he tolt me when he got to Heaven, maybe he'd see could God send an angel down to watch out fer me."

Rab hugged her tighter and ran his hand slowly up and down her arm, warming her, silently reassuring her it was okay to hurt, that he understood. She tipped her head back and lifted her gaze to his.

"That first day I met ya," she began. "When ya cold cocked Paw, I figgered maybe you was that angel, the one Henry sent down fer me."

Rab smiled, his mouth pulling up on one side,

slightly derisive, yet wide enough to show off the dimple in his cheek. "And if I remember correctly, the other night I believed you to be an angel as well."

"Reckon we was both wrong."

He rested his chin on top of her head. "Yeah, I reckon we were."

They lay embraced in silence for several minutes. Down the hall a door closed. A horse nickered from the street below, and a wagon rattled past. Johnny thought the deputy had fallen asleep until she suddenly felt him kiss the top of her head. Surprised, she looked up.

He stared at her through half lowered lids, with dark brown eyes that smoldered with the slow burning heat of a banked fire. He wanted her. She recognized the desire in his eyes. Yet he held back, watching her face. And in those moments, he offered Johnny the right to say no, a choice she'd never seen her father, or any other man, give to a woman.

An unfamiliar heat rushed to her cheeks. She'd never been kissed by a man, and she suddenly ached to discover how it would feel to press her lips together with his. Slowly, he tipped his head toward her.

His lips were warm and dry as they briefly touched hers. He paused and kissed her again with a long, lingering pressure that teased her mouth and caused her to tingle inside. She squirmed. His hand slipped around her shoulder, gently imprisoning her against his side. His tongue came out and traced the outline of her lips, sliding along the corners of her mouth.

Curious as to what he was doing and longing to know more, her lips parted. His tongue slipped inside. She stiffened at this new intimacy, of what he was going to do next, and afraid of how far she'd allow him to go. But caught up in the wonder of him, she relaxed. His skin held the scent of sandalwood soap but with an acrid trace of sweat. She wondered if he'd found a way to wash his arm, and while she felt a twinge of guilt for not helping him, she knew his pride wouldn't have allowed him to ask.

The breath from his nose streamed warm against her cheek. The stubble around his mouth scratched and pricked as his tongue delved deep into all the secret recesses of her mouth, hot and wet, and mingling the bitterness of coffee with the taste of eggs and toast. His arm held her snug against the side of his chest where his heart thumped softly, in harmony with the steady beat of her own.

Her hand crept upward, investigating his chest, then his left shoulder, fascinated by how hard the muscles there felt, even though he hardly used them.

Sliding her finger tips down his left bicep, she investigated each ridge of scar tissue that webbed the end of his stump.

He stiffened and broke the kiss. Confused, she pushed herself back and searched his face.

The muscles along his jaw bulged where he clenched teeth. Tension radiated from him like heat waves on the distant prairie.

"Is yer laig a-painin' ya?"

His brow pulled together as he studied her.

She'd been so lost in the pleasure of his kiss, now she wondered if she'd been doing it wrong.

After a long moment he said, "Sickening isn't it?"

"What?"

He raised all that remained of his left arm. "It repulses you, doesn't it?"

Her breath escaped in a sign of relief. He didn't refer to her kiss. She levered herself up on her elbow and propped her chin in her hand. She looked at his arm then studied his expression, a bit surprised he was so serious.

"I reckon I don't know what re-plus-es is, but

iffin yer a-tryin' to say yer arm ain't the purttiest part of yer body, yer right. But we all got somethin', Rab. If it ain't chickens it's feathers."

He continued to search her face, but she stared right back. Then gradually, his gaze softened. He offered her a brief smile, then looped his arm around her neck and pulled her down on top of him. For a moment their mouths were a mere whisper apart, then he claimed her lips in a bruising kiss, that went on and on, as though he were clinging to some part of her soul with the desperation of drowning man. They kissed until she could no longer discern the line between his essence and her own.

He flinched when she bumped his thigh, so she swung her leg over his hips, straddling him for a moment, then without breaking the kiss she lifted herself across his torso to his left side.

He rolled with her, so they faced each other. His hand touched her face, cradling her jaw. Her skin tingled as his thumb brushed back and forth across her cheek bone. She never knew the touch of a man could be so gentle, and her insides grew warm from the tenderness of his caress.

Gradually, his hand slid down her neck. His thumb stroked the base of her throat as his fingers slipped beneath her shirts to graze her collarbone. Shivers rippled down her back, and she heard herself whimper against his lips.

His mouth left hers to kiss her chin and jawline. His hand slid lower, grazing the top of her breast.

Unbidden, fear extinguished her pleasure like a blast of north wind. Her body stiffened and for a few moments her breathing stopped.

His dark gaze locked with hers, but he didn't remove his hand. "Let me touch you, Johnny."

She shook her head, and though she wanted to pull away from him, the honesty in his brown eyes, held her motionless.

"Only with my hand," he stated softly, in a timber of voice that caressed her as gently as his touch. "You've given me so much. Let me give you this. Let me show you that being a woman doesn't have to be like what you saw."

Her heart pounded against her chest, against his hand. Image fragments flashed through her mind in a single blink of her eyes; slaps, cries of pain, her mother moving stiffly after one of her father's visits, Morning Song with bruises on her face and arms, and that young girl in the yellow dress, staring hollow-eyed at the sky as bare-assed men shoved inside her.

Another blink and there was only Rab's face, with his stubble-coated jaw and stray lock of hair falling over his forehead. This man, with the deep dark brown eyes, waiting for her to say, yes. Giving her the gift of choice; asking her to trust him. And she did. Only him. For always—only him.

"Rab," she whispered.

And he kissed her. With his lips, he explored her mouth, her cheeks, her eyes. She relaxed and gave herself to him as he slowly unbuttoned her layers of clothes as though she were a precious gift.

His hand once more sought her breasts, teasing first one and then the other until her nipples hardened and peaked, as her body strained toward something it never knew, yet craved. His hand slid lower across her belly to her hip as his mouth moved to where his hand had been.

Her back arched against the mattress, thrusting her breast toward the mouth that suckled and teased her nipple. She clutched his left bicep with one hand and pressed her lips to his shoulder, sucking and teasing his salty skin the same way he did her breast. Her other hand wrapped around his neck, holding him close while her fingers slid into his thick, silky hair.

His hand delved lower, to touch the soft curls inside her cotton drawers, first with firm lazy circles then long deepening strokes. She shifted her mouth to just below his ear, squirming against him, seeking release for something she couldn't define.

A moan escaped her lips, and she turned into him, pressing her thigh against his hardened shaft. This time the soft sound came from him, but she didn't have time to wonder why, because every muscle of her body had tensed as the strange sensations inside her, intensified. The aching built as his fingers increased their pressure, until she reached some inner pinnacle, and her body stiffened as wave after wave of sensation shuddered through her body. She cried out his name, but he swallowed it with his kiss.

Heart pounding, she lay beside him marveling in all that had just happened when the pressure began to build again, and she realized his hand had not stopped its stimulation.

Three times she cried out his name until, limp and drained, he withdrew his hand. He reached down to pull up the quilt from the end of the bed and kissed the top of her head as she snuggled into the crook of his left shoulder and dozed.

****

"Why did your mother give you a boy's name?" Rab asked, lazily trailing his index finger up and down Johnny's arm.

"She didn't. She named me fer the Johnny-jump-ups what bloom every spring."

"Johnny jump-ups?"

She turned her head toward him. "Maybe ya ain't got none up north."

"Johnny, I haven't lived up north since I was nineteen. And I still don't believe I've heard of them."

"They's the little purple flowers what are the

first to poke through come spring. They was a-growin' when I was born an' my maw she said they was the same color as my eyes."

"Violets. Yes, that's exactly the color." Those wide, blue eyes, with their tiny flecks of midnight blue had mesmerized Richard that day in the corral, and even now he could easily become lost in their depths.

"Maw used to call me her little Johnny-jump-up, septin' when Paw come home. She tolt me, Paw, he wouldn't like it none fer her to call me that."

"No, I imagine he wouldn't." Now that her face was washed and her bruises healed, he could easily see she was a beautiful young woman. He shuddered to think what would have happened to her, alone with her father's men. "Your mother was smart to have thought up your whole disguise. She probably saved your life."

Johnny shifted closer in his arms. "My maw tolt me wunst that she birthed a baby girl afore I was born. But Paw, he figgered it were Maw's fault she didn't birth no boy-child, so he smacked her around and hurt her bad. Then one night baby Mary jest up an' died. Maw tolt me Mary died in her sleep, but they was times I wondered, if Paw didn't jest put his hand over her face till she quit breathin'.

"So when I come along, Maw, she was too scairt to tell him I was a girl, an..."

Richard wrapped his arm tight around Johnny and buried his face in her hair, cutting off her words. Images of his brother's young daughters flashed through his mind, laughter and singing, pretty dresses and bows, dolls and jump ropes. He recalled his sister-in-law braiding their hair before school, and his brother pushing them on the swing after supper. His chest swelled with the anguish of unshed tears for that lonely, little girl Johnny once was.

He could almost picture her, dressed as a boy, hiding from her drunken father in the corner of a dirty cabin, staring at pictures inside someone else's locket.

And he silently vowed that if it was the last thing he ever did in his sorry life, he would make sure Johnny had a chance to have that family, and to find someone who would love her the way she deserved.

A knock, loud enough to wake the dead, rattled the door of their room, as though someone pounded the wooden portal with the side of their fist instead of their knuckles.

"Hey, marshal!" A familiar voice bellowed from the hallway. "You in there?"

Wide-eyed, Johnny stiffened beside him, shoving against his chest. "Let me go, ya damn lawman." As soon as he lifted his arm from her shoulders she scrambled off the bed.

"Just a minute!" he called, waiting as she stood in the corner of the room hastily buttoning her clothes. When she finished tucking in her shirt and pulling up her suspenders, he said, "I guess you'd better let Mr. Hobbs in, before he shouts our business for the whole town to hear."

She snatched her hat from the floor and jammed it back on her head, completing her disguise before opening the door. The freighter barely looked her way as he strode across the room and dropped his great bulk into the wing chair.

"Is there a problem, Hobbs?"

"Nope, I was just wonderin' if you was dead. Hadn't seen ya in a while and you wasn't lookin' too good last time I seen ya."

"Well, I'm feeling much better since I got some sleep."

"Glad to hear it, marshal. No offense, but ya still look a mite peaked." Hobb's leaned back in the chair and extended his legs, crossing them at the ankles. "I was wonderin' how long you was plannin' to hold up here. If ya don't mind me sayin' so, after that ambush, I'm feelin' a mite itchy to move out."

Richard frowned and rubbed his forehead. "Don't worry, everything's under control. I sent a telegram to Fort Smith the day we arrived, and someone should be here in the next couple of days to escort the prisoners back. You can go with them. I'll follow as soon as the man at the doc's is ready to travel."

Hobbs nodded. "Sure enough, marshal. What about the kid here?" He jerked his head in Johnny's direction. "Does he go with us, too?"

"I'll worry about Johnny. You go on downstairs and see Mrs. Sittel. Save her a trip and take some dinner over to the prisoners."

Once Hobbs left, Richard switched his attention to Johnny. She stood in the corner, watching him with a look of suspicion, like that of a stray dog who didn't quite trust humans. Part of him winced, from the pain of knowing that despite all they'd shared she still didn't quite trust him.

Yet as their gazes met across the room, he could see she knew what he was going to say. She was just waiting for him to prove her wrong. He wished things could be different. He didn't want to be lumped together with every other man in her life, who had hurt and betrayed her.

But he had to go about this the right way, within the parameters of the law he was sworn to uphold. He took a breath.

"I'm sorry, Johnny. I wish you could stay with me, but you'll have to go back with the deputy who arrives."

She caught her lower lip between her teeth and dropped her gaze to the floor. "I done tolt ya, I ain't no outlaw."

If someone had stabbed him in the chest and given the knife a twist, he couldn't have felt any worse.

"And I believe you. But everyone thinks you're Bodine's son. Witnesses put you at the scene of several robberies."

"It weren't me."

"Even so, a girl was killed, Johnny. I can't ignore that. As soon as I get back, I'll talk to Judge Parker. I'll tell him how you've helped me. I'll pay for the best lawyer in town. I'll do everything I possibly can, but I will not take the law into my own hands. I walk a very fine line between right and wrong as it is. I won't cross it. Not for you, not for anyone. I can't cross it, or I'll become just as much an outlaw as your father."

Her head jerked up. "Yer nothin' like my paw," she snapped.

"You don't understand, Johnny. You think, because I punched your father, I'm some kind of goddamn hero. Well, I know what I really am."

"Yer a lawman. Ya do what's right."

He laughed, but it sounded as sharp and bitter as he felt. "I'm nothing more than the crazy, empty shell of a man, trying to maintain my sanity long enough to do some good in this world, with whatever time I have left." He threw his arm across his eyes and blew out a weary sigh that rose from deep within his soul.

"But that's the difference 'twixt you an' my paw."

"What?"

"That yer always a-tryin' to make up to God, fer the wrong ya think ya done."

"You don't have any idea what I've done. Hell, I don't even know."

"Since that first day, I seen how somethin's always a-gnawin' on ya."

Richard shifted his arm to his forehead, pushing back his hair then opened his eyes. Johnny had moved closer and stood beside the bed, chewing on her lower lip, twisting her index finger around the long cuff of her shirt sleeve.

"Even when ya was feverish, yer mind wouldn't let go a whatever it was ya done. My paw, he never give a damn. The more folks cried an' begged, the more he laughed. Nothin' he done ever gnawed on him."

He shoved himself up higher against the pillows. "Guilt? You think my feeling guilty absolves me of all I've done?"

She narrowed her eyes and met his gaze straight on. "No, I reckon guilt don't solve nothin', but at least ya feel it. Iffin maybe ya'd try ta remember, ya'd see what ya done ain't as bad as ya think. Reckon it was God planted them trees, not you."

"I don't need to remember because I feel it—right here." He poked himself in the chest a couple of times with his index finger. Each thump drove his skin into his breastbone with enough force to bruise, but he didn't care.

"Day and night I feel it, this dark side of me, you don't want to see, a monster, a trained killer who disavowed every moral and commandment my brother and I were taught. I was a sharpshooter, Johnny. Do you know we were considered murderers even by our own army?"

"It was a war, Rab. They was a-shootin' at you, too. But they ain't yer enemies no more. And iffin ya took a shine to a watch some Reb was a-wearin' ya wouldn't knock 'em upside the head an' take it. Ya wouldn't shoot 'em fer twenty dollars and a horse.

"No, ya ain't nothin' like my paw, Rab. An' yer a God damn sonofabitch fer a-thinkin' it." Abruptly, she spun on her heels, snatched her doeskin bag from the floor, and headed for the door.

He tossed aside the covers and swung his feet to the floor. "Where the hell do you think you're going?"

"Down to the Injun jail with the other pris'ners!"

"Damn it, Johnny, wait!" But the door slammed behind her with enough force to rattle the window.

Chapter Ten

Richard dug his fingers into the edge of the mattress and closed his eyes. Was Johnny right? If he tried real hard to remember...

Fleeting visions of trees, and dense underbrush flittered through his mind. *Smoke.* The veins in his neck pounded, and his palms grew sweaty. No. Don't think about it. He shoved the images aside and limped across the room to the chest of drawers. Bracing himself on the tall piece of furniture, he lifted his saddlebags from the floor and withdrew his bottle of Old Crow. Only a few swigs remained. Using his teeth, he spit the cork on the floor and downed the contents before he took himself back to bed.

Sleep claimed him a few minutes later. When he opened his eyes the corners of the room had darkened with afternoon shadows. He checked his wound when he relieved himself, grateful most of the swelling and redness had disappeared. He owed his leg to Johnny. How could he ever repay her for that?

Maybe they could all go back together. He should be feeling almost normal in a couple of days. And if the man at the doc's wasn't ready to leave, whoever came out from Fort Smith could stay and wait. Feeling better than he had in a week, he dressed, intending to let Johnny know his decision.

Later, he'd talk to Hobbs and check on the prisoners. He gulped down a cup of cold coffee and finished the rest of the food on the tray wondering why she hadn't returned it to the kitchen.

With his hand wrapped in a firm grip on the banister, he carefully hopped down each stair. Though the pain in his leg had receded to a dull ache, he knew excessive walking would send him right back where he was when they arrived.

He asked, but neither Lena or Edward Sittel had seen Johnny, nor had the man at the livery where Richard thought she might have gone to check on Jack. Wondering if she was trying to prove a point, he started toward the Tobucksy Courthouse.

Limping past the billiard hall, he glanced through the front window and noticed Hobbs inside, a glass of beer in one hand and a cue stick in the other. Curious, Richard opened the door and stepped inside.

"Howdy there, marshal!" Hobbs called, waving him over. "You're lookin' better every time I see ya. I reckon you can't join me in a game with only one arm, but if you want to back my next shot with a silver dollar, I'll double your money for ya."

Richard shook his head. "No thanks, I believe I'll just head on down to the courthouse and check on the prisoners. By the way, have you seen Johnny? I know sh..." His voice trailed off when Hobbs began shaking his head. "What's wrong?" A foreboding shudder rippled through his body leaving him suddenly chilled.

"Nothin's wrong. I reckon no one told ya, that's all. Those deputies you was tellin' me about come for the prisoners already. They was up in Eufaula when they got a telegram from Fort Smith and jumped on the train. Said they wouldn't need my help and paid up what you owed me. Johnny was down there tendin' Bishop and Machler when they came. Kid likely left with them."

Dread slammed into Richard's chest like a mule kick, snatching the breath from his lungs. He stiffened to keep his feet from staggering back under the force of its impact. Eufaula had no telegraph office. Nor could he imagine any of his fellow deputies not stopping to see him before they left town.

"Can I see you outside for a minute?"

He waited as Hobbs lay down his cue stick and finished off his beer then stepped out front.

"What's the problem, marshal?" Hobbs asked. Confusion etched horizontal lines across his forehead.

"When did they leave?"

"Well now, let me see." He rubbed his thick fingers across his chin. "I seen you around noon. Then I brung the prisoners their dinner, so I reckon it was nigh unto two o'clock that the deputies showed up."

"What did they say? What made you believe they were deputies?"

"You mean they wasn't?"

"Just start at the beginning."

"They wasn't the same fellas that ambushed us was they?"

"I don't know. Just tell me what happened."

"Well, like I said, I was just collectin' their plates when Johnny come by with his bag of medicines to tend the prisoners. We was standin' out front talkin' to a couple a Indian police, when these three men come up an' asked where you was."

"They asked for me by name?"

Hobbs shook his head. "No. As I recollect, the red headed one asked, where was the deputy marshal that brung in the prisoners. I told 'em you was laid up over to the Elk House. I seen one of 'em was wearin' a badge—"

"A badge?" Richard frowned and looked off down the street. If the man claiming to be a deputy marshal was one of Calvin's men, where had he gotten a badge? Richard couldn't help but glance down. Yes, his own silver star was securely pinned to his vest. That left Brady's badge. Had the other deputy still been wearing it when Richard wrapped his body? He rubbed his forehead, trying to remember.

There'd been smoke, and he couldn't see so he'd aimed at their muzzle flashes. No, that wasn't right. Think. He remembered lying beside Brady and putting his hand on his friend's bloody chest. No. That was wrong, too. He recalled looking down at Brady. Had the deputy been wearing his badge? Damn, why couldn't he remember?

He turned back to Hobbs. The big freighter stood watching Richard as though he was as odd as a three-legged calf.

"Damn it, Hobbs, quit gawking and tell me what they said?"

"Nothin' much," he muttered.

It was bad enough Richard believed himself to be crazy, having other people look at him as if they believed it as well, just made him mad.

Hobbs continued. "I asked if they was the deputies sent down from Fort Smith. They said they was, so I asked 'em how they got here so fast, an' that's when they said they was up in Eufaula when they got the telegram."

"What about Johnny?"

"They said they had a warrant for Johnny Bodine."

Richard slammed his open palm against the rough, board-and-batten siding of the Billiard Hall and Bakery.

"Damn it. I have the warrants," he ground out between clenched teeth. "And there was no warrant issued specifically for Johnny Bodine, because no one knew Johnny's name."

"I'm sorry, marshal, how was we to know? All the kid was worried about was his horse. He wanted to fetch him, but the dep—whoever the feller was, said he wouldn't need it."

Richard had to go after them before someone saw through Johnny's disguise. And with the bruises on her face healed and her skin washed clean, it wouldn't take much for someone to realize those wide, violet eyes belonged to a beautiful, young woman. He would not let her end up like the girl in the yellow dress.

They already had a substantial lead. To keep up the pretense of being lawmen they would've had to take the wagons. That would slow them down. Although they would probably abandon the wagons for horses once they got far enough from town.

"How many were there?"

"Only three, that I seen."

He did some quick calculating. That meant Calvin Everett and the man called Breed probably waited at a designated rendezvous point with extra horses, those five, plus Warren and Machler. He should wait for help, but that would be at least two more days.

Physically, he was in no shape for this. He couldn't possibly hope to catch them. But he had to try.

"I'm real sorry, marshal."

"It wasn't your fault. I underestimated Everett."

"Are ya goin' after them now? Let me get my gear an' I'll come with ya."

"No, it's not your job, it's mine. Just stay here and keep your eyes out for the real deputies. They're coming from Fort Smith. My brother's name is James, ask them to tell you."

"Well, if you're sure ya don't need me."

"I don't. Just let them know what happened."

"Okay, marshal, good luck."

"Thanks." Richard left Hobbs and hurried back to the hotel room. He shoved their few possessions

163

into saddlebags, paid the bill, and headed to the livery. There he saddled Johnny's big paint, and his own dark bay, Billy. If he rode hard, he could probably locate the wagons before night fall.

Five miles south of town, he found the abandoned prison wagon and ransacked chuck wagon. Dozens of fresh hoof prints indicated this was where they'd held the extra horses. He only stopped long enough to scrounge a sack full of supplies from what the outlaws left behind. He picked up some extra ammunition from the locked box, and gathered up the piled handcuffs and leg irons. He spent another few minutes rummaging for the length of chain they used to secure the prisoners at night, and tied it on behind the cantle of Johnny's saddle. It was nearly dark, and he wasn't the best tracker, so he couldn't tell how many men there were, but not counting Johnny, he hoped he was facing no more than seven.

He followed them for another hour, heading south, skirting the edge of the Ouacita Mountains, then made camp. His leg ached, but all he could do was change the dressing with the clean bandages Johnny had left drying in the room. He ate a cold supper and put out his fire as soon as he'd heated some coffee. The thought of spending the night beside a burning fire amidst all this scrub oak and pine made his chest tight.

Throbbing in his leg woke him just before dawn. He swallowed down the last of the coffee and mounted Billy. Everett and his men were following a trail south, toward Denison. Richard pushed his horse hard, keeping his few rest stops brief. By late afternoon, he caught up to the outlaws. Circling their left flank, he scouted for the best place to keep watch. The hilly land grew thick with box elder, pines, and oaks. He blew out a shaky breath and wiped his sweaty palm on his thigh.

Damn woods.

He tied Billy and Jack in the trees behind a ridge about two hundred yards from the outlaws' camp, hoping the wind wouldn't change. He didn't want the other horses to catch their scent. He loaded his Winchester and filled his gun belt with extra ammunition then climbed the ridge and moved forward into position.

The rocks and ledges loomed in shadows around him as trees and bushes rose from the gullies and crevices, surrounding him, closing in on him. All he could see was darkness, and all he could smell was the muskiness of moss and loam. *No. Don't think about it. Johnny needs you.* With the back of his wrist he wiped the sweat from his brow and drew a deep breath. At least there was no smoke.

He peered through a v-shaped opening between the rocks. Tethered in the shadows of the tress, to the left of the fire, he counted eight horses. There were too many men for him to overtake alone, so he resigned himself to keep an eye on them until his reinforcements could catch up.

Next, he located Johnny. She sat alone, on the far side of the camp fire, with her back against a tree and her knees drawn up close to her chest. Somehow he sensed her fear, accelerating his own breathing and causing his palm to sweat.

One man sat against a rock, with the brim of his hat tipped down to his nose. And though he appeared to be dozing, Richard sensed that the man was aware of every movement in the camp. Making a guess, Richard assumed this was Calvin Everett.

Warren and Machler lay sprawled on the ground with a third man, a blanket spread between them, and a fan of cards in each man's hand. A dark skinned man with braided black hair and moccasins entered the area with a fourth man. Both men carried an armload of wood. The sticks and broken limbs clattered together as they dumped them into a pile on the ground. That left one man missing.

"Johnny," the half-breed called. "Get over here an' get this fire goin'."

"I ain't got no Lucifers," she snapped.

"Lucky for you, I got me a flint and steel, so haul your sorry ass over here an' start this fire."

She stood and started toward the pile of wood, dragging her feet as she walked.

Richard scanned the area once more. Calvin Everett could have stationed that eighth man almost anywhere. If he stumbled upon the horses, Richard would be facing more trouble than he could handle. He had to locate that sentry before the man found him. He checked his revolver, slung his Winchester over his shoulder, and limped back the way he came, assuming any guard would start by scouting their back trail.

Richard didn't want to overtake him; that would only alert the outlaws to his presence. He just needed to be sure the man hadn't discovered the tracks left by the two horses Richard had hidden, or his position on the ledge. Several minutes later, he spotted a scruffy man with long hair, settled in behind a half-dozen red bud trees on a low hill, with a full view of the back trail.

Confident his own hiding place was relatively safe, Richard returned to the rock ledge. His stomach rumbled as the aroma of bacon, coffee, and rabbit wafted his way. While a good meal would probably make him feel better, what he longed for was a strong cup of hot coffee, with a generous splash of whiskey. He smiled to himself. He could hear Johnny's mountain dialect in his head, sputtering and complaining until he relented and drank a cup of her bitter tea instead.

He shifted on the hard ground, the pain in his leg keeping him from getting comfortable. Shadows lengthened, and gradually hid the movements of the outlaws. He could hear them though; their low tones resonated by the damp night air, as tree frogs peeped in the distance. Thankfully, once the food was eaten the outlaws let the flames dwindled to the low, red glow of coals and gradually the soft rumble of snoring began.

He rose numerous times throughout the night to check his perimeter and make sure the horses hadn't wandered off or been discovered. He cleaned his guns by rote, the task easy even in the dark. Twice, he heard Calvin order the guard changed, but no one came his way.

A beam of sunlight heating his face woke him, and he half-opened one eye to see three chickadees pecking at bits of lichen on the same rock that pillowed his cheek. He groaned as he lifted his head, and they flew into the branches above.

He set his Winchester on top of the rock and used his hand to lever himself upright. He didn't have to look down to know his leg was swollen. The snugness of the bandage around his thigh told him what he didn't want to know. He rolled his stiff neck and shrugged his shoulders, then limped away a few yards to relieve himself.

When he returned, he watched Everett gesture to Warren and another man, and order them to bring back wood for the fire. Warren tromped off into the trees near the string of horses, while the skinny man headed in Richard's direction. It wasn't likely the outlaw would be ambitious enough to climb the ledge to gather sticks, but if he wandered around the back of the rocky outcropping, he'd definitely find the horses.

From above, Richard swung his rifle over his shoulder and slipping through the cover of trees, he followed a path parallel to the man below. However, each time the outlaw stopped to break-down a dead branch, or add another stick to the growing pile in the canvas sling he carried, he advanced a few steps closer to the hidden horses. Richard wondered just how big a bundle the man planned to carry. Hoping each addition would be the last and the man would return to camp, Richard wasn't surprised when one of the horses nickered.

The outlaw froze, then quietly set down his bundle of kindling, and slipped his Colt from his holster. Cautiously, he crept forward and peered around the rock, behind which the two geldings stood. Seeing the horses, he quickly scanned the area, then, tipped his head back to check the ledge above. He must have sensed Richard's presence rather than seen him, because he grabbed the nearest bush with his free hand and cautiously pulled himself up the incline.

But even if this skinny outlaw didn't spot him, the man had found the horses and any moment would report back to Everett. Richard stepped behind a cedar tree and waited for the outlaw to pass. Then, noiselessly, he inched along behind him. A small stone, loosened by his boot heel, skittered across the mulch of dry leaves covering the ground.

The outlaw swung around, and Richard drove his fist straight into the man's chin. The outlaw's whole body stiffened, and he fell flat on his back without uttering a sound.

Pain radiated up Richard's arm from the force of the impact, and as he took a moment to shake out his hand, the strap of his rifle slid off his shoulder. He shoved his weapon back as he whirled around intending to grab some handcuffs from his saddlebags. In his haste, his foot skidded out from under him, and he slid down the hill, unable to stop himself by grabbing onto any of the bushes or trees. He lay on his back for several minutes, blinking at the pale-blue, morning sky, through a lacy canopy of green leaves and pine needles.

What the hell was he doing? Now, not only did his right leg feel warm, as though it was bleeding, but his back hurt. He could barely catch his breath. He was exhausted, outnumbered, and likely to die before noon. Oddly, on any other day he wouldn't have cared. Today he did. If he was killed, who would protect Johnny?

Heaving a sigh, he rolled to his feet. He searched the path of his decent until he spotted his rifle, then, limped to the horses for as many sets of hand cuffs as he could loop through his suspender straps.

After he'd climbed back to the outlaw and handcuffed the man's arms around a tree, Richard gagged him, crept back to the rocks, and checked the activity in the camp below.

Johnny stirred something in a pot, while nearby Machler and a skinny red-headed man sipped coffee. Everett and the half-breed lay on their bedrolls, and from the trees near the horses, Warren returned dragging a single, dead tree limb. Now, as long as the man on guard duty stayed away, Richard only had to contend with five outlaws. Maybe he could work his way around the clearing and drive off the horses before Everett and his men made their get-a-way.

"Where the hell's Stringer with the rest of the wood?" Warren complained several minutes later as he snapped sticks off the limb and tossed them into the fire.

Machler glanced around. "Stringer!"

Everett rolled to his feet. "Red," he ordered the man drinking coffee. "Go."

Johnny watched Red check the pair of guns he wore strapped to his hips and stride toward the trees where Stringer had last been seen. Keeping her hat brim low, she knocked the large spoon against the rim of the pot and placed it in the grass.

Rab was out there. She could sense him in the breeze, the way she could feel an impending storm in the cooling of the air, and see its approach in the trees, as the leaves turned over and the boughs moved up and down. Uncle Cal and the others sensed him, too, though she doubted they knew the cause of their unease. They moved about the campsite, their heads swiveling back and forth as restless as the tip of a cow's tail, while they searched for something they couldn't see.

She inched away from the fire, hoping to reach the tree where she'd left her doeskin bag before anyone noticed her disappearance. But the hair on the back of her neck tickled. Turning her head slightly, she saw Machler watching her through narrowed eyes.

"It's that sonofabitch, one-arm deputy!" he yelled as he drew his gun and raced for cover. A single shot rang out and before he had run ten feet, he fell to the ground clutching his lower leg.

Galvanized into action, the rest of the men fired their guns, but couldn't find a target. Dewey, the man who had taken the last shift on guard duty, ran into the clearing with his gun drawn.

Johnny sprinted for the trees, but someone charged up behind her. She glanced back and saw Uncle Cal gaining ground. A moment later, he slammed into her back, knocking her face down in the grass, the same way Rab had on the day they met. However, this time her attacker radiated an aura of malice that made her blood run cold.

Desperate to escape, she wrapped her fingers around tufts of grass and tried to pull herself out from under him. Then surprisingly, his weight lifted off her back. She pushed to her knees but felt him grab the back of her over-size duster the instant before he jerked her to her feet. Instead, she raised her arms and allowed her uncle to lift the loose garment right over her head.

Free, she dashed for the trees, but she could hear his labored huffs of breath coming closer as his longer legs gained the distance. His arm wrapped around her waist, lifting her feet right off the ground. She squirmed and shoved at his arm, but he held her tight. He stiffened, with his hand just below her breast, and she knew.

"I'll be damned," he whispered.

She'd been so mad at Rab when she left the hotel room she'd forgotten to bind herself flat. Uncle Cal chuckled, but the low sound that rumbled against her back lacked the lightness of any humor. Terrified, she elbowed him in the ribs and kicked his shins with her boot heels.

The report of another rifle shot rang out, and the rest of the outlaws aimlessly returned fire while she struggled against her uncle's hold.

"All this time—Did your paw even know?" He chuckled. Keeping her close to his body, he pulled her backward toward the cover of the trees, moving them toward the horses.

Leaning close he whispered. "I bet that marshal knows."

Revulsion rippled through her body in a nauseating wave as his stale breath swirled inside her ear.

"Ya been a-givin' him what ya been denyin' me?"

She reached behind her head and tried to claw his face, but he drew back, and all she managed to do was knock his hat from his head. They had nearly reached the horses when Rab's voice rang across the clearing.

"Let the kid go!"

Breed and Warren fired in the direction of his voice, but the brilliance of the morning sun blinded them to Rab's position. Another shot echoed through the clearing. Warren screamed, clutching his hand as the gun he held flew from his grip.

The nervous horses pulled back on the picket line, and oddly able to slip free, they scattered into the trees. Uncle Cal cursed and shifted his hold on her, using one arm to secure her body tight in front of him like a shield. He pulled his pistol from his holster and pressed the barrel against the base of her jaw.

The soft bulge of his swelling cod pressed against her backside, and her stomach twisted like a balled up wash rag. Unshed tears choked the back of her throat. She had to get away from him. She'd seen what he'd done to the girl in the yellow dress. She searched for Rab, but the white glare of the sun was so painful, she was forced to drop her gaze to the grass at her feet.

"Rab will kill you."

His hollow laugh vibrated against her back. "Reckon we're nigh unto a hundred feet from where he made that last shot, and we got trees fer cover. He'd have to be a damn good sharpshooter to make his shot an' not kill ya." He dragged her to the left, inching his way around the edge of the camp site. From the corner of her eye, she spotted a loose horse a few yards away.

Another rifle shot cracked the air, and Dewey, who had been zig-zagging toward the trees, fell to the ground.

Breed raced in the opposite direction. Again came that single shot, more ominous than ordinary gunfire because of its deliberation. A clod of dirt kicked up in front of Breed's boot, and his arms stretched toward the sky. "We give up, deputy."

"Everett, drop your gun and release Johnny!"

Uncle Cal laughed aloud. "This one's mine now, deputy," he called. "And I ain't a-givin' up this prize to no one."

The heat of his breath against her neck sent a shudder rippling through her body, and she renewed her struggles to escape his hold. But Uncle Cal only laughed as she dug her fingernails into his arm and kicked his shins. They had moved far enough to the side of the camp to ease the glare of the sun in her eyes.

Rab's voice rang out again, but from a different location. "Let-Johnny-go!"

"Me and the kid got other plans, deputy!" Uncle Cal continued pulling her toward the loose horse, the cold iron barrel still pressed into the soft underside of her jaw. A bullet thudded into the tree beside them, frightening off the horse and scattering bits of bark over Johnny's shoulder.

Her heart missed a beat as she tried to throw herself toward the ground, but Uncle Cal held her tight even as he laughed at her fear.

"Ya shoot me and my finger squeezes this trigger," he called out.

She tried sliding out from under her uncle's forearm, but his hold was too rigid.

"I'm a-lightin' outta here, deputy, and ya cain't stop me. 'Sides, ya got enough rightchere to keep ya busy. Me and Johnny, we's a-goin' to have some fun together. Ain't we—boy?"

There was no further response from Rab, and she wondered if he would risk the rest of the outlaws escaping in order to come after her. Bringing in his prisoners was almighty important to him, and the only value she'd ever had to anyone was her skill with yarbs and healing. No one had ever wanted her for any other reason. Until now...

Uncle Cal chuckled, and keeping her in front of him, he stepped backward into the trees.

Maybe she could run off once he relaxed his guard. But where would she go? How would she find her way? The familiar vise of panic squeezed like an iron band around the sides of her chest. No, she had to escape before then or...

A rifle shot cracked the air. Uncle Calvin jerked backward, pulling Johnny with him. They landed with a thump, and she found herself sprawled on top of him, staring at the sky. The arm that had held her tight, while still crossed just below her breasts, went slack. She pushed it aside and scrambled to her feet.

Uncle Cal lay flat on his back, with his dark eyes open, and his uppity grin still spread across his face. But just above the bridge of his nose, in the center of his forehead, was a small black hole. On the ground, like a shiny shadow, a thick, dark puddle pooled on the leaves beneath his head.

Repulsed, she lifted her gaze only to find the trees and bushes behind where they stood had been splattered with red. Bits of bone, hair and brain glistened on the leaves and bark. Saliva pooled around her tongue, forcing her to swallow repeatedly. She backed away, half expecting Uncle Cal to jump up and grab her again.

She bumped into a bush and whirled around, swatting the leafy tentacles as she stepped around it. She lifted her head. Rab stood at the opposite edge of the clearing, his Winchester slung over his shoulder. He tossed manacles at the men and ordered them to handcuff themselves around the smaller trees.

She longed to charge across the distance, throw her arms around his neck, and never let go. But doing so would reveal her secret to Machler, Breed, and the others. Part of her wondered if they even now suspected.

Drawing a deep breath, she lifted her chin and started forward. Her white duster caught her eye, and she walked toward it, looking neither to the right or the left, terrified she would see in their following eyes what Uncle Cal had seen. Leaning over, she picked up the garment and without wasting the time it would take to undo the buttons, she slipped it over her head, turned up the collar, and snatched her hat off the ground.

"Johnny," Rab called as she jammed the Stetson on her head and pulled the brim low. "See if you can catch any of those horses."

She raised her gaze to his and wondered if he'd guessed how much her knees shook.

With a jerk of his head, he gestured toward the trees. "Go on," he urged.

The steady reassurance in his tone held her paused for just a moment, before she veered off toward the trees where the picket line was strung.

"I'll help you in a few minutes."

She didn't wander too far from the camp; enough to be out of sight, but still within earshot. She dropped behind a large gray rock and drew her knees up tight to her chest. Images of the girl in the yellow dress crowded her mind to mingle with the odor of Uncle Calvin, and the weight of his body against hers when he knocked her to the ground. She pressed her spine against the stone until her bones hurt, forcing her to focus on the pain. The inside of her nose burned and tears stung her eyes, but they never fell.

Slipping her hand inside the neck of her shirt, she pulled out the locket. Her fingers squeezed tight around the worn silver. Beneath her breastbone, her heart hurt for all she'd never known. She lowered her head and repeatedly thumped the side of her fist against her forehead, wishing she could relieve the tension twisting her insides by crying, yet hating herself for wanting to.

Then she heard his uneven gait shuffling through the leaves. She lifted her head and there he was, frowning down at her, so damn dependable in his quest to always do the right thing.

"Are you okay?"

Yes, no. She was so torn up and confused inside she didn't know what to say to keep from falling apart. Her breath shook as she sucked in a deep gulp of air, then let it escape in a rush of bravado.

"Well, hell, Rab, I weren't raised in the woods to be scairt by no owls. I seen dead men afore."

The dimple flashed in his left cheek for just an instant, before he turned and eased himself down beside her. With a soft groan, he stretched out his leg; then surprised her by draping his arm around her shoulder.

She bit her lip. Scooting closer, she nearly curled into his lap, needing to feel the warmth of him pressed against her side, content to breathe faint traces of soap and gun oil which blended with the musky scent that was Rab.

He squeezed her tight. "Well, I was scared." He held his hand out level in front of her.

Even in the shade, she could see his fingers tremble. Then he lowered it across the front of her chest.

"I haven't made a shot like that since the war. Don't suppose you have a bottle anywhere in this baggy coat of yours?"

She shook her head.

He chuckled, but it was a bitter sound. "Damn."

Chapter Eleven

Turning her head, she studied his face as he stared at some invisible point beyond the trees. Purple shadows darkened the hollows beneath his brown eyes, and a slight flush tinted the cheekbones of his pale face.

Since the day she met him, she'd never seen him take a life. She'd watch him struggle daily through his job as a lawman, to make up to God for the wrongs he thought he'd done. And yet today, for her, he'd killed. Her heart swelled tight inside her chest.

She removed her hat and rested her cheek against his shoulder. The crook of his elbow squeezed snug against the side of her neck, and the weight of his chin settle on top of her head. She didn't understand why or how, but clinging to this man eased all the tension and the churning inside her. He was warm, and solid, and safe. And just his presence silently reassured her that nothing would happen to her, not while he had breath. She rested her hand over his heart and watched her fingers rise and fall with each inhale and exhale.

His thumb teased the top of her breast through her underwear shirt, in a slow back and forth arc. She wondered briefly when his hand had worked its way beneath her duster, beneath her vest and two shirts. She squirmed against him, being careful not to bump his leg, and aching for him to touch her the way he had in McAlester. She wanted her body to quiver in anticipation, and then explode like a crack of thunder during a mountain storm. She needed him to chase the memory of Uncle Calvin from her mind, needed him to make her feel, for the first time in her life like the woman she was never allowed to be.

A breeze sifted through leafy canopy overhead swaying the thinner branches back and forth. Birds chirped in the trees and hopped across the ground among the shifting patches of sunlight.

Richard dipped his head and kissed her temple. And somehow, sitting here in the woods with Johnny curled all soft and warm in his arm, his heart didn't race and his palms didn't sweat.

He lifted his hand and lightly brushed the backs of his fingers across the delicate blush of her cheek bone. His thumb traced the outside curve of her ear then swooped lower to graze her jawline.

Slowly, giving her the opportunity to pull away if she needed, Richard leaned close and pressed his mouth to hers. She responded tentatively at first, barely brushing his lips. Her hand rested against the center of his chest, her thumb slipping back and forth across the fabric of his vest. He took the kiss a little further, lightly tracing her lips with his tongue. He needed her desperately, yet he knew if she pulled away in fear, the monster inside him would have won. Her hand stilled on his chest. He lifted his mouth from hers.

"You're so beautiful," he whispered.

He coaxed her onto her back and claimed her mouth once more. She yielded as he teased her lips apart and delved inside. A groan rumbled deep within his throat in response to a throbbing that had nothing to do with his swollen leg. Never had he been consumed with such urgency to be part of someone as completely as he did Johnny. He needed to be inside her, to feel like a whole man again instead of this crazed, broken, half-man shell, he had become. He swallowed convulsively through a throat so choked with emotion he could barely breathe.

Her hands roamed up his shoulders and down his back as he worked free the buttons of her vest, shirts, and underwear top.

"Are you sure you want me to do this?"

She nodded. "I need to feel ya, Rab."

"I don't want to hurt you, Johnny, but if we do this, there is no way to avoid it. I promise the pain will pass, and I'll try my best to make it perfect."

He prayed what her uncle had done hadn't renewed her fear of him. Her hair smelled faintly of smoke from the campfire, but no images of war pushed through. There was only this beautiful young woman staring up at him, eager for his touch, now working free the buttons of his vest and shirt.

"I trust ya, Rab," she whispered as she pushed his suspenders off his shoulders, then his shirt.

He rolled off to sit beside her, while he took a moment to pull off his clothes. He glanced over. She watched him with an expression akin to wonder. He smiled back as he kicked off his boots.

Beside him, she removed her duster and spread it over the ground.

He studied the smoke stains, holes and singe marks. "I think you need a new one."

She looked back and shook her head. "I can patch the holes and scrub out them stains wunst I get me some time. It was Uncle Henry's and it's all I got left a him."

He nodded. Though the linen coat might have sentimental value for her, he also knew how greatly she depended on the over-sized garment for protection. He just hoped that one day she would feel safe enough to dress as the beautiful young woman he saw.

He unbuttoned his pants and loosened the tie-string of his drawers, but left them both on, recalling the last time she'd seen his body aroused. He shifted onto his left side, as Johnny lay beside him.

Reaching out, his hand cupped her face. Seemingly of their own volition, his fingertips slipped across to trace her lips, then trailed down the line of her throat. Her head tilted back, and she closed her eyes. His fingers drifted down between her breasts, around, and across them. Each soft mound fit perfectly in his palm. Her nipples hardened at his touch, and he leaned over to trace them with his tongue. Lightly, he nipped the hardened buds with first his lips, then his teeth. She shivered and arched her back in response. A tiny convulsion rippled through her body as a soft moan escaped her throat.

He lifted the edge of her shirt with his thumb and index fingers. "Can I take these off?"

She stiffened for a moment, her gaze searching his face. He didn't know what she saw, but when she sat up and removed her vest and shirts, he slowly released the breath he didn't realize he'd held. Once she'd kicked off her boots and scooted close, he leaned in to claim her mouth, pushing his tongue inside, searching deep, and twining it with hers even as his hand slipped past her navel, beneath the waist band of her britches.

She wedged her hand between their bodies and tickled the hair on his chest with her fingers. Her other hand cupped the back of his head then drifted forward to trace the shape of his ear.

Blood surged through his veins as he grew hard with the need to possess her, but she wasn't ready, so he swallowed and continued the kiss.

His hand slid to the apex of her thighs. He slowly stroked her and teased her with lazy circles that had her pushing against his hand. A groan rumbled in his throat, and he slipped his finger inside her moist warmth. A soft mewling sound escaped her mouth, lightly vibrating against his lips.

The moisture of her arousal increased at his

touch. She was ready, but he wanted to give her pleasure first, before he took her virginity. Her hand at the back of his head clenched into a fist, pulling painfully at the roots of his hair. With a moan, her hips arched against his hand. He broke the kiss and dipped his head to tease her breasts with his mouth as he withdrew his finger and increased the pressure of the tiny circles he made against the nub at the top of her cleft.

She moved against his hand, pressing herself harder and faster against him. Then she stopped as her breathy gasps blew into his mouth, and her body shuddered beneath his.

His own need swelled inside his pants, and he withdrew his hand to hastily shove down the rest of his clothing. When he glanced back, her hungry gaze roamed his entire body then stopped as she stared at his full arousal.

No fear widened her violet eyes, only a blatant curiosity.

"Please, Johnny," he whispered, warmed by her reaction. "I need to be inside you."

Without taking her gaze from his face, she slowly peeled away each layer of clothing. Each inching away of fabric sent goose bumps prickling over his body. By the time she lay naked beside him, he ached so much for release, he worried he would lose control and come all over himself.

Her gaze shifted, drifting lower, down his chest to his waist, and then his groin, where his manhood rose, full and hard.

Lifting her gaze to lock with his, she whispered, "Only you."

"Johnny," he groaned, rolling himself over her, positioning himself at her entrance. Her hands slid up his rib cage, under his arms to press flat against his shoulder blades.

She felt so warm and tight around his shaft, as

he entered he almost couldn't wait. "I'm sorry," he whispered as he closed his eyes then pushed through her barrier. Her fingers dug into his skin. He paused, breathing deep and slow, giving her a moment, waiting for the pressure of her fingertips to ease.

As it did, she began to breathe again, and he moved inside her, slowly at first, then faster until sweat popped out across his forehead. He became so focused on the growing pressure inside him he was unaware of anything else. Then when he thought he could hold back no longer, he rolled off her with a groan, and spilled his seed into the leaves.

He lay on his side, his back to her, just breathing, wondering if she hated him now, if she saw him as a man no different from the rest. Then he felt her fingertips touch his left bicep. They slid up his shortened arm to his shoulder and back down. Relieved, he blew out a sigh and rolled toward her, lying on his back.

She shifted onto her side and let her fingers wander lazily through his chest hair. He met her gaze and she smiled. He wanted to hug her, to wrap his arm around her and pull her close, but she was on his left side. Of its own volition, his arm lifted and pressed against the center of her back.

She sighed and snuggled against him, sliding her hand across his waist. He shifted and reached his right arm out to cup her face. His thumb brushed back and forth across her cheek.

"God, I wish I had two arms so I could hold you the way a man is supposed to hold a woman."

She smiled softly and met his gaze, as though she were able to see deep inside him. "Rab, ain't no one ever held me like you."

"Johnny," he whispered.

He searched those deep blue eyes of hers, seeking solace in the simple understanding that was

Johnny. And what he found was acceptance. A simple acknowledgement of the whole him, as broken and confused and lost as he was, there was Johnny silently saying it was okay.

And suddenly, he couldn't imagine another day without her in his life. He pulled her tight against him and buried his nose in her silky blonde hair. Nothing, and no one else mattered—only Johnny.

He always believed Caroline, through her purity and innocence would be the one to give direction and balance to his life. He never once dreamed a young outlaw, living on the other side of that line he was so afraid to cross, would be the one to give him back his soul.

****

Just past noon, Richard headed everyone northeast toward Fort Smith. He debated about going back for the prison wagon, but they were still four days from Fort Smith, and he couldn't afford to waste the time. The prisoners were tied on their horses with their wrists handcuffed to their saddle horns. He wrapped Everett's body in the ground cloth from his bedroll, so Johnny wouldn't have to deal with the image, and tied the body on the back of the extra horse, which brought up the rear of the procession. Beside him, Johnny held the rope from the halter of the first horse in the line.

Despite the pain in his leg, he pushed hard until dusk, but the hills and woods made travel slow. Keeping his Winchester trained on the prisoners, he acted as a guard, poised to shoot if any one of the men so much as looked crossways at Johnny while she secured them to a tree. He took time before it was completely dark to hunt. Everett had a pack horse with some supplies, but they were low on meat.

Darkness had fallen when he returned with a grouse, two squirrels and a rabbit. He waited until everyone had eaten and he'd taken a quick scout of their back trail, before he finally allowed Johnny to clean his wound.

He said nothing while she expertly applied the new poultice and dressing.

"How bad is it?"

"Well, ya ain't had no whiskey, so I reckon some of the sweats and shakes is bottle fever. Then all that rock climbin' an' runnin' around in the woods ya done today weren't the best thing for it, so it's festerin' a mite."

He fell silent as Johnny packed up all her herbs and salves. Then he spoke, his voice floating into the dark, so softly it was no more than a whisper. "I can't lose my leg, too."

She swung around, her expression hidden in the flickering shadows of the campfire. She set aside her bag and scooted up beside him. "Ya ain't a-goin' to lose yer laig, Rab."

"Do you promise?"

"I promise."

Exhausted and oddly reassured by her quiet conviction, his eyes drifted closed. "Johnny?"

"Yeah?"

"Lie beside me."

"I cain't."

"Please, Johnny. I'm tired, my leg hurts, and I'm cold. I'm so damn cold."

"I cain't Rab, I'm afeared that worthless bunch a no accounts will see. They'll know I ain't no boy."

He opened his eyes. She sat beside him, her back straight and her chin tucked to her chest. Johnny had sacrificed so much for him, given him back a small hold on his sanity, he couldn't ask any more of her.

"It's all right. I'm just being selfish." He forced a grin. "Now that I've had you in my arms, I don't want to let you go."

She cocked her head and smiled back. It wasn't much of a smile, very small and a bit lop-sided, but it warmed the cold places inside him.

"Good night, Johnny," he whispered as he pulled up his blanket. He checked the revolver beside his leg and sighed. The throbbing had eased thanks to Johnny's poultice. His eyes closed, and his breathing slowed.

"Rab?"

"Hmmm?"

"Fer what ya done today, a-savin'me from Uncle Cal like ya done. Thank ya."

"Don't mention it."

"Rab?"

"What?"

"Maybe that monster inside ya ain't as bad as ya think."

****

Determined to reach Fort Smith before his strength gave out, Richard kept rest stops to a minimum and handed everyone a stick of jerky at mid-day. As he had the day before, he kept moving until dusk; with his Winchester pointed at the prisoners, he had Johnny unlock them one at a time before securing them each to the length of chain already fastened around a tree.

"Hey marshal, you ain't lookin' so good." Warren jeered.

Johnny threaded the chain through the ring in the leg irons shared by Dewy and Red.

"You're weaker than a sick kitten marshal." Warren continued.

Beads of sweat popped out across Richard's forehead. Ignoring Warren's threat, he waited as Johnny unlocked the man they called Breed.

"What do you think Machler?" Warren continued his taunt. "We could rush him with no trouble and knock him right off his horse."

Johnny stepped back as the half-breed dismounted.

The man lunged forward, and in one smooth motion yanked Johnny against his chest with the chain of his handcuffs pulled tight around her throat. "Throw down yer guns, marshal, or I'll snap his neck."

The thrust of an invisible knife pierced the center of Richard's chest as his gaze met the wide-eyed terror in Johnny's eyes. How could he have allowed himself to be so distracted by Warren and Machler? The half-breed moved so fast Richard barely caught a glimpse of the motion. Swallowing his mounting panic, he drew a deep breath and raised his Winchester a notch.

"You should have picked a taller shield," he said. He forced a rough chuckle from his throat. "At least that would have been a challenge." He blinked to focus the images that blurred and swayed before his eyes. Fighting the urge to swing his rifle over his shoulder and rub his eyes, he continued his bluff.

"How far away was Everett? And there were trees. This is too easy. I can close my eyes right now and still send a bullet through your brain so fast you'll be dead before you hit the ground. So let Johnny go, or try it and die. It's up to you, because right now you're not worth the two dollars I'll get for bringing you in."

His pulse throbbed against the sides of his neck, counting the seconds it took the breed to make a decision. Sweat trickled down the sides of Richard's face, as he struggled to keep the heavy rifle raised and level. He wished he had a left arm to help hold it steady, while he prayed the outlaw wouldn't call his bluff. Richard doubted he could even muster the strength to pull the trigger. But his ruse worked, for after staring him down for several long moments, the man released Johnny.

"All right, marshal," he relented, and went willingly to the next place in line, where Johnny slid the chain through the ring in his leg irons. "You win this time, but you ain't gonna last much longer. At this pace you'll never see Fort Smith."

Judging from the way he felt at the moment, Richard didn't doubt the half-breed's prediction.

"That's right." Machler added as Johnny chained him with the others. "Then Johnny'll let us go. He'll help his old pards, 'cause he's too damn scared to be alone. We'll light out for Mexico an' leave your carcass to bloat an' rot in the sun. Buzzard's will peck out your eyeballs. Coyotes'll drag your innards all through these woods. An' nobody'll ever know what happened to ya."

With the prisoners secured for the night, Johnny tethered the horses to a picket line and stripped the saddles from their backs. Once she'd finished that task, she began pulling supplies from Everett's pack horse.

Satisfied things were calm, Richard moved his horse, Billy, off into the trees, out of sight from the prisoners. Then leaning forward, he hooked his right arm around the saddle horn. As carefully as possible, he kicked his feet from his stirrups then eased his right leg over the back of his horse. He slid to the ground landing with all his weight on his left leg. But despite his care he was forced to keep his arm hooked around the saddle horn in order to keep himself from falling. He pressed his clammy forehead against Billy's neck and swallowed down the waves of nausea that threatened to erupt at any moment.

After several minutes, he mustered his strength enough to undo the cinch. With a tug, he pulled the heavy saddle from the horse's back and let it drop to the ground with a thud and a clank of buckles. He swayed.

Johnny appeared beside him, her arm around his waist, her right shoulder supporting him under his left arm pit. He blinked several times as the top of her wide brimmed hat swam before his eyes. His stomach rolled again. Even with her help, he barely staggered to the bed roll she'd spread out. Too exhausted to stand, he swayed for a moment, then collapsed in a heap, barely aware of the snickers coming from the prisoners before blackness claimed him.

****

Johnny leaned forward to remove the damp cloth from Rab's forehead and replace it with a cooler, more soothing one.

"Johnny?" he mumbled weakly.

"Rightchere, Rab," she whispered on a sigh, relieved no more than twenty minutes had passed. His eyes opened. He rolled onto his right side, bracing himself with his elbow as he searched the campsite. Apparently satisfied, he blew out a slow breath as his dark gaze came to rest on her face.

"Been crying for me outlaw?" he teased, the imprint of his dimple barely visible in the stubble of his left cheek.

She straightened and snorted. "I'd have to care fer ya powerful bad, lawman, to be cryin', fer ya. Why ya been givin' me nothin' but grief since the day I laid eyes on ya. 'Sides, boys don't cry."

All traces of his dimple vanished. "But you're not a boy, Johnny."

She turned away and began fussing with the pots on the fire. "I know that lawman," she snapped. "What do ya thank I am, stupid? I ain't stupid. Reckon I know'd who I was my whole life.

"I meant babies. Babies cry an' I ain't no baby." She slapped a piece of fried rabbit on a plate with a biscuit and scooted back to his side.

"Johnny, it's okay to cry. Everyone cries

sometime, even grown men."

She shook her head. "Yer jest a-funnin' me lawman. I ain't stupid. Men don't cry. They don't get scairt an' bawl their eyes out over somethin' dumb."

"Sure they do. They just pretend they haven't."

"I bet you ain't never."

"Sure I have, Johnny. I cried when my folks died. I cried when my best friend was killed in the war. And I cried when I woke up and discovered they'd taken my arm."

She stared at the tin plate in her hand for several long seconds then shook her head. "But they ain't dumb things, lawman. I bet ya ain't never cried 'cause ya was scairt. Scairt a gettin' lost. Not knowin' which way ya come or which way to go. Ya ever been so scairt yer knees shake an' yer chest squeezes so tight ya cain't breathe? Ya ever been so scairt to be alone that ya'll stay with folks ya hate 'cause yer too a-feared to leave?"

"Johnny, everyone's afraid of something. You know what scares me so bad that when I think about it my stomach rolls like I'm going to be sick?"

She shook her head.

"Maggots."

She grunted in disbelief. She expected him to actually admit how much he hated the woods, but maggots, they were so insignificant, her mouth dropped open in surprise.

"I know, to you it's nothing, but to me...I can't stand the thought of them, their wiggling, white, segmented bodies—" He shuddered, closed his eyes and swallowed.

"I was shot through my wrist during the Battle of the Wilderness and lay there, pinned down all night." He turned his head, shifting his gaze to his left arm and the shortened blue sleeve.

"They took my arm off the next afternoon. My stump filled up with pus and swelled. Flies crawled all over the bandage laying their eggs. I could look down and see the maggots wiggling and crawling around underneath the cloth. I'd take off the wrapping, and walk around camp, squeezing my arm, watching maggots and pus fall out. I was in pain all the time, but I refused the morphine. I didn't want to sleep, because I was afraid to dream. After a couple of days, I believed the maggots would crawl their way inside my body and eat out my insides. So I kept walking, kept squeezing." He shifted and lay down, resting his head against his saddle.

"God, Johnny, I hate maggots."

"Them maggots prob'ly saved yer life, Rab. They ate out the poison that would a kilt ya. They'd prob'ly be a good thing fer that laig a yers right now"

"No." His eyes flew open, and his hand snatched her wrist. "Promise me, Johnny, no maggots."

She twisted her arm, but he held her fast. "I promise, Rab. I won't let no maggots in yer laig. Now let go a my damn hand."

"I'm sorry." His crushing grip loosened its hold.

She snatched her arm back and massaged the sore area of her wrist.

"Johnny?"

"What now, lawman?"

His eyes were open, his gaze locked on hers. "Promise me you won't let them take my leg."

"They won't."

"Promise me, Johnny. I've learned to get by with only one arm, but if I lose my leg, too...Johnny, promise you won't let them take my leg."

"They won't. Yer laig ain't that bad. A good poultice will fix it up right proper."

"Don't lie to me, Johnny," he snapped. Light from the fire caused the sweat on his neck to glisten. "I know it's bad. I saw doctors amputate so many limbs during the war, that it looked like cord wood piled outside the surgery tent. And most of those wounds weren't this bad."

"I ain't a-lyin' to ya. I done tolt ya, I know more about doctorin' bullet holes than a jackrabbit knows about runnin'. The bullet didn't hurt the bone none so they ain't no reason to am-pin-tate. The reason yer feelin' like ya was rode hard and put up wet, is 'cause ya won't keep offin it and let yer body time to heal."

"We can't stop now. We're only about three days from Fort Smith. Once I deliver these prisoners, I'll take the time to rest."

She frowned. Pure orneriness was the only thing that kept Rab moving. He wouldn't tell her the last time he'd eaten, and she doubted he'd slept much since McAlester. "I fried up that brush bacon ya shot."

He shook his head. "I can't Johnny. I'm not hungry."

"Ya want to save that laig a yers, ya got to eat."

He sat up, and she watched as he forced down her meal. But a few minutes later he vomited everything back up. Scared for him, but afraid to let him know, she cleaned him up and helped him change his shirt, grumbling the whole time. She then encouraged him to drink some of the willow bark tea she'd just brewed.

"Come on Rab, jest a few swallers. It'll take the pain an' bring down yer fever."

Obediently, he managed a few sips before he shook his head. "I can't. No more, Johnny."

He cleaned his guns while she passed out food to the prisoners. Later he insisted she go with him while he checked the perimeter. He had left his vest off after he changed his shirt, and by the time they returned to his bed roll, the red shirt he wore had darkened with sweat.

She handed him a cold cup of tea, and he drank

half before he handed it back to her.

"Okay, but ya best take some more later."

"So damn tired." He lay down, and his eyes closed.

Carefully, she tucked a blanket around his waist and placed a fresh compress over his forehead.

Once he'd fallen asleep, she got up to check the horses and carry back some more water. The prisoners sprawled across the ground, snoring softly. She grinned knowing how furious they'd be if they knew she had drugged their food.

Returning to the fire, she prepared some more flax seed and cornmeal for a new poultice to draw the infection from Rab's leg. She changed the dressing frequently throughout the night. She removed his shirt when his fever climbed and forced him to drink more of the willow bark tea. Late in the night chills wracked his body.

"Johnny?" he called weakly.

"Rightchere, lawman." She spread her own bed roll on top of his blankets to keep him warm.

"Johnny?" He called again.

"Hush yer mouth lawman, or yer a-goin' to wake that bunch a no-accounts by the trees."

"Johnny?"

"I'm rightchere. What the hell do ya want?"

He chuckled to himself and opened his eyes. "I'm cold."

"I know. Why the hell do ya think I'm a pilin' on all these blankets?"

He shuddered. "Sleep with me Johnny. I'm so damn cold."

"All right, Rab." She lifted the blankets and scooted up against his left side.

"Hold me, Johnny. I'm freezing. I can't feel you."

Though he radiated enough heat to make her sweat, she snuggled closer, wrapping her arms securely around him. She felt another wave of shudders rack his body. His teeth chattered.

"You never promised."

"Promised what, Rab?"

"Don't let them take my leg."

"I promise."

"Promise me, Johnny. Don't let them take my leg. I won't live without it. Promise me."

"Is yer ears broke? I promise. Ain't nobody a-goin' to take yer laig whilst I got breath in me. First man to try is a-goin' to find a hole in his chest big enough to drive a mule through."

He chuckled. "God, Johnny, I love you."

Her heart skipped a beat causing her breath to snag inside her chest. She searched his flushed face. He didn't mean it. Between the bottle-fever and his infected leg he was delirious. But what if he had? She caught her lower lip between her teeth. Dare she hope? Could Deputy Marshal Rab Bennick truly love her, worthless little Johnny Bodine?

"What'd ya say, lawman?"

"Don't let the maggots get me."

Her heart plummeted into her stomach with enough force to make her sides hurt. She swallowed against the tightening in her throat. Of course he didn't love her. No one ever had. Why should he?

"Johnny?"

She squeezed her eyes tight. "All right, Rab." She managed to choke out. "I promise. No maggots neither."

Some of the tension eased out of his body. She laid her hand against his hot face. The rough stubble of his cheek pricked her palm. Tenderly her fingers sifted through his damp brown hair. She drew him closer, as though by holding him she could protect him and keep him safe through the night.

Eventually, she drifted into a light sleep, waking every few minutes to reassure herself that Rab was still breathing, hoping that he'd be better in the morning.

But when the sun came up his thigh was swollen to twice its normal size. Fever glazed his brown eyes and tinted his cheek bones with pink. Though the sun had barely risen, sweat dampened the hair around his ears and at the back of his neck.

Johnny urged him to eat but he refused. He sipped some herbal tea, but that was all.

"Rab, yer laig's swoll like a poisoned pup. I need to lance it so's it can drain. An' ya got to rest up. Just one day."

Stubbornly, he shook his head. "No. If we push, we can make Fort Smith day after tomorrow. Then I'll rest. I promise." He tried to smile, but his dimple barely dented his left cheek.

"But yer a-wobblin' like a newborn calf." She swore and called him six ways a fool. He staggered so much on his way to his horse, she wondered if she should tie him there. She swung up on Jack and gathered the reins then waited patiently for Rab to urge his horse forward, but he didn't move. His head nodded forward, and he swayed in the saddle. Machler and the rest of the lazy pack of no accounts began to laugh.

"Hey, lawman," she called, unsure how far to allow him to push himself. "Which way?"

He roused at the sound of her voice and shook his head. "East."

"But, Rab, ya know I cain't reckon which way is east."

He turned in the saddle and blinked at her as though trying to focus his thoughts. "The sun, Johnny. East is toward the morning sun."

Warren and Machler snickered. "Hey marshal, are we goin' or stayin?"

Rab gave his head another shake and nudged his horse forward. The prisoners' horses were tied together in a line and Johnny jerked on the lead rope, trying to keep abreast of Rab.

She hated the way Breed watched them with that cocky smirk tugging at his lips. With him riding the first horse in the line, he saw and heard every exchange between her and Rab and knew how weak the deputy had become.

A little more than an hour after they broke camp, Breed's horse charged forward, crashing straight between her horse and Rab's. The lead rope burned through her palm then jerked from her grip as Breed raced ahead. Strung out behind him, the rest of the prisoners struggled to keep their horses from veering off the trail and tangling the rope around a tree.

Instantly alert, Rab yanked his Winchester from his scabbard and kicked his bay into a gallop, crashing through brush, and weaving through trees to get ahead of them. Johnny's horse eagerly thundered after them and quickly passed, Dewy and Stringer, as Rab's horse struggled to overtake Breed.

Breed's horse stepped on the end of the dragging lead rope, yanking his head down. The horse stumbled to one knee and scrambled to find his footing. If Breed hadn't been tied to the saddle, Johnny imagined the outlaw would have been pitched right over the horse's head and broken his neck. Instead, the mishap gave Rab the extra seconds he needed to get his Billy ahead of Breed's horse and force him to stop.

Johnny rode up alongside Breed and leaned out of the saddle in order to grab the rope with her uninjured hand, while Rab sat on Billy with his Winchester pointed at Breed's chest. Less than four feet spanned the distance between the end of the barrel and the buttons on Breed's vest.

"Go ahead." Rab's words slurred a bit, but his tone was low and threatening. "Try it and there'll be a new face in Hell tomorrow."

Breed's cold stare locked with Rab's burning gaze. "I seen enough dying men in my time to know ya ain't never gonna see Fort Smith. I can wait."

"Yeah? Well, I've been to hell and back before, and I'm a lot tougher than you think."

Chapter Twelve

Near noon they came upon a small creek running through woods. Rab was nearly unconscious and burning with fever. Making the decision to camp, she halted the horses at the only place the bank sloped down to the water. While the horses drank, she roused Rab long enough for him to keep his rifle trained on the prisoners. One by one they dismounted, and she chained them to a tree.

Then she led Rab's horse into the creek, upstream, away from view. She unbuckled his gun belt and tossed it onto the grassy slope of the bank. Then trying her best to support him, she helped him dismount into the water. By grabbing him under his arms, she tugged him backward until his shoulders rested securely against the bank and his lower body lay submerged in the creek. Satisfied he wasn't going to slide into the water and drown; she hobbled the horses, gathered some wood, and rolled out his bedroll in the shade of a blackjack tree.

Warren and Machler taunted her from the far side of the camp site. "Hey, Johnny, that marshal dead yet?"

"Hey Johnny, we're goin' the wrong way."

"That deputy's so sick he don't know he got us lost."

"Shut the hell up, or I reckon ya can all go hungry!" she yelled.

They were low on supplies. There were some beans and enough flour and sourdough starter to make biscuits but that was it.

They laughed as she stomped off toward the

creek. "Let us know as soon as he dies."

"He ain't a-goin' to die!" She yelled over her shoulder.

"Johnny?" Rab called weakly as she sloshed into the water.

"Rightchere, lawman." She sat in the water behind him and drew him close.

"What happened?" he asked as she wrapped her arms around his chest and pulled him up a bit. "Did I fall off my horse?"

"Ya sure as hell would have iffin I hadn't decided to stop. I tolt ya to get rested up, but no, ya ninsisted on pushin' yerself. Ya damn lawman. Ya ain't got a lick a sense. It's plum amazin', it purely is, that ya ever managed to stay alive this long."

He chuckled softly. "Insisted."

"What?"

"Insisted, not nin-sis-ted."

"Ninsisted, sisisted, ya must be feelin' better."

"I'm thirsty, Johnny."

"Well, hell, yer a-settin' in the middle of a damn creek."

He chuckled and she used her own hand to scoop up water and trickle it into his mouth. He drank greedily before he drifted off again. Johnny continued to hold him, reluctant to let him go, but she needed to go back to camp and fix something to eat. Carefully, she scooted out from behind him and eased his shoulders against the bank.

"Johnny?"

"Rightchere, Rab."

"Where are you going?"

"To fix some vittles and check yer prisoners. Then I'll be back. Ya'll have to help me Rab, to fetch ya outta here. But I'll fix ya up a nice place by the fire an' help ya outta them wet clothes so's ya don't take a chill. Then I got to open them stitches. I reckon ya don't want me to, but I got to let the poison out. Ya'll feel better Rab, I promise. Ya think ya'll be up to eatin' some broth? I'll fix ya some special from that grouse ya shot, so's it won't bother yore belly none."

"I am feeling a little hungry."

Heartened, she smiled. "That's good, Rab. Yer a-doin' better. An' yer pistol is rightchere iffin ya need it." She picked it up and set it beside him before she turned and started up the bank.

"Johnny?"

She stopped.

"Take my rifle. Keep it with you, but don't get close to the prisoners. They'll try to take it from you. Shoot them if they try anything. I mean it, Johnny. Don't hesitate. We're getting close to Fort Smith, and I guarantee they don't want to hang."

"I'll be careful, Rab." She scrambled back up the bank. At the top he called again.

"Johnny?"

"What the hell do ya want now, lawman?"

"The sun's in my eyes."

She cursed and stomped back down to his side. "Ya sure are the whinnin'est lawman I ever did meet." She picked up his Stetson and dropped it over his face. "Better?"

"Yes, thank you." His muffled laughter rumbled beneath the hat.

"Good. Now shut the hell up so's I can tend to my chores, else I reckon ya'll be settin' in that creek 'til ya turn blue." She wheeled around and climbed back up the bank, his amused chuckles echoing behind her. "Damn, lawman," she muttered.

"Johnny, my hand's hurtin' real bad." Warren complained when she returned to the campsite.

The prisoners sat in a semi-circle, and though they were shackled in pairs and attached to the length of chain, Rab's warning made her wary. She stopped just outside their reach and raised the rifle.

"What's wrong with it?" She'd checked everyone the day before and all their wounds were right as rain. Rab's shot had only grazed the top of Warren's hand.

"I don't know, but it's throbbing powerful bad."

"Well, take off the wrappin's and let me see."

She waited while he unwound the strip of bandage. Even though he wore handcuffs he still moved slower than sorgum. Impatient, she stepped toward him then stopped. They'd only grab the rifle if she got close. She turned and leaned the weapon against a tree trunk, well out of their reach.

"Johnny, my hand." Warren cradled it close to his chest.

"Let me see," she said as she approached.

Then from the corner of her eye she spotted Dewy lunging toward her just as a warning bell rang out in her mind. He latched onto her pant leg and yanked. Her foot flew out from under her, and she fell backward. As her butt slammed against the ground the rest of the prisoners were on her, grabbing at her clothes. She kicked out, the toe of her boot connecting squarely with Stringer's chin.

"Give us the key," Machler demanded as he dug through the pockets of her duster.

"I ain't got no key!" she cried, hitting and shoving at his arms.

A set of hands dug into her pants pockets as another unbuttoned her duster and someone else patted the pockets of her vest and shirts.

She tried to kick out, but the weight of other hands held down her legs.

"Rab got the keys. Leave me alone!"

What if they didn't believe her? Though her binding cloth was securely wrapped around her breasts, she wondered how long before their groping hands, discovered the truth. She redoubled her efforts to escape, thrashing and clawing at their faces. She even managed to bite someone on the arm.

A gunshot exploded nearby, echoing through the trees.

Startled, her heart jumped to her throat. The groping hands stilled. She twisted her head around, trying to see between the outlaws that surrounded her. For a moment she believed more of Uncle Cal's men had arrived. But slowly the men lifted off her and backed away.

Johnny scrambled to her feet, jammed her hat back on her head, and swung around.

Two men sat on horses at the edge of the small clearing. One man was black skinned, broad, and very big. He sat on a tall red roan horse with a white blaze. He had two Colt revolvers, one was in his holster, butt forward, the other held in his right hand, pointed straight at them.

The other man was lean, with the crown of his hat barely reaching the shoulder of the black man beside him. A faint wisp of smoke swirled around the barrel of the gun he aimed in their direction.

She eyed the strangers suspiciously as she inched her way toward the Winchester by the tree.

"What do you want?" she demanded of the two men.

The shorter man squared his shoulders and scowled at her. "I'm U.S. Deputy Marshal Wade Hollister and this is Deputy Marshal Bass Reeves."

She took two steps toward the tree. "Let me see yer badges."

Both men pulled back the lapels of their coats to expose the tin badges pinned to their vests. She realized then that these two were the actual deputies Rab had said were coming from Fort Smith. Yet a bit of doubt remained.

"How do I know ya didn't steal them badges from dead deputies?"

The two men exchanged worrisome glances.

"What dead deputies?" asked Hollister, his voice cold.

Behind her, Machler laughed. "The ones that are nothin' but buzzard bait by now."

"They ain't all." Johnny snapped, taking another step toward the tree.

"Hold it!" Hollister ordered. "What's your name, boy?"

"Johnny Bodine." She reached out and grabbed the rifle, but held it pointed at the ground. Both deputies stiffened and swung their guns in her direction.

"Shoot 'em, Johnny!" Machler called out.

"Bodine? You Pierpont Bodine's kid?"

"Yeah, so?"

"Come on, kid." The big black deputy coaxed. "We been trailin' all of you since McAlester. We just want you to answer some questions is all. Now put down that rifle."

"Why? Ya still ain't proved ya'll is lawmen. I ain't stupid. Ya'll could be friends a theirs." She jerked her head to the side, indicating the outlaws. "An' stole them badges like ol' Dewy here done when him an' the rest a Uncle Cal's men rode straight to the courthouse in McAlester with all the nerve of a government mule."

Hollister frowned. "Don't you know the men in your father's gang?"

"I know'd the men what rode fer Paw, an' some what rode fer Uncle Cal. But them varmints yonder got kin under every rock in the Nations."

"Look, we don't have to prove anything to you," Hollister snapped.

Johnny ignored him, instead focusing her attention on the big black man. "What was the names a them deputies what rode out after Paw?"

The two men exchanged glances. The shorter

man nodded and the big deputy, Reeves, answered. "U.S. Deputy Marshals Brady and Bennick."

Satisfied, they were the lawmen Rab had said were coming, she gave Reeves a quick nod then tossed him the rifle in a high smooth arc. He caught it easily as Johnny swung on her heels and started toward the creek. Rab was awful quiet considering the ruckus.

"Hold up there, boy," Deputy Reeves called.

Turning around she saw he held the rifle stock so she could see the carved letters, R-A-B.

"This is Bennick's rifle," he said. "How'd you get it?"

"He give it to me."

Machler and Warren laughed.

"Johnny shot Bennick," Machler taunted. "How else ya think he got it?"

She shot the outlaw a quick glare before swinging her gaze back to the deputies. "Ya damn fools, Rab ain't dead. Don't go a-listenin' to them varmints." Annoyed with everyone, she wheeled around and started toward the creek.

"Hold it, kid," Hollister ordered stepping in front of her. "You're not going anywhere except over there with the others." He nodded with his head to indicate the prisoners chained to the tree.

"I ain't no outlaw."

"Sure ya ain't, Johnny." Warren yelled.

"Shut yer damn mouth. Ya know I ain't."

"Both of you, shut up." Hollister snapped. "I know there was a warrant issued for Bodine's son. That's you, and that makes you our prisoner."

"Just cause he's my Paw, don't make me no outlaw. Iff'n yer maw's a whore does that make you one?"

Deputy Reeves shook his head and chuckled. "Calm down, kid."

She shoved her hand inside the pocket of her

baggy duster. Hollister tensed, raising his revolver. "Take your hand out nice and slow."

She scowled then slowly withdrew her hand.

Hollister grabbed her arm. "You're under arrest."

"Fer what?" she demanded her body instantly tensing at his touch.

"For the murder of U.S. Deputy Marshal Bennick."

"Ya stupid lawman." She pulled back to free her arm from his grasp. "I done tolt ya he ain't dead. Warren an' Machler an' Breed, now they-all is killers. Why would ya believe them over me?"

"Because Bennick was my best friend." Squeezing her upper arm, he gave her a harsh shake. "Why the hell did you have to shoot him?"

"That's twixt him an' me." She tried again to jerk her arm free of his grip, but he held her fast. "Let me go, ya damn sonofabitch." Her heart raced as panic intensified her struggle.

With the line of prisoners cheering her on, Johnny kicked Hollister in the legs. She tried for his groin, but he'd pulled her too close to his body for her to do him any harm.

"Rab!" she yelled.

Reeves moved in with a set of handcuffs.

She tried to run, but Hollister jerked her back. Desperate she sank her teeth through his coat sleeve, into the flesh of his forearm. He yelled and swore, but instead of releasing his hold, he brought his other hand up and from the corner of her eye, she glimpsed the dark wood of his revolver just as it descended toward her head.

Pain exploded through her skull, and her world went black.

****

The crack of a gunshot jerked Richard awake. Instinctively knocking his hat from his eyes, he rolled over and peered through the foliage at the top of the bank. He searched for movement in the shadows and glimpses of Confederate gray between the trees. If it weren't for the silence of the birds, he would have thought he'd dreamed the gunshot. He reached for his Sharps. It wasn't there. A wave of panic crashed against the inside of his chest. Quickly he scanned the ground around him. Where was his weapon? On his left lay a revolver in a leather holster. He reached to pick it up, but his arm was gone!

No, no no! His silent scream reverberated inside his head. He rolled onto his back and squeezed his eyes tight. It had been thirteen years since he lost his arm. What was wrong with him? Don't think about it. Don't think about it.

He blew out a ragged breath. He was a U.S Deputy Marshal. His right hand grabbed the leather holster and pressed it tight against his chest. He told himself this was his .44 caliber, Smith and Wesson, Top Break revolver. Yet, he was terrified if he'd open his eyes he'd see his old .36 caliber Navy Colt.

He silently counted to three then forced his eyes open. Relief escaped his lips in a single whoosh of breath. Johnny had given him his gun and—

Johnny! He snatched the weapon from his holster and flipped open the chamber. Then he tossed the gun belt with its extra ammunition, over his shoulder, and gun in hand, he crawled forward.

Raised voices drifted to him through the trees, but he couldn't make out what they said.

He levered himself onto his left knee, then pressing himself against the gray trunk of a chinkapin oak he pushed himself to standing. His whole leg hurt, and he bit his lip against the pain as he took a breath and hopped forward.

At the edge of the clearing, his gaze immediately sought Johnny, but he didn't see her. The line of men across from where he stood, blurred and swam before his eyes. He blinked several times, trying to bring them into focus.

Two men, one tall and broad the other short and lean, stood with their backs toward him, as they looked down at what first appeared to be a large, white canvas sack. Were they more of Everett's men?

The blood drained from his face and a deep chill shook his body. The gunshot—*Johnny was hurt!* He raised his gun and hobbled forward.

"Hold it right there, you sonsabitches."

The two men stiffened and lifted their hands shoulder high.

"Drop your guns and turn around real slow."

As the men complied, Richard blinked and gave his head a shake, trying to focus their images. But the ground tilted, and he brought his right foot forward to keep from falling. Intense pain shot up his leg and radiated through his hip. The faces before him swirled together with the trees, melding into a mass of green. His knees buckled and his revolver hit the ground with a thud as his world faded to silent black.

****

When Richard next roused himself, darkness surrounded him. His throat felt like it was coated with burlap, and he could barely form enough saliva to swallow. He shifted his hand under the blanket to touch his leg. Enough heat radiated from his thigh to warm his hand, even before his fingers touched the thin bandage which had been wrapped around the wound. Odd, he thought, Johnny usually applied thick dressings with a strong herbal smell.

Johnny! An image of her crumpled on the ground flashed through his mind. His fingers stretched out, seeking his gun. *Gone!* Dread slammed into his chest as his heart thudded painfully against his breast bone. His eyes flew open

206

as he sought to orient himself. A small campfire burned a few feet away. A dark shadow sat on the opposite side; the glow of the flames obscured the person's features.

"Johnny?" His voice was hardly more than a raspy whisper.

The figure's head turned toward him. Uneasiness stiffened every muscle in Richard's body. This wasn't Johnny. His gaze darted around the area, seeking a weapon of some kind.

The person rolled to his feet and walked around the fire. *Damn!* Richard cursed. He should have kept quiet. He closed his eyes, feigning sleep. He could feel the heaviness of the approaching footsteps through the ground. The person stopped beside him.

"Bennick?" The man's voice was close, as if he'd squatted down, and it sounded familiar. Some of Richard's anxiety eased.

Cautiously, he opened his eyes and blinked. Wade Hollister was hunkered down beside him, his friend's brow furrowed in concern. Richard sighed. He didn't have to worry anymore. He didn't need to be alert every moment of the day and night.

"Bennick?" His friend watched him intently.

"Wade?"

"Yeah, it's me. How are you doing?"

"Johnny. Where's Johnny?" Richard struggled to sit, searching the area for the familiar baggy duster and floppy hat.

"Whoa there, Bennick. Take it easy." Hollister reached out to press him back against his bedroll, but he resisted the pressure of the deputy's hand.

"You looking for the kid? He's right over there."

Richard strained to see where Hollister pointed. Johnny lay on her back, perpendicular to Richard's feet, with her head turned away. A blanket covered her up to her chin. It struck him as strange not to see her curled into a tiny ball. "There was a gunshot...Is Johnny..."

"Don't worry the kid is fine. He's sleeping."

As long as Johnny was all right, Richard lay back and closed his eyes. She had been pushing hard the whole trip, aside from the late nights nursing him. Now that help was here, she'd probably succumbed to exhaustion.

"Bennick?" Hollister prodded. "You've been out a long time. Can I get you anything? Water? The kid made soup. You want some?"

He shook his head. He was thirsty, but the thought of cold water on his stomach made him queasy. As much as he complained about it, what he really wanted was some of Johnny's tea. Bitter though it was, it did settle his stomach and eased the pain in his leg.

"Maybe in the morning." Johnny would be awake then, swearing at him, forcing him to eat. She had said she was going to fix up his leg. He wondered if she had. He drifted into sleep wishing Johnny was beside him to chase away the nightmares.

Muzzle flashes and fire. He could feel himself burning, surrounded by trees, unable to crawl away. Maggots crawled in and out of his leg. He called for Johnny, but she never came.

****

Johnny woke to the warmth of the sun on her cheek and a pounding in her head that caused her to wonder if she'd been mule-kicked. Her stomach rolled, and her head spun as she tried to sort out all that had happened up to this moment. She sat with a groan and discovered her hands cuffed together and her feet bound by a pair of shackles.

Deputy Hollister was beside her in an instant, his gun drawn. Ignoring him, she pushed unsteadily to her feet and glanced around for Rab. Off near the trees, Deputy Reeves was laying Rab on a travois, behind Rab's horse, Billy. She started toward him.

"Hold it, kid," Hollister ordered.

"I ain't a-goin' nowhere's," she said, turning. "I jest need ta fetch my bag a yarbs so's I can poultice Rab's laig, after I lance it with my knife."

Hollister laughed. "I'm not letting you within ten feet of him, let alone give you a knife." He gestured her forward. "Now go get on your horse."

"But his laig needs ta be opened so's the poison can get out."

He shoved her forward.

She took a few quick steps. "I was a-fixin ta do it yesterday, but ya went an' knocked me upside the head with yer damn pistol."

He pushed her again. "Shut up and get over there."

She shuffled up alongside Jack. "I got some willow bark fer tea, to bring down his fever. And some blue cornmeal fer a poultice."

The deputy undid her leg irons so she could mount.

"Ya gotta let me doctor that laig."

"You shot him. I don't want you anywhere near him."

"I'll stay rightchere on my horse and tell ya what needs doin'."

"Enough from you. Now shut up or I'll knock you on the other side of your head."

They moved out a few minutes later. Hollister rode in front. Behind him came Machler, Breed, Warren, and Stringer. Johnny rode near the end of the line, between Dewy and Red. She turned in her saddle numerous times, hoping for a glimpse of Rab, but he remained hidden from her view.

She loudly cursed the stupidity of the deputies and threatened their lives, as Machler and Warren cheered her on. And though Reeves seemed inclined to stop and let her help Rab, Hollister was adamantly against it. After an hour the damn fool rode back and gagged her with his sweaty bandana.

****

The next afternoon railroad workers, riverboat men, and fancy-dressed women, lifted their heads and stared as the deputies and prisoners were ferried across the Arkansas River. Warehouses, stores, saloons, and houses stretched out in every direction, in a town even bigger than the one Johnny imagined for her family in her locket.

She could only gawk as Deputy Hollister led the procession down the wide, dusty street. Shopkeepers stepped from doorways and watched. Johnny hunched her shoulders, trying to curl inside her duster as jeering boys ran along on either side of the horses, taunting the prisoners from beyond the dust clouds, which billowed around the horses' feet. Breed and Machler snarled back and promised to haunt the boys from their graves.

Ahead, Hollister turned his horse between the low, heavy stone walls of an old fort, passing through the wide entrance, and leading them toward an imposing brick building with two rows of windows, and a wide front porch.

Johnny swung her head around, searching for Rab, but Deputy Reeves continued up the street, taking Rab away from her. A great chasm seemed to split through the core of her being as she watched him go, and she was forced to bite down on her lower lip to keep from crying out. Rab had been so still and quiet this morning, worry had twisted her stomach into one big knot.

And that damn fool lawman, Hollister, wouldn't let her anywhere near Rab. Would he be all right without her help? What if they took his leg? She'd promised, and all she'd done was fail him.

A minute later, they stopped near the wide front steps where two guards emerged from a basement door. Along the foundation were small, square windows. From inside, men pressed their faces against the bars, hooting and yelling as Deputy Hollister unchained Breed and Machler. After they dismounted, one guard logged their names and possessions in a book and the other guard escorted them through the door.

Once the rest of the men had been turned over to the guards, Hollister approached Johnny and removed her gag.

"Ya cain't leave me here," she sputtered as soon as the cotton cloth was untied. "I ain't no outlaw." Panic raised the pitch of her voice. She tried to be brave, but her breaths escaped in short little puffs of air, causing her chest to hurt.

"You're Bodine's son, and there is a warrant for your arrest." He inserted the key, and removed her leg irons and handcuffs.

Dismounting, she decided Hollister was not only a fool, but mule-headed stubborn.

She lifted her gaze to meet his. "But Rab needs me."

Yet, at this moment, she needed Rab a heap-sight more. If only she could feel the weight of his arm around her shoulders, holding her tight, letting her know things would be okay, she could face this basement prison filled with men.

"Sorry kid, tell it to the judge."

The guard grabbed her arm and shoved her forward, down the steps, and through the door. The smell of sweat and human excrement assaulted her senses. She slapped her hand over her nose and mouth and stepped forward into a small area partitioned off between the outside door and the inside of the jail. He handed her an itchy wool blanket and opened the inner door to the crowded basement cell.

The only light came through small, ground-level

windows. She stood for a few moments as the crowd of men stared back, sizing her up. She wished she could turn and run, back outside, back the way they'd come, back down the wide street, searching every building and alley until she found Rab. With cold finality, the door of iron bars clanked shut behind her.

As much as she hated Warren and Machler, Johnny scurried forward, sticking to them like a leech. At least their familiarity offered some measure of protection. Dewy and Red found a spot near the fireplace, but she wouldn't have chosen it, because most of the odor in the room seemed to come from the large tub inside the unused hearth. Breed and Stringer found some men they knew from somewhere and stopped to talk.

Tears clogged her throat and silent sobs swelled tight inside her chest. This tiny room was filled with thieves, murderers and rapists. She bit down on her lower lip.

Don't cry. Don't cry, she chanted to herself as she worked her way through the crowd behind Machler. Eventually, they found a tiny area along the wall. She huddled there on the stone floor, her arms wrapped tight around her up-drawn knees. Even Warren and Machler were subdued, talking quietly between themselves.

How was she ever going to protect her secret in here? She could almost feel the hands of these men milling around, touching her body, holding her down, as they pulled off her clothes. She wiggled her back against the damp stone and pulled her blanket tight around her, wishing that somehow the wall would swallow her up. She shivered, but her baggy layers of clothing did nothing to warm her.

Afraid to reach for her locket, she closed her eyes and thought about a big white house surrounded by a strong iron fence, or maybe pretty, white pickets, like the one at the Elk House. She imagined the smell of pies cooling on a window sill, and a swing hanging from the limb of a large oak tree. In her mind, she heard the laughter of a man and woman and saw a table overflowing with food.

"Hey, there, boy."

Johnny's eyes flew open. A man with dirty clothes and graying whiskers stood looking down at her with one ice blue eye. His other eye, his left, was stuck in the outside corner of his eye socket so that he appeared to be looking in two places at the same time.

"Got a name?" the grizzly man continued.

She swallowed down her fear and lifted her chin. "Johnny Bodine." At the mention of the name Bodine, the prisoner's black eyebrows rose.

Then to make him think twice, she added. "An' I'm kin to Calvin Everett, so's ya best jest stay away from me or Uncle Cal'll gut ya in less time than it takes ta skin a badger."

The man chuckled. "But yore paw an' yer uncle ain't here."

"They ain't, but the men what ride fer them are." She slipped her hand inside her boot and pulled out her small skinning knife. "Now stay away from me, or I'll gut ya my own self."

The man chuckled. "Damn it, kid, where'd ya get that little toad sticker? Didn't anyone search ya?"

Machler laughed. "Johnny's our little pickpocket. Whatever ya want, Johnny'll get it fer ya."

The big man's smile vanished. "What I want is that knife a yourn. So why don't ya pass it over?"

The thought crossed her mind to just give him the knife, maybe then he'd leave her alone. But if she did would he use it on her later? And how would the other men treat her if she backed down and they perceived her as weak?

"Didn't yer paw teach ya nothin'?" Warren

213

whispered as he inched away. "Never show yer hand."

The big man reached for the front of her duster, as though he were about to jerk her to her feet. Instead, she jumped up and ducked under his arm, bolting toward the other side of the room. She heard him swear as she jumped over the legs of men sitting on the floor and darted around those who stood in clusters, talking. Behind her, she heard heavy boots thump against the stone floor along with the grunts and curses of the men the big man must have shoved aside in quest to reach her.

Chapter Thirteen

Keys rattled somewhere near the entrance. The big door creaked opened. "Johnny," a deep voice called. "Johnny Bodine."

She froze and turned toward the entrance.

Deputy Reeves stood there with a guard. "Hurry up, kid!" the guard called.

The man with the strange eyes charged up behind her.

She looked across and met Deputy Reeves's dark brown gaze. Had something happened to Rab? Her heart seemed to miss a beat, fluttering like a butterfly with a torn wing.

"DuBois, go sit down," ordered the guard. "What are you doing chasing this kid?"

Behind her Dubois whispered, "I'll be right here when you get back."

Trying to ignore his threat, she stepped toward the deputy on shaky legs.

"You're comin' with me," Reeves explained tersely as the guard let them out of the smelly basement.

Johnny blinked against the afternoon sunlight as she climbed the steps, and Reeves ushered her into the back of a prison wagon.

An aching pain crept through her heart as the wagon rolled down the wide, dusty street. Deputy Reeves hadn't said a word about where they were going. The numerous ruts jarred the wagon and bounced her around on the hard seat. Was he taking her to hang?

She knew nothing of courts and trials, only that

Judge Parker was called the Hanging Judge. Wherever they were going, she hoped it would be over soon. She only wished she could have seen Rab one more time.

The wagon turned down a shady street with rows of large, beautiful houses and picket fences. Each one similar to the house in her imagination. She touched her locket through her shirts. Imaginary people and an imaginary life.

In reality, she was going to hang, just because her father was a killer. So much for wishing. Unshed tears clogged her throat. She wondered if the judge would show mercy if she cried. She drew a breath and tried to make tears come. But nothing happened. Life had destroyed that ability.

Life and Pierpont Bodine.

The wagon rolled to a stop in front of a big blue two-story house with a covered front porch. Deputy Reeves was so tall, he jumped easily from the high seat, then walked around and unlocked the door.

She didn't know much, but she did know that if she was going to hang, this wasn't the place. Reeves ushered her up the steps to the front door. She threw him a questioning look but he said nothing.

Once inside the foyer, she heard the muffled sound of her name coming from somewhere overhead. Her breath caught on a gasp. *Rab!* He'd called for her, and they brought her to him. Relief that she wouldn't hang, twisted together with her fear for Rab, and like a tornado across the plains— the force of it grew so powerful that, for that instant, she didn't know what to think or where to go. Then with a burst of energy, she bolted for the staircase and the security that was Rab.

At the landing, she caught a glimpse below into the open doorway of the parlor. A neatly dressed man with a beard, paced behind a sofa, upon which a young woman sat, sobbing into the wide bosom of a gray-haired lady. But focused on finding Rab, she dismissed any thoughts of who they were and raced up the second half of the stairs. At the end of the hall, where the door was only partially closed, she could hear the voices of several men. Bursting into the room, she skidded to a halt.

Her beloved Rab lay stripped of his clothes on a bed that had been partially protected by an oil cloth. A folded sheet covered him from his navel to the top of his thighs, and was anchored under the mattress on either side of the bed. Linen strips around his ankle tied his good leg to the brass foot rail. His arm and even his stump were secured to the headboard with more linen strips.

His voice grated hoarsely in his throat as he called her name and writhed against his restraints. She ached to throw herself on top of him, to both cry and kiss him, but she held herself back. She glanced around the room. Deputy Hollister stood anxiously at the head of the bed.

Against the wall, to her left stood an older man with his graying hair slicked back. She'd never seen him before, but he wore a Marshal's badge pinned to the lapel of his dark suit. Concern etched lines across his brow and around his mouth. These two men were not a threat to Rab. She turned to the right and her whole body stiffened as though a bucket of ice water had been dumped over her head.

A saw! On a small table, amid surgical instruments, small bottles, piles of towels and bandages, lay a bone saw. And looming beside the table, like a ghoulish specter in black, stood a whisker-faced man wearing a frock coat.

"Johnny," Rab called weakly.

"He's right here," soothed Hollister. For the first time since she met him, Johnny saw a gentler side of the man.

At that moment, Reeves barreled into the room

jostling her from behind. The marshal glared at him as Reeves holstered his gun. Johnny took a step back, brushing against the big deputy's right side as she moved.

"This him?" The marshal demanded.

"Yes, sir, Johnny Bodine," the black man answered.

The marshal's gaze narrowed as he turned toward her. "Personally, I believe you should be locked up, away from God-fearing citizens, until the day Judge Parker sentences you to hang. I lost a very fine man out there because of you and your father. But my deputy here has been asking for you. I don't care if you're the son of Satan himself, if you can give him some measure of comfort before the doctor takes his leg, then, I myself will put in a good word for you with the judge."

She jerked her chin up and glared right back. She didn't like this man, standing there in his fancy suit, looking down his nose at her. She opened her mouth to tell him she wasn't an outlaw, when Rab called to her from the bed.

"Johnny?"

Instantly, the marshal was forgotten as she adjusted her baggy coat and strode to the side of the bed. "What the hell do ya want now, lawman?"

At her gruff words, each man in the room took a step toward her, like a flock of mother hens protecting their chick. But they stopped short when Rab ceased his struggles and opened his eyes.

"Sweet...as ever," he whispered as his dark brown gaze, bright with fever, sought and found her face.

"An' yer bossy as ever." She dropped beside him on the bed and began to tug loose the bonds that held his shortened left arm. "I swear to God, Rab, the way ya was a-bellerin', a body could'a hear'd ya clean across the Nations."

"I'm cold, Johnny."

"No ya ain't. Yer hot."

"Don't go."

Swallowing back a sob and the nearly overwhelming urge to pull him into her arms and cry, Johnny forced her voice to maintain its usual surliness. "I ain't a goin' no wheres. So hush yer mouth an' go to sleep."

His eyes drifted closed for a moment, and she stretched across the bed to work loose the knot of the binding that held his right hand.

His eyes flew open. "Johnny, the maggots are back. I can feel them crawling—"

"They ain't no maggots, lawman." Vigorously, she rubbed the hot, dry skin of his upper arm, trying to restore the circulation. "Yer arm jest went to sleep cause them damn fool friends a yourn tied it to the bed. I swear, the lot of 'em together ain't got the brains God give a squirrel."

His head rolled back and forth on the pillow. "No, Johnny. My leg. I can feel them crawling around in my leg."

She glanced down at his right leg, swollen and grotesque. The skin around the stitches where she had removed the bullet was stretched tight, oozing yellow pus. Some of the skin had turned gray, and she detected the sour bite of rotting flesh. Her stomach clenched, her mind spinning as she sought the best way to treat the infected limb.

"They ain't no maggots in there neither. Ya ain't got no poultice, an' yer laig filt up with poison ag'in. Them maggots wouldn't be sech a bad thing. Like I tolt ya, they eat up the poisons an' clean the wound right smart."

"Don't want maggots."

"I know ya don't, so's I reckon I best fix ya up another poultice. What'd ya do with yer saddle bags?"

"They're on my horse." His eyes drifted closed.

"Yer horse? I don't see yer damn horse. No wonder ya got yer name carved in all yer gear. It's so's folks'll give it back to ya after ya lose it."

Rising from the bed, she intended to free his good leg from the foot rail, but his eyes flew open, wide with panic.

"Johnny."

"I'm rightchere, lawman." She dropped back beside him, reached across his torso, and drew his right arm across his chest so she could rub the circulation back into his hand.

"Don't go."

"I done tolt ya, I ain't a-goin' no wheres. Jest to mix up a new poultice fer that laig. Ya get some sleep an' ever'thing'll be right as rain come mornin'."

Slowly the tension seeped out of his body, and his eyes closed.

"Now hold up there, son." The doctor spoke, stepping up beside the bed. "This man will die unless I amputate that leg."

She swung around and glared at him. "Says you."

"Now look here, you young ruffian. I am this man's physician. Even now it may be too late, but if he's going to have any chance at all to live, that leg needs to come off—now."

Helpless she turned to the marshal.

The older man stepped closer to the bed. "I can see how fond you are of Deputy Bennick, but the doctor here has had the finest training. He knows what's best. No one wants Bennick to die. You can stay if you like. He seems to take comfort from you, but I will not allow you to interfere with the doctor's decision."

Johnny glared at the marshal. "Yer daft as a brush." She looked around the room, her gaze capturing that of the two deputies. "All his fancy book learnin' an' all this sawbones knows, is how to cut off folks's limbs."

She swung her attention to the doctor. "Iffin' a-savin' Rab's laig is above yer huckleberry, then ya best leave me to do what I know, an' either help or stay outta my way."

The marshal took another step toward the bed, his narrowed glare directed straight at Johnny. "I've had just about all the interference I will stand. Either you cooperate or you will be forcibly removed. The doctor needs to administer the chloroform before the operation—unless you prefer to see him operate without it."

"No!" Richard screamed, bolting upright in bed.

His eyes widened with a terror so palatable Johnny tasted his fear and shuddered.

"Johnny! Don't let them take my leg. Johnny, where are you?"

"I'm rightchere, lawman." Gently, she pressed her hands against his hot shoulders and pushed him back against the pillows. "Didn't I promise ya, Rab?" She soothed. "Ain't nobody a-goin' to take yer laig whilst I got breath in me."

"You promised." He relaxed.

She crooned on. "Don't be afeared Rab. I'm here now, an' that sonofabitch sawbones ain't a-touchin' yer laig. Now go to sleep an' trust me."

"I trust you, Johnny," he mumbled, so exhausted his words slurred together.

"Marshal Upham," demanded the doctor. "Do something."

The marshal moved toward her, but before he had taken his second step, she whipped a Colt .45 from under her baggy duster and pointed it across the bed directly at the doctor's chest.

"What in the world?" Upham exclaimed as she clicked the hammer back. "Where did you get that gun?"

Hollister instantly drew his gun on Johnny.

"From yer dumb deputy." Ignoring Hollister, she nodded toward Reeves, who stood glaring at her. The Colt from his left holster in hand, and whose empty right holster earned him a censuring scowl from the marshal, the doctor, and Deputy Hollister.

"Now get this damn sawbones outta here, afore I put a hole through his head, an' he has windows where his ears was."

Paling considerably, the doctor gathered his instruments, dropping each one twice, before his shaky hands managed to stuff them all into his black bag.

"I wash my hands of this whole thing," he said as he backed toward the door, his bag held tight to his chest. "I told you what needs to be done. This man's death will be on your conscience."

"Damn it, Doctor, wait a minute." Angry, the marshal swung toward Johnny, but halted when she raised the barrel a notch.

"Drop that gun," Hollister ordered, "or I'll shoot you."

Maintaining her aim on the marshal, she said, "Try anything an' I reckon I'll shoot the marshal here. Yer so all fired anxious to see me hang, makes me no never mind how many men I kill, no how. Like my paw always said, 'ya can only hang me wunst.'"

She shifted her gaze and caught a glimpse of doubt in Reeves dark eyes. Did he know how nervous she was? Did he suspect she was bluffing?

He must have, because he returned his gun to his holster and gave her a slow, easy smile. "Hollister, there's no need. Johnny ain't goin' to shoot no one. He's just tryin' to help. Now let's all calm down and let Johnny do what he can for Bennick. And, Johnny, give me back my gun."

While Reeves and Marshal Upham visibly

relaxed, Hollister seemed reluctant, and since he had conked her on the head, she didn't trust him any farther than she could toss a bull by the tail.

Reeves frowned at Hollister. "Put your gun up, Wade."

"Not until he gives you back your gun. The kid is still a prisoner. He should be in shackles and handcuffs. I don't know why you and Bennick are so trusting of the brat."

Reeves looked to Johnny. She heaved a weighted sigh. "I reckon yer right, all this argufyin' ain't a-helpin' Rab none." She stepped toward Reeves and placed the gun in the wide palm of his extended hand.

Then leaning across the bed, she pulled free the sheet, and spread it out over Rab's lower half, affording him the dignity of being properly covered in this room full of people.

Fairly confident they wouldn't stop her from doctoring Rab, she turned to Reeves. "Rab says his saddle bags is on his horse. Can ya fetch 'em? My bag a yarbs an' sech is with 'em."

Reeves started for the door then hesitated. In his deep, Southern drawl he asked, "Are you sure you can save him?"

"Rab ain't a-goin' to die. Ya been listenin' to that damn fool sawbones. Alls we got to do is get the poison out an' his fever down"

"No offense kid," interrupted the marshal, "But his leg looks bad. If this is an example of your care..."

"Why ya God damn sonofabitch. No wonder ya'll couldn't catch my paw. The lot a ya ain't no smarter than a box a rocks. 'Course this ain't no example a my care. This here's what come from them dumb deputies a yourn. They done took off my poultice an' didn't give Rab nothin' fer his fever. 'Course it looks bad. It's damn bad. I ain't ever seen it like this, even when Uncle Cal fetched us outta that jail and Rab was a-chasin' us half way to Texas."

Hollister stepped forward, regret etched his features as he watched his friend moving restlessly on the bed. "What do you need me to do?"

"I'm a-goin' to need boilin' water. Reckon I can use these here towels an' sech, the doc left. An' when that big, black deputy fetches back Rab's saddle bags, I'll need me a place to cook down my yarbs."

Hollister nodded. "I'll go see what Mrs. Walker has in the kitchen.

Once the deputies left, Johnny turned to Marshal Upham. "Was ya a-goin' to help or jest stand there a-growin' roots?"

A grin, quirked up one corner of his mouth, and he stepped toward the bed.

Turning, Johnny leaned over, pulled up her pant leg and removed her knife from her boot.

"Damn," Upham swore. "Didn't my deputies search you for any weapons?"

"I done tolt ya. Ya got a bunch a dumb deputies."

Ignoring the marshal, Johnny removed the glass chimney from the bed side table and lit the lamp. "Now, I'm a goin' to need ya to help hold him down." She raised the wick and heated the knife blade. "I got to slit open them stitches I put in, so's the poison can get out."

She shed her duster, tossed it to the floor, and climbed on the bed to straddle Rab's right leg. Sitting on his shin, she pulled back the sheet to expose the wound and leaned forward, her knife poised over the wound.

Grunting and groaning, Upham climbed onto the bed to straddle Rab's opposite leg then dropped forward to splay his hands on Rab's shoulders.

Johnny glanced over meeting his gaze. "Ya best watch yer self now. Rab jest might pitch ya offin the bed."

The marshal gave a quick nod.

She drew a steadying breath and slowly released it before using the tip of the blade to carefully slice through the first tiny stitch.

"No!" Richard screamed, bucking and thrashing.

The marshal bounced around a bit, but the old man surprised her by keeping his hold and not tumbling to the floor.

"Holt still, Rab," she snapped, not wanting to injure him anymore than necessary.

"No. Don't cut it off."

"I ain't a-cuttin' it off. I'm a-fetchin' out them maggots ya hate so much."

Whether her reply reassured him or he had lapsed into unconsciousness, she was grateful he couldn't feel her cut through the rest of the stitches. While he was still, she sliced off the ragged edges of dead skin.

Hollister returned with a kettle of hot water. He set it on the floor and joined her in helping Marshal Upham off the bed. The two men watched as she used hot moist towels to draw out as much of the infection as she could. When Reeves came back with her doeskin bag, she smeared the last of her piñon over the wound. She didn't have much of the ointment, but Morning Song insisted the white pitch was amazing for drawing pus from a wound.

Later she would use a mixture of chia, flaxseed, and blue cornmeal. Though she changed the poultices every hour and most of the infection had drained from the wound, Rab's fever continued to rise.

Afraid, Johnny wiped him down with cold water and spooned willow bark tea through his cracked lips. Her mother had died of a high fever, and so had Morning Song, and now she could only watch Rab's every breath, helpless to do more.

The clock at the bottom of the stairs chimed

three times. The only sounds were the soft snores of Deputy Reeves, sprawled in an upholstered chair, and the water sloshing in the basin when she wrung out her cloth.

She brushed back the lock of hair Rab always found so annoying. His fever was so high and his breathing so shallow, Johnny was terrified she was going to lose him, too.

"Damn it, Rab." Her fingers combed through his hair. "I need ya so much. Don't ya dare leave me alone."

Behind her someone coughed. She jerked around, pointing a Colt revolver at the open doorway and Deputy Hollister's chest.

"Whoa!" he cried, raising his hands. "Where'd you get another gun?"

"Ya dumb lawman, don't ya know no better than to sneak up on a body like that."

"Look, kid, no one is going to amputate Bennick's leg, so just give me the gun."

She released the hammer and held out the weapon. "No wonder they give Rab the job a-huntin' down my paw. I swear, you an' Reeves together ain't got the brains God give a goose."

Stepping forward, Hollister snatched the revolver from her hand and checked the chambers.

Reeves roused at the sound of their voices, groaned and stretched.

Hollister stepped toward him. He handed him the Colt. "Quit letting that kid steal your gun."

Reeves slipped the revolver back in its holster. "Your turn. See if you do any better. I's goin' home to my wife."

While the two deputies whispered about her by the door, Johnny wrung out a cloth and returned to the task of wiping it over Rab's chest and shoulders.

Hollister came up on the other side of the bed and watched for a few minutes.

"Too bad it ain't winter," she said as she slid the cloth over Rab's shoulder and down his arm. "I could pack him in snow, like I done fer Uncle Henry when he got shot."

"Snow?" Hollister asked.

Johnny lifted her head and met his gaze across the bed. "Yeah, snow brung down Henry's fever right quick, but I couldn't fix what that damn whiskey peddlers bullet done."

"How about ice?"

"Sure, but I ain't got none. This here's summer."

"But there's ice in the ice house." Hollister offered weakly.

She blinked at him in disbelief. "Ya got a whole house full a ice?"

"Yes, I assumed you knew that. The iceman cuts blocks of ice from the river in the winter and stores it packed in straw and sawdust for use in the summer."

"How the hell would I know that? I ain't never lived in no town afore. I was raised by a bunch a no accounts who was born tired an' raised lazy. How the hell would I know ya got a house full a ice in the middle a summer? It's plum amazin' ya can get yer self outta bed in the mornin'."

Hollister started backing toward the door. "I suppose you'd like me to get you some."

"A course I'm a-wantin' ya to get me some ice. Lots a ice!" she shouted as he scurried away down the hall. "Damn, Rab," she muttered turning back to the bed. "I don't think them friends a yourn could pour water from a boot iffen the 'structions was on the bottom."

Within an hour they'd covered the bed with an oil cloth and every inch of Rab's body except his leg was packed in ice. All morning, Johnny kept her vigil, but there was no change. She was terrified of losing him. The ice kept him cooler, but the fever refused to break. The wound remained infected and though the poultices were working, because Johnny changed them so frequently, she quickly depleted her supply of herbs. She thumbed through her book racking her brain for an alternative.

At mid-day, Mrs. Walker, the sister of Benton Caldwell, the man who owned the house, stopped to bring Johnny a glass of milk and a cold beef sandwich. Staring at the two thick slices of fresh yeasty bread triggered the memory of a time when she tended a laceration on the leg of one of her father's nicer men. The man had told her that his mother always used a poultice of white-bread mold to prevent infection.

Johnny jumped up and ran after the older woman.

Mrs. Walker was more than willing to help and volunteered to search the neighborhood for a supply. Meantime, she set a loaf of bread in the cellar where it was damp enough to grow mold for the days to come.

An hour later, Johnny applied the new poultice. Reeves and Hollister came in and out that afternoon replenishing the ice. They had little to say, but their hopelessness was reflected in their bleak expressions. Mrs. Walker brought her supper, but Johnny had no appetite.

Several hours later, she fell asleep in the chair she'd pulled up beside the bed. Somewhere in her dreams a soft moan drifted into her consciousness. With a groan, she lifted her head and blinked. Yawning, she rubbed one hand along the ache in her lower back and with the other, reached out to turn up the wick in the lamp. Disbelief widened her eyes to discover Rab covered in sweat, his teeth chattering.

Her hand shaking, she cupped his stubble-coated cheek. She blew out a shaky breath as unshed tears clogged the back of her throat. A smile spread across her face for just a moment before she leaned over and kissed first his damp forehead, and then his dry, cracked lips.

She gave him one more kiss then spun around and dashed across the room to a second chair where Hollister dozed.

Grinning, she drew back her fist and punched him in the arm. He jumped straight up, his gun drawn as his gaze flew around the darkened room.

She smiled and pointed toward the bed. "Look, Rab's fever broke."

He shoved his gun into his holster and rubbed his arm as he pushed her aside on his way to the bed.

She followed and stood beside him, gazing down at Rab, one more time, reassuring herself with each rise and fall of his chest that he was going to recover.

Hollister seemed to forget how much he hated her, for he grabbed her in a rough embrace, and gave her a couple of quick thumps in the center of her back.

Instinctively, she stiffened and pushed away. "Let go a me, damn you."

He didn't seem to notice as he stepped back, a smile on his face. "I'll be right back. I'm going to grab some clean sheets and a couple of buckets so we can get rid of this ice."

He swung away from her and strode down the hall before she had time to agree.

After Mrs. Walker changed the linens and Rab slept comfortably, the older woman managed to tempt Johnny away from Rab with the promise of a sandwich and of a hot, tub-bath. Though her fear of discovery kept her from enjoying a long soak, her bath was the most enjoyable one she had ever taken.

With extra blankets and pillows, Johnny fixed a

pallet for herself on the floor. She longed to crawl into bed and curl up close to Rab, but with Mrs. Walker and that sneaky deputy popping in and out at all times, she didn't dare. So she curled up on her bed of blankets and closed her eyes. Exhausted, she fell into a sound asleep.

Chapter Fourteen

"Johnny?"

She bolted upright at the sound of her name.

"What are you doing down there?" Rab asked in a raspy voice, turning his head in her direction with an effort that seemed to cost him. "I'm thirsty."

She grabbed the cup of tea she'd been spooning into him earlier. It had grown cold, but she thought it more strengthening than plain water. She propped him up with pillows so he could drink. He never even complained about the taste. He drank greedily then lay back against the pillows.

"I'm cold."

"Oh, ya ain't neither," Johnny declared, setting the cup on the end table. "Ya only say that when ya want me to sleep with ya."

"Will you?"

"Will I what, lawman?"

"Sleep with me, outlaw?"

She didn't hesitate. She climbed in beside him, her heart swelling inside her chest from the sheer joy of knowing Rab was alive and grinning with that endearing dimpled smile which melted her heart.

"Have I been sick long?"

"Naw, a couple days is all."

"I called for you. You didn't come."

"I came, lawman."

"There was a doctor. People holding me down. They were trying to cut off my leg." His smile vanished, and he struggled to sit, but his weakness wouldn't allow it. He tried again as sweat broke out across his forehead.

"What the hell are ya doin'?" she asked, fighting to keep him still.

"My leg..."

"It's still there. I promised ya didn't I?"

"I need to see."

"Yer a-goin' to make yer self sick, Rab. Cain't ya feel it?"

His head dropped weakly into the pillows. "Yes, I...feel it. Hurts...like hell," he panted from the effort.

"I tolt ya."

"But for a long time...after...my arm...hurt like hell. Sometimes...I still feel it. Sometimes...my fingers...itch. Please, Johnny."

She had no idea how someone could feel an itch on an arm that wasn't there, but she didn't argue. Desperation radiated from every inch of his body. She knew he would never rest until he was sure. Rising to her knees, she levered him to sitting and shoved pillows behind him for support.

She threw back the covers, removed the bandage, and allowed him to examine the wound. By the time she reapplied a new dressing and adjusted the covers, he had fallen into a deep sleep. Giving in to her own exhaustion, she snuggled up beside him and was soon sound asleep.

****

Fierce whispers from two people somewhere in the room, stirred Johnny into a vague state of awareness. The man spoke with quick, sharp words, while the woman spoke in low soothing tones. Johnny wanted to open her eyes, but she told herself it was only a dream. A door clicked shut. She opened one eye but saw nothing and snuggled closer to Rab. She fell back to sleep almost immediately.

****

The penetrating heat of a sunbeam warmed her face and slowly roused her from her first good night's sleep in weeks. Yet, it was the steady thrum of Rab's heart, beating beneath her ear, which warmed her insides. Her fingers sifted through the soft hair sprinkled across his chest. Slowly, she lifted her head, and with a smile tugging at the corners of her mouth, she studied his face. That lock of hair he always found so annoying had dropped over his forehead, brushing the tops of his dark brown eye brows as he slept. Using a light touch so as not to wake him, Johnny trailed her index finger over his stubble coated cheek, across his chin, and down his throat.

Rab sure could use a shave. He didn't much like having a beard. She sniffed. A bath wouldn't hurt either. He hated being dirty, too. She eased out from under his arm and slid off the bed. She took a minute to check his wound and change the bandage, before she drew the sheet and blanket up to his chest. She pulled on her boots, grabbed her duster, and jammed her hat on her head.

Quietly, she eased open the door. She'd go down to the kitchen and see about cooking Rab a pot of soup and brewing some more willow bark tea. After that she'd fix up a new bread-mold poultice and heat water for his bath and shave.

Focused on her mental list, she almost tripped over Deputy Hollister's extended legs, where he'd been dozing in a chair. He jumped up when she banged into his knees. As she pulled the door closed, he stole a quick peek into the bedroom.

"How is he?"

"Sleepin'," she replied, wondering why he'd been outside the door. She started down the hall, her apprehension growing as Hollister trailed her all the way to the kitchen.

Marshal Upham sat at a small table near the window with the same bearded man she'd seen pacing in the parlor the afternoon she arrived. A cup and saucer had been placed before each of them.

Mrs. Walker stood in front of the large cast iron stove stirring something in a big pot. She flinched as Johnny walked in.

"Oh," she cried softly. "G-good morning."

Johnny nodded in reply, but watched the older woman's nervous movements. Something felt wrong.

Marshal Upham rose from the table. "How is Deputy Bennick this morning?" The warmth she'd felt from him yesterday had vanished.

Uneasy, she backed closer to the wall. "Rab's sleepin.'"

"Good. Good." Upham gestured toward his now empty chair. "Relax, Johnny, sit down. Have a bite to eat."

The hair on the back of her neck tickled, and suddenly here she stood, the only jackrabbit in a room full of bobcats. She glanced at the chair and shook her head.

"Reckon I'll jest head on back to Rab."

The marshal glanced first toward the man at the table, then to Deputy Hollister, before refocusing his attention on her.

"I want to say how much we all appreciate what you've done. You saved Deputy Bennick's leg when the doctor wanted to amputate. But you are a prisoner, and after what Mrs. Walker and Mr. Caldwell here, witnessed early this morning, I'm sure you can understand why, in a household of gently-bred ladies, it would be best for everyone concerned if you returned to the jail."

She shook her head, at a loss to understand any of what the marshal was saying, except for the very clear words, "...return to the jail."

"But I got to—"

"Look here, Bodine." Mr. Caldwell rose from his chair. "We all realize you were raised by a group of men with little or no morals, and have had no

Christian teachings to guide you, but when we walked into that room this morning—I can only pray that Bennick, in his weakened state was unaware of such immoral debauchery. For my own dear sister to have witnessed such sin was bad enough, but if my daughter were to learn what—"

The back door swung open, and a beautiful young woman stepped inside, a basket of eggs hung from her arm. Her gaze went immediately to Mr. Caldwell.

"I have your eggs for breakfast, Papa." Her gaze shifted to Marshal Upham. "Good morning, marshal."

She set the basket on the sink near the pump and removed her bonnet.

It was then Johnny recognized her as the young woman who'd been crying in the parlor the other afternoon. Perhaps only a few years older than herself, the young woman's thick brown hair had been twisted into a bun at the back of her head. Her eyes, as she stared down her nose at Johnny, were as blue as a winter sky. She wore a dark rose print dress with a high lace collar and bustle.

Johnny glanced down at her own tattered, dirty, too-big, boys clothes in shame. Even if her hair grew long and she put on a dress exactly like that one, she would still be a mule in a horse harness.

The best thing she could do was get back to Rab. She started toward the stove. "I'll just fetch me some hot water fer some willow bark—"

Mr. Caldwell gestured toward his daughter. "There is no need. Caroline and her aunt will be seeing to Deputy Bennick's care from now on."

Caroline Caldwell's nose pulled up in disdain as she perused Johnny from head to toe.

Johnny shook her head in denial. "Well, that's right nice of ya ma'am, but Rab, he needs me, an' well, I jest as soon keep a-watchin' out fer him." She

235

squared her shoulders and stepped to the stove. "I reckon I'll brew some tea fer his fever an' fix up another poultice for his laig."

Caroline drew herself up indignantly. "I assure you, I am quite capable."

Johnny swallowed a lump of inadequacy. Caroline was so beautiful. She didn't seem to have trouble remembering how to say big words.

"But Rab needs me."

"Why do you persist in referring to him by that ridiculous name?"

Johnny frowned. A funny weight pressed into her chest. "Reckon that's his name. He got it carved in all his gear." But even as she heard herself speak the words, she recognized their sudden lack of conviction.

Caroline laughed. The sound sliced through Johnny, right to the marrow of her bones.

"You stupid boy. Those are his initials. R for Richard, A for Albert, and B for Bennick." She laughed again.

Johnny felt as though she had been gut shot, as pain ripped through her stomach leaving her torn and bleeding. She couldn't breathe. The agony was so intense, she wanted to wrap her arms around her middle and slump to the floor. His name wasn't Rab. She glanced around the room. Marshal Upham's gaze was on his cup. Harriet Walker briskly stirred the contents of the pot. Near the table, Hollister stared out the window.

They'd all known! Every time she called him Rab, they'd known. And they'd laughed. The stupid, outlaw brat, who'd thought she was as good as everyone else. The stupid kid who'd briefly believed she had worth.

And *Rab!*

The realization was so powerful she nearly doubled over from the force of its impact. No wonder she made him laugh. Each time she said his name he was reminded of what a stupid, stupid girl she was. Just like the way he corrected her mispronounced words.

But these people would never glimpse the anguish ricocheting through her insides, for she had had years of practice masking hurt. Years of standing straight and tall, looking people in the eye and tamping down the pain, tucking it away into the secret recesses of her soul, hiding it so nobody knew they had the power to hurt her. And in those brief seconds after learning the truth, Johnny skillfully drew her emotions under control.

"What the hell do I care what his name is?" she declared. "He ain't nothin' but a Goddamn, sonofabitch, Yankee lawman anyways."

Marshal Upham's head snapped up. Hollister watched her with narrowed eyes. Mrs. Walker looked relieved. They all did.

Well hell, she was glad her affected attitude could so easily absolve them of that inkling of guilt they each might have felt. She hated each one of them, standing there as uppity as a herd of government mules. She wished her paw were alive. He'd kill them all for hurting her, just like he shot that whiskey peddler.

Mrs. Walker spoke hesitantly. "We only thought...well, you've been so tireless, so devoted to Deputy Bennick's care...we believed you'd grown rather... er...fond."

Johnny snorted. Her heart pounded beneath her shirts. "Fond? Well hell, that's a good one. I was jest a-watchin' out fer my own self. Takin' care a that deputy so's he'd put in a good word for me with the judge." She peered into the pot on the stove. "Fond of a lawman? Why my paw's spirit would rise up and haunt me from the grave."

Marshal Upham's jaw clenched. Both ladies

paled visibly, which gave Johnny some small measure of satisfaction. Only Hollister's frown looked skeptical.

"Yes, well," Marshal Upham began. "It is high time things were restored to their proper order. You my boy, while we appreciate the great service you have done for our deputy, whatever the reason, are still a prisoner. Consequently, Deputy Hollister will return you to the jail from whence you came, until your arraignment before the judge. Meanwhile, I am certain Miss Caldwell is more than capable of overseeing the care of her fiancé until their wedding."

Johnny stared at the marshal confused. He spoke too quickly and used words she didn't understand. However, two facts slowly became clear. She was going back to jail and—Rab was getting married.

The agony she'd felt minutes before was nothing compared to the pain tearing through her heart at this devastating news. She felt like a chunk of fire wood that had been split in two with an axe, with one thin splinter barely holding the two halves together. Each time Rab had been holding her, kissing her, loving her, making her feel things she had never felt before, he had been using her. Just like every man she'd ever known used women. Except, this was worse; she had trusted him!

And here stood Caroline Caldwell, the embodiment of everything Johnny knew she could never be. Caroline was beautiful and smart and ladylike. And Johnny hated her for that. And she hated Rab for choosing her.

But Johnny hated herself the most. For believing in Rab, for believing in her own dreams, and for giving her fragile heart to a man who only managed to grind it in the dirt.

Paw was right. She really was a worthless piece

of shit.

She needed to lash out and hurt someone. Anyone, anything, just to ease the mounting pressure that threatened to explode inside her.

"Well, I hope to hell ya know what yer gettin' into with Rab," Johnny snapped flippantly as she moved toward the end of the sink.

Mrs. Walker gasped.

Johnny withdrew an egg from the basket and tossed it back and forth between her hands. "He gets all fired bossy and ornery when he don't get his way. An' when he gets riled he cusses hot enough to fry bacon."

She smiled inwardly at the shocked gasps which hushed the room. Caroline had even clamped her hand across her mouth.

"An' Rab, he hates to sleep alone." She grinned, satisfied with the mortified expression on Caroline's face. "He gets cold an' whines like a mule 'til ya crawl in beside him."

"That's quite enough, Bodine," Marshal Upham snapped, gesturing Deputy Hollister forward. "Mrs. Walker and Miss Caldwell are ladies."

Johnny laughed. "Oh, 'scuse me ma'am."

Hollister advanced in her direction, but she tossed the egg into the air and let it smash on the floor. Marshal Upham gestured for Hollister to stop, as he himself, moved closer. Johnny side-stepped toward the stove. Their faces pale, the two women stepped aside.

Johnny pointed at the pot. "What the hell are ya cookin' in there?" she demanded of Caroline.

The young woman drew herself up indignantly. "That is chicken and rice soup. It is very fortifying to those of a weakened constitution."

Johnny huffed and said, "Them white things is dis-tusk-ting. Rab ain't a-goin' to eat it." Secretly, she hoped Caroline fed him bowls of the stuff, and he gagged on every one.

"How dare you! You disgusting..."

Johnny flinched and swallowed.

"...illiterate, brush-ape, to presume to tell me what is best for my fiancé!"

Johnny had to get out of here. To run far away and never look back.

Caroline continued. "You don't belong in this house with decent, God fearing people. You belong in jail, with the rest of that abhorrent congregation of useless, murdering outlaws."

Johnny snapped. And surprising herself the most, she drew back her fist and punched, driving the anguish that tore through her heart, straight into Caroline's jaw. With a small cry, the young woman fell backward into a senseless heap.

Hollister lunged forward and grabbed Johnny's arm. Spinning her around, he snatched her other wrist and pressed them against her lower back. Ignoring the pain, she braced herself against the deputy's chest and kicked out at Marshal Upham, who had sprung forward to assist Hollister.

Harriet Walker dropped to her knees beside Caroline. "Oh, mercy!"

With a set of manacles in his hand, Marshal Upham stepped close.

She couldn't let these men get the handcuffs on her. She couldn't go back to that jail with all them outlaws and the man with the weird eyes. When Hollister switched both her wrists into the grip of one hand in order to accept the handcuffs from the marshal, Johnny straightened, then threw herself forward, bending at the waist, dropping her shoulder, and thrusting her pelvis back. Hollister flew over her head and landed with a whump, flat on his back.

She spun away and bolted for the doorway. But a dark silhouette loomed in the threshold. She skidded to a stop as Upham's voice rang out behind her.

"Stop him!"

Johnny swung around just as Deputy Reeves's hand reached for the back of her collar. Instead, his fingers grazed her neck and caught in the string of rawhide. As she jerked away, the rawhide snapped and the locket hit the floor with a ping. Deputy Reeves lunged for her again, and she whirled away. But Hollister rolled to his knees and threw himself forward, wrapping his arms around her lower legs. Johnny crashed into the table, scattering silver and china across the floor.

Desperate, she snatched up a piece of broken dish and twisted around as Hollister struggled to maintain his hold on her legs. In a flash, she lashed out with her make-shift weapon and sliced through his left cheek. Blood gushed from the wound. Hollister released his hold, and she scrambled to her feet. Passing the sink, as she ran for the back door, she grabbed the basket of eggs and threw them at Deputy Reeves. She heard him skid into the table as she reached for the door knob.

She flung the door wide and vaulted over the railing of the stoop. Without a backward glance, she raced around the corner of the house into a neighbor's yard. She heard yelling and changed direction, zig zagging through yards and down side streets. She looked back as she dashed around the corner of another house. Though she saw no one behind her, the volume of their voices warned her they were close. Fortunately, it was early enough in the day, she saw no one who could point out her direction to the deputies.

With her arm pressed against a stitch in her side, she searched for a place to hide. Ahead was a small house with a weedy yard and a sloping back porch. Careful not to trample a path, she skidded to a stop and picked her way across the yard, crawled under the steps, and wiggled herself up tight against the stone foundation.

A few minutes later, she heard shouts and footsteps hurrying past, but no one seemed to notice her hiding place.

With nowhere to go and no idea what to do, she stayed where she was, curled into a ball, watching a couple of black beetles scurry across the dirt and into a crack in the foundation.

Paw was right. You couldn't trust a lawman. She'd been a fool to believe Rab was different. He didn't care about her. He didn't love her. Her whole life she'd clung to stupid, foolish dreams and look where they'd gotten her. Alone, afraid, and unwanted; her biggest fear come true. The pressure inside her chest built until the tears that had been bottled up inside for so long leaked from the corners of her eyes, to silently trail across her cheeks and drip into the dirt.

Chapter Fifteen

Evening shadows filled the room when the throbbing in his leg roused Richard from his peaceful oblivion. Goose flesh prickled across his arms, and his tongue was stuck to the roof of his mouth. He turned his head on the pillow, searching the room. Where was Johnny? On a small table, a basin of water with a cloth draped over the edge sat beside a glass lamp. A wooden rocking chair had been pulled up close to the bed and an abandoned needlework sampler lay on the seat.

Johnny didn't sew. Richard frowned, struggling to separate dreams from reality. Johnny had been here. She had saved his leg hadn't she? Or had it all been part of his crazy sequence of dreams?

Urgently needing reassurance, he struggled to prop himself up on his elbow. He stared down the length of his body and saw the long shape of both legs beneath the blankets. But he wasn't satisfied. He levered himself upright with the stump of his left arm, and used his right hand to jerk aside the covers and reveal the thick bandage wrapped around his bare thigh. Exhausted, he dropped against the pillows. He ran his shaky hand across his eyes and down over the thick stubble on his face. Damn, how long had he been sick?

He thought Johnny had been here during the night, showing him his leg was all right, keeping him warm. Where was she?

The bedroom door creaked as someone slowly pushed it inward, bathing the bed in a beam of hallway light.

"Oh dear, Lord! Richard!" Caroline cried. She swung around and ran from the room, her hands lifted to the sides of her face like blinders on a carriage horse.

He'd forgotten to cover himself back up.

As Caroline fled, her aunt Harriet marched in. Behind her trailed a whiskered man wearing a frock coat and carrying a black bag. Richard's pulse rate accelerated. Cold sweat broke out across his brow.

"No." His voice rasped through his dry throat. "Get the hell away from me. Johnny!"

"It's all right, deputy," soothed Caroline's aunt as she stepped beside the bed and lit the lamp. "You're keeping your leg."

Though he struggled to control it, panic raced through his body, pounding against his chest, and temples.

"Where's Johnny?"

"Calm yourself, deputy. The doctor just needs to change the dressing." She leaned over him and pulled the blankets across leaving just his right leg exposed.

His body stiffened, and his hand clenched into a fist as the elderly doctor slowly unwrapped the bandages.

"Amazing," he muttered, as he checked the healing progress and reapplied a new dressing. "I never would have believed it possible."

Richard didn't let himself relax until the doctor closed his black bag and Harriet Walker readjusted the covers.

"Now you just rest," the older woman soothed. "Caroline should be back shortly with your supper tray. I'm sure you must be hungry. If you'll excuse me, I'll see the doctor out." She lightly patted his good leg as if he were a small boy then left with the doctor. He released a long sigh and closed his eyes.

****

"Here we go!" Caroline announced cheerily.

Her voice jarred Richard from a light doze, and he opened his eyes as she entered the room carrying a bed tray. She set it at the foot of the bed then came forward to help him sit up adjusting the pillows behind him.

The aroma of chicken wafted from the bowl and for the first time in a long while he realized he actually felt hungry. Caroline placed the tray across his lap, and he looked eagerly into the steaming bowl of soup before him. He blinked at the contents and swallowed the saliva that instantly pooled around his tongue. He looked up.

A bright pink blush crept up Caroline's cheeks as she spread a large linen napkin over Richard's bare chest. She picked up the silver soup spoon.

"Would you like me to feed you?"

He swallowed several more times, though he hadn't taken so much as a sip.

"Richard?" She queried. "Darling, are you all right?"

"Can't eat this," he croaked.

"Of course you can, darling. It's good for you. Chicken and rice in a nice hearty broth." She dipped the spoon in and brought it to his mouth.

He tried. He really did. He closed his eyes so he wouldn't have to see them, with their tiny white bodies floating beside the bits of chicken.

"Come on darling, open up. You need to build your strength."

He told himself it was only rice. He needed to eat. He opened his mouth. The hot liquid felt wonderful against his dry throat as he swallowed, but he could feel the rice.

She offered him another spoonful. He kept his eyes squeezed tight and swallowed quickly. He swallowed again. Had something squirmed inside his mouth? No. Rice didn't move.

Caroline encouraged him to take more. His leg throbbed. This time he could feel each tiny grain as it slid down the back of his throat. Saliva filled his mouth. He squeezed his hand into a fist around the blanket. Another spoonful. His stump began to tingle. The rice was alive. No. It's only rice. He swallowed it down. His stomach rolled up against the back of his throat.

"Come on, Richard, please try a little more."

He shook his head, afraid to open his mouth to speak. He gulped down more saliva. His stomach lurched. His face broke out in a sweat.

"Richard?"

"Sick," he croaked. "Gonna be sick."

"What?"

But it was too late. He vomited Caroline's soup right back into the bowl. She screeched as it splashed onto her dress.

He dropped back against the pillows panting, his face clammy.

Caroline snatched the napkin off his chest and used it to dab at the spots on her dress, then gave his chin a cursory wipe.

He turned his head and met her stricken gaze. "Sorry," he murmured. "It's the rice. I just can't eat it. Looks like...never mind."

She frowned. "It's all right darling. Would you care to try some tea?"

He nodded. Tea would be good. Johnny's tea always soothed his stomach. Maybe he could eat later, when his insides didn't hurt so bad. Caroline held the cup while he sipped. It didn't have the same bitter taste of Johnny's usual tea, but it felt good sliding down his throat.

"There you go, darling, drink up. Next time I'll strain the rice from the broth." She readjusted the pillows so he could lie down again.

She picked up her needlework and sat in the

chair. "Do you realize there are only four weeks left until our wedding?"

Only four? A low groan escaped his throat, and he dropped his arm over his eyes.

"Richard? Are you feeling all right?"

"Yes." He yawned. "Caroline, how would you feel if we postponed the wedding for a while?"

Just one month ago, he believed marriage to Caroline was the only way to save his sanity. He assumed her innocence and purity the only way to give balance to the evil that lurked inside him. But over the last couple of weeks, Johnny had shown him it wasn't balance he needed, but acceptance of himself, as damaged and confused as he might be.

"Postpone? But I've made so many plans. Besides, you'll be fine by then. Why, has something come up? Won't your brother and his family be able to make it?"

Her words seemed to slur together, and Richard forced his eyes open then rubbed his hand over his face.

"No, he's coming," Richard said. "But James also"—he hesitated, uncertain how to broach the next subject—"expressed concern about me trading my badge and gun for a suit and tie. He's worried I won't like working behind a desk."

She laughed. "Of course you will. Why Papa just loves it."

"But James says his ranch is expanding rapidly, and he'd like to offer me a partnership. How would you feel about moving to Montana? He says it's beautiful open country, with endless blue sky and mountains topped with snow even in summer. We could build our own house, anyway you'd like. I've saved enough money so we—"

Her laughter rose to fill the room. "Oh, Richard, don't be silly. Montana? How positively ridiculous."

His eyelids drifted closed, and he forced them

open again. He wasn't surprised by her response, but some small piece of him was relieved. It proved he wasn't right for her either and eased the guilt he felt at having to break the engagement. He just needed to find the right words. If only it wasn't so hard to think.

"Life will be perfect once you're living here with Papa and me, instead of that dirty, old cabin you share with that other deputy."

"Hollister." He yawned.

"Pardon me?"

"Wade Hollister is the name of the deputy...I share...the cabin with."

"Yes, of course.

He couldn't believe how tired he was. He intended to ask her about Johnny, but Caroline's voice seemed to drift to him from far away.

"You rest now. The laudanum will help."

"No. No laudanum. Not that bad."

"I'm sorry darling, but I put it in your tea. You've already taken it."

He shook his head but couldn't fight the effects of the drug. Caroline slipped from the room, and he drifted into a deep sleep a few moments later.

****

All day, Johnny lay under the porch afraid to move. From inside the house came the voices of an older man and woman. Outside, dogs barked and children ran up and down the street.

Johnny had gone without food before, but the aromas that wafted from the kitchen window that evening set her stomach to rumbling. And while she probably wouldn't have emerged from hiding so soon, she desperately needed some water and, if the cramping she felt in her lower abdomen was any indication of what was to come, some rags.

When all murmurings and creaking floorboards ceased, she crawled from under the small porch.

Shadows swathed the town in black and roof tops gleamed with the pewter luminance of a moon just past full. Even the dogs and cats had ceased their prowling. Mindful of knocking down too many weeds, she moved stiffly, her lower back aching as she headed to the corner of the yard where the man and woman had gone throughout the day to use the outhouse.

Once she'd relieved her bladder, she took a couple of towels from a neighbor's clothesline then returned to the yard, where she sat beneath a tree, and with her small knife, sliced the toweling into a pile of strips. She tossed the loose threads down the outhouse hole so no one would suspect her presence.

When she finished her task, she returned to the porch, intending to crawl underneath again. But the hollow pain in her stomach held her back. She stared longingly at the back door and wondered if she could somehow swipe just one piece of bread.

Setting her pile of rags at the bottom of the stairs, she cautiously mounted each step and tip-toed across the porch. She turned the knob, the door swung open.

Enough moonlight shone through the windows to outline the stove, table, sink, and side-board. Glancing around, she searched for a small room like the one at the Elk House, where Lena Sittel kept her leftover food. To the right of where she entered stood another door. There were no windows in this area on the outside of the house. She hoped this was the right place. The door creaked, but she pushed it wide open, for she needed the moonlight flooding the kitchen to illuminate the long, narrow room.

Inside, a counter ran the length of one wall with drawers below and cupboards above. At the very end, opposite from where she stood, sat a large copper tub. On the wall to her right hung pots and pans, a wash tub, and washboard. The first two cupboards she opened were lined with rows of quart jars; tomatoes, green beans, corn, and peas.

She reached to the very back and eased out a jar of green beans. Next, she spotted a basket of yeast rolls wrapped in a towel. Greedily, she popped an entire roll into her mouth. She stuffed another into her shirt pocket and wrapped them up again.

Half a strawberry-rhubarb pie tempted her next. Johnny rummaged through several drawers before she located a fork. She only intended to eat a narrow slice, but the sweet and sour combination tasted so good, she ate almost a third of what remained in the pan. She opened a crock on the floor at the end of the counter hoping to find pickles and discovered pickled beets instead. Spearing them with her fork, she ate three before her stomach had had enough.

When she finished, she grabbed a glass and stopped at the kitchen pump for several glasses of water, then slipped out the back door.

After hiding under the porch for another day, Johnny raided the pantry again. The next night, there was a plate on the counter with fried chicken, potato salad, and a slice of pie. The night after that, the plate of food was set on the table along with a glass of buttermilk.

The following morning, the back door squeaked open. Heels clicked above her head. As the person came down the steps, the black shoes were visible first, then the hem of a black dress. At the bottom the woman stopped.

"All right," she demanded. "Whoever you are, come out from under my porch."

Afraid the woman would go for the marshal if she didn't do like she said, Johnny crawled out on her hands and knees, bringing with her the woman's dishes and silverware.

The woman stood with her arms crossed over her ample bosom, peering at her through wire rimmed spectacles. Her faded blue eyes assessed Johnny from the top of her head to the toes of her boots.

"Landsakes, look at you."

Not knowing what to say, Johnny gnawed on her lower lip and dropped her gaze to stare at the white puffs of dandelions around the bottom step.

"What's your name?"

"Johnny."

"Johnny, ummm? Run away?"

That seemed as close to the truth as anything. "Yes, ma'am."

The woman seemed to mull this over for a moment. "All right then, get yourself inside and clean up. I'll not have any young lady sitting down to my breakfast table looking like a rag-a-muffin who just crawled from beneath my porch."

Johnny jerked her head up and met the woman's steady gaze. Her answering smile radiated a warmth Johnny wasn't sure how to accept.

"I raised seven girls, all of them a handful. Not much gets by me. We'll have a chat while we eat, and take it from there."

The bath Johnny was forced to endure a few minutes later was wonderful, despite the fact the woman, who introduced herself as Flora Pickens— who, while wielding a bar of lye soap in one hand and a bristle brush in the other—nearly scrubbed the hide right off Johnny's back. Although, once Mrs. Pickens finished, even Johnny was reluctant to don her usual baggy clothes.

"I'll look through some of my things later and see if I can't find a corset to fit you. Meanwhile"— Mrs. Pickens draped a dress over the screen dividing the wooden tub from the rest of the kitchen—"here are some things from my younger days. I'm sure the dress is sadly out of fashion, but I believe it'll fit fair to middlin'."

Johnny pulled on the chemise and drawers. She'd seen her mother wear garments like these, but had never felt such feminine underclothes against her own skin. She traced the bits of eyelet lace along her neckline with a trembling finger then turned each of her legs this way and that, admiring the ruffles around the knees of her drawers. A tingle of excitement raced through her body and she smiled. She already felt like a different person.

The oven door creaked open and banged shut. The aroma of bacon filled the room.

Gnawing her bottom lip, Johnny quickly pulled on the single petticoat Mrs. Pickens had given her and followed it with the dress.

A row of tiny buttons down the front kept her fingers busy as she pushed each cloth-covered orb through its corresponding hole. The collar felt tight around her neck. For a moment, she was tempted to open a few buttons, but she worried that fine ladies didn't loosen their frocks and Mrs. Pickens would think poorly of her for doing so.

Johnny slid her hands down the front of the skirt, smoothing the wrinkles and twirling the width of material from side to side. Tiny violet and dark blue flowers covered the light green fabric and brought to mind the green of the prairie in summer, dotted with blue sage, wind flower, and musk thistle.

From beneath the hem, peeked her bare toes, all pink and squeaky clean. She wondered if she should put her boots back on, but her mother never wore shoes in summer so she reckoned it was more lady-like without them.

"Don't you look lovely," Mrs. Pickens said when Johnny stepped from behind the screen.

Heat flooded her cheekbones at the compliment, and she bit her lip, fighting the sting of tears. She'd never heard herself described as lovely, didn't believe anyone would ever think her pretty.

Would Rab also think her lovely? Would he now regret laughing at the way she said her words, or for believing her to be nothing more than a stupid backlander?

Apparently unaware of her churning emotions, the woman popped muffins from a pan into a cloth-lined basket. Turning, she passed Johnny two potholders and a ceramic pan filled with baked sweet potatoes and bacon.

"Come along, dear." Mrs. Pickens then led the way out of the kitchen, a platter of scrambled eggs and ham in one hand and the basket of muffins in her other. "I'm serving breakfast in the dining room today."

A well-dressed, older man entered the dining room through another door. His hair and goatee were white and a pair of spectacles sat on his nose. A pleasant smile spread across his face.

Mrs. Pickens placed the food on the table. "Johnny," she said gesturing toward the man. "Allow me to introduce my dear brother, Mr. Charles Emory."

Johnny stepped forward, extending her hand for him to shake. "Pleased to meet ya, sir."

He smiled as he gently grasped her fingers instead, and turned her hand, palm down.

"Delighted to meet you, my dear," he said giving her a slight bow.

"And, Charles," Mrs. Pickens continued. "Allow me to present to you, Miss Johnny, the young lady who has been living under the porch."

"Unusual name for a girl. And do you have a last name?"

Johnny glanced at the rose pattern on the carpet. She didn't want to go back to jail, nor did she want to lie to these nice people. "Lee," she said, meeting his gaze. "Johnny Lee."

Charles Emory raised his bushy eyebrows and

looked past her toward his sister. When he said nothing more, Johnny breathed a sigh of relief. Then as Mr. Emory stepped around her, to pull out a chair for his sister, Johnny sat herself in the opposite chair.

Mrs. Pickens gave her a slight frown. "My dear, when a gentleman is present a lady always waits to be seated."

Johnny stared at the flowers painted around the outside of the pretty white dishes. She wasn't sure why it mattered when she sat, but she stored away the information so she wouldn't make the same mistake again. Mr. Emory prayed a blessing then passed her the basket of muffins.

They were so moist, Johnny ate one before she learned there was fresh butter in the crock, something she hadn't had in years. When she spread it across her second muffin and it melted, she didn't think food could taste any better.

"My sister tells me you claim to have run away from home," Mr. Emory began. "Do you mind my asking, why?"

Johnny set her fork down and twisted her fingers in her lap as she tried to decide which pieces of the truth to share. "Well, after my maw died, my paw, he come an' drug me off to the hind end of creation to live with him. It weren't too bad, ceptin' fer paw's brother, Uncle Cal. Wunst he learnt I weren't no boy, well he reckoned on a-keepin' me fer his own sinful pleasures."

Mrs. Pickens gasped, "Oh dear Lord, in Heaven." Her sagging face paled.

Johnny seemed to have shocked Mr. Emory as well, for he stared at her wide-eyed for several seconds. "Did he..." He cleared his throat. "Did he..."

She took pity on him and shook her head. "Naw, he was a-fixin' to, but he got shot through the head afore he could do anything."

Mrs. Pickens squeaked and clamped her hand across her mouth.

Mr. Emory breathed deep and squared his shoulders. "We must all thank the Lord that through his divine intervention you were spared from enduring such an unconscionable act."

She wondered how Rab would feel knowing these people thought him God's divine indi-ven-shun, especially since he believed God hated him.

When the meal ended, she offered to do the dishes. Mrs. Pickens agreed, and she and her brother sat in the front parlor room talking. When Johnny finished, they invited her to join them.

Chewing on her lip, she perched on the edge of a large upholstered chair and ran her hand back and forth over the fabric until her palms burned.

"Johnny," Mr. Emory began. "Let me share with you a bit of our situation. Eight months ago, my brother-in-law, Flora's husband, Harold, passed away. My sister had thought to stay on here alone but found herself unable to maintain a house this size. Through correspondence we decided she would sell the house and come to live with me.

"I have a large home in St. Louis, where I teach English Literature at the Cresswell Acadamy for Young Gentlemen. My own wife died several years ago, and I have found myself longing for simple conversation at the end of the day. Flora also plans to act as my hostess for any faculty dinners or holiday parties.

"I say this only because we would like to offer you an opportunity for temporary employment. This house has sold, and Flora needs to be out by the end of the month. I arrived last week to help her pack. But for the two of us the task has proven to be a bit more than we can handle. If you want to stay and help, we will pay you a small sum when we are finished.

"And if things work out amicably, we can discuss the possibility of your coming with us, to companion Flora as she moves about the city. Since her own daughters are grown, tutoring you in the finer points of being a lady will occupy her days and, in turn, perhaps groom you for a suitor and eventually marriage."

Johnny's gaze shot from Mr. Emory to Mrs. Pickens and back again. They watched her, waiting for her to answer, but she had no idea what to say.

"Ya want to give me money fer a-helpin' ya pack up yer things?"

"I'm certain the task will be far more arduous than you suppose and will entail sorting through the many trunks in the attic. And yes, aside from the moving of heavy furniture, we would like to pay you for your help."

"Well, hell, ya aint got to give me no money, no how. After all the vittles I ate, I'd surely admire to help ya."

Mr. Emory leaned back in his chair and steepled his fingers. "*Thou hast spoken no word all this while. Nor understood none neither, sir.*" A soft smile warmed his expression as he lifted his gaze to meet hers across the room.

"Love's Labour's Lost, Act five, scene one. I apologize, my dear, for spouting Shakespeare in the middle of our discussion, but your marvelous Elizabethan, double negatives have brought to life the poetic beauty of Old English."

She blinked, understanding him "none neither." But from the way he grinned at her like a mule in a thistle patch, she couldn't help but smile back as she realized, this wonderful, fancy dressed man liked the way she talked. He was a teacher, yet he didn't laugh or call her stupid.

She swung her gaze to Mrs. Pickens who, ignoring her brother continued the conversation.

"...the sum we are offering will be small, so proper room and board will be included."

Johnny nodded her agreement. All she'd known her entire life was stolen property and stolen money. If she wanted something she took it. The idea of earning lawful money of her very own sent a tingle straight to her toes. She hopped to her feet and extended her hand to Mr. Emory.

The old man rose with a smile spread across his face and reached out to grasp her palm in his.

"I reckon we got us a deal, Mr. Emory, sir." She gave his hand a quick shake.

He laughed. "Yes, Johnny, I believe we do.

****

Richard slept most of the next two days. Caroline continued to dose him with laudanum, and he was powerless to stop her. He tried to learn what had become of Johnny, but Caroline repeatedly put him off. Johnny was taking a walk. Johnny was eating in the kitchen. Anything to appease him long enough to eat his next meal and subsequently consume his next dose of laudanum.

But this morning when Caroline brought his breakfast, Richard feigned sleep. It had been difficult to suppress his moans when that clumsy doctor visited to change his dressing. Even now he had to relieve himself so bad he thought his bladder would explode. But if Caroline followed her usual routine, she would soon set aside her needlepoint to have lunch with her father when he returned from his office at noon.

Eventually, she rose from the rocking chair. She stood beside the bed for several long moments.

"Sleep well, Richard," she whispered. "I shall return shortly."

He waited to be sure she wouldn't come back then tossed aside the covers and eased his legs over the edge of the bed. While he'd been sleeping that first day, someone, probably Mrs. Walker, had dressed him in a night shirt. The garment was too tight and too short, obviously one of Benton Caldwell's cast offs, and Richard detested it.

While he waited for the dizziness in his head to clear and his rolling stomach to settle, he wondered if Caroline would ever be comfortable with his naked form. Vaguely, he remembered how she averted her eyes from having to look at the ugly scar tissue on the end of his left arm, when she brought the rice soup the first day. She even used to flinch, if he accidentally bumped her with that arm when he was fully clothed.

Damn what was he going to do? He was supposed to marry her. Well, the first thing he needed to do was get out of bed and start moving. Maybe then she would bring him something heartier than laudanum and soup.

He stood, careful to keep his weight off his leg. The room spun and tilted. Without thinking, he stepped down on his right foot to keep from falling. White-hot agony shot up his leg like a lightning bolt. He sucked in a gulp of air. The room tilted wildly in the other direction. He reached out to grab the bed post, but missed, and he crashed to the floor.

"Well, hell," he murmured when the world had ceased spinning, and he opened his eyes to find himself looking under the bed. "At least I found the chamber pot."

By the time Caroline returned, all he'd managed to do was lever himself back up to sit on the edge of the bed where he started.

"Richard! Merciful heavens, what are you doing?" Caroline set the tray on the chest of drawers and rushed to his side. "You are far too weak to get out of bed." She eased him back against the pillows.

He offered no resistance because he found himself exhausted. He hated not being stronger and resented Caroline for pointing it out.

"I need to start getting up."

"Oh no," Caroline began, plumping his pillows. "Dr. Winters recommends two weeks of bed rest and you've only been here five days."

Five days! "I'm not staying in this damn bed for two weeks."

She gasped. "Richard, please. Your language."

He closed his eyes as his head sank into the pillows. He hated lying around or being fussed over.

"Sorry."

"I forgive you." She drew up the covers and smoothed out the wrinkles. "I understand. You've been very ill. You are not yourself. Now, I'm sure you must be hungry. You didn't eat any breakfast. How about a nice bowl of beef broth?"

"I don't want any more of your damn broth. I want meat. How the hell am I ever going to get my strength back when all you feed me is laudanum and soup?"

"Richard, please. You are becoming overset." She turned to retrieve the luncheon tray from the dresser. "You must remember it was only four days ago that you were unable to even hold down my soup."

He scowled. "Only because your damn soup had maggots in it."

"Richard, I am trying to make allowances because you've been so ill, but I cannot bear much more of your vulgar profanities." She set the tray on his lap and tucked the napkin into the collar of his night shirt.

Frustrated, he reached up and snatched her wrist away. "Will you please stop all this fussing. I can take care of my own damn napkin."

Caroline let out a small squeak and jumped back. She held her wrist to her breast and rubbed it with her other hand.

"I'm sorry, Richard. I was only trying to help." Her small voice trembled.

He closed his eyes and blew out a ragged breath. He was an ass. "No, Caroline, I'm the one who should apologize. There's no reason for me to take out my frustration on you. I'm sorry."

She hung back for a minute then asked tentatively, "Would you like me to feed you?"

"Caroline, I can feed myself. I appreciate your concern, and all you've done for me, but please stop fussing."

"I-I'm sorry, Richard." She hovered by the bed for a minute, irritating him even more by standing there with her hands clasped at her waist. "Is there anything else I can get for you?"

"How about some soap and water? Maybe a wash and shave would improve my mood." He took a few sips of tea.

Caroline brightened. "Yes, that's an excellent idea, and since your beard has gotten so thick perhaps we could begin shaping some nice chin whiskers like Papa's."

"I've told you, I don't like a beard."

"And that's fine for the job you have now, out among the savages and riff raff. But once you start working for Papa in the prosecutor's office, you'll need to present yourself in a manner that is more prestigious and refined."

"Leave my face the hell alone and stop trying to turn me into a replica of your father."

She gasped at his new outburst and withdrew another step.

Immediately, he regretted exposing her fragile spirit to the ugly monster that lived inside him. Feeling so much older than his thirty years, he blew out a ragged breath as he shoved down his demon and pushed it back into its dark corner.

"Forgive me," he apologized. "I don't know what

came over me. No doubt too much time out among, 'the savages and riff raff.'"

"I-I'm sorry, darling." Tears filled her blue eyes. "You can keep your face just the way you like it. I'll get the water. After you wash up and have a nice nap you'll feel more yourself."

Richard drew a deep breath and let it out slowly, rather than yell at her again. He hated the way she talked down to him, like he was a small boy. Had she always treated him like this? Why hadn't he noticed before?

Then something she'd said captured his attention. His eyes narrowed on the empty bowl of soup and the half-full cup of tea. "Caroline, you didn't put laudanum in my food again did you?" But even as he asked the question he knew. A heavy lethargy had already settled into his limbs.

"God damn you." With a clumsy sweep of his arm, he sent the whole tray of dishes crashing to the floor. Caroline screamed and ran from the room. Her sobs receded down the hallway as his eyes drifted closed.

Chapter Sixteen

When Richard next opened his eyes, deep shadows filled the corners of the room. Thanks to Caroline he'd slept away the entire afternoon. His mouth felt like someone had wiped it out with cotton. He turned his head looking for the pitcher of water. He was somewhat surprised to find Hollister in the rocking chair, reading the newspaper, his ankle atop his opposite knee. The lamp light cast one side of the deputy's face in darkness. The newspaper rustled.

"So, Miss Caldwell finally learned what a sorry sonofabitch you really are." Hollister folded the paper and laid it on the table.

"Do you think I could get some water before you lecture me?"

"Sure." The deputy rose and poured half a glass of water from the pitcher. He passed it down to Richard who eyed it dubiously.

"No laudanum?"

Hollister shook his head. "Is that what this is all about?"

Richard gulped the water then passed back the glass. He flopped against the pillows and threw his arm over his eyes. "I can't marry Caroline."

"What's the matter? Cold feet?" Hollister asked from the direction of the chair. "The girl has been steadfastly by your side since we brought you in. And today you decide you can't marry her. Forgive me, Bennick, but I don't follow. What'd she do?"

"She's always fussing."

"Well that's reason enough right there. Fussing.

Of all the nerve."

"Go to hell, you don't understand."

"You're right. I don't understand. I never did. When I was a kid, my folks would dress me up for church. I was always on my best behavior because if I wasn't my pa would take a switch to my backside when we got home. And that preacher and his wife always told my folks what a sweet, well behaved boy I was. But that was only at Sunday service and church socials. They never saw me throw rocks at my sisters, or steal my ma's pies, or toss chickens off the barn roof.

"You've always been so proper and well behaved around Caroline, I wondered how you managed it for so long, or if Caroline had ever met you when you weren't dressed for church."

"She did today."

"I figured, when I got here and found her crying in Mrs. Walker's arms then saw the mess you made in here."

"She's always giving me laudanum. I think she likes being my nurse, but doesn't want to deal with me when I'm awake. I'm beginning to think she would have been happier if they'd taken my leg."

The rocking chair grated against the wood floor as it tipped back and forth, but Hollister said nothing.

"It's the same with this damn nightshirt." Richard grabbed a fist full of the fabric and lifted it away from his chest. "She doesn't want to risk seeing me as a man. She enjoys treating me like a little boy."

"Caroline is a genteel lady. You know that. Seeing you in all your glory the other day probably shocked her sensibilities."

"And my arm. She always keeps it covered up so she doesn't have to see how ugly it is."

"If it's as ugly as the rest of you, it's probably

best."

Richard ignored him. "She always notices my arm isn't there."

"We all notice that."

He sighed. "I know." A half smile tugged back the left corner of his mouth. "Except for Johnny," he said softly. "Johnny sees an arm where there is none."

"So what are you going to do? You obviously can't marry Johnny, and Caroline has been by your side since we brought you in more dead than alive."

Richard scratched his chest. He could have sworn Johnny had been here with him, curled beside him in this bed. The damn laudanum had him so addled he wasn't sure which memories were real.

"Caroline was with me the whole time?" He turned toward Hollister.

"Well, the first couple of days she was crying in the parlor. But once your fever broke—"

"What the hell happened to your face?" Richard exclaimed, noticing for the first time the row of stitches along Hollister's right cheek.

"That little outlaw you're so fond of sliced it open on Sunday morning with a broken dish. Nine stitches."

Richard couldn't help himself. He laughed; loud and hard and long. He laughed until his ribs ached and it hurt to breathe. And it felt wonderful.

Hollister drew himself up indignantly. "I sure as hell don't think it's funny. Look at the scar I'm going to have."

"I'm sorry," Richard chuckled. "But I've been hit, kicked, bit, shot, cussed at, and traveled half way across Indian Territory with a band of outlaws who wanted me dead, and that's not even the half of it."

"He also sent me sailing across the kitchen."

Richard laughed again. "How the hell did you manage to get Johnny so riled?"

"Reeves and I were trying to catch him after he punched Caroline in the jaw and knocked her senseless."

"Johnny punched Caroline?" Richard asked incredulous. "Why?"

"I'm not sure. Caroline was making you soup and Johnny said something about you not eating it because the rice was disgusting. Then Caroline called Johnny a disgusting brush-ape, and Johnny hit her."

"That's my Johnny." He grinned.

"Now that I think about it," Hollister continued. "Johnny might have gotten riled earlier, when he referred to you as Rab. Caroline called him stupid and told him your name was Richard."

"What?" Richard shot upright in bed. He threw aside the covers and struggled to shift himself to the edge of the mattress. "Caroline can be so damn thoughtless."

Hollister was out of the rocker in an instant, his hand pressed firmly against Richard's shoulder. "Hold up, you're not going anywhere."

"Let me go, Wade. I've got to find Johnny." Richard pushed him away and swung his legs over the edge of the mattress. "Where are my pants?"

"Your pants?" Hollister echoed dumbly, stepping back.

Richard stood, swaying slightly as the room swirled around him. "Yes, damn it. My pants. I've got to find Johnny. Caroline has no idea how cruel her remarks can be."

"Uh, Rich," Hollister began hesitantly. "Johnny's gone."

Richard felt the blood drain from his face. The floor tilted, but he looped his arm around the bedpost before he toppled to the floor. "Gone? What do you mean gone?"

"The kid took off the morning he cut my face,

and no one's been able to find him. He's probably half way to Mexico by now. Any deputy going on scout in the Territory will keep an eye out for him, but so far no one has heard a word."

"That warrant is a mistake. Johnny wasn't part of that gang."

"What are you talking about? He was identified at several stage robberies. He matches the description on the warrant you had in your saddlebags. If it wasn't Johnny, who was it? Besides, the kid never denied it was him. He only said that he was helping you so you'd put in a good word for him with Judge Parker."

"Damn it, Hollister, it was more than just 'help,' can't anyone see that? Johnny saved my life then helped me bring in six prisoners when I could barely fork my horse."

"I'm sorry, Bennick, I truly am. You went through hell out there and I can understand how close you got to that kid. There is something likeable about him I hate to admit, in spite of what he did to my face."

A brief grin tugged at the side of Hollister's mouth which wasn't swollen. "You should have seen him when the doctor wanted to amputate your leg. He stole Bass's gun right out of his holster then pointed it at the doc. He fought for you like a wolverine taking on a grizzly bear. He had us all believing you would live, even when the doc said there was no hope left.

"Parker's been by every day to see how you are. He knows what Johnny did, but the kid is gone and there's not much we can do, except to go out, hunt him down, and bring him back."

His thigh muscles trembling, Richard dropped to sit on the edge of the mattress. In four short weeks, Johnny had become so important to him he could no longer imagine living his life without her. She wouldn't have gone far, but where?

"I've got to get dressed."

"Bennick, slow down. It's the middle of the night, and you're so weak you're about to fall on your face."

"I'll be fine, but if you don't get me my clothes, I'll look for Johnny dressed like this."

"Don't be a fool. Now lay down, we've got more important things to talk about."

Richard fixed his gaze on his friend. He was amazed by how these brief moments standing had drained all his energy. "What things?"

"We need to talk about what happened out there." Hollister rose. "Stop being stubborn and let me help you."

Once Richard was tucked back under the covers and propped up against the pillows, Hollister returned to his chair and continued.

"Brady is dead, and so are a driver and two guards. Bodine and Everett have been killed, plus how many wounded? You know Parker, if even one prisoner is killed he wants the death investigated. And I don't know what you did to rile Caldwell, but from the way he's been stomping around downstairs, I don't think you'll need to worry about being engaged much longer."

"So that's why you're here? You want my statement?"

"Sure." He picked up a small notepad and pencil from the bedside table. "While it's fresh, tell me what you remember."

Richard blew out a long sigh and stared at the circle of lamp light on the ceiling. "I can't."

"What?" Disbelief laced Hollister's voice.

"I can't remember." Richard drove his fingers into his hair, shoving the hair off his forehead.

Hollister tipped the rocker forward and braced his forearms on his thighs. "What do you mean, you can't remember?"

"I can't remember, Wade. It's all a mix of images that don't make any sense."

"What are you talking about?"

Richard turned his gaze toward Hollister. "I mean some things are blurred together with what happened to me a long time ago, and in other places chunks of time are missing from my memory."

The other man remained quiet for several long seconds, then he slowly rose from the chair and stood beside the bed. "You damn well better start remembering. Those prisoners we brought in will be asked what they know about it. And you sure as hell don't want that. Parker has always liked you, but you know he holds us to a higher authority. If you can't explain what happened, Caldwell will take the investigation to the Grand Jury."

Richard draped his arm across his eyes, but it did little to block the jumble of painful images which filled his mind, or erase the memory of how he last saw Brady, lying in the grass, covered in blood.

God, he needed a drink.

****

The next morning, before the rooster in the neighbor's yard had even crowed, Benton Caldwell shoved open the bedroom door and marched straight up to Richard's bed.

"I am withdrawing my consent for a marriage between you and my daughter." He gave the bottom of his suit coat a sharp tug, emphasizing his announcement. "My sister, Mrs. Walker, will be seeing to your needs until you are strong enough to leave this house."

Richard opened his mouth and took a breath poised to disagree but thought better of the idea and snapped it shut. He no longer wanted the marriage, so why argue?

"I always believed my daughter could do better

than a deputy marshal, but Caroline wanted you, so I have tried to be accommodating. I ignored your poor financial condition and provided you a job opportunity which would allow you to be home every night instead of gallivanting across the Nations for months at a time, leaving Caroline home alone, anxious and afraid.

"I even tried to excuse that unholy display of debauchery my sister and I witnessed on Sunday past, by reminding myself how ill you were and that the incident only occurred because that young rapscallion of an outlaw, had taken advantage of you in your weakness."

Richard shoved back his hair and rubbed at the ache growing just above his left eye. What was the man talking about? Had Richard done something to Johnny while he was out of his head with fever? Was that the reason she'd run off? Why couldn't he remember?

"But since then, your constant inquiries into the young outlaw's whereabouts have given me reason to believe that something went on out there between the two of you, so horrendous, I dare not contemplate its evil. Aside from that, serious questions have been raised regarding your conduct as a lawman in the Nations. These things, coupled with your blatant disregard for my innocent daughter's sensibilities, your rudeness and outbursts of violence, have over the last few days shown me your true character as a man."

Richard blew out a sigh of relief. He almost laughed. Caldwell thought him a Sodomite. In some perverse way, Richard found it amusing to let him go on believing it. He never liked the man, and now he wondered why in the world he ever thought marrying into this family was a good idea.

Somehow Johnny, with her simple, pragmatic acceptance of life, and of him, had shown him that

269

he didn't need Caroline, or her innocence, to balance the evil in his soul. There was no evil, only guilt, and for now, not remembering was okay.

Caldwell drew himself up indignantly. His cheekbones splotched with red above his beard. "I do not find this to be funny."

Richard hadn't realized he was smiling. But Johnny did that to him. She wasn't even here and he was laughing.

"I want you out of my house." He whirled on his heels and strode from the room, pulling the door closed with a slam that rattled the window.

****

Without the numbing effects of laudanum, Richard felt strong enough to leave the Caldwell house the next morning. Hollister arrived with a buggy to transport him and his belongings back to the cabin they shared on the outskirts of town.

Conversation between them was minimal, and it crossed Richard's mind to wonder if Caldwell had shared his suspicions with Hollister, because as soon as Richard was settled, Wade left the cabin without a word. Losing Hollister's good opinion should have mattered, but all Richard cared about was finding Johnny.

Restless energy had him pacing the length of the cabin despite the ache in his leg. She wouldn't have gone far. And with her skill as a pick-pocket, if she did find a place to hole-up, she could probably survive quite a while right here in Fort Smith.

He grabbed his hat and stepped onto the porch. How long could she hide before she was caught—caught and sent to jail? If she was in trouble, she certainly wouldn't seek him out for help. Especially believing he had betrayed her then laughed at her behind her back.

He stepped off the porch and started toward the road. If only he knew where she was, he'd make her understand that while she made him laugh, he never once laughed at her—he loved her.

He would talk to Judge Parker and make him understand how much Johnny did to bring in the prisoners. Caldwell would have to drop the charges. Once Johnny was free, Richard would ask her to marry him. He'd take her to Montana. Johnny wanted to be part of a family and that was one thing he could give her.

He limped along the narrow road until the ache in his leg radiated into pain and sweat beaded his brow. He turned around and sighed, disappointed to see the cabin less than a quarter mile away. By the time he made it inside, he could barely stand. Exhausted, he fell across his bunk and closed his eyes.

****

A bullet slammed into the tree beside him, shattering chips of bark against his ear. He dropped to his stomach behind a decaying log and took aim at the Rebs positioned on the high ground in front of him. He propped the barrel of his Sharps on the log and focused on the muzzle flashes. He held his breath and squeezed the trigger. Again, he waited for the muzzle flash and fired.

"Stop! No, stop!"

Richard jerked awake, covered in sweat. His heart pounded as loud as the gunfire which reverberated in his head. He rolled to sit on the edge of his bed, and with a shaky hand shoved his damp hair off his forehead. He drew a deep breath then limped across the room to the pie safe along the wall near the table. Reaching up, his fingers stretched behind a tin of flour then closed around the narrow neck of a bottle.

The pulse throbbing wildly against his jaw seemed to slow just by looking at the golden liquid and the familiar black bird on the label. He set the bottle on the table and pried free the cork. He'd hoped he could manage the monster—that darkness inside himself—without the bourbon, but without Johnny he couldn't face the memories. Tipping the bottle to his lips, he swallowed one quick gulp and sighed. It slid down his throat as smooth as ever.

He replaced the cork and set the bottle aside. Limping back to his bunk, he thought he'd kill some time cleaning his guns. Hollister had dropped all Richard's belongs from the Caldwell house on the floor in front of the bedside table. Richard sat on the edge of his bunk and leaned forward. Lifting aside his rain slicker and bedroll, he spotted his saddle bags, but instead of reaching for them, his fingers closed around the soft doeskin strap of Johnny's beaded bag.

He kicked off his boots and scooted back to lean against the log wall. Pressing the bag into his face, he closed his eyes and inhaled—deerskin and herbs—the essence of Johnny. He drew another breath, savoring the blend of scents as they filled his nose and drifted down to erase the lingering taste of bourbon.

Where the hell was she? He lowered the bag to his lap and removed her book of drawings. Flipping through the pages, it was easy to see the gentleness of Johnny's nature in the delicate turn of each leaf and petal she'd drawn. When he came to the section related to gunshot wounds, the pages were worn and smudged. He swallowed the lump that rose in his throat. They'd gone through hell out there together, and she never once complained.

"Damn fool, lawman."

He smiled—well, except about him.

"Hell, Rab, iffin ya wasn't as stubborn as a Missouri mule…"

He rubbed his aching leg. God, he hated sitting here doing nothing when she was out there somewhere, lost and afraid. With a yawn, he lowered himself to the pillow and fell sound asleep.

****

"What do you have to say about this?" Marshal Upham asked the next morning as he slid a folder filled with papers across his desk toward Richard. "You know Parker, he holds all you deputies to a pretty high moral standard, and he won't tolerate any abuse of that authority. He wants these deaths investigated and resolved before those men you brought in go on trial. We need you as a creditable witness."

Reluctantly, Richard leaned forward and opened the file. As he suspected, the words, Investigation into the Death of U.S. Deputy Marshal Martin Brady, were written across the top. The other men were listed on subsequent pages, Tyler, Miles, the skinny cook, and Hobbs.

"Hobbs is fine, sir. I last saw him in McAlester. Hollister and Reeves should have talked to him when they passed through."

Upham made a note on a piece of paper. "Can you tell me what happened to Brady? It's been a few days since you talked to Hollister. Remember anything more?"

"No, sir. It's like I told Wade, there are gaps, and the images I do remember are mixed together with battles from the war, and I can't tell which is which."

"Well, do you remember how you were wounded?"

"It was an accident. Johnny tripped and the gun went off."

"And how did a prisoner happen to gain possession of this gun?"

Richard leaned back in the leather chair and rubbed his forehead. It all seemed so long ago. Strange to think it had been less than a month. The woods were dark and thick with gun smoke. He'd been hiding behind a log shooting at muzzle flashes. No. That was wrong. His pulse thrummed wildly against the base of his jaw. *Don't think about it. Don't think about it.*

Bodies lay slumped beneath trees, curled in brush and bent over logs. From everywhere, they accused him, their chests soaked in blood, their eyes vacant and wide. Brady, Tyler, Sergeant Boyle. Inside his head his own voice rang out, ordering Johnny to shoot him, to put him out of his misery, while he advanced on her and she begged him to stay back.

His stomach churned and sweat popped out across his brow. Even now the guilt still lingered. He'd done something, something very bad, he just didn't know what. He didn't want to think about it, but Brady was dead, and he had a feeling it was his fault.

God, he needed a drink.

"Bennick?"

Richard blinked and blew out a shaky breath. Upham had asked a question. What was it?

"Deputy, I think this is too much for you right now."

"I'm fine, it's just hot in here."

"No, you don't look well. Go home, get some rest, and we'll talk again in a couple of days. Meantime, you may want to hire yourself an attorney. If this goes to the grand jury, he can have Hobbs and Johnny Bodine subpoenaed. I'll send as many deputies out to find them as I have to." Upham stood and stepped around his desk.

Richard rose and they shook hands.

"Now don't worry, deputy," Marshal Upham said as they walked to the office door. "You've been very ill. Just give it time. The memories will come back to you."

Richard said good-bye and limped down the hallway. That's what he was afraid of.

Outside, he mounted his horse and sat, his gaze captured by the gallows on the south side of the parade grounds.

The platform rose seven feet high, just enough to keep a man's feet from touching the ground when the lever was pulled. A twelve foot beam supported by heavy timbers, ran the width of the floor, and was strong enough to allow six men to simultaneously drop to their deaths.

Although hangings attracted hundreds of people who camped out near the grounds and brought picnic lunches, Richard had never watched an execution. He'd seen too much of the reality of life to find death entertaining.

How would it feel to stand up there, looking out across a crowd of gawking spectators? Would he choose to wear the hood, or would he stare defiantly over the tops of their heads as the weight of the finest hemp was dropped around his neck.

He could almost imagine the prick of the fibers pressing into his Adam's apple as the well oiled hemp was pulled snug. He swallowed against the imaginary pressure. The knot would lay heavy behind his left ear, in the hollow of his jaw bone. Then when the trap opened, and his body shot down, the rope would snap taut and break his neck.

The hangman, George Maledon, once told Richard that he had never preformed a "bad" hanging. He had a trick when positioning the rope so men didn't strangle, thrashing and kicking until they died.

Richard tightened his grip on the reins. Would hanging be his fate if he couldn't remember; if Johnny couldn't be found? Though he struggled daily to do right, maybe in the end, this had always been his destiny.

He shook away the images and headed his horse through the gate. More than thirty saloons populated the busy river town. He trotted Billy toward one of the finest. The hitching rail was full, so he tied his horse across the street in front of a dry goods store then he went inside to grab a drink and buy a bottle.

A few minutes later, as he shoved the bourbon into his saddle bag, two women came down the walk, and stopped to look through the front window.

"Oh, what a pretty locket," the woman in green said to her companion.

"My mother had one like it except hers was engraved with roses," the friend replied.

They chatted for a few moments then moved on down the board walk.

His interest piqued by the word "locket", Richard stepped to the window and peered through the glass. A small, cloth covered table held a display of ladies items; gloves, combs, a silver hair brush, a music box, and a silver locket on a chain. Unable to help himself he went inside and asked the clerk to see it.

"This piece is solid, sterling silver, it's not silver plated," the clerk stated as he peered at Richard over the top of his spectacles.

Richard held the locket in his palm and ran his thumb back and forth over the design. Somehow just holding it connected him to Johnny, and for the first time today, he didn't feel quite so alone.

"Hand engraved. Notice the extra bright polish."

Richard nodded.

The man leaned close. "If you open it, you will see a number stamped inside. That tells you this is a one of a kind piece. Your special lady can be sure no one else will have a locket like this."

"How much?" Not that he cared. He had to have it.

"As I explained this is crafted of the finest quality and—"

"I'll take it." He turned and limped to the cash register at the back of the store, leaving the babbling clerk to hurry after him. He traced the design one more time before the clerk dropped it into a little velvet bag and wrapped it up.

Taking the tiny package, Richard slipped it beneath his vest into his shirt pocket and left the store. He felt better just keeping it close, and until he found Johnny, it might just bring him good luck.

Chapter Seventeen

Sun beat down on Richard's shoulders a few days later. He stood before a large white house just two blocks north of Benton Caldwell's home. Suspended from a post, hung a white sign with the words, Evan Stewart, Attorney at Law. Below the lettering, a red arrow pointed toward a stone path which disappeared around the side of the house.

Richard had been cross-examined by this lawyer many times and had talked to him briefly whenever they met at the courthouse. Funny how he'd always planned to hire the man to represent Johnny.

He limped along the path and climbed the steps of the side porch. Maybe he should just lie, create a story to fill in the gaps and be done with it. After all, he was a U.S. Deputy Marshal. It was his word against theirs. But he was a U.S. Deputy Marshal and U. S. Deputy Marshal Richard Bennick did not commit perjury.

He drew a deep breath and rapped his knuckles against the wood. A moment later the door opened, and a balding man in a rumpled suit gestured him inside.

"Good to see you up and around, deputy." He pushed his spectacles up his nose and extended his hand.

Richard's hand enveloped the lawyer's soft palm as he grasped it in a firm shake. "Thank you."

They entered a large room to the right of the side entry. Floor to ceiling shelves were crammed with books and periodicals. A large desk, overflowing with thick legal tomes and files, held a position near the single window. Evan Stewart gestured toward a long table in the corner, covered with more books and piles of papers. Richard waited as Stewart shoved aside the clutter at the end of the table and lifted a large orange cat off one of the chairs.

Smiling, Richard sat down and extended his leg underneath. Stewart snatched a pencil and several sheets of blank paper off his desk and carried them to the now cat-free seat. He pushed his spectacles up the bridge of his nose and met Richard's gaze across the table.

"What can I do for you, deputy?" The cat jumped into the old man's lap. He scratched the animal under the jaw as Richard related his story. Aside from an occasional, "Hmmm," and "Uh huh," Stewart said nothing until Richard asked if the man could represent him.

"Of course I will, young man. Fine morals, always by the book. I never could shake you in a cross-examination. Integrity. Always liked that about you. Now..." He shoved the cat to the floor and grabbed a sheet of paper. Pencil in hand, he scribbled a few notes.

Richard rubbed his thigh. "The problem is I can't remember what happened. And I can't see how anything I say will stop Caldwell from going to the Grand Jury."

"Let's not get ahead of ourselves." He shoved up his glasses again. "First, we'll do as the marshal advised and see if we can't locate this man Hobbs, and of course Johnny Bodine. If we're lucky their statements will fill in the blanks, confirm your innocence, and we'll be done with this."

Richard wasn't sure how much Hobbs knew, and he didn't think Johnny would be easily found. Something of his skepticism must have been reflected in his face, for Stewart offered him a reassuring smile.

"Don't worry, deputy, if worse comes to worse and this goes to trial, we'll enter a plea of not guilty. Your law enforcement credentials are impeccable. And you have an exemplary record of arrests, not only as a deputy marshal, but as a detective for the railroad.

"These men in the jail, have not only had ample time to conspire their story, they have obviously done so with bias. Nor is there a credible witness among them. I'll file a motion that their testimony be inadmissible because of their prejudice."

Stewart made a few more notes and set down his pencil. Folding his hands, he leaned forward and looked at Richard over the top of his spectacles.

"Don't worry. We'll use plenty of reputable character witnesses. Then we'll play up your injury and remind the jury how ill you were. If there are gaps in your memory they'll understand. We'll keep you off the stand so Caldwell can't exacerbate your blackouts and create any doubt in the jurors' minds that you could have done this. Meantime, don't leave town."

Though Evan Stewart sounded confident and reassuring, Richard remained skeptical. And when he stepped outside a shadow moved across the bottom steps and side walk. Looking up, a single black cloud drifted across the sky to block the sun, then appeared to follow him as he left the house and walked to his horse.

****

"Come along, Violet," Mrs. Pickens called from the bottom of the stairs.

Johnny reached out to trace one of the roses which decorated the wall paper of the bedroom she'd been using since she arrived. She'd never had a room of her own, and this one was so pretty, and bigger than their whole cabin back home. Her fist clenched around the handles of a small satchel, and she gave the now empty room one last look. The heels of her new shoes clicked loudly against the floor of the hallway and echoed through the house as she descended each tread of the staircase.

The packed trunks and odd pieces of furniture Mrs. Pickens had chosen to keep had been freighted to St. Louis already. The remaining household goods and furnishings had been sold at auction yesterday.

Mrs. Pickens turned from the doorway of the parlor at Johnny's entrance. A sheen of tears glazed the old woman's eyes. This was the same cozy room Johnny had sat in just two weeks ago; now its warmth was gone.

"Sure do hate a-leavin'," Johnny said as she glanced longingly around the empty foyer. "I reckon this here's the grandest house I ever seen."

She followed Flora Pickens onto the porch. Mr. Emory locked the door and checked the latch one last time.

"Where is your bonnet?" Flora asked, dabbing her eyes with her handkerchief.

Johnny frowned for a moment then dropped to sit on the front step. Rummaging through the satchel, she muttered, "Now where the hell did I put that damn thing?"

Mrs. Pickens heaved a weighted sigh. "Please don't swear, dear."

Johnny pulled a blue bonnet from her bag, set it on her head and tied the ribbon under her chin. "Sorry, ma'am, I'm a-tryin' not to."

With a grin on his face, Mr. Emory put the key in his pocket and stepped toward the edge of the porch as though on a stage. "'Now might I do it pat, now 'a is a-praying.'"

"Oh, good Lord, Charles," Mrs. Pickens exclaimed. "Will you please stop quoting Chaucer every time this poor girl says something."

"I was quoting Shakespeare. Hamlet, to be more precise."

"Charles, please," she argued as she brushed past him on her way down the steps. "You undermine everything I'm trying to teach the girl. I don't care if Moses himself taught her to speak. Ladies and gentlemen no longer speak Old English, and we do Violet a disservice to encourage it."

Charles handed his sister into the waiting buggy.

Mrs. Pickens had given Johnny the name Violet after she agreed to help them.

"Johnny is such a masculine name," Flora had said. "I thought maybe we could call you Violet, for your beautiful eyes."

Johnny didn't much like the name, after all she'd been called Johnny her whole life and her new name felt rather odd and uncomfortable, like her new dresses and shoes, but these people cared about her and wanted her to be part of their lives, so any changes they wanted to make, well, she could adjust.

Mr. Emory tied Johnny's satchel on the back with their bags, then came around and squeezed into the seat. Mrs. Pickens put her arm around Johnny's shoulder and pulled her close. "You just wait until you see Mr. Emory's house in St. Louis. It's three stories tall, painted yellow and green, with a beautiful wrap-around porch, all trimmed with intricate gingerbread scroll work."

The horse trotted smartly down the street as she told Johnny all about the new house.

"Up in the attic is a copula with windows on all four sides where you can look out and see all over the city. Around the house are colorful flower gardens and a tall wrought iron fence to keep out stray dogs."

Mr. Emory told her all about his friends and neighbors then gave her a sly wink, as he mentioned the wonderful character of a young man who was the son of a fellow teacher.

At the train station, Charles climbed from the buggy and went inside. A few minutes later, he returned with a porter who pushed a large flat cart.

"I'm sorry, my dears, but the stationmaster informs me the train is running late. Nothing unusual I take it, for these western states, but it will give us ample time for a bite to eat."

Once he and the porter finished unloading their trunks and bags, Mr. Emory made arrangements to have the buggy returned to the livery then he escorted his sister and Johnny to a nearby restaurant.

They had just taken their seats when an older man approached their table.

"Hello, Flora."

A wide smile spread across Mrs. Pickens's face. "Why, Ephraim Fitch, how wonderful to see you. You remember my brother, Charles. And this is Violet, his niece by marriage."

Mrs. Pickens had created Johnny's identity as her brother's niece the day after she gave her the name Violet. Johnny found the lie even easier to believe than the one she had made-up for the people in the locket. Immediately, she began calling Mrs. Pickens and Mr. Emory, Aunt Flora and Uncle Charles.

Flora turned to Johnny. "Violet, this is my dear friend, Mr. Ephraim Fitch. He and my Harold were best of friends." She lifted her gaze back to Ephraim. "Is Grace with you?"

"Yes, she is, and we would love to have you all join us. We have a table over by the window." He gestured toward the front corner of the room. "Please."

They all stood and wove their way around and between the other tables. Introductions were made once more and everyone scooted their chairs closer together.

Johnny chewed her sandwich in silence as conversation flowed around her. Uncle Charles laughed at a story Ephraim told about a mischievous neighbor boy, and meeting her gaze across the table, Charles gave her a quick wink. His gesture flooded her with warmth. She smiled back. With her new identity and new clothes, it was almost as if her old life had never existed. She vowed she would let nothing jeopardize her future with this family.

Without much to say, Johnny fiddled with the napkin in her lap, idly watching the people as they passed outside the window.

Then she saw Rab.

She shot to her feet, her stomach in her throat. Conversation ceased. Charles and Ephraim stood along with her.

"What's wrong, Violet?" Flora asked.

Johnny glanced down, confused by the nearly overwhelming urge to charge out the door and race down the street after him. He had laughed at her, made fun of her. He wanted to marry someone else. She hated him. So why did this glimpse of his wide shoulders and dark hat cause her cheeks to heat and her heart skip a beat?

"I jest seen...er...saw a friend a mine."

Maybe she needed to see him—one more time— to tell him what she thought of him, to show him that she was a lady now and doing just fine without him in her life. She would simply tell him good-bye, then get on the train, and never look back.

Not wanting to embarrass Flora and Charles in front of their friends, Johnny took a moment to choose her words. "Please excuse me, I got...have to go. I'll be right back."

"Violet, dear, your bonnet."

From the corner of her eye, she saw Flora hold

out the dreaded hat, but Johnny pretended not to hear as she sidled around the tables on her way out.

A group of people stepped through the door as she approached, and she scooted outside.

She'd learned enough this week to know ladies didn't shout after a gentleman, but afraid she would lose sight of him, she lengthened her stride and called, "Deputy Bennick!"

As the feminine voice carried down the street, Richard stopped and turned. A beautiful young woman with blonde hair, wearing a blue dress, stood in front of the gun shop, watching him. Curious, he walked toward her.

A winsome smile tugged at the corners of her mouth as though she found his confusion amusing. He stopped and cocked his head. An elusive image fluttered around the periphery of his mind.

"Can I help you?"

"Hello, Richard."

The tone of her voice rang familiar, but her words were stilted and didn't flow naturally. Besides, no one but Caroline ever called him Richard.

She lifted her chin, and her wide, violet gaze searched his face.

A funny pressure swelled in his chest. He was almost afraid to believe... "Johnny?"

"Johnny!" He stepped forward, reached out and pulled her to him. His arm snaked around her waist, and he leaned down pressing his cheek against her hair. "Johnny, thank God you're all right. I searched all over town. Where have you been?"

He lifted his head and studied her face. She blinked up at him, her mouth gaping slightly, as though she wanted to say something, but couldn't find the words.

"God, you're so beautiful," he whispered, amazed that she was here, warm and healthy, and wrapped in his embrace.

His mouth swooped in to claim her parted lips. His tongue delved deep, absorbing the lingering flavors of coffee and bread as he intimately explored every bump and crevice. She sagged against him as her tongue touch his, tentatively at first then boldly tracing the smooth underside before moving up to swirl around the tip.

He groaned and squeezed her tighter.

Her tongue stilled, and her hands slipped up between their bodies to press against his chest. At first he didn't notice the pressure, he was so focused on kissing her lower lip, but when she twisted her head away and shoved, he stepped back.

"What's wrong?" he asked, a bit hurt by her rejection.

"A proper gentleman does not acrossed a lady in...in..." She frowned.

"Accost."

"Jest get yer damn hands off me." Whirling, she started back the way she came.

His stomach lurched. "Johnny, wait." He lunged toward her, grabbed her arm and spun her around. "I'm sorry. I never should have corrected you. It's just that it always got you so fired up." A small smile quirked at the corner of his mouth. "You make me laugh. If you only knew how long it's been since I..."

He shook his head feeling as disoriented as he had the first morning he got out of bed after being sick. He tried a different approach.

"You look so pretty—It's such a surprise seeing you here. I've been so worried and—Can't we go someplace and talk?"

She shook her head. "I'm sorry, Richard," she said in that carefully modulated voice. "I just wanted to see how your leg was feeling and say good-bye."

He rubbed his forehead and exhaled with frustration. What had happened to his Johnny? The drawl still slowed her words, but her speech sounded so rehearsed and formal he had no idea what to think. And the dress, while it looked nice on her, it seemed to have changed her into a different person. A person who didn't want him, who had only stopped him to say...

"Good-bye? Where the hell are you going?" He gestured past her shoulder. "Look, there's a restaurant right here. I'll buy you some dinner, we'll talk."

She glanced back. "I don't believe it would be proper. 'Sides, our train leaves soon. I'm sorry, Richard."

"Damn it, Johnny, stop calling me that!" He slammed his palm against the wall of the gun shop. "My name is Rab. Don't ever call me anything else."

"I'm sorry, Rab."

He shifted his gaze back to her. Her complexion had paled, and her gaze had dropped to the board walk, her lower lip caught between her teeth.

Remorse slammed into his stomach like a medicine ball. He'd acted just like her father. No wonder she wanted nothing to do with him.

"God, I'm sorry." He reached out to touch her shoulder, but she shrugged away from him. His heartbeat quickened.

An older gentleman in a dark suit stepped up behind Johnny. "Violet, is everything all right?"

Johnny turned and smiled. "I'm fine, Uncle Charles."

Violet? Richard knew his mouth hung open, but couldn't seem to remember how to close it.

"Uncle Charles, may I present, Deputy Marshal"—she lifted her chin a notch and narrowed her gaze in Richard's direction—"Richard Bennick."

He almost smiled at that glimpse of the Johnny he loved.

"And Richard, this is my uncle, Mr. Charles

Emory." She turned slightly as Flora approached. "And this here's his sister, Mrs. Flora Pickens."

They exchanged a brief greeting then Charles removed his watch from his vest pocket. "If you will excuse us, deputy, I'm afraid we have a train to catch."

He felt like an hour glass that had just been flipped over. For an instant he was full, then, he was suddenly turned upside down, and like the sand, Johnny was being rushed from his life. He had to stop her.

He presented his arm. "It would be my pleasure to escort you, Miss Violet."

She shot him a narrow-eyed glare that made him want to smile. He tucked her hand over his arm.

Charles walked ahead of them with his sister, while Richard and Johnny followed in silence a few paces behind.

The train whistle screeched as they stepped onto the platform. Puffs of steam floated around the engine. Other passengers milled around the platform, saying good-bye to family and friends. Porters loaded baggage into a car farther down. Johnny withdrew her hand and stepped back, seemingly more interested in all the activity than in him.

"It was real good to see ya Ra—Richard," she said, her gaze on the toes of her shoes. "I'm happy your leg healed up right nice. But we both got different lives now. I thank ya for all ya done fer me, but I got me a family now."

He wanted to grab her close and never let go. Would she stay if he told her he wasn't getting married, that he desperately needed her help one more time? That if they got through this one last difficulty he could give her a real family, with children, who would grow up with an aunt and uncle and cousins. He opened his mouth to do just that, when Charles interrupted.

"Violet, your Aunt Flora and I will wait for you on the train."

They seemed to care about Johnny, and she apparently cared for them. Her speech had improved, and she'd looked so beautiful in that dress he almost hadn't recognize her. How could he have ever thought her a boy?

This moment was her chance for the life she never knew, the life she deserved. If she stayed, her testimony might help him, but she would go back to jail. She would face charges for stage robbery and the murder of that young girl. What if she was found guilty? She'd go to prison. He would never ask her to take that chance.

The only way he could save himself was to remember what happened that day. To do that he would have to face his past.

The whistle blew again.

"All aboard!"

Johnny swung her attention to the conductor then back. "I gotta go."

"Johnny, wait." He reached into his pocket and pulled out the velvet bag. "This is for you."

She stared at his extended hand.

"Take it. I saw it in a store and I bought it..." His voice trailed off into nothing.

Her hand shook as she reached for the bag. Pulling the drawstring she first peered inside then emptied the contents into her palm. She lifted her gaze to his, her violet eyes welled with unshed tears.

His own eyes stung at the sight. He couldn't do this. He couldn't watch her leave.

"Can ya put it on fer me?" she whispered. "I ain't never worked no fancy hitch. All I done was loop a strip of rawhide over my head."

"I don't know if I can." Without his left hand, he had no idea how, yet here stood Johnny, once again believing he could do anything. He swallowed down the lump in his throat.

"Miss!" the conductor called. "It's time to go."

She swung around, presenting her back and holding each end of the chain at the back of her neck. To make it easier for him, she bowed her head. Her hair had been pulled back with combs and pinned, exposing a pale, slender neck that he longed to nuzzle and lightly brush with his lips.

Taking the end of the chain between his fingers he slipped the little s-hook through the tiny loop Johnny held. He leaned close and lightly touched his lips to the hollow behind her jawbone. The fragrance of lilacs filled his senses.

"Be happy," he whispered in her ear.

She shivered and turned, their bodies mere inches apart. He leaned close for one last taste of her lips.

"Miss!"

She pulled away and hurried to the steps. Unable to let her go, Richard followed.

The whistle blasted again, and the train began its slow acceleration, wheels turning and chugging.

"You can put pictures of your new family inside," he called as he walked alongside the train.

Clutching the rail of the steps with one hand, she stretched out and touched his cheek with the other. "Yer a fine man, Rab, and I'm right proud ta call ya friend."

He clasped her hand with his, jogging alongside, nearly out of platform. He placed a quick kiss in her palm then let go as the train moved on down the tracks.

"I never laughed at you!"

****

Johnny stared after Rab, standing alone on the end of the wooden platform, until the black dot that was him became nothing. Those beautiful dark brown eyes had grown so sad when the train pulled away it nearly broke her heart. Feelings stirred inside her then took off like leaves in a whirlwind, spinning so fast it became impossible to tell which emotion she actually felt.

Part of her wanted to launch herself into his arms, breathe deep of that familiar sandalwood scent, and hang on for the rest of her life, but years of stomping down her emotions and being wary of men, had kept her feet rooted to the steel platform at the end of the car.

His actions confused her. If he had secretly chuckled every time she called him Rab, why was he so furious when she used the name Richard? She believed he thought her a joke when she mispronounced her words, yet even now she could still hear his voice in her ears, "I never laughed at you!"

Flora Pickens corrected her speech all day long, so why did it bother her when Rab did it?

And the way his mouth claimed hers, like he wanted to taste her forever and never let her go. His kiss consumed her with a passion he ought to save for his betrothed. Maybe he thought to use her as he had before, as if he considered her too stupid to know about Caroline.

Well, the damn fool was wrong. She wasn't stupid, and she hoped he was happy with his choice. She'd said good-bye. He was out of her life, and it was time for a new beginning. She blew out a sigh as she turned and opened the door.

But the air inside the car caused her eyes to sting, and as she made her way down the aisle to her seat, the faces of the people who looked up as she passed blurred.

"Is everything all right, dear?" Flora asked.

Johnny slid into the rear-facing seat across from Flora and Charles without a word. They stared at her for a moment then resumed their conversation, while Johnny turned her attention to the scenery flying past her window and blinked back her tears.

When Rab had walked past the restaurant she'd been so happy to see him she'd almost forgotten to breathe. Then he called her beautiful, gave her this expensive locket, and said "I love you." Why would he do those things if he didn't care? Why would he say that if he were marrying Caroline?

A piece of her wanted to believe in him, believe he cared, but her realistic side reminded her Rab was a man, like every man she'd ever known, who lied and used women for their own pleasures. Rab wasn't the imaginary man in her locket. He wasn't good or noble, and he didn't love her.

She looked down. The new locket lay flat against the bodice of her dress. With her thumb and forefinger she lifted it for a closer look. Tiny spring flowers had been engraved on both sides of the silver oval. *Little Johnny jump-ups!* A tiny gasp escaped her throat, and she clamped her lower lip between her teeth. Tears filled her eyes and clogged the back of her throat. *That goddamn, Yankee lawman.*

She slid her thumbnail along the seam and popped apart the two halves. Despite the fact that he'd told her she could put pictures of her family inside, she somehow expected to find his photograph within. Maybe a picture showing one of his rare smiles, with that big dimple and that piece of hair he hated so much falling over his forehead.

Instead, it was as empty as her heart, with only a skewed reflection of herself staring back, blurry and distorted in the shiny silver.

Her chest tightened, and her lungs ached for the air of another shallow breath. Sweat coated her palms.

As the train chugged farther and farther down the track, she was seized by an overwhelming sense of despair, as if she'd been left alone in the middle of the flat, empty prairie, where the wide, blue sky reached down in every direction and brushed the tips of the swaying grass.

Chapter Eighteen

Richard swallowed the lump in his throat and swiped at the inside corners of his eyes. He stared until the train was nothing more than a tiny dot on the horizon. Then it was gone and nothing remained but two long rails stretching into the distance.

The mournful wail of the whistle drifted back to his ears, echoing the loneliness inside him. Slowly, he turned and walked back along the platform. He checked with the station master and learned the train was heading east, to St. Louis, but with countless stops along the way, Johnny could be getting off almost anywhere.

His leg ached by the time he returned to his horse and rode to his cabin. He tossed his hat on the table, grabbed his bottle from the top of the pie safe, and downed a hefty swallow.

He missed her already. He missed her grumbling bluster and her sage mountain wisdom. He missed her simple acceptance of life and of him. All this time, he imagined her hiding somewhere alone and afraid. He'd wanted to find her and save her. He wanted her to need him as badly as he needed her.

Instead, she'd apparently landed on her feet. Whoever Uncle Charles and Aunt Flora were, they appeared to care for her. Johnny seemed happy. She had a new identity and a new family like she'd always wanted.

Richard just wished he knew these people. He'd feel better knowing she was safe. What if they were no good?

She had introduced them as Aunt Flora and Uncle Charles, but after Calvin died, Richard believed Johnny to be all alone. She'd said she was from the Ozarks, and now he wondered if these people were taking her back there. But if Charles and Flora were family, how had Johnny found them?

She mentioned once that her mother kept track of the family tree. He put the bottle back where it belonged then limped across the room to his bunk. Leaning down, he grabbed the doeskin bag from the shelf under his bedside table. Inside, he felt for the worn leather Bible and flipped it open.

Just past the front cover, on a page with small rectangular boxes, were the births and deaths of several generations of Tagetts, Bodines, and Everetts, but no record of either a Flora or a Charles. He sat on his bed and scooted back against the wall.

He started with the entry for Johnny's mother. Katie May had been a Tagett and had married Pierpont Bodine in eighteen-fifty-six, when Katie was fourteen and Bodine twenty-three. A baby girl had been born within the year and died at one month.

Johnny was born the first of May of eighteen-fifty-nine.

Richard stared at the date for several minutes. He'd never given much thought to Johnny's age. She had such an open pragmatic outlook on life that made her wise beyond her—eighteen years? God, he was a cradle robber. He was going to be thirty-one in two months. What was he thinking, taking her innocence, and harboring the crazy notion that if he were cleared in this investigation, he and Johnny could somehow be together? Johnny deserved better than an old cynical, half-insane, half-shell of a washed-up, ex-deputy marshal.

With a sigh, he started to close the Bible when

the name Henry Bodine caught his attention. If Henry hadn't been so important to Johnny, he probably wouldn't have given the name a second look. But curious about the man who seemed to be the complete opposite of his brother, Richard read the dates. No one had entered the date of Henry's death, but his birthday seemed to leap right off the page—April tenth, eighteen-fifty-three—just six years before Johnny. Henry must have been raised by Johnny's mother after Ellen Bodine died when Henry was three.

Richard closed his eyes and let his head fall back with a thump, trying to assimilate the facts. Henry had been the one who'd stolen the big brown and white paint Johnny always rode. Henry had given Johnny the locket after he returned from a stage robbery. And Henry once owned the white linen duster Johnny always wore. The man couldn't have been more than twenty-three when he was killed. If Henry had had blond hair, then that warrant should have been issued for Bodine's brother, not his son.

He slammed the Bible closed with a quick yell. He wanted to find Johnny and tell her, but she was gone and his joy fell flat.

****

When Richard stopped at Marshal Upham's office on Monday, the marshal told him that Benton Caldwell was taking the investigation to the grand jury. Upham also felt that since Johnny Bodine was a necessary witness and he already had deputies out looking for the boy, that the warrant would stand.

"I'm sorry, Bennick. I know the kid means a great deal to you, but hang on to your evidence. You can present it if they bring him in. Meantime, I hope you have a lawyer, you're going to need it."

****

A week later, with his palm sweating, Richard

stood in the courtroom of Judge Isaac Parker, who after only two years on the bench was known across the country as the hanging judge. Over six feet tall, with broad shoulders, a square jaw, and piercing blue eyes, Judge Parker was a formidable presence in the court room.

How many times had Richard sat in that witness chair, on the right side of that high, cherry panel desk, looking toward this same table, where countless defendants listened as he testified against them? To Richard's right stood Evan Stewart, his face expressionless as the seemingly endless list of charges were read aloud.

"Deputy Richard Bennick, you are charged with three counts of murder in the second degree in the deaths of Deputy Martin Brady, Greyson Tyler, and Samuel Miles. And with three counts of assault with a deadly weapon with intent to kill or maim..."

The wall clock on Richard's left steadily counted the passing seconds. Tick-tock, tick-tock; his starched collar seemed to draw itself tighter around his neck, choking him so he couldn't breathe, reminding him of George Maledon's oiled lengths of hemp.

He ran his finger around the inside of the starch band, trying to ease the snugness. Even now, all he had to do was lie, claim his memory had returned, come up with a plausible story, and everyone would believe him. It would be his word against theirs.

"How do you plead?"

Evan Stewart's voice rang out, "The defendant pleads not guilty on all charges."

Maybe that was a farce as well, because down deep inside some gnawing sense of unease warned Richard that maybe he really was guilty.

"Your Honor," Benton Caldwell interjected, "the people request bail of one thousand dollars."

"Your Honor," Evan Stewart spoke up. "Defense

finds the prosecution's request unreasonable. Mr. Caldwell knows my client already met his bail and cannot afford such an outrageous increase. Deputy Bennick would have to be held in jail with the very men that he not only put there, but who made these charges against him. This would be tantamount to a death sentence.

"My client is a man of upstanding character. He is well known in the community and is still recovering from a near fatal wound which he received while bringing in the very prisoners who now accuse him of these ridiculous crimes. He is not a flight risk. We would respectfully request that Deputy Bennick be released on his own recognizance."

Caldwell argued, "Your Honor, the people are concerned with not only the severity of the crimes, but the abuse of the deputy's power as a representative of this court."

Judge Parker nodded. "Thank you, Mr. Caldwell. Your objection is noted, but I will allow Deputy Bennick to be released on his own recognizance, on the condition that he check-in with Marshal Upham once a day and he agrees not to leave Fort Smith for any reason until after a decision regarding these charges is rendered."

"But, Your Honor..." Caldwell argued.

Parker glared at him. "I've made my decision."

In the court room, few men dared to argue with the Judge. Yet, whenever Richard had seen Parker outside of court, he was approachable and friendly and always carried a bag of candy in his pocket for the children.

Parker gestured for his clerk and whispered with him for a few minutes before addressing the courtroom. "I want this business settled. We will go right to trial. Any pre-trial motions will be heard at ten o'clock, Tuesday next. Jury selection will begin in two weeks. Trial date set for thirty days." He brought his gavel down with a sharp thwack.

Evan Stewart spoke up, "Your Honor, we have witnesses we are still unable to locate. We need more time to prepare."

Judge Parker leaned forward over his desk; his tawny hair gleamed in the sunlight. "I dislike this whole business of a U.S. Deputy Marshal being charged with murder. I want the matter resolved. Find your witnesses, Mr. Stewart." He gave his gavel another quick bang. "Next case."

****

"Violet?"

Johnny looked up from her breakfast plate as Charles lowered his copy of the Fort Smith Western Independent. He'd ordered a subscription to the newspaper so his sister would be able to keep up with news of her old friends and neighbors, but he seemed to read it more than Flora.

"The friend you were talking to outside the restaurant the day we left Fort Smith, what was his name again?"

A tiny flutter of apprehension tickled her stomach. From across the table Flora sneezed for the third time since they sat down to eat.

"God bless you," Johnny said, though her attention remained on Charles. "Richard Bennick," she replied.

"Hmmm. Well, if this is the same man, he's going on trial for murder."

Johnny shook her head in disbelief. "That can't be the same man. The Richard Bennick I know wouldn't never kill no—anyone. He's too honorable."

"You're probably right. They say this man killed a deputy marshal in Indian Territory."

"Charles," Flora reprimanded in a tone as stuffy as her nose. "I hardly think murder an appropriate topic for breakfast conversation.

"Rab never kilt no one, Lord's eye on it!" Johnny declared, jumping to her feet.

"Oh dear," Flora exclaimed, then sneezed. "Violet, please remember your lessons."

Charles refolded the paper. "Leave the child alone. I find her speech delightful. 'I hear America singing, the varied carols I hear,'"

"Are you quoting from that blasphemous, piece of trash again?" Flora rose from her chair, her chin tipped upward.

Johnny had heard this same argument all week, ever since Charles brought home the collection of poems Flora though to be filth.

"Walt Whitman is not blasphemy," Charles declared also pushing to his feet.

"You can't teach that filth at school. You'll lose your position and never teach again."

"You're being melodramatic. I can read whatever I wish in my own home."

Johnny wondered if they actually enjoyed baiting each other like this. Charles had brought the book, *Leaves of Grass*, home and left it in the parlor, right on the seat of Flora's favorite chair. He knew her love of poetry would prompt her to pick it up. The two of them left the room, still arguing about the book. Johnny snatched the newspaper from the corner of the table and hurried after them.

She caught up to them in the front foyer. "Uncle Charles, tell me what the paper says about Rab."

He turned away from the mirror, where he had just put on his hat. Flora sneezed again.

"I'm sorry, Violet." He took the paper and flipped to the article he'd been reading then quickly scanned the page. "Evidently, this deputy, Richard Bennick, was on an assignment in the nations with a Deputy Martin Brady. There was apparently a shooting incident in which Deputy Brady and several others were wounded and killed. Your Deputy Bennick is

300

being charged with murder in the second degree, for his involvement in their deaths."

"It ain't true!" Johnny declared.

The gazes of both Flora and Charles shot to her face.

Johnny closed her mouth and bit her lip.

Softly, Charles asked, "Is Deputy Bennick the man who killed your uncle?"

She nodded.

"Yes, that's what we suspected. At the time you joined us, Fort Smith was humming with gossip about the young outlaw, Bodine, who had brought in prisoners with a deputy marshal, then saved his life and vanished." He picked up his leather satchel from the table beneath the mirror. "I have to leave for school now, but I'd like you to think very carefully about what you want. Because if what I suspect is true, there will be severe consequences, which ever decision you make."

"But I cain't let Rab hang for somethin' he didn't do."

"And what of you, my dear? What will happen to you if you return to Fort Smith?"

She shifted from foot to foot and studied the roses on the hooked rug beneath the toes of her shiny black, lace-up shoes. She'd almost forgotten she was an escaped prisoner. She looked up, meeting Charles's steady gaze as he watched her through his spectacles.

"I reckon I'll go back to that jail, and maybe they'll want to hang me fer things my paw done."

Charles glanced at Flora and nodded. They knew, Johnny realized. They'd always known. And still, they'd taken her in like she was family.

"Are you willing to give up all you have here, all you will have in your future for this man?" he asked.

She didn't want to leave. This big house with its many rooms and tall black iron fence were as she always imagined a house should be. Charles and Flora were two of the nicest people she'd ever known. They'd given her clothes and a place to live. They had embraced her as part of their family. Flora taught Johnny to speak properly so she would never have to feel ashamed again. Charles teased her and read aloud every evening; beautiful poetry and wonderful stories, of adventures and faraway places Johnny had never known existed.

Now, Flora had a cold, and Johnny wanted to be here to fix the herbs for tea and a poultice for Flora's chest.

But if she stayed, Rab might hang. The image of his warm body lying cold and lifeless, of never seeing that dimpled grin again, or hearing him laugh, sent a chill rippling through her body.

He must have known he was in trouble that day at the train station, yet he never said a word. She wrapped her fingers around the locket and squeezed. All he'd said was to be happy and to fill her locket with pictures of her new family. Yet, her locket remained empty, because what she longed for was a photograph of him. A picture that captured a glimpse of his smile, a treasure to lock safely inside and keep close to her heart for always.

She had no choice. She had to return to Fort Smith. It didn't matter that he married Caroline. After all he'd done for her, he deserved his chance to be happy.

Charles and Flora must have both sensed her decision, because Flora began to cry and Charles gave her a brisk nod.

"Are you absolutely certain this is what you want?"

"Yes, sir."

"I commend you for making the choice, though we will be unable to accompany you to Fort Smith. Flora is not feeling well, and I have just started the new term. You've brought warmth and laughter into this big old house. We'll both miss you very much. Let us know how you fare. If you need anything, Violet, anything, money, an attorney, just send us a wire."

He stepped toward the door then turned. "The trial starts on Monday. You'll have to take a train to Springfield and from there to Fort Smith. I'll check the schedules on my way home this evening."

"Thank you, Uncle Charles."

He gave her a nod and stepped out the door.

****

Flora had sniffled and dabbed at her eyes while she helped Johnny pack. Though Flora claimed it was only her head cold, Johnny pretended to believe her and tried not to cry herself. Uncle Charles took her to the station the next day. He gave her money and a bear hug, and made her promise to send a telegram as soon as the trial was over.

Unfortunately, there was no train to Fort Smith until Monday so she had to spend two nights in a hotel. Her room wasn't as nice as the one she had at the house in St. Louis, but it was perfect because she didn't have to leave the building to find a place to eat, and in the evening she sat in a wooden rocking chair on the front porch and watched the people walk by.

Flora and Charles both assured her she would be safe traveling that short a distance alone. When Johnny wanted to make the trip dressed in her baggy clothes and duster, Flora insisted it was unnecessary, because gentlemen did not accost women in public, and even western men held women in high regard.

All the way to Springfield, men bowed politely, held doors, gave up their seat, and offered to carry her bag.

Then at the second stop after leaving

Springfield, two men boarded the train and made their way down the aisle in Johnny's direction. The first man, tall and thin, wore a low slung gun belt and had a pair of saddlebags tossed over the shoulder of his tattered wool coat. The man who followed was short, with a thick waistline. He wore no gun and his clothes were rumpled and his shirt tail untucked. He, too, carried a pair of saddlebags, but instead of moving smoothly down the aisle, this man bumped into the seats and knocked people in the head with his saddle bags.

Keeping her gaze averted, she gnawed on her bottom lip and watched as they made their way toward her, blatantly avoiding each empty seat until they dropped into the one behind hers. Her stomach tensed and she swallowed. She'd almost forgotten how it felt to constantly live with that knot of fear twisting her stomach.

Behind her the two men chuckled. She inched forward on her seat.

"Look, Lem, ain't this the purtiest gal you ever seen."

"Sure Pudge, her hair looks just like gold dust," replied the second man.

She should have worn her bonnet. Aunt Flora insisted a lady always covered her head outside, but Johnny hated the calico headwear with its big ribbon tied under her chin. It felt like she was being choked, and without the need to hide her femininity she saw no need to wear it. Now she wished she had.

"Lem, do you think she'd know if I touched it?" The two men whispered, but Johnny heard every distinct word. Goosebumps crawled up her arms as the thought of Pudge touching her hair.

She stood and froze when she felt someone grab a fistful of material at the back of her skirt.

"Where are ya goin', purty lady? We jest want to talk to ya."

Down the length of the car the passengers facing the front of the train were unaware of her plight. A few others were seated so they looked toward the rear of the train, but they could only see her standing. They didn't know about the hand holding her skirt.

Would they help her if she called out? Many were well-dressed gentlemen. She twisted around, her gaze following the dirty sleeve of the offender right to his face.

"Release me at once," she snapped in her best impression of Aunt Flora's indignant tone.

"Pudge, let go of the lady." Lem flashed her a toothless grin in apology.

The heavier man released his grip. "I jest want ta touch yer hair. I ain't never seen hair so purty."

Johnny narrowed her gaze on his face. Pudge didn't seem quite right, but unsure whether he was harmless or not, she stepped into the aisle and moved up and over a few seats.

When they didn't follow, she relaxed and looked out the window.

As the train chugged into the mountains, the terrain changed. Trees of cedar, oak, and pine hugged the edge of tracks which curved around hills and crossed steep hollows that reminded Johnny of the area where she and her mother lived when she was little.

At the next small town, passengers got off and a few new people got on. In the confusion, she didn't realize the two men were beside her seat until it was too late. Instead of continuing up the aisle, Pudge slid into the rear facing seat across from her and Lem followed beside him.

Johnny stood, intending to move to the front of the car, but Lem grabbed her wrist.

"Now, you got no call ta be rude." The sour smell of alcohol and rotting teeth wafted from his mouth.

"Pudge here don't mean no harm. Why don't ya jest sit down an' let us visit with ya fer a spell."

"I ain't a-settin' down, an' ya can get yer damn hand off me." She gave her arm a yank that freed her from his grasp, but the momentum coupled with the rocking of the train, knocked her off balance, and she had to press her hand against the window glass to keep herself from falling backward into the seat.

She noticed she'd caught the attention of a few of the closest passengers, but no one seemed certain enough of what was happening to interfere.

Aunt Flora wouldn't let Johnny tuck her knife into the top of her lace-up shoe, but she did sew nice big pockets into all of Johnny's dresses and told her, "A lady can keep all sorts of useful items in a pocket."

Lem braced his foot on her seat, blocking her escape. Pudge smiled like a boy with a new toy and reached out with his dirty fingers to stroke the fabric of her skirt. Johnny slid her hand into her pocket and burrowed straight to the bottom where her fingers closed around the familiar grip of the knife Henry had given her.

She tried once more to get them to leave her alone.

"I don't want no trouble, now let me pass."

Lem smiled mockingly, as if her words were a challenge to see what she would do next.

In one quick motion, Johnny whipped her hand from her pocket and jammed the blade right into the back of Pudge's hand. He yowled like a tom cat on the back fence.

Lem grabbed her opposite wrist in an iron grip as she yanked the blade from Pudge's hand. The few male passengers who heard the commotion, called to her and scrambled down the aisle in her direction.

Pudge held his bleeding hand to his chest and whimpered.

"Bitch." Lem's sharp whisper held an edge of steel. "You had no call ta do that. He weren't gonna hurt ya none."

But Johnny refused to back down. She held her knife close to her body with the tip of the bloodied blade pointing right at Lem's throat.

"My paw is Pierpont Bodine. Ya touch me ag'in an' I'll slit yer throat like I was a-guttin' a catfish."

"Miss," a young man called out as he and another man approached her seat. "Are you all right? Do you need any help?"

She took a deep breath and slipped her knife back into her pocket as she tried to refocus her mind on her new manners and lady-like talk.

"No, thank you," she said carefully. "But I believe these gentlemen would like to leave the train."

As she scooted past Lem and stepped into the aisle, he shot her a poisonous glare that promised revenge if he ever saw her again, but she didn't care.

A third man, a little older than herself suggested she join his aunts at the front of the car, while he went for the conductor.

"Come sit with us dear." An older lady with blue tinted hair said as she patted the empty seat beside her. "My name is Winifred, and this is my dear cousin, Lucy."

Grateful, Johnny sat and said hello, nodding to the second aunt, a tiny little woman with tight curly hair. "Nice to meet you. I'm J-Violet."

"It's a pleasure for us as well." Winifred's gaze fell to the lace on the front of Johnny's dress. "What a pretty locket. Do you have a picture of your sweetheart inside?"

"No, ma'am, it's empty."

"Oh, what a shame. And then to be accosted like this, what is this world coming to, that such uncouth vermin should be allowed on a train with decent, civilized people."

"I'm fine, thank you, and I seen my share of vermin."

"I see that you stabbed him with your little knife. Good for you my dear." She gave a sharp nod of approval.

Lucy leaned forward then and said timidly. "Maybe we should carry one, too, Winnie."

"Marvelous idea," Winifred agreed. "Always be prepared and all that."

Lucy turned to Johnny and whispered. "If we purchased our own knives, could you teach us how to use them?"

"Yes," Winifred chimed in. "Think how wonderful it would be to travel about the country without a man constantly underfoot. We'd be strong independent women like you, Violet." She reached out and patted Johnny's hand.

Johnny lifted her head and smiled. She didn't have to hide beneath layers of baggy boys clothes anymore. She could be herself and manage just fine.

Chapter Nineteen

"Doctor Hendrickson, did you have an opportunity to examine the bodies of Deputy Martin Brady, William Tyler, and Samuel Miles?" Benton Caldwell asked from where he stood behind the prosecutor's table.

Richard decided this was not a good morning. His trial had started promptly at eight a.m., and by the time opening remarks were finished, the starched collar around his neck once again felt like a hangman's noose.

"Yes, sir, I did. Deputy Bennick had the bodies shipped to Fort Smith by train. Marshal Upham asked me to examine them real quick at Harold Elder's funeral parlor before they were buried."

"And from your brief examination; were you able to determine how each man died?"

"Yes, sir. They all died from gunshot wounds."

"Thank you doctor, but could you please be more specific and tell the court in what area of the body each man received his fatal wound?"

"Samuel Miles and Greyson Tyler died from gunshot wounds in their upper abdomen and Deputy Brady died from a chest wound."

"And doctor, from these examinations, did you conclude that the person who shot these men did so with accurate precision?"

Evan Stewart popped to his feet. "Objection. The doctor doesn't know if one person or seven people were involved in the shooting, nor can he know the intent of the shooter. For all we know they could have been ricochets."

Judge Parker leaned forward in his chair. "Mr. Caldwell, stick to questions relevant to the doctor's first-hand knowledge."

"Sorry, Your Honor." He picked up a sheet of paper from the table in front of him, glanced at it and continued. "Doctor, I understand you were a surgeon during the war."

"Yes, I was attached to Hancock's Second Corps."

Richard shifted on the wooden chair. He'd been a sharpshooter under Major General Birney, a part of Hancock's Second. For a fleeting instant, he wondered if this was the doctor who'd taken his arm. There'd been so many doctors it was unlikely, still, his arm began to itch. He rolled his shoulder and rubbed the end of his stump.

"And doctor, during your years serving in the war, did you see many wounds like those sustained by Martin Brady, Greyson Tyler, and Samuel Miles?"

"Well, not often. That type of wound is usually fatal, and I'd have no reason to treat those men."

Caldwell turned toward the jury, where two rows of six men sat in wooden chairs on a raised platform. "And during your time in the army, did you ever hear of an elite group of marksmen called Berdan's Sharpshooters?"

"Yes, they were men who were exceptionally accurate with a rifle."

"And what was their purpose as a unit?"

"To kill—"

Evan Stewart shot to his feet again. "Objection. Your Honor, any man who ever battled an enemy during a war has killed. Doctor Hendrickson was attached to the Medical Corps. Any specific knowledge of the orders the men of Berdan's Sharpshooters received would be speculation. Nor does what happened in a war twelve years ago have any bearing on this case."

Judge Parker stroked his goatee for a moment then gave a slight nod. "Objection sustained." He swung his attention to the jury. "The jury will disregard the doctor's last statement. Mr. Caldwell, confine your questions to those of a medical nature."

"Doctor, have you ever seen what happens to a man who has gone without sleep for days at a time?"

"I've heard of cases where men had been awake so long they couldn't sleep and other men who saw things that weren't there."

"They suffered hallucinations?"

"Yes. One young soldier had been sent to me because he thought he saw haystacks in the road and tried to march around them."

"Thank you, doctor. No further questions."

Evan Stewart stood as Benton Caldwell took his seat.

Richard marveled at the differences in the two men. Caldwell's dark suit was neatly pressed, his shirt a pristine white, and his tie knotted with precision. Evan Stewart on the other hand, looked as though he'd slept in his suit and knotted his tie on the way out the door. "Strategy, my dear deputy," Stewart had explained one day. "The men on the jury are working men from all over the area. We don't want to appear better than them."

Stewart bent down to pick his pencil from the floor where it landed when it rolled off the table. Richard wasn't sure how much was for the jury and how much was natural.

"Doctor Hendrickson, you told us a minute ago that you examined the bodies of Martin Brady, Sam Miles, and Greyson Tyler. How long had these men been dead before you examined them?"

"Deputy Bennick had their bodies shipped home by train. I'd say four or five days."

"So the bodies had begun to decompose."

The doctor nodded. "Yes."

"And how much time did you spend examining each body?"

Doctor Hendrickson gave his shoulders a quick shrug. "A minute or less. I needed information for identification, and the bullet holes were the obvious cause of death."

"Doctor, was it possible to tell, from your lengthy examination, exactly who shot these men?"

"Well, no, I don't know who shot them. I can only say, from the area of the body and the amount of blood on their clothes, that they all received mortal wounds and died quickly."

"Thank you, Doctor. Now, were you one of the citizens who turned out on the first of June to watch Deputies Reeves and Hollister return with Deputy Bennick and... Excuse me a moment while I check my notes." Evan Stewart adjusted his spectacles then flipped through some papers on the table in front of him. He then lifted his gaze to peer over the top of his spectacles, and address the doctor. "And seven prisoners?"

"No sir, but I heard about it."

"Then how long after his arrival in town did you have the opportunity to see Deputy Bennick?"

"About a half an hour. Tommy Nordstrom, neighbor boy of Benton Caldwell's, came running into my office, saying I was to come quick, someone was badly hurt."

"And what did you find when you arrived at the Caldwell house?"

"Deputy Bennick was gravely ill from an infected gunshot wound in his right thigh."

"Did Deputy Bennick have a fever?"

"He was delirious."

"And from your examination were you able to make any kind of determination as to how long Deputy Bennick had been ill?"

"That serious an infection took some time to develop, maybe a week or longer."

"And what was your prognosis for Deputy Bennick's recovery?"

"I believed the deputy would die unless his leg was amputated."

Evan Stewart gestured toward Richard. "Deputy Bennick, could you please stand?"

Richard's chair slid against the floor as he pushed it back and stood. Warmth washed through him from the sheer joy of actually being able to stand here with his full weight on both legs. He could never repay Johnny for all she'd done. No one deserved to be happy more than she, and he hoped her new life was everything she wanted.

"Thank you, Deputy." Evan Stewart turned back to the doctor as Richard sat.

"As we all saw, both of the deputy's legs are intact. Could you please explain to the court how you were able to perform such a miracle?"

Caldwell came to his feet. "Objection, Your Honor. How is this relevant to what happened at the time of the shooting? We can all see that Deputy Bennick recovered."

Judge Parker turned his blue-eyed gaze on Richard's attorney. "Mr. Stewart?"

"I'm sorry, Your Honor, I'll rephrase the question." Evan Stewart turned back to the witness chair.

"Doctor, have you ever met Johnny Bodine?"

"Yes."

"And who is Johnny Bodine?"

"He was one of the prisoners brought in by Deputy Bennick. Johnny is Bodine's son."

"And could you please tell us how you met?"

"I was getting ready to perform surgery on Deputy Bennick's leg..."

Richard rubbed his thigh. He knew Johnny had

been the one to save his leg, but he'd never realized exactly how close he'd come to losing it. His throat closed off as the doctor talked.

"...and when he threatened to shoot me through the head, I packed my instruments and left."

Richard felt his lips twitch. He could almost hear Johnny sputtering now. God, he missed her.

"No further questions."

Judge Parker inclined his tawny head toward the doctor. "Witness is excused."

To the right of the Judge's large desk, a fly bounced around the upper glass of an open window, in front of which sat two deputies. Richard knew the men, but not well. He wondered what they thought, looking over here at him, the crazy deputy now accused of murdering one of their own. Maybe he should have spent more time cultivating friendships. But even Hollister, who was the closest to being called a friend, now stared at him with suspicion.

Voices droned on in the courtroom. The doctor walked past. Evan Stewart sat down. Richard wondered how the man could ever hope to win this case. It was basically Richard's word against the outlaws, and he still couldn't refute anything they claimed. He wondered if on some level, part of him wanted to be punished.

Caldwell called Machler to the stand. This would be interesting.

Evan Stewart shot to his feet. "Your Honor, I object to this witness being called. He is one of the prisoners Deputy Bennick brought in from Indian Territory. He is facing felony charges and would benefit greatly if Deputy Bennick is found guilty. Not only that, but he and the other men brought in with him, have had ample time together to conspire their story."

"Mr. Stewart, I already denied that motion in pretrial. Your objection is noted, but overruled."

Handcuffs and leg shackles clanked together as Machler was escorted to the witness chair by the bailiff and two deputies. The clerk held out a Bible and Machler swore to tell, "nothing but the truth."

Richard glanced at the men of the jury, wondering if they would believe anything that came out of this man's mouth.

"State your name for the record."

"Calvin Abernathy Machler."

Benton Caldwell rose and began his preliminary questions, careful not to put the man in a negative light, as he established how Machler came to be at the scene. If the jury hadn't seen the outlaw come into the courtroom in chains it might have sounded like Machler and the rest of Richard's prisoners were innocently riding across Indian Territory on their way to church before they were arrested.

"Now, Mr. Machler," Caldwell began his next question. "Could you please tell us what happened after you stopped to water the horses."

"Well, most of the extra horses were run off by Bodine's son, Johnny. That's why the deputy there"—Machler nodded his head in Richard's direction—"went chasin' after him."

"And then what happened?"

"The other deputy, Brady, decided to make camp. The skinny guy, who was the cook, started making a fire, and the driver of the other wagon unhitched the mules to take 'em down to the stream."

"And where were you?

"Me and the other men was sittin' on the ground."

"What happened next?"

"There was a gunshot and one of the guards went down."

"Did you see who had fired the shot?"

"No, sir, we never seen him, he just started

shootin'. Picked us off, one at a time, 'til everyone was dead or wounded."

"Were you also wounded, Mr. Machler?"

"Yes, sir, I was shot in the leg."

"Mr. Machler, if you did not see Deputy Bennick, how do you know who did the shooting?"

"'Cause no one else was around, and when it was over he come walking into camp, right up to Bodine, who was gut shot, an' fired his Winchester next to Bodine's head, then told him he wasn't gonna kill him cause he liked watchin' him die a slow death. Then when Bodine died, that one-armed deputy said he was glad he was dead."

"That's rather unusual, don't you think, for a deputy with such an excellent reputation as an officer of this Federal Court, to gun down his prisoners then take delight in their deaths?"

"I reckon it don't sound right, but that deputy hated Bodine and tried to kill him before, when we was crossin' the Washita."

Caldwell stepped around the table and leaned against the front. "Could you please tell us about that?"

Machler turned his head and gazed straight at Richard. A gleam of triumph lit his eyes, but Richard stared right back, waiting stubbornly until Machler looked away first.

"Well, we was all in the river, tryin' to push out one of the wagons that was stuck in the mud. Johnny an' Willis was chained together. One a them must'a slipped an' they both went under the water. Bodine tried to pull them out, but the deputy—"

"Excuse me, by deputy you mean..."

Machler gestured toward Richard. "Deputy Bennick there."

Caldwell stepped closer to the jury box. "And then what happened?"

"Bennick musta thought—"

"Objection." Stewart's voice rang out from beside Richard. "Mr. Machler cannot know what Deputy Bennick thought."

Judge Parker leveled a stare at Caldwell. "Sustained."

Caldwell turned back to his witness. "Just tell us what Deputy Bennick did and said."

"He jumped off his horse and punched Bodine. Then said, 'I ought ta kill you.'" Then Bennick grabbed Bodine around the throat and started choking him."

"What happened next?"

"Nothing, Bennick just walked away."

"No further questions," Caldwell said and returned to his seat.

"Mr. Machler," Evan Stewart questioned from his chair. "What happened to the man who slipped in the mud?"

"He drowned."

"That's a shame." Stewart shook his white head. "What happened to Johnny? You mentioned Bodine's son was chained together with this man... I'm sorry, what was his name?"

"Willis, Colby Willis."

"Thank you. And why didn't Johnny get pulled under and drown along with Mr. Willis?"

Machler sat quietly for a moment. "Johnny was okay. He hauled himself to shore."

"Chained to a dead man?"

"Yeah, Johnny's a pretty tough kid."

"But not tough enough to keep the man he was chained to—the man who every time he went under the water, pulled Johnny under, too—not tough enough to pull that drowning man's head up out of the water so he could breathe?"

Stewart stood and moved to the front of the table. "Wasn't it the truth that Bodine held the man's head under the water as a punishment for falling asleep on guard duty, and that Bennick rushed in to save Willis's life? When Bennick could only save Johnny he did indeed yell at Bodine, but instead of trying to kill him, Bennick hauled Johnny and the dead man to shore. Wasn't that what actually happened, Mr. Machler?"

Machler shifted in his chair. "Now, I couldn't exactly see every angle from where I was standin'. I might'a mixed up a couple a things."

"Yes, I'm sure that's it. It's certainly easy to mix up the facts in all the confusion of you trying to save your friend, instead of standing there watching him drown. Isn't it true that Bodine used just such acts of violence to threaten you and the other men who rode with him? And you knew if you had tried to save Mr. Willis, you probably would have died yourself?"

Machler said nothing.

"Mr. Machler, answer the question please."

He shifted in his chair, and glancing down, muttered, "Bodine was strict, but I wouldn't call him a murderer."

Evan Stewart walked back around the table and sat. He shot Richard a wink and sorted through a couple of pages of notes before looking up. "Now, Mr. Machler, do you know a man named Calvin Everett?"

"Yeah, but I didn't see him 'til he come to McAlester and got us away from the Indian Police."

"I'm sorry, that's not what I asked you. I asked if you knew him."

"Yeah, he's Bodine's brother. I seen him a few times."

"Thank you. And before Deputies Brady and Bennick arrived at the sod house, had you been aware of any plans for Bodine and his brother to meet up someplace?"

"No," Machler quickly replied.

"Did you know a man named Pike?"

"No."

"Are you sure? I understand he rode with Bodine's brother, Calvin Everett."

"I told ya, I never seen him before."

"Odd. He was dropped at the doctor's office in McAlester two days after this alleged shooting by Deputy Bennick. I believe Pike had been shot twice."

"Maybe he was waterin' his horse the same time we was there."

"Maybe? You didn't see him watering his horse before the shooting started?"

"No. Like I said, it all happened so fast, we was all tryin' not to get killed."

"Then afterward, did you see this man having his wounds treated?"

"Yeah, I reckon Johnny saw to him. Johnny's good at doctorin'. He tended to all of us."

"Then why do you suppose Deputy Bennick tried to kill everyone in the camp then minutes later, allowed Johnny to treat all your wounds? And why would he take this badly injured man to the doctor?"

Mr. Caldwell called out, "Objection. Mr. Machler can't know what Deputy Bennick was thinking."

"Never mind, Your Honor." Evan Stewart gave his hand a quick wave, as though shooing at a fly. "No further questions." He sat down beside Richard and flashed him a reassuring smile as Machler was ushered from the courtroom.

Benton Caldwell then called Milford Warren to the stand. As he'd done with Machler, Caldwell tried to portray Warren as an innocent victim. Then he asked Warren essentially the same questions as Machler, and Warren in response, gave the same answers.

"Other than the afternoon of the shooting," Caldwell said several minutes later. "Had you ever seen Deputy Bennick do anything which might seem odd for a United States Deputy Marshal to do?"

"Well, he has a bottle in his saddle bags, he's always takin' a drink from."

"So you saw him drink a lot."

"Reckon, so."

"Anything else? "

"He was always ridin' out to check our back trail."

"During the day or at night?"

"Both. He was always in an' out."

A few more questions and Caldwell finished his examination. He tugged on the bottom of his coat, smoothing the wrinkles before he sat.

Evan Stewart glanced up from his chair.

"Mr. Warren, have you ever seen Deputy Bennick drunk?"

"I don't know."

"Have you ever seen him stagger around camp, have a hard time mounting his horse, begin yelling, or singing boisterously?"

"No."

"When you saw Deputy Bennick take a drink, did you ever see how much he drank?"

Warren shifted in the chair and looked around the room.

"I mean was it half the bottle or just a sip? Was he holding the bottle while he looked for something in his saddle bags?"

"I seen him take a sip now an' again."

"A sip." Evan Stewart turned toward the jury and nodded.

"Mr. Warren, were you also wounded during this shooting?

"I was shot in the hand."

"The hand. Unusual place to be shot if Deputy Bennick's intent was to kill you."

"I reckon he missed."

"He missed. You were indeed a lucky man. Did

you try to get away before he realized his mistake?"

"No, I played dead so's he wouldn't kill me when I moved."

"That was probably a smart idea; that way, when the shooting stopped you would be easy to recapture. Because you had no idea that this crazed deputy, who was shooting to kill, would instead, suddenly decide to let you live, and take you all back to Fort Smith."

"Bennick was crazy. We never knew what he would do."

"If I was a deputy marshal and you were my prisoner, I don't think I'd tell you what I was going to do either. Now on this journey to Fort Smith, how were you transported?"

"We rode in the wagon some a the time or marched alongside," Warren answered quickly, as though he knew the answer to this question and didn't have to take a moment to think first.

"So you must have been pretty tired at the end of the day."

Warren nodded. "Reckon I fell asleep after supper most nights."

"So you don't actually know how much time Deputy Bennick spent checking the back trail."

"Well, I seen him leave camp at night an' come back first thing in the morning."

"Mr. Warren, you just testified that you were asleep. So you can't know if the deputy rode out for an hour, came back and slept, then went out again early in the morning, can you?"

"Well, not exactly."

"Thank you, Mr. Warren." Evan Stewart sat down.

After Warren stepped from the stand, Caldwell called Breed, Stringer, Red, and Dewy to testify, but as they denied any involvement in the ambush, Caldwell could only ask them questions related to

Richard's whiskey consumption and his sleep patterns.

When Caldwell finished, he rested his case and Parker called a break for lunch. When they returned an hour later, Evan Stewart called Hollister to the stand.

"Deputy, how much money do you make for every prisoner you bring in?"

"We get an arrest fee of two dollars."

"How much for a dead prisoner?"

"Nothing."

"Deputy Hollister is there a book of rules or a code of conduct for deputy marshals going into Indian Territory?"

"There is a booklet, 'Laws Governing U.S. Marshal and His Deputies.'"

"And are you aware of any time when you and Deputy Bennick worked together, where Bennick broke any of these rules."

"No, Bennick wouldn't take a pencil that didn't belong to him. He's the most 'by the book' deputy Parker ever hired. One time he forgot to pack his shaving gear. A whiskey peddler we picked up offered him to use his soap an' razor, but Bennick said, no, he wasn't allowed to use the property of any prisoner in his charge."

Richard shifted behind the table. Everyone thought he had such an admirable sense of integrity. How could he tell them it wasn't a noble character, but rather fear, that held him accountable to the truth. Fear of that damned invisible line; fear of crossing it and becoming lost forever.

"Is Deputy Bennick a good shot?"

"Yes."

"Can you recall a time you saw Deputy Bennick's skill with a gun?"

"Yes. We'd been out on the scout for about a month picking up prisoners. We were heading back to Fort Smith and were ambushed by Curly Wyatt's brother, who turned out, used to be a Confederate sharpshooter. We took cover in a dry river bed, but we were pinned down and couldn't move. Bennick said he'd get him then pointed his Winchester toward a bluff about a quarter mile away. I asked him how did he know where the fellow was, and he said, 'That's where I'd be.' He aimed that rifle nice and careful then pulled the trigger. Wounded Curly's brother in the shoulder. Since I've known him, Bennick's never killed anyone."

"Deputy Hollister, have you ever seen Deputy Bennick drunk?"

"No, he likes his bourbon, but I've never seen him drunk."

"That's all. Thank you, deputy."

Caldwell stood and cleared his throat. "Deputy Hollister, have you ever been involved in the investigation of a shooting where a prisoner has died?"

"Yes," Hollister glanced up at Judge Parker, who looked even taller than six-foot-two, sitting behind the tall paneled desk. "The Judge will also order an investigation whenever there is an excessive use of firearms."

"And were you involved in the investigation of Deputy Brady's death."

"Yes."

"And what did Deputy Bennick tell you when you asked him about the incident?"

"He said he didn't remember and got upset when I pushed him to try."

Murmurs flowed around the courtroom. Parker banged his gavel to restore order. Richard glanced toward the jury box. Everyman stared at him. His stomach clenched. Why couldn't he remember? For both incidents his mind was a blank. Maybe he had killed Brady and the other men. Maybe he had crossed that line of sanity and didn't even know it.

"Deputy Hollister you testified that Deputy Bennick always followed the rules of conduct for deputy marshals." Caldwell picked up a small book from his table and opened it. "Are you aware, Deputy Hollister, that it is a violation of the revenue law to introduce ardent spirits into Indian Country?"

Richard's heart dropped straight into his stomach. He could use a good swig of Old Crow right now, and from the way things were going today, he probably wouldn't be able to appreciate the taste much longer.

"But that applies to bootleggers and peddlers, not a single bottle in a saddle bag for medicinal purposes."

"I'm sorry, but that's not what it says here. Seems to me your by-the-book deputy chooses which laws he wants to follow and which laws he doesn't."

Chapter Twenty

"I thought you said I wouldn't have to testify," Richard whispered to his attorney during a ten minute recess.

Stewart had put Hobbs on the stand mostly as a character witness and to show the jury the hardship they'd endured getting the prisoners to McAlester. Since Hobbs had been unconscious during the entire ambush, he was no help with regards to Brady's death and could only testify to what he saw the next morning.

"I've been watching the jury. Each of Caldwell's witnesses is essentially telling the same story. And while I might be able to cast doubt on their testimony, the men in that jury are looking at you wondering why this investigation even came to trial. They're wondering what truth is being hidden and all that doubt is being cast on you."

"But what am I supposed to say? I don't remember? They aren't going to believe me."

"If you don't remember, say so. We don't want them to think you're hiding something. Be honest and that honesty will come through to the jury."

This was not a good idea. Richard knew it in his bones.

While his attorney asked the questions there wasn't a problem. Richard just told the court how he'd seen riders shadowing them and how Johnny's behavior had heightened his sense of foreboding. He had no problem with his memory until he and Johnny charged into the woods after the first shots were fired. Evan Stewart didn't push him to remember and left Richard a few minutes later to face Benton Caldwell.

"I don't remember," Richard replied for the third time to Caldwell's repeated questions about the ambush.

"A U.S. Deputy Marshal and three men are dead, and all you can say is, 'I don't remember.' How convenient."

"There was an ambush." He spoke carefully, trying desperately to put the pieces together in his mind. "I didn't kill them. I wouldn't."

"And how do you know this when you have repeatedly told this court that you can't remember?"

"I don't know, I—"

"You must know something deputy, tell us."

"I can't remember, damn it."

"Objection." Stewart called. "Mr. Caldwell is badgering my client."

"I'll rephrase, Your Honor. Deputy Bennick do you remember where this alleged ambush took place?"

"West of McAlester, about two days out."

"And how many men were there"

Richard's head ached as he tried to assimilate the jumble of images in his mind. Nothing made sense. "I don't know," he groaned.

"What time of day was it?"

"Late afternoon."

"You're sure?"

"Yes, late afternoon, evening. We'd been fighting about an hour when the sun started going down. The woods were so dark we could barely see."

"And you're sure there was an ambush?"

Richard laughed but it sounded as cracked and brittle as he felt. "There had to be. I wouldn't just shoot my own men."

Even as he said the words the evil voice inside his head whispered, Maybe you did. *Don't think about it! Don't think about it!* He wasn't a killer, he wasn't! Johnny would have told him. Damn it, why couldn't he remember?

He ran his finger around the inside of his collar, brushing the tender area where the starched cloth had chaffed the skin below his jaw line. There was an ambush. There was. But the doubt rose in the back of his mind like the bile climbing up the back of his throat. They were all lying. Sitting in that jail together, they wanted nothing more than to get even with him.

He rubbed his hand over his face. He wasn't a murderer; was he? The doubt swirled around him like thick fog. The wispy tentacles enveloped his feet then swallowed his knees. Maybe he had killed Brady and the others. He rubbed his temples until the pressure of his fingers against his skull radiated pain across his head so that the roots of his hair hurt. Remember, he ordered himself.

He drew a shaky breath and continued. "I chased Johnny through the trees, across the stream, and out the other side, into the open grassland. Johnny's horse was fast and had gone pretty far before I caught up and we started back. We were almost to the tree line when we heard the first shots."

"And what did you do?" Caldwell asked.

"I was holding the reins to Johnny's horse until we got close enough. I grabbed my Winchester and jumped off my horse. Gun smoke hung between the trees, and I couldn't see. I dove behind an old log. When I lifted my head I could see their muzzle flashes, where they were firing from a low ridge. I had to stop them from killing us. I'm a sharpshooter, it was my responsibility, so I aimed and..."

He pressed the heel of his hand against the throbbing pain in his forehead. The next thing he remembered was waking up to find they had taken his arm.

No. That was wrong. The cold chill of insanity whispered across his skin. He shivered.

"Deputy Bennick?"

"I jumped off my horse and zig-zagged closer. I got off two shots without taking aim, just to draw their fire. Two bullets whizzed past my head. A couple more kicked up dirt in front of my boots. I dove behind the log and fired my Sharps. It was so dark with the smoke and the sun going down, I couldn't see, but when I looked up, I saw their muzzle flashes."

"Whose muzzle flashes, Deputy? Who was shooting at you?"

"The Rebs, sir. I killed them all." *No, no, no!* That was wrong. Had he said it out loud? He blinked and looked around. Every eye in the courtroom was focused on him. The room was so still, the sound of his own breathing sounded like the huffing of a blacksmith's bellows. His skin chilled and sweat broke out across his forehead. The faces stared back with rude condescension, their expressions silent and condemning, as though they thought him truly crazy.

"No further questions." Caldwell returned to his table with a satisfied grin on his face.

"Witness is excused. You may step down deputy."

Richard could barely put one foot in front of the other as he limped back to the table. Engaged in a whispered conversation, with a young man Richard had seen around the court house, Evan Stewart barely cast Richard a glance as he dropped into his chair. The young man hurried away.

"Mr. Stewart?"

"Yes, Your Honor. Defense would like to call Miss Johnny Bodine."

Richard's whole body stilled. Johnny? Here?

His chair creaked as he twisted around, searching the back of the courtroom.

The soft murmurs of the spectators droned like bees around a hive. When the door opened and she stepped through, a burst of energy surged through him, lifting the dread that had been pressing down on him.

She wore a simple lavender dress with a lace collar and cuffs. Her skin though tanned, was clear of bruises. She was as lovely as the last time he saw her, standing on the train platform, just after he'd kissed her. There was simplicity in her movements as she walked to the front of the courtroom. Even her boyish stride was as open and practical as her outlook on life.

He glanced at Caldwell, whose mouth hung open. Amused, Richard couldn't help a smile.

Johnny passed between the tables, and meeting his gaze, she stumbled.

Evan Stewart reached out to steady her, and in true Johnny fashion, she shrugged away from his touch and went straight to the witness chair.

Stewart hadn't mentioned finding Johnny. While a part of Richard thrilled to see her again, the other part didn't want Johnny to see him here—like this.

The clerk approached the witness chair, and she was sworn in.

"Could you state your full name for the record, please?" Evan Stewart asked from behind the table.

"Johnny Lee Bodine." Whispers hissed through back of the courtroom.

"Bodine. Are you related to the man known as Pierpont Bodine?"

"Yes, sir. He was my father."

"Was?"

"He was gut-shot this summer."

Richard frowned. She was back to talking like a

refined lady again. Considering all the times he corrected her speech, it was odd that he missed the passion in her voice when she spoke using her mountain dialect.

"Was that during the time you, your father, Machler, and Warren were all in the custody of Deputy Bennick?"

"Yes, sir."

"And were you with Pierpont Bodine when he died?"

"Yes, sir."

"Gut shot did you say?"

Johnny nodded. "Yes, sir."

"Do you know who did it?"

"No."

"You said you were with him when he died, but you don't know who killed him?"

"I wasn't with him when he got shot, just when he died."

"Where were you when he was shot?"

"Hiding behind a log with Deputy Bennick."

"Hiding?"

"I was hiding; the deputy was reloading."

Richard smiled at the memory, because she'd been yelling at him for not doing it fast enough. Funny he just remembered that.

"Reloading? Sounds as if there was an exchange of gunfire. Why don't you tell us what you saw?"

"I didn't see anything. I had my head down so I wouldn't get shot."

Evan Stewart sighed and rubbed his hand over his face in frustration.

Caldwell rose from his chair. "Your Honor, this witness obviously has nothing to add to the testimony we've already heard."

"Your Honor," Evan Stewart interrupted. "I would ask the court to allow us a bit of latitude. We have not yet had time to depose this witness as she has only just arrived in Fort Smith."

Judge Parker's sharp blue eyes bore straight into Evan Stewart's gaze. "Granted for now."

Stewart turned back to Johnny.

"And can you please tell us how you met the defendant, Richard Bennick?"

"He and the other deputy came out to the place we were staying to arrest us," she replied in that slow, carefully modulated tone Richard hated so much.

"And were you arrested?"

"Yes, sir."

Stewart nodded. "Then could you please tell the court why you are not in jail right now."

"'Cause I ran away from his house." Johnny pointed to the prosecutor, Bennett Caldwell. Another round of whispers rippled through the crowd.

"I see. Then are you in danger of being arrested by coming here today?"

"Yes, sir."

God, he wanted to wrap his arms around her and never let go. Did she know how much her sacrifice meant to him?

Evan Stewart smiled. "Are you aware, Johnny, that the warrant for your arrest was actually intended for your uncle, Henry Bodine?"

At least he'd done that much for her. Richard nodded when her blue eyes widened and her gaze shot straight to his.

"Henry, not me?" she squeaked.

"Yes, Johnny," Evan Stewart continued. "You are free to come and go."

"Your Honor," Caldwell whined.

Parker frowned. "Mr. Stewart, proceed."

"Johnny, as briefly as possible, could you please tell us what you did see the day your father was killed?"

"Well, Paw told me Uncle Cal's man, Breed,

331

passed the word that they were a-comin' for us the next day. Paw wanted me to get the keys from Deputy Brady and when Paw got the signal from Breed, I was supposed to cause a ruckus so Paw and his men could get to the horses."

With only a few interruptions from Evan Stewart for clarification, Johnny carefully told how she tainted the water, stole the keys, and drove off the horses. Next, she explained how Rab snuck around the outlaws and pinned them down near the creek. She related the conversation she heard between her father and his men and how they tried to create a smoke screen so Rab couldn't see them.

"Thank you, Johnny."

As soon as Evan Stewart sat down and Benton Caldwell stood, Johnny dropped her gaze and drew her lower lip in between her teeth.

"So, Johnny," Caldwell began. "You never saw who shot Tyler, Miles, or Deputy Brady?"

"No, but it wasn't Rab."

"Rab?"

Johnny shifted in the wooden chair. "I know that isn't his real name, but it's what I call him."

"Yes." Benton Caldwell nodded and gave her a sympathetic smile. "The two of you became very close during those weeks you spent together."

"'Bout as close as two coats a paint."

Caldwell chuckled. "Yes. And we know how diligently you nursed Deputy Bennick when he was ill and even held off the doctor at gunpoint when he wanted to amputate the deputy's leg."

"I promised Rab I wouldn't let 'em take his leg."

"And you kept your promise didn't you?"

"Yes, sir."

"You'd do anything to protect Deputy Bennick."

"Yes, sir."

"Even lie to protect him."

Richard stiffened.

"I ain't lying."

"No, of course not. I'm sorry. That's a very pretty dress you have on. Where did you get it?"

"Mrs. Pickens give it to me."

He nodded. "Just that one?"

"No, she give me three."

"Three dresses. That's a lot. Didn't you have any dresses of your own?"

"No."

"Why is that, Johnny? Have you ever even owned a dress? When I met you, you were wearing britches and presented yourself as a boy."

Richard frowned as he watched Caldwell. The man seemed to be taking it personally that Johnny had lied to him about her true identity.

Caldwell stepped toward the witness chair. "How long have you disguised yourself as a boy?"

"My whole life."

"Your whole life? Did any of your father's acquaintances know you were a girl?"

"No, sir."

Evan Stewart shot to his feet. "Objection. Your Honor, Mr. Caldwell is badgering the witness. Johnny is not the one on trial here today."

"Over ruled, Mr. Stewart."

The hint of a smile played on Caldwell's face as he refocused his attention on Johnny.

"Was your father, Pierpont Bodine, even aware you were not his son, but in fact, his daughter?"

"No."

"No. So you're telling us that no one, not your father's closest friends, not your Uncle Calvin, or even your very own father, knew you were girl, because for... How old are you Johnny?"

She shrugged.

"Seventeen, eighteen?"

She shrugged again.

"So every hour of everyday, for let's say—

eighteen years—you lived a lie. A lie so great your own father was unaware."

"But I seen how Paw and them others is with women... I seen what they done to the girl in the yeller dress. I didn't help her cause I was too scarit, but I ain't a-goin' to let Rab—"

"The question please, Johnny. Just answer yes or no. Did you, or did you not, lie about your identity every day for eighteen years of your life?"

"Yes, sir, I reckon I did." She looked down and gnawed on her bottom lip.

Caldwell picked up something small and shiny as he stepped around the table to approach the witness chair. Richard's spine went rigid when he recognized the loop of rawhide hanging from Caldwell's hand.

The prosecutor stopped in front of Johnny and extended his arm. "Could you please tell us if you have ever seen this locket before?"

She nodded.

"Please speak up, Johnny."

Richard's hand clenched tight around the wooden arm of his chair. He hated the way Caldwell attacked her.

"Yes, sir."

"And could you please tell us where you got it?"

"Uncle Henry give it to me."

Caldwell nodded. "And do you know where your Uncle Henry got this pretty piece of jewelry?"

"He got it off some folks that was on a stage they was robbin'."

"Could you open it please?"

Johnny popped the clasp and for a moment, stared at the halves.

"Could you tell us please who these people are?"

Johnny shrugged. "Don't know."

"You don't know. Have you ever pretended to know? Just made up a story about them and told that lie to another person?"

"I reckon I tolt the story more to myself, than anyone else. But I tolt some of it to Rab wunst."

"And what lie did you tell him about the people in your stolen locket."

"I tolt him they was my real maw an' paw."

"And how did Deputy Bennick react when you told him this falsehood."

"He was right glad I weren't part a that bunch a no accounts. Said my warrant was a mistake an' he'd see to it the charges ag'in me was dropped."

"I see. So, you've made a habit of lying about your identity, to your own family, for eighteen years. You threatened an unarmed doctor with a stolen gun to save Deputy Bennick, a man you yourself said, you would do anything to protect. Then you lied to that same man, so he would feel sorry enough for you to see that the charges against you were dropped." Caldwell crossed his arms over his chest and glared at her.

Richard shifted in his chair and leaned forward. Despite her bravado, he sensed her fear, the way he had at the dugout, when her father belittled her and called her names.

"Can you explain why three other men have sat here in this court room, in the exact spot where you sit now, and have all told a very different story?"

"I reckon they's lyin'"

"And how do we know you aren't the one lying? We all know how close you and Deputy Bennick are. Could it be you are lying now, in order to protect him?"

"Could be, but I ain't."

"And why would we believe you, when all you've done is tell lie after lie?"

Richard's grip shifted to the edge of the table. The muscles of his arm grew as stiff as the wood his fingers pressed against. Why wasn't Evan Stewart leaping to his feet in protest of Caldwell's badgering?

"I ain't a-lyin!" Johnny declared. "I know'd Uncle Calvin my whole life an' he an' Paw was the kind a men what would steal the pennies off a dead man's eyes. An' them what rode with 'em is the same."

"But that doesn't explain why we should believe you are suddenly telling the truth, when by your own admission you've done nothing but lie your entire life."

Richard jumped to his feet. "Leave her alone, Caldwell. If you're angry with me for not marrying Caroline, fine. Don't take it out on Johnny."

Judge Parker's arm shot out across his desk, his index finger pointed like an arrow, straight at Richard's chest.

"Sit down."

A tug on the sleeve of his suit coat dropped him onto his chair.

Evan Stewart leaned close and whispered, "Johnny's doing fine. You aren't helping."

Richard's gaze shot to Johnny. She stared at him with the same stunned, wide-eyed, open mouth expression, he'd seen that first day, after he'd cold cocked her father.

I love you, he silently mouthed.

Johnny's eyes widened, even as Judge Parker admonished sternly, "Deputy Bennick, I hope that sentiment wasn't intended for me."

Heat flooded his cheeks, and Johnny's mouth quirked up at the corner. Caldwell's gaze swung between the three of them, his annoyance etched in the frown across his forehead.

"Miss Bodine, by your own admission, you did not see who shot Tyler, Wilt, or Deputy Brady, correct?"

"Yes, but—"

"No further questions."

Evan Stewart stood. "Redirect?"

Parker inclined his head with a nod.

"Johnny, if you did not see who shot Deputy Brady, Mr. Miles, and Mr. Tyler, how can you be so sure it wasn't Deputy Bennick?"

"'Cause Rab can shoot the egg out of the nest without rufflin' the chicken. When Rab saved me from Uncle Cal, he kilt him with one bullet rightchere." Johnny pressed her index finger to the center of her forehead. "I helped wrap them bodies. Brady was shot three times. Iffin Rab wanted him dead it wouldn't a took him three tries. An' iffin he'd a-wanted to kill Machler an' Warren they'd be dead as beef."

She had such blind faith in him, Richard couldn't help but smile. No matter how this turned out, Johnny would always be his hero.

"Now Rab, he done somethin' back in the war that hurt his heart so bad, his mind just figgered it'd be best to ferget it happened. Maybe he'll remember one day, maybe he won't. Reckon it don't much matter. He jest thinks it was bad, so he's been a-spendin' his whole life a-tryin' to make up to God fer what he done.

"I reckon the reason he don't remember that ambush is 'cause what happened in them trees is too close to what happened in the war. His mind don't want to remember neither one. Some wounds from war ain't so easy to see as his missin' arm."

****

The jury returned a half an hour later. Richard glanced at Evan Stewart, sitting beside him as the twelve men filed into the courtroom.

"Don't know," Stewart whispered. "It's either very good or very bad."

Richard glanced over his shoulder, searching for Johnny in the sea of faces. Judge Parker asked him to rise.

"Gentlemen of the jury, have you reached a

verdict?"

"Yes, Your Honor, we have."

The seconds ticked by as Richard blocked all from his mind, straining his ears, listening for those specific words, waiting, waiting...

"We find that the defendant, U.S. Deputy Marshal Richard Bennick, acted in accordance with the discharge of his duties, and we find him not guilty on all charges."

Richard's knees gave out, and he dropped heavily into the chair.

Judge Parker thanked the jury and closed the case with a sharp bang of his gavel.

Evan Stewart pumped Richard's arm up and down and patted him on the back.

Richard managed to murmur some vague words of appreciation before he stood and looked around. A few people nodded in his direction then blended into the crowd as it filed slowly from the courtroom.

Johnny stood alone at the back of the room waiting until the crowd thinned.

Out in Indian Territory, Rab had been confident and sure of himself. Now, he stood beside that wide table looking a bit confused and lost. Then his gaze met hers. He hesitated for a moment, searching her face then held his arm wide.

She sprinted toward him as he passed through the little gate. A moment later, she threw her arms around his neck. His arm wrapped around her waist, and he held her tight, just swaying back and forth while she breathed deep the scent of sandalwood.

"Damn it, Johnny," he murmured into her hair. "I can't believe you came." He drew back and searched her face as though memorizing every inch. "I thought you were settled someplace with your new family."

"I tolt Uncle Charles an' Aunt Flora I had to come. I reckon they was disappointed, but they didn't stop me. Uncle Charles even bought my ticket."

He stepped back. "You're so pretty let me look at you."

She gave him a quick little spin.

His left cheek dimpled when he grinned, and his hungry gaze devoured her from head to toe. Suddenly his grin faded as his gaze focused on the side of her lavender skirt.

"Is that blood on your dress?"

She glanced down at the dark stain where Pudge had grabbed her skirt. She shrugged. "It ain't mine."

"Then whose blood is it?"

"Jest some lazy, no-account I stabbed fer a-puttin' his grimy paws on me."

"You stabbed someone? Damn it, Johnny, you never should have come."

"Ya ungrateful lawman." She took a step away from him and swatted the side of her skirt instead giving him a much deserved shove that would have knocked him all the way into next week. "Iffin I'd a done that, I reckon you'd be a-settin in that jail a-waitin' to get yore neck stretched."

The stiffness in his posture seemed to wilt. He drove his hand into his hair, shoving back the piece that constantly fell forward. "You're right, I'm sorry. I'm very glad you came." He shifted his gaze to meet hers. "Does this mean you forgive me for hurting you? I never meant—"

"Forgive ya?" She frowned. "Fer what? Ya cold cocked Paw. Ya stuck up fer me with that other deputy. Ya went ag'in ever'thing ya was a-feared of to save me from Uncle Cal. Ya talked to that judge about Uncle Henry so's I could go free, an' ya tolt me I was beautiful.

"Ain't no one ever took up fer me like you do. I never been worth much in my life, but ya make me feel like somebody, Rab. Ya make me feel like I matter."

He stepped toward her and grabbed her wrist. "God, Johnny, you do matter, more than anything in this world. I'd tear the stars out of Heaven for you."

He tugged her close. "I love you, but you've got your whole life in front of you. You're so beautiful and you seem so happy. Your new family must be very special."

Her heart did a little flip, and suddenly, she wasn't sure what to do. She glanced down, gnawing on her bottom lip. "Is that what ya want, Rab? Fer me to go back?"

"What I want doesn't matter."

"It does to me."

He let go of her and walked to the partition behind the tables then turned. "I don't know, Johnny. I'm so... wrong... inside. It's not fair to you. I need you so much; I'll suck you dry. And I don't want to use you like your father did."

She lifted her chin and searched his face. "There ya go ag'in, a-thinkin' yer jest like my paw. Paw never give me no choices. You are. If I've a mind to, I can go back to Uncle Charles and Aunt Flora. But I need ya, too, Rab. I need ya to hang onto and show me which way is east."

"My brother offered me a partnership in his ranch. I'm going to Montana. I want you come with me, but not if you're doing it because you're afraid to be alone. I need you to come because you love me."

She blinked against the sudden burn of tears. "I don't reckon I know how." If she were braver, she would have thrown her arms around his neck and kissed him, said the words he wanted to hear. Instead, they tumbled around inside her queasy stomach and when she opened her mouth nothing came out.

He swallowed and searched her face. "Tell me

what you feel," he whispered hoarsely.

She glanced down and lifted the locket. "I feel like this here locket ya give me. All fancy an' pretty on the outside, but empty without no picture in it. An' I want a picture a you."

"There must have been someone at your new home, whose photograph you could put inside."

"I reckon I didn't want nobody else's."

"Johnny, are you sure you want mine?" He took a step toward her.

"It's what I come all this way fer."

"I do have a small photograph. I had intended to give it to Caroline, but she didn't want it. She said it was too worn out and ragged around the edges."

"I want it, Rab," she said softly.

His Adam's apple bobbed up and down. "There is a big wrinkle through the center, where it almost tore in half."

"I want it."

"You might not be able to tell who it is."

"I'll know."

He closed the distance between them. "It might not fit."

"Iffin ya give it to me, it'll fit."

"Damn it, Johnny," he rasped. "I'm so cold at night without you."

"Is it cold yonder in that Monty-ana?"

A grin quirked the corner of his mouth. He nodded. "Very cold."

She heaved an exaggerated sigh. "Well, I best come with ya then. Yer likely to freeze to death come winter iffin I ain't there to keep ya warm."

A chuckle rumbled inside his chest. He kissed the top of her head.

"Does this here place have trees? 'Cause ya ain't a-goin' to be happy lessin' the trees is so far apart the woodpeckers got to tote lunch."

He laughed then kissed the tip of her nose. "My

brother tells me it's mostly open range, but the trees are tall pines and aspens with white trunks." He brushed his hand along her jaw.

Her pulse skittered through her veins. She lifted her gaze to stare straight into those beautiful dark brown eyes.

"Besides," he continued, "as long as you're with me, I don't think I'll have to worry about trees again." He leaned close and pressed his lips to hers, melding her mouth with his. His tongue slipped inside, sucking and tasting hers with such intensity, she sagged against him, praying this kiss and this moment would never end.

He lifted his lips from hers and Johnny raised her gaze to meet his, surprised by how serious he looked.

"And, Johnny..."

Her heartbeat quickened.

"...it's Mon-tana."

A word about the author...

Kathy Otten began making up stories as soon as she learned to write them down. Growing up with a mom who loved antiques and a dad who loved cowboys, she naturally grew into a love for westerns and later western romances. She grew up with horses and married a dairy farmer. Once her kids were in high school, Kathy pulled the notebooks from under the bed and seriously began the quest for publication. She joined critique groups and bought lots of books, studing the craft of writing enough to rewrite some of her old stories and create many new ones.

Lost Hearts is Kathy's second novel, and she is currently busy with a third.

Kathy loves to hear from readers.
You can contact Kathy through her web site at
www.kathyotten.com
or through email at
jersey.vt.1774@hotmail.com
(Just put the name of the book in the subject line
so it isn't accidentally deleted.)

Thank you for purchasing
this Wild Rose Press publication.
For other wonderful stories of romance,
please visit our on-line bookstore at
www.thewildrosepress.com.

For questions or more information
contact us at
info@thewildrosepress.com.

The Wild Rose Press
www.TheWildRosePress.com